The Art of Salvage

LEONA THEIS

COTEAU BOOKS

© Leona Theis, 2006. First US edition, 2007.

All rights reserved. No part of this publication may be reproduced, stored in a retrieval system or transmitted, in any form or by any means, without the prior written consent of the publisher or a licence from The Canadian Copyright Licensing Agency (Access Copyright). For an Access Copyright licence, visit www.accesscopyright.ca or call toll free to 1-800-893-5777.

This is a work of fiction. Names, characters, places, and incidents either are the product of the author's imagination or are used fictitiously. Any resemblance to actual persons, living or dead, is coincidental.

Edited by Sandra Birdsell.
Book and cover design by Duncan Campbell.
Cover image by Austring Photography.

Printed and bound in Canada at Tri-Graphic Printing Ltd.

Library and Archives Canada Cataloguing in Publication

Theis, Leona, 1955-
　　The art of salvage / Leona Theis.

ISBN 1-55050-348-0

　　I. Title.

PS8589.H4517A78 2006　　　C813'.6　　C2006-903075-8

1　2　3　4　5　6　7　8　9　10

COTEAU BOOKS
2517 Victoria Ave.
Regina, Saskatchewan
Canada　S4P 0T2

AVAILABLE IN CANADA & THE US FROM
Fitzhenry & Whiteside
195 Allstate Parkway
Markham, ON, Canada, L3R 4T8

The publisher gratefully acknowledges the financial assistance of the Saskatchewan Arts Board, the Canada Council for the Arts, the Government of Canada through the Book Publishing Industry Development Program (BPIDP), Association for the Export of Canadian Books, and the City of Regina Arts Commission, for its publishing program.

for Murray

PART I

HERITAGE PROPERTY

In an upstairs suite in a house on Temperance Street, Amber dragged a box out of her closet and through her bedroom, bumped it over the edge of the carpet and pulled it across the kitchen tiles. Sat down on the floor, knees bent, feet on either side of the box. The tiles were cold and she slapped her bare feet against them, left right left right left right, to juice the circulation to her toes. She made a fist and punched the box, her knuckles landing smack on the green condensed milk logo stamped on the side. My life in a box, she thought. Ha. Condensed.

She reached into the pocket of her jeans and pulled out a small oval of ornate brass – the doorbell plate from the house that had been torn down this morning. Empty round hole in the middle where the doorbell's button should be. She let the plate drop to the floor, where it made a small clang. She'd hoped for a bigger noise.

"Forget it, Del," Amber said to the bit of metal and her feet and the cold floor. "Who needs you?"

How could that *be?* she thought. All those months I lived on the second floor of that old house and Del never said spit. Keeping people at a distance was one of Del's everyday talents, for sure, but a feat like this, the withholding, and for so long, of the information she'd finally let out this morning was athletic in its achievement. A personal best. A woman capable of that form of silence wasn't to be trusted.

Who needs you Del?

Del her "sister." Del her birth mother.

Birth mother. You can take a fat, rich word like "mother," and when you add "birth" in front of it the whole big idea shrinks down to a dictionary definition. The distance Del maintained. The way she rationed words. Even the way she walked – her rapid, abbreviated stride. And her arm's-length smile, the sense Amber got from her that she had Amber on a list of things to be periodically checked. As if when Del had given her child over to her own parents to raise, someone had told her love abhors a crowd.

For instance, on the telephone this past Christmas day. Amber had counted twenty rings, then hung up. Dialled again: Damn, I'll *force* a conversation. Twenty-six rings. Rubbing the smudges from the pebbled plastic base of the telephone as she waited. Coax, coax.

"Hello."

"Del?" Amber had said.

"Yes. Oh, Amber. Yes?"

"You weren't answering."

Pause.

"Are you all right?"

"Of course, Amber. I'm fine."

Pause.

"What is it then, Amber?"

"What *is* it? It's *Christmas*."

Knock, knock against the handset after she hung up. Nobody in there. If you're nobody, and I'm your child, who does that make me?

It's no big deal, Amber used to tell herself. But not any more. She'd soon be twenty-five, and two and a half decades seemed a long time to be on earth without having your fundamentals sorted out. Twenty-five: a milestone, a time of reckoning.

Amber writhed her shoulders as if to slither out of here and now. Get back to the way she'd felt this morning – before she had encountered Del at the demolition. Back to the feeling of waking into a world that was clear and ready for her to write whatever she chose onto its walls. She couldn't count on waking up feeling like that.

Just yesterday for instance, Amber had stood in her bedroom looking at the mess, and the word *sloth* had surfaced in her mind. The swampy, rank odour of the idea itself. An ancient, deadly sin, ticket to hell and damnation. Thank God I'm an atheist, she'd thought, earning herself a fleeting grin. "Thank God I'm an atheist," she'd repeated aloud, but it was a flimsy joke and didn't survive the second pass, didn't counter the dismay she'd felt when she considered the room. The room and, in fact, the world beyond it.

When she'd woken up this morning it was to the same room, the same litter – the hill of laundry behind the door, the plate and the greasy fork on the rug, the dresser-top scattered with coins, CDs, socks, a half-full pop bottle with one hoop earring around its neck – but during the night the frame of reference had shifted. The muddle and clutter had become vital signs, evidence of life. A whole mess of possibilities. To get back to *that* feeling – that's what Amber wanted. She slapped her feet, left right, against the cold tiles; the box on the floor between her knees; left right. Get back to nine o'clock in the morning, eight hours ago:

Early to be up on a day off. Showered and towelled and pulling on jeans, getting ready to go see the Burton house come down, the house where not so long ago Amber had lived on the second floor – with, and then without, a man named Cal. She'd heard they were going to let people pick through the wreckage. She'd go looking, then, for some small object to bring away and add to her hoard. Maybe something as everyday plain as a cupboard door handle, chrome, tapered, a groove cut down the centre, like the handle she'd gripped in a white-knuckle squeeze the night Stuart called to say about Dad. A souvenir of the place that had been her walls and roof through two enormous griefs; one tumble into love; one climb back out; more than one wary visit with Del.

Bring it home and add it to the congregation in her slumpy cardboard box: a crockery shard, an old soldier's badge, a single earring, a broken fish hook, a dozen other items. Her inventory. Some days you need one.

No danger Cal would be there to watch the wrecking this morning: he counted nostalgia among his worst enemies. But nostalgia was only one of Amber's reasons for going. She'd never seen a house taken to pieces, roof torn off, walls pulled open. She liked the idea of a thing being split apart like that.

She leaned across the clutter on the dresser, face to the mirror. Took out the upper of the two small hoops she wore in each ear and slid in a pair of amber studs. Amber – it was a name she'd come to terms with, but only after years of wishing to be rid of it, embarrassed by the people it showed up on: centrefold girls, exotic dancers, heroines of romantic novels – Amber Sunrise, Amber Sea, Amber Sands. What could Del have been thinking? Out of a universe of names...

But Amber was over that now. She'd adopted a new relationship with the word; she'd read about it, amber the substance, that is: its properties, its history, its uses as a charm. Why shouldn't she be precious?

Her unruly russet hair. She gathered it into a careless twist, rough against her fingers, and clipped it high on the back of her head. She swept the change that lay loose on the dresser into the bowl of her hand. Silver-painted fingernails. Curly strands of hair had escaped already from the clip and floated around her head as if they were live things. Spring sunlight glanced off the crystal of her watch and the movement of her wrist sent a bright small searchlight flashing over the walls. Appropriate, she thought; she often felt as if she were searching, if only she knew for what. Security, maybe. A sense of direction. The feeling she was worth the space she took up. The same things everyone wanted, right?

She crossed to the laundry heap and ducked her hand into the pockets of yesterday's pants. No change, no bills. Nevertheless she was having one of her good days, one of her things-are-possible days, her mind a new white room, clear and full of light. Out on the street, she shook the coins in her pocket to make money noises, to coax a big sound from small wealth. Jingle, jingle. Even six bucks' worth of coins, give or take, can ring optimistic on the right day.

The world was like that for her, as if she moved in a private atmosphere that would change of its own accord; change so she'd find herself breathing in a new outlook, for better or worse. She knew the name for this, found it at a website: cyclothymia, a muted version of what would, if you took it and gave it a powerful yank, be bipolar disorder. Small ups, mostly downs, a style of temperament that wasn't garden variety but wasn't truly exotic either. Inherited, she was convinced, her own working out of the family's heirloom depression. Her father had suffered his own toxic version. And Del – she had her own wonky manifestation. Chinese women used to have their feet bound; Del's whole personality was bound, wrapped like an onion inside a taut stretch of skin. Of course, with an onion, there's always the chance that some still-green force could split it open and expose a glistening inside.

The walk to the Burton house was short. Fractured sidewalk bordered by twiggy elms with their buds ready to burst. Close to the river, close to the bridge, Amber stopped opposite the pale yellow two-storey named after the man who had built it almost a hundred years earlier. Two silent women held a paper banner: Our Heritage Destroyed. In a city as young as Saskatoon there weren't more than a handful of buildings this age. Half a dozen people stood on the grass, talking, gesturing with their thermal mugs. Most were middle-aged, but one was younger, mid-twenties like herself; he was long-haired, as if he wished he'd been born a generation earlier. Now why would he wear his hair that way? She pictured him with a Caesar cut, blond and short above his eyes. Better.

Workers in overalls and light jackets waited near the house; over their jackets they wore bright orange vests with yellow reflector tape. Sunlight slanted from the east while a single, blue-dark cloud shed late, unhurried flakes of snow that settled on the hardhats of the wreckers, on their bright vests, on the waiting machinery. Amber took her sunglasses from her jacket pocket. The coincidence of weather: so often, her good days would be studded with odd combinations. Or was it just that on a good day she was in a position to appreciate the unusual?

The people who worried about local history had tried to save the Burton. It was built by one of Saskatoon's early settlers, a lumber merchant, a civic leader, an original Temperance Colonist. Others argued, just as noisily, that the old rat's nest had to go. There it stood, old colours and original wood exposed in places where the paint had flaked away – a history in layers. The siding hadn't been painted in years, but a stylish shade of dark green had been slapped on a year or two ago around the window frames and eaves. They'd got it wrong: it made the walls and roof look worse by comparison. You can't just tart up a place and pretend it's different, the dry rot still there under the paint.

Last Saturday's paper ran a shot of the house the way it had looked eighty years ago: a gracious verandah, wide windows that overlooked the river, and on the roof, just for show, a widow's walk with a wrought iron rail – a widow's walk you couldn't even get to; no stairway, no door. Too bad such a funky old place had been left to ruin. The Burton was divided into suites in the late sixties, fridges and old gas ranges and sofa beds hoisted on pulleys through high windows and wedged into corners in former bedrooms. No one had put much money into it since. If you wanted a heritage tragedy, Amber thought, that was it – the loss of potential that happened years ago, not what the wrecking machines were about to do this morning. These people with their paper banner were years too late. By the time

Amber had moved in, the slump in the verandah and the gaps in the shingling already signalled the beginning of the end.

She'd seen the classified ad and made the call. *Two-room suite in character home. Shared bath.*

"Character home," she'd said to the landlord when he met her by appointment on the front walk. "Who are the other characters?" He'd refused to play. Now why can't people just be nice? What would it cost? He wore a tan suit and a well-made coat and walked the halls and stairways of his property with his toe rubbers still on.

"Two suites on the main floor, two on the second, a bachelor at the top. You're on two. You share the bathroom with your next-door and with the bachelor. Quiet after eleven."

Bachelor at the top. Amber had asked if she could take that literally, ha-ha. He might have smiled a little that time, she couldn't just say.

Looking past the bent elbow of the track-hoe now, Amber saw that the oak front door of the house was missing. Maybe the heritage people had hauled it away. She hesitated, then walked onto the lot, expecting someone to shout at her to clear out. She slipped past the machinery unnoticed and stepped onto the verandah. The carved trim that had framed the doorway was gone, exposing unpainted wood that looked startlingly raw. From the small round hole where the doorbell used to be, wires stuck out like fingers wrapped around thin air.

Maybe the door and its trim had been hauled out to the Western Development Museum. Letters to the editor over the last few months had argued for controlled demolition. Salvage *is* possible, people wrote. Hear, hear. Amber peeked in at the front hallway. The maple floorboards had been lifted and taken away. It looked as if salvage had been possible after all. She should have come on an earlier day and talked her way in, found something in her old suite worth taking. They'd start the wrecking any moment. Now that she saw the crude muscle of the machines, she couldn't imagine them leaving rubble worth picking through.

A truck door closed; workers pulled on serious leather gloves. Amber turned to leave. A bit of metal, knocked off the step by her foot, made a ting against the cement walk. She stooped to pick it up and recognized it as the faceplate for the doorbell – a brass oval with a tracery of leaves and vines skirting the hole in the middle. She slipped it into her pocket.

"What are you doing?" One of the orange-vested men.

"Nothing, dropped something."

"Clear out now." He gestured toward the wrecking machine. "Do you know what that claw can do?"

"Sorry."

"You people don't get it." He waved impatiently at the spectators with their banner. "It's a *house*. Houses can be replaced."

"Sure thing," Amber said, and she walked back across the street. The man climbed into the cab of the wrecking machine and sunlight flashed off the door as he pulled it closed. Amber blinked to clear her eyes of the yellow spot. Noise and vibration and belch as he roused his machine, pig of a beast. She stood on the sidewalk opposite the house, flexing one knee and then the other, as if she were warming up for a run, wondering whether and when to expect the discombobulation that sometimes followed the bright-white-room feeling – the rapid multiplication of thoughts, twisting off from each other in paisley shapes, one generation after another. The sense that her mind was boiling over.

The machine extended its track arm and pulled at the eaves. Dust and diesel smoke rose together. The wood as it splintered made a crackling sound like fire. The arm extended section by section to pull at the top of a wall. It was fun to watch. Somewhere in the lizard part of the human brain is that throbbing little thing that loves destruction, and here was a time and place Amber could let it out from under its tarp. Just an old house and no one getting hurt. The claw of the machine rose and made grasp after clumsy grasp, its five steel fingers tearing at the roof. The rafters gave way, blue shingles falling, and giant splinters. The slats of an orange venetian blind from an upstairs window bent like twist-ties. With a crude, dinosaur-like motion, the machine shaped a hill of rubble into a ramp, then climbed it, caterpillar wheels on the roof of the crushed back porch. The arm reached up to the third storey, extending and retracting, gathering the parts of the house to itself in a gesture that looked strangely protective. A second machine around the other side of the house took over, punching at the remaining brick walls on the north and east sides of the main floor. The fireplace succumbed and a plume of soot billowed out, a last flourish.

The leveling had taken no more than three-quarters of an hour, the house reduced to a hill of has-beens: the double-hung windows, the creaks in the fourth, fifth, and ninth stairs, the corroded bathroom on the second floor where Amber had learned to lean to the right so the crack in the toilet seat wouldn't pinch her butt. The countertop where Cal, in one of his rare lapses into sentiment, had printed her initials in a heap of spilled sugar.

The faces of the heritage people showed resignation. The younger one, the man-boy with the too-long hair and snowflakes melting in it, took a slow pull from his coffee mug and put his arm around the woman – his mother? – who stood beside him.

Amber looked past them toward the bridge. What should she do next on this bright day? Below the bridge, the sunlight scattered as it hit the river. It isn't a deep river, but it has a tricky current, a current people sometimes forget to take seriously. Sunbathers like to play on the sandbars; once in a while someone ventures too far into the water and is swept away.

A woman turned off the bridge and came in the direction of the Burton house. She walked in the same quick, small-stepping way Del walked, hardly any motion in the shoulders. No, don't worry, there'd be no need to deal with Del today. She'd be at work, clock-punched and efficient behind her machine inside the five-storey factory on Twenty-second. But it looked like Del. Dark hair in that drastically short style she'd adopted. It *was* her. Her signature sweats, the kind with elastic at the waist and ankles, as if they were tailored for a skinny, sad clown.

Why would she be here?

Amber fidgeted with the doorbell plate in her jacket pocket. Her legs, her legs, restless underneath her, as if they argued with each other whether to bolt or stay. She always felt so helpless in the presence of Del's blue enamel eyes. Conversations that played out like solitaire. What would bring Del to this place on this day? She was no heritage activist.

She was closer now. A barely perceptible startle when she spotted Amber, and then the small smile, the recognition for official purposes.

"So you came too," Del said.

The sun too bright now for Amber, hurting her eyes even through her sunglasses. Her visual field fracturing the way it always did before her mind boiled over. She did her best to look at Del's face despite the fracturing.

"I thought I'd watch. But what brings you?"

Del looked across at the remains of the house. "It's down already."

Small talk, their established pattern. Tiny talk. "It was a good show," Amber said, "but it wasn't a long one. Two of those machines and it was done with in no time."

Del nodded.

"So that's the end of my old place," Amber said. She was doing it again, speaking into the space between herself and Del as if the responsibility were hers alone.

"My old place too," Del said quietly.

Amber leaned in. "What did you say?"

"I lived there too. Way back."

"Where?"

"There." Del made a small motion with her head. "Third-floor bachelor."

"You never said. All that time I lived there and you never *said?*"

Del moved her shoulders. Apologetic or dismissive?

Across the street, the door of the Cat on top of the rubble heap opened and the driver picked his way to the ground, lit a cigarette, and beckoned to the group of watchers. Putting on work gloves as they walked, the thin line of people crossed to the remains of the house, where they began to pick loose bricks from the rubble. Del seemed absorbed by their movements, maddeningly so.

"When?" Amber said. "When did you live there?"

"Way back." Del's voice was barely more than a whisper. "When I came to the city. My first place." She was looking, still, at the crumpled house, at the people rummaging in the wreckage.

Jesus. Del in there, Amber thought. Del in there with Phil. The two unknown quantities. Does that mean I was conceived there? How did he look, Phil, walking up that staircase? The man who, be he alive now or be he dead – for he might be alive somewhere for all she knew – had contributed half her complement of genes. Did he have to duck his head the way Cal used to do when he turned on the first landing?

And Del hadn't said spit. Never would have said spit if Amber hadn't seen her here and called on her seldom-used ask-Del muscles. Amber stared until finally Del glanced at her. But it was only a glance. Del shifted her gaze immediately to the flakes of snow melting as they hit the sidewalk.

Look at her. Standing there, skinny, like sticks wired together. The Rumpelstiltskin voice that lived inside Amber said, Didn't you think I'd care to know? Do I figure so small that nothing about your history is worth mentioning to me? What makes you such a goddamn *miser*?

But she couldn't say that out loud. This tradition of accommodating Del, of leaving her be: Stuart did it, Mom and Dad too, when they were alive. This was the thing Amber had never figured out how to split open. She recognized the choice before her: either figure out how to say things out loud to Del, or decide once and for all not to care.

It was time to be somewhere else. Amber flexed her knees by turns, almost running on the spot without lifting her toes. "I have to go," she said. "Work," she lied, her muscles straining. She could see better now; the fractures in her vision had resolved.

"Yes, sure, I'll talk to you...later." Del made an awkward movement with her elbows.

Amber raised a hand and trailed it behind her for a step or two, then ran a few yards. She looked back to see Del not looking her way, and continued running along the bank to a bench above the river. From here the view of the Burton was screened by a thick clump of bushes that had begun to leaf out. This was her comfort bench, her familiar bench. Often she'd stop here for the view, even on a freezing winter day, stand for a moment with her hands on the backrest before carrying on across the bridge to be at Poor Man's by ten. The name of this valley is Meewasin, the Cree word for "beautiful." From this vantage, Amber had seen the valley in all seasons: the colours on the snow from a late-morning sunrise in winter; the current undercutting the last of the ice in spring; the summer pelicans circling in the sky; the yellow poplar leaves swirling on the wind in October. This was where she came when she needed beauty and its power to calm her, as she did now. Unable to be still, she braced her hands on the back of the bench and stretched her long legs one at a time, behind her, then to the sides, then knee to chest.

Still the duet of sun and snow. A breeze blew south along the riverbank and Amber faced into it. She had a history with wind. She was twelve that summer when the rogue wind rushed through the campground near the creek late on a July afternoon and lifted Amber off her feet. She'd been struck by a heavy wooden beam that had been lifted by the same powerful gust. They used to play, she and her friend Tamara, in the ghost-town emptiness of the rarely used campground. The blow put Amber to sleep and kept her there for four days. Tamara ran for help.

Stuart got her to the hospital within minutes, a good brother, and organized shifts of sitters: Mom, Dad, himself, their neighbour Old Glad, even Del, who, according to Stuart, made it down for a day and then took the bus back to the city and called for updates in the evenings after the long-distance rates went down. Eventually Amber had emerged, good as new, with no sign of neurological damage. There was no blaming the wind and the wooden beam for her swings from low to high to low again.

Looking at the river now, Amber moved her head from side to side, then up and down and at angles, playing with the changes in light through the lenses of her sunglasses. The dark green river was embellished with flashes of yellow. She thought of a dress, emerald green, that had belonged to Mom – to the grandmother she'd always called Mom. Her best dress, the one she put on for the Lodge Christmas party or for a wedding dance; the one that meant lipstick and earrings and a showy twirl in the kitchen at Amber's request before her parents put on their coats. The fabric was called shot taffeta, so-named, Mom told her, because it was shot through with a bold orange thread. The orange contradicted the green and changed the look of the fabric when the light struck in a certain way. Where was that dress now? Amber used to take it to the window to look for the orange, moving the cloth forward and back and upside-down, looking for the glimmer, as if that was where the joy was stored.

The third-floor bachelor. At least it wasn't the same suite. At least Del hadn't lived in the same damn suite. Growing up in Ripley, Amber had slept in the same bed as a long-ago Del had, looked out the same windows, put her T-shirts away in the same stubborn, screeching drawers, not finding out until she was eight years old what the accurate shape of her family was. She swallowed. Breathed. Swallowed again. At least her rooms in the Burton house had been her own.

Amber needed to run, wanted to zipper open her skin and kick free of it. She ran back up the bank and along the asphalt path, passed the memorial to the long-dead pioneers and hung a right, onto the bridge. A rag of crazy hot sax music rose up from under the bridge and she knew that the guy who liked to bring his instrument and his camp stool and sit on the gravelled slope was down there now. At least there's that, she thought – and it made her feel a little better for the moment – at least there's a man who brings his saxophone and stands on the riverbank and makes music.

She wasn't in shape; still, her muscles knew from years of racing how to do this on their own. The long downslope from the east bank to the west. Dashing past pedestrians and babies in strollers, over flattened paper coffee cups, around spilled milkshakes. Moving, moving, barely able to keep up with herself. She was made of elastic and springs; she was shuddering tires on gravel; she was the stones shot out to the side. She was the ring in a ring toss, the whirl in a whirlpool, a game without rules, unplayable. Inside her head a midway of speed rides, the roller coaster barely clasping the rails, clattering past switches, cresting the rise, plunging without permission.

Two hours were gone, just like that, as if time had run ahead to meet itself. Here she was, back in her little suite. Presto. Except for the anger, she could remember little of what had come between stretching her tendons by the bench above the river and walking back into her kitchen. What she did recall was the feeling that downtown there had been too much too much too much of everything. She'd come home with the six dollars in change still jangling in her pocket. She shucked her shoes and peeled off her socks, feeling suddenly hungry. Crackers. Wheat Thins or Bretons or those little garlic toasts. With salsa. No. Jalapeño jelly. It didn't matter because budget soda crackers and imitation Cheez Whiz were what she had. She set a plate of crackers and this morning's flat half-Coke on the kitchen floor.

She went to the closet in her bedroom, pulled out her cardboard box, dragged it to the kitchen and sat down on the floor. Her stuff box, that's how she thought of it – both noun and verb, because she stuffed things into it that didn't belong anywhere else, things that were too important to throw away. She kept them, she told herself, because, when you're weird like I am – when your mood can slide without warning from high noon to stale midnight, when your own beginnings are indistinct – once in a while you need tangible evidence of who you are. And I have collected a carton full.

"Forget it, Del," Amber said again. She folded back the cardboard flaps. Her muscles and her mind less jumpy now, beginning to relax. Yes. This heap of artifacts, the people and events concentrated in them. She wanted to let the air at these things, to see their shapes and feel their surfaces. On top was the stuffed doll Aunt Lenore made two decades ago, and which reminded Amber of the father who raised her – the attenuated legs, the pleasant, soft, winter-wool face, the dark embroidered eyebrows, fuzzy now and stitched on not quite straight. He was always old, her dad, the dad she knew. She set the doll on the floor next to the untouched Coke and crackers.

Also in the box: the fish hook that was her souvenir of Cal. He'd have a good laugh if he knew what she was thinking right now — her idea that the junk in this box might amount to the person who was Amber. Cal didn't even grant that there was such a thing as a self, just a lot of what he called "Spencerian brats jostling for the real estate in your head." Okay. But not much use if what you need is to discover how to love who you are.

In a corner of the box was a thick red zodiac candle, one of the leftovers Amber had found in the Ripley bedroom she inherited from Del. There'd been other vestiges in that room — a purple cotton blouse hanging in the closet, a game of Trouble with several pieces missing, two dozen books ranged along wall-mounted shelves: *The Call of the Wild, Robinson Crusoe, Tom Sawyer,* the Anne books and the Emily books, *The Black Stallion,* all of which Amber read and loved, sometimes even slept with the way other kids slept with teddy bears. And in addition to these leftovers, she used to imagine there were fingerprints on the zodiac candle she'd adopted; she used to sit on the floor watching the flame burn a deep recess in the centre, while the stiff outer blanket of wax embossed with the astrological signs retained its shape, hardly melting.

Hardly melting, Amber thought now. Del. Del and the man named Phil living in the Burton house together. Just one floor up. Del sitting at Amber's kitchen table in that same house more than once, and never saying a thing.

The man named Phil had died a long time ago, too long ago to be still grieved. That's what Mom and Dad had told Amber, and they were just repeating what Del had told them. That was what they said, though frequently Amber had needles of doubt. Making the father into a dead man would have simplified life for a pregnant girl in 1974. Did he die, really, or did he just walk out the door one day – the door of the third-floor bachelor, as it turned out – descend those slippery wooden stairs, swing onto his bike, and pedal off across the bridge to someone else?

Del and her shut-tight silence: yes, a personal best. Amber had been tricking herself into thinking that because technically, biologically, they were mother and daughter, something could be made of their relationship. Wishful thinking. Pretending. Baby sister – Del had adopted their official relationship and refused the natural one. It's possible for sisters, if they're separated in age by a span of nineteen years, to travel indefinitely in their deep, separate grooves; to go on that way for a lifetime, always parallel, never touching.

She grabbed her stuff box by its worn side flaps and tried to upend it. The cardboard began to tear away in her hands. She let go, slid her fingers underneath one end and lifted so the remaining contents tumbled onto the floor. Into the open. She liked the spilling, the noise, the clatter and roll.

Since grade school Amber had known how people behaved if they wanted to keep secrets. The trick was to say as little as possible, so they didn't get tangled up in their own dissemblings. That was the idea, but Amber herself wasn't all that good at it. The time she and Tamara stayed with Tamara's cousins in Winnipeg and the group of them went shoplifting (cheap plastic jewelry, for the cheap thrill of taking it) and raiding gardens (fat, muddy carrots), they thought they'd gotten away with it. The next morning after they'd eaten their cereal at the kitchen table, passing their new bracelets, rings, earrings from hand to hand, trying them this way and that, Tamara's aunt and uncle called all of them into the living room and said they were disturbed and ashamed. The next thing the aunt said was, "I'm so disappointed in you kids," and the next thing the uncle said was, "What do you think is a suitable punishment?"

"But I brought this bracelet from *home!*" Amber blurted out. It was a ridiculously desperate defence; up until then, the only thing that had concerned the aunt and uncle was the half-dozen wilting, contraband carrots they'd found beside the hedge.

"You couldn't just keep quiet?" Tamara's older cousin had said.

There's more than one kind of silence. The kind of silence Dad had maintained had been steady and gentle and sincere. It flowed around you and held you up. Del's, on the other hand, was like a sheet stretched tight across a doorway. If Del could keep quiet about such a simple fact as where she used to live, what else wasn't she saying?

BODY MEMORY

Del had seen and heard from a distance the last tumble and thud of the lower brick walls as she crossed the bridge; she'd seen the wrecking machine climb the heap of former rooms and fixtures and stop squarely on top of the widow's walk where no one ever walked. *Widow.* She didn't qualify for the title – never had – either emotionally or in fact. Even now, she didn't qualify.

Now that Amber had gone, Del felt freer to look more closely at what was left of the house. The sight of Amber this morning, loose locks of hair spiraling in the wind, had taken her by surprise. Del was upset with herself now – the way she'd let Amber's presence disarm her. She pressed down hard on that feeling until it diminished.

The Burton had been a big house; its remains were dwarfed now by the bare lot around it, by the flood of sky that filled the space the walls and rooftop used to occupy. She'd come here with a ridiculous hope that the end of the old house would lay things to rest, but she was experiencing the opposite. Seeing the walls fallen in on each other unnerved her – all that air floating loose where there used to be a structure.

She saw a rag of wallpaper clinging to plaster, crouched and tilted her head, trying but failing to spot an older layer, the orange geometric pattern from her and Phil's days in the house. She straightened and began poking with her toe at a tough caragana root sticking out of the soil; the disturbance released the smell of wet dark earth. Sunshine melted the snowflakes that fell on her running shoes. Spring and winter in the sky, the smell of summer in the soil: this crowding of seasons, the one walking up the heels of the next, as if she might need a reminder of the speed of time. The sense of acceleration you can't escape once you're into your forties, life piling up like a stack of bills before you can get to them. Overdue.

Two women, each with a single brick in each hand, edged past Del intending to deliver their bricks to a truck parked in the alley. She stepped back to give them room. Two more women, also each carrying a single brick in each hand, followed. At this rate they'd be at it for hours.

She shouldn't have come today. She'd woken with a headache and phoned in late, a rare occurrence. After swallowing two pills spiked with codeine, she'd headed out the door but opted to cross the river instead of going to work right away. If you're already late punching in, there's a point where it's hardly worth bothering until after lunch.

She'd come to the house last week, too. Someone at work had mentioned the fuss over that derelict wreck coming down. And then she'd had the phone call from Duncan and Vivien in which they'd reprised their old roles as the bearers of news, telling her that Phil had died. Before the phone call, the idea of coming for a last look had been just an idle notion; the call had transformed it into a need. The man from the development company had let her walk through once she'd explained to him up, down and around that she wasn't one of those heritage people. Not an activist by any stretch. She'd climbed the stairs and studied the blankness of the empty bachelor suite. Filled the spaces with images of sofa bed, round-cornered fridge, books lined up along the baseboards, the plastic drawer liners with the pictures of blue stoves and orange teapots, the red fuzzy mat on the floor by the window. And Phil sitting cross-legged on that mat, looking out at the river, lighting a smoke.

She'd visited twice during the year or so that Amber lived here. The first time, she'd started up the stairs to the third floor without thinking and had to correct herself. She'd sat, then, at the kitchen table in Amber's second-floor suite, unsettled by the thought of where her feet had wanted to take her. Body memory. As if decades hadn't passed. But it was a silly bit of emotional trickery the house had been playing on her, bordering on nostalgia.

The ad hoc salvage crew finally regrouped and organized itself, two people piling and sorting, a third person loading bricks into the arms of those who carried them to the truck. Their stubborn optimism, their salvaging of bits and pieces looked pitiful, and Del turned her back on their efforts.

She stepped off the curb and out of the way, moving carefully, placing her foot just so, adjusting her focus so she wouldn't trip. She was getting used to what Dr. Misanchuk called "progressive" lenses. Such a positive term for such a negative development, the achievement of being simultaneously nearsighted and farsighted. The new glasses helped at work – if she held her head at the proper angle she could thread her machine more easily than she'd been able to before – but they made it hard to tell where the ground was, made her unsure of herself on stairways.

Her first intention as she left the wreck of the Burton house was to walk through downtown and home without stopping. She'd get herself something to eat and go to work later. Once she'd crossed the bridge, though, she turned north along the brick path that ran above the river, then east through downtown until she was standing in front of the Colony Hotel where the Student Prince had once been, before the ground floor was renovated and divided into a faintly English pub on one side and a coffee shop on the other. Hardly a wall or a light fixture was left from the days when Del worked at the Prince. Such a short part of her life and so long ago, and it would mean so little if it weren't for what came of it – the young woman who was separated now from Del by the river and by an expanse of no-one's-land that had nothing to do with geography.

It was Del's responsibility to keep watch, of course, but from the proper distance. She was ready in case Amber needed anything – help with the rent, tuition if she decided to go back to school – but she'd relinquished emotional rights the day she handed Amber over in her yellow terrycloth sleeper. It was remarkable what you could get used to. It would be a waste to play at imagining a different trajectory for a course that originated so far in the past. Sometimes, though, the imagination will do as it pleases. The trick, then, is to elsewhere occupy your mind, to elsewhere occupy your self. There are ways.

Across the street from the Colony was a wooden bench. Del jaywalked to get to it. She stepped up to the sidewalk, miscalculated, and her toe caught the curb. Both hands shot out to break her fall and a moment later she was sitting on the edge of the sidewalk brushing grit off her palms.

"Are you all right ma'am?"

Ma'am. Not her favourite form of address, but he was only being polite, this shaved-to-a-shine young man with a loose-hanging suit and a briefcase and a friendly look on his face.

One ankle hurt a little, nothing serious. "I'm all right," she said. "It's the new glasses."

"Right, ma'am," he said, looking baffled. "So you're okay?" He put out a hand, but she'd already braced her palms on her good knee and was pushing herself up.

"Fine. Thanks." This was so embarrassing. To prove how fine she was, she stood steady and balanced until he turned to go, and then she limped to the bench. It was a minor twist; it would recover in a moment. She rested.

This was a city block in transition. The department store on the corner had closed six months before and there was no new tenant in the building. Department stores were supposed to be dependable, supposed to go on forever. Things were not supposed to change this way. Between the hotel and the papered-over windows of the old store were narrow storefronts where tiny businesses bloomed and wilted every few months. This sidewalk no longer carried the amount of traffic it had before the big store closed. The shop that was tucked in closest to the hotel had been toughing it out for at least a year, though: Terra Firma, the store that claimed to carry "all things to bring you back in touch with the earth."

Del had wandered into Terra Firma only once. The store felt like a repetition: incense was back in style, evidently. A lot of things were back in style from twenty-five years ago: candles stamped with the signs of the zodiac, patchouli oil, rags and feathers, Indian cotton blouses with tiny mirrors that looked out through embroidered eyelets. Everything old is new again. A woman who looked to be, like Del, in her mid-forties had stood, smiling, behind the counter, a long silver braid resting on her shoulder. Del had wanted to say to her, "Didn't we already do this part?" But as she browsed she saw the differences. Yes, there were the incense, the inlaid hash pipes, *The Illustrated I Ching*, the yoga mats, the small handmade books of poetry. But there were also books of a different tone, one, for instance, entitled *Discovering the Path to Riches*; the meaning of "riches" didn't appear to be entirely spiritual. On another shelf was a boxed kit that promised to instruct the buyer in how to release the energy of ancient Chinese coins (supplied) by lacing them together in a precise way with red ribbon (supplied); and this would lead to wealth. As calibrated by the goods of this world. Today, from the bench across the street, Del could read a blue and yellow poster taped in the window of Terra Firma, inviting the public to meet a "Prosperity Shaman." Promises. Someone should take a pen and stroke out the "an".

Del saw herself reflected in the glass front doors of the Colony as an indistinct arrangement of basic shapes and angles. Back when she worked at the Prince, she didn't use the front entrance. Staff went in and out the alley door. Policy. These days, a different collection of people would be opening and closing that back door, tormenting and taking care of each other the way Del and Phil and the others did when it was their turn. The way Amber must be doing over at Poor Man's.

Del flexed her twisted ankle. Not bad. She stood and tested it. Not great either. The idea of getting home, let alone to work, seemed to call for the discovery of a new source of energy. She hobbled to the bus stop.

At home she drew the curtains in her tidy little house and slept off and on. Towards six she roused herself, made a tomato and peanut butter sandwich, washed a carrot and a stick of celery, put it all on a tray and carried it to the living room. She sat in her old velour chair with the tray on her lap and her feet up. The ankle was steadier already. She picked up the remote and skipped from channel to channel. Game shows from California, sitcoms from New York and LA. The cable feed funneled the American networks through Detroit, and so, between shows, Del caught the local headlines from that faraway city. She'd have to watch later for the full story of the curious assortment of characters, among them a man with a braided beard, whose rooming house had been robbed. The way the time zones dovetailed with her hours of waking and sleeping and working, Del saw and heard more of Detroit than she did of Saskatoon. In the summertime, *News at Eleven* came on at nine. She'd come to prefer watching the Detroit local news over keeping track of what was happening here. The distance, the remove, made it more like a set of stories – items to watch purely for the sake of diversion. She could tolerate drama if it was half a continent away.

She had her television, she had her work, the occasional visit from Vivien or Tracy and once a week or so a coffee after work – sometimes even dinner at the Grille – with Larry. There were the end-of-the-month gatherings at the Roundhouse with a few co-workers from the second floor – a chance for the others to practise speaking English. It was a small, adequate, comfortable-enough life, or so she managed to think of it until the call last week from Duncan and Vivien – Duncan whom she still thought of as Scavenger, his nickname from the seventies. They were the bearers once more of bad news, telling her that Phil was dead. Or was it really bad news, this time, given the circumstances? She'd dared to say this to Vivien, who stayed on the line after Scavenger ran out of words.

"I'll ignore that ridiculous question," Vivien said. "I'll put it down to your state of shock."

They were silent for a moment, and it felt to Del like a silence full of old conversations, old questions.

"What?" Del finally said.

"I was thinking about Amber."

"Thinking what about Amber?"

"How she won't even know. This event will pass right by her as if it never happened."

"No," Del said, "as if it happened years ago." She paused. "Vivien..."

"Yes?"

"You aren't going to go and say anything?"

"No, I just... All right."

After she hung up, Del did her best to quell her emotions by reaching for the remote. A bubble of uneasiness rose at every commercial break. Vivien was her oldest and dearest, but she put too much stock in truth, prized it even when it was the booby prize. Vivien had trouble keeping her mouth shut. She wouldn't go to Amber now, would she? In the beginning, Vivien used to argue that Amber should be told about Phil, maybe even be taken to visit him. Have the opportunity to see his face, or at least the opportunity to choose not to, was how Vivien had put it.

First the phone call; and now, today, across the river – with timing that surely was unnecessarily cruel – a machine with a steel claw had ripped into the past. Everything old is indeed new. Every sliver of glass and cloying stick of incense. There should be rub-on anaesthetic for eruptions of old grief; there should be a Buckley's Mixture for the soothing of sore regrets. There should be refuge in sarcasm.

Del ran the bath and climbed in. She soaped her underarms, her thighs and her skinny ribcage and contemplated the slow transformation the body works on itself: the roundness below her bellybutton, so out of place on her small frame, as if it had been pasted on after the rest was finished; the morphology of breasts. She and Tracy have made jokes at work about how they should call head office and tell them to design a new line of shirts with lowered bustline darts, what with all the baby boomers.

She turned on the tap, soaked a washcloth and draped it warm across her shoulders. Yesterday her tense muscles had bothered her so much she'd left for work early, gone down to the lunchroom where she knew she'd find Larry with his before-the-buzzer coffee and asked for a shoulder rub.

"With pleasure," he said. Rarely did she allow him that close; she was still making up her mind about Larry – his niceness, the attention he paid her even when she didn't want attention. He arrived in the cutting room at work a year ago, when the accounting firm where his wife worked transferred her from Winnipeg to Saskatoon. He'd been a cutting room man in Winnipeg too, and didn't have much to lose in the move; his wife was the big earner. Ex-wife now, though Larry said it came as a surprise to him. Apparently the marriage had been in its last days even as they loaded the van. She could've *said* something.

He was an earnest shop steward who lately had begun to worry out loud about the World Trade Organization, specifically, the *Agreement on Textiles and Clothing*, of which he had a copy marked up with yellow highlighter. He went to meetings, sometimes even out-of-town meetings, to talk about the status of garment industry workers at home and abroad. "You wouldn't believe the politics of it all," he'd said once to Del. But of course she would believe it. That's what you got, she supposed, for being the quiet one. Just because you don't have a lot to say, people think there's nothing going on inside.

Still, keeping your mouth closed was the safest bet, and let people think what they want. It was opening your mouth that got you into situations. She'd made a mistake that night a couple of weeks ago at the Roadhouse, telling Larry about Amber, letting him into her business that way. It was the two and a half beers that did it. She'd admitted that the dimensions of her family as she'd first set them out for him were inaccurate; told him that her baby sister was in fact her daughter. Once he'd seen that opening he'd got his fingers in and pulled the whole idea wide and started stuffing the cavity with advice. Larry was blessed with so many opinions he didn't lack for spare ones to give away. If he thought – after that behaviour – she was about to let him in on the rest of it, No.

Del had never been a heavy drinker at the worst of times, but by the time she got into bed that night – alone, make no mistake, she hadn't let her guard down *that* far – she'd decided never to drink again if that was the kind of confessional episode it lead to. Best to abstain. She'd renewed her promise the next morning and kept it since, despite the Scotch in the cupboard, despite the four beer still standing in the fridge beside the milk. Someone else would drink them.

"Full of knots," Larry had said yesterday as his fingers worked their way across Del's shoulders and up her neck, past the nape and up the back of her head, moving through her short hair. His touch lost its force and verged on becoming a caress.

"Further down," she'd said, and his hands had returned to their straightforward working of her shoulders.

At nine, Del tuned in to watch the Detroit news. Here was a resident of the rooming house she'd heard about earlier. He pulled at his braided beard as he described how a masked man had cleaned out everything of value while the landlord crouched, quaking, in the hallway. In another part of the city, at a high school, police were dealing with a suspected arson. Downtown, a gang of children had jumped a man at a banking machine. So much going on, so distressing. In a food court two girls with a knife had kidnapped a woman and told her to take them shopping. The TV stories were supposed to be there simply for the sake of story, to satisfy Del's need to be interested or amazed by some faraway incident. She counted on them. But tonight they were difficult to take in. She wanted a way to keep the stories in line, pin them, manage them.

Del turned off the set, went to her bedroom and changed into her nightgown. Flurries of memory and unseemly emotion, as if things that had been held secure inside the walls of the Burton house were now set free to roam. If she'd been the sort to marry under those circumstances, this would be the year of the silver anniversary. She walked around the foot of the bed, smoothing the covers with the flat of her hand. Palm down, she made her way along the far side closer to the wall and back again.

Downtown after work the following day, Del edged past a display table at the entrance to the bookstore in the Midtown. Hardcovers flashed their shiny jackets at her: cookery, history, islands in the sun. She headed further into the store and made her way along the wall, looking for maps. She passed a metal stand tiled with aphoristic fridge magnets: *The square root of joy is faith; The square root of apathy is selfishness; The square root of generosity is imagination.* Evidently life was a matter of factoring back down to essentials.

She walked past rows of books under the sign that said Self-Help. She could almost hear the noise they made. A decade ago, in the days when Vivien was seeking her inner child, Del and Vivien had met for drinks one afternoon on a hot cement patio downtown and then, on Vivien's impulse, stopped at the library before separating to go home. Del had followed Vivien to the appropriate section and waited while her friend scanned the shelves.

"Help yourself," said Vivien, gesturing to the books on either side.

"Pun intended?" said Del.

"What? Oh, I see." Vivien smiled.

"Anyway, I never touch the stuff."

"Have a seat then, I won't be long."

Del, who had a light buzz in her head from the combined effects of the afternoon sun and the quick half-pint, sat down right there on the floor amid the three hundreds of Dewey's decimals.

Vivien looked at her with a raised eyebrow. Warm brown eyes, soft brown hair parted in the middle, as she'd been wearing it since the seventies, sometimes longer and sometimes shorter. Longer, that day ten years ago, as she looked at Del and said, "Wouldn't you be better off in a chair?"

"Thanks. I'm fine right here."

"There's a chair by the wall."

"I'm *fine*."

Del ran her finger along the corrugation of spines. Entire fields of psychology were bound up between covers. She waited until Vivien disappeared around the bank of shelves, then took down a book. Italicized twelve-step lingo littered the text. She wedged the book back into its tight space, bumped her fingers along the row, took down another.

Vivien came back around the corner hugging half a dozen volumes and Del snapped her book shut and shelved it too quickly, thinking how she must look to Vivien, as if, like a three-year-old, she were under the illusion she could replace it without anyone seeing.

With half a laugh, Vivien said, "I caught that."

"Busted."

She resented those books, the way they made a psychology out of ordinary troubles; their message that she should consider herself sick. *Excessive need for control. Learned helplessness.* That isn't how life is at all. People get over things. People are like springs – resilient that is, not twisted.

"Victim books," she said to Vivien.

"Yeah?" Again, the raised eyebrow. Vivien's gaze moved from

Del to her own cargo of books, then back to Del.

Oops. She hadn't meant to offend. "No, no," Del had said. "For you it's something you're adding on top, not something you're using to fill a hole."

Vivien had shrugged, "I'm interested, that's all."

"Exactly," Del had said.

In the bookstore now, Del lowered her eyelids to limit the amount of information coming in. Moving past the self-help section, she found a tall metal rack filled with maps. She adjusted her glasses and brought the print into focus: Ottawa, Toronto, Winnipeg. She rotated the wobbly rack: Montreal, Vancouver, Regina. Close to the bottom, where she had to do a deep knee bend to read the titles, were the American cities: Palm Springs, Miami, San Francisco. She caught the dry smell of paper as she fingered through.

"Can I help you?"

"Detroit."

"Pardon me?"

"I need a map of Detroit."

The woman removed a handful of maps and fanned through them, did the same with another handful. She was looking in precisely the places Del had already searched. Couldn't she go look somewhere else – a secret drawer in the back, some place the customer wasn't perfectly capable of looking on her own? But no, the woman riffled through another handful and said they didn't have much call for Detroit.

"If it's important, we can order it."

"Yes."

The rain began as she left downtown. As always, she was prepared; she paused to take her shell out of her backpack. Yesterday's twisted ankle had been minor, had recovered overnight as she'd known it would. She walked quickly, listening to the patter of the drops against her waterproof hood. By the time she reached home it was pouring. She shook her jacket over the tub and hung it from the shower head to drip dry. The storm made a great noise, flung sheets of water at the living room window. Del poured herself a glass of water. Until her recent vow of abstinence, her drink of choice had been Scotch. She sipped her water and decided she didn't miss the whiskey. She knew how to do without.

Her house was on high ground, but in other parts of town people would spend the following days mopping their basements and calling in the insurance adjusters. Captivated by the storm, Del moved her old velour chair in front of the window and watched as the rain swept down, making a lake in the low area further along the street. A storm like this after all this time could still bring with it a sense of dread.

The summer she was pregnant there had been one of the most violent rains the city had ever seen, but that time Del had missed the better part of the show because she'd been sitting in a dark corner in a windowless west-side bar, talking with a disengaged Phil about the approaching birth. He was working split shift that day, agreed to meet her during the in-between.

He: "You're still giving it up?"

She: "I'm still giving *her* up."

"You don't know it's a her."

"I know she isn't an *it*."

"Sorry."

The rain and thunder had sounded small and far away as they sat in the pub, and they came out unaware into the aftermath. The parking lot shone slick in the premature darkness and the street lights were mirrored in the puddles. All over town, she would later hear, cars were abandoned and basements flooded to depths of four feet. Tree branches fell through front porches. In one of a handful of accidents associated with the storm, a small boy drowned in a pedestrian tunnel under the freeway.

Phil unlocked his bicycle and used the side of his hand to squeegee the water off the seat. "I guess that's it," he said. Then, as if he thought that was too short a remark for the occasion, he added, "For now. I'll call. Don't get wet."

As he'd pedalled away, she'd watched the curve of his backbone where it showed through his red work shirt.

Today's storm tapered off to a drizzle. Del turned on the TV to watch *News at Eleven* (at nine). The camera lens framed a Detroit shopkeeper standing in front of a blazing building, surrounded by cigarette cartons and kitchen towels, welcome mats, plastic dishes, chocolate bars – all the merchandise he could drag out before the fire department forbade him to go back in. He had no insurance, he said. He gestured toward what was left of his inventory, knocking over a flimsy rack of gum as he did so. His existence a shambles. Del could almost have cried. The storekeeper disappeared from the screen; the newscast shifted to politics and Del turned off the set, thinking of the sorry man on the wet sidewalk, his white hair against his dark skin, the tremor in his hand.

"Who will help me now?" he'd said.

In sympathy Del said, "No one but yourself."

PART 2

OUT FROM UNDER

It seemed so simple in the beginning, this moving to the city and finding work, the relief of being here rather than there. And the job – the job was like an invitation to a party every night.

"What's the new girl's name?" said the guy with the single caterpillar eyebrow. He stood, shaggy-haired and half-shadowed in the diluted light from the shuffleboard table and directed his question not to Delorie, who was right there in front of him delivering his Molson Canadian, but to Scavenger, who was behind the bar pulling glasses out of the dishwasher; his short, muscled arms moving quickly to keep up with the speed of the belt. The eyebrow man held a number of coins in his hand; he turned and sorted them as he spoke.

"Delorie," Scavenger said, still reaching for glasses, the wisp of black hair in front of his bald spot drifting forward in front of his eyes, "meet Shuffleboard Mike."

Mike tossed seventy-five cents on her tray, more by half than the price of the beer. "Welcome to the Prince," he said. "I start you off with a good tip. After that it depends on the service."

The word "proprietary" came to mind, and Delorie smiled to herself. If Mike thought she was smiling at him, fine.

Anna walking by said, "Don't be fooled. That's the last decent tip you'll get from him."

The regulars sat at the front, close to the bar – Mike, Twitch, Stan the Hippie Indian, Sheilah the Bear and an assortment of others – handy to the challenge boards for pool and shuffleboard. Because she was the new girl, Delorie discovered, the regulars accorded her special status. Twitch found out she liked "Long Cool Woman" and he played it on the jukebox so often that by the end of her first week she could sing it by heart and wished she couldn't. Ajax gave her a two dollar tip to congratulate her on making it through Saturday, the biggest tip anyone scored that night.

"The significance of a two dollar bill," said Phil. The old joke about whore money. He goosed her spine with a pushed-out knuckle as they waited at the bar for Scavenger to fill their orders. Phil: dark brown hair with a glint of red; a wiry build; triangular sideburns that were close to being out of style; a wide grin that might even be genuine. Like Delorie, he was a few months out of a small-town high school. Delorie shrugged off his comment and slipped the rust-colored note into her apron pocket. Don't look a gift horse. She intended to enjoy being the new girl.

Hammer, a muscular pool player, insisted she bring his drinks even when she wasn't assigned to the front. For the fun of it, Delorie complied for a few days; but on busy nights it was a nuisance and on Saturday she refused, told him there'd be no more special service.

"I can't serve you. Professional ethics – those are Max's tables, Max's tips."

Max, however, said, "Don't do me any favours," and Hammer whined and pouted, said he *required* she speak with him. She walked over.

"What's your problem?"

"A matter of great importance, Delorie-baby." He straightened, looked her in the eye, took her free hand in both of his. She let him hold it, let herself enjoy his grip and the way he moved his thumb back and forth across her palm.

"Well?"

"You have to marry me."

"Because...?"

"Because...I'm pregnant." Deadpan. "And you're the mother." Mustache curling into the corners of his mouth and she wondered if it didn't get in the way when he ate.

"Har-dee-har." She withdrew her hand and slapped his arm. Some people think they're very funny when they're outside of four beer. Still, the warm feeling where his thumb had crossed her palm.

"Delorie-baby, come back." She shook her head as she walked toward the bar to call her order to Scavenger; flipped her straight, dark hair over her shoulder. She'd washed it that afternoon, knew how it shone, how it swung between her bony shoulder blades as she walked away.

Phil clinked his tray against hers. "Hammer's in love."

"Should I be worried?"

"Not one bit," Vivien said. She was taking a smoke break, leaning against the wall beside the cupboard where they stashed the empties. "It doesn't last more than a few days with him."

Vivien: long limbs, bangles at her wrist, expert eyeliner. Soft brown hair in a single braid; flash of earring as she turned her head. Already Delorie knew when she looked at her that she'd found both a friend and someone to admire.

"Scavenger!" Hammer shouted. "If Delorie doesn't personally deliver my next beer I'll commit a drastic act." Delorie, biting back a smile, picked up her whiskies and mixes, arranged them on her tray, distributed the weight so it would balance.

"Drastic like what?" Scavenger said. Heads turned. Scavenger laughed and looked at the faces of the people sitting close to the bar. He raised his hand to brush back his orphan wisp of hair. His manner showed the confidence of a man who — even if he was only five six and his best facial feature was a finely carved mustache — was broad-chested and moved the way a guy does when he's in command of his muscles and the space around them.

Hammer looked at the faces too. Delorie set a final two draft on her tray.

"If she doesn't come over," Hammer said. "I'm gonna lift the pool table off the floor."

"You'll wreck your back," Scavenger said.

"You know, Scavenger," Hammer said, "for a young guy, you're pretty old."

Scavenger returned to the taps, poured glass after glass of draft and lined them up fresh and foaming along the bar. "I guess I am."

Delorie picked up her tray. She was pleased with how the muscles in her left arm, her carrying arm, were already growing into the job. "Be good, now, Hammer," she said. As initiation rites went, she'd been through worse. In high school, her senior had made her wear a bone in her hair like Pebbles Flintstone, and a gunny sack for a dress. He'd also tried (but failed) to make her carry a plastic vinegar jug he'd marked with XXX, in reference to her father's drinking habits. The rites of passage were far more fun here at the Prince, where nobody knew the first thing about her. This feeling of being out from under, in a place where she could breathe freely, move about, laugh out loud.

Hammer stood, rolled his shoulders, flexed, and started for the pool table. Sheilah the Bear and Stan the Hippie Indian moved aside, cues in their hands.

Scavenger came around from behind the bar. "Sit down Hammer."

Phil tapped Delorie on the shoulder. "Better watch this, Delorie – I mean, Delorie-*baby*."

A man in a purple jacket halfway down the house shouted for his Scotch and ginger and she ignored him. Anyone who put ginger ale in Scotch could wait. Hammer bent his knees like a weightlifter and braced himself, his hands under one end of the pool table. He strained and reddened; his neck muscles quivered and his blonde hair trembled above his forehead; a finger of ash dropped off the cigarette he was biting and landed on the felt. Is he doing this in honour of me, thought Delorie, like with knights and damsels? How did it come about that skinny Delores Woods from Ripley, Saskatchewan had been transformed into a damsel worthy of attention? What to do, wave a handkerchief?

One end of the pool table rose the slightest bit off the tiles.

"A-fucking-mazing," said Shuffleboard Mike.

"You crack that slate, Hammer," Scavenger said slowly, "and hotel management will kick your ass into next November."

"He really did it," Delorie said. "Some people." No one, not even under the influence of alcohol, had ever performed a feat of physical prowess for the purpose of impressing her.

Hammer lowered the table, relaxed his grimace and leaned against the wall until his arms stopped shaking. Scavenger walked over to him, took the cigarette from his mouth, guided him back to his chair. Delorie made her way to her section. The point of Hammer's exercise was exactly what? To show that he *could*? To get her attention? More likely this: to show that he could get her attention. Just don't mistake it for affection.

None of which made the flattery any less fun.

When she came back to the front, Phil was unloading glasses from his tray into the dishwasher. It was overfull and the belt wasn't moving. "Damn! Don't you people know how to load this friggin' thing?" A highball glass slipped from his hand and broke on the tile.

"Shit-shit-shit," he said. "Leave that, I'll get it next time." He looked at Delorie and said, "Know what Hammer did when Anna was the new girl? Sat on the counter in the women's can eating barbeque potato chips until she went in there to talk him out. He does these things."

But of *course* Anna would raise a reaction. Anna: voluptuous at her hips, her breasts, even at her lips. She wore her sleeves folded back, showing the translucent skin on the insides of her forearms. Those six inches of skin could make her look half undressed if she moved an arm in a certain way. And hair with a natural wave and naturally blonde. Delorie hadn't much for natural waves in either physique or hair.

Sheilah walked up to the bar with her pool cue. "What about our game? We paid for that game."

"Hammer," Scavenger said, "buy these two a new game."

"Delorie-baby," said Hammer, "light of my life, bring me two draft and I'll gladly pay these two for a new game."

"Christ's sake," Phil said, lifting two full glasses from the bar and taking them to Hammer. "It'll go to her head."

Well it already *had* gone to her head, and now Phil's agitation did too, his response out of all proportion when he'd broken the glass. You had to expect a little breakage in a place like this. Delorie picked her way around the shards of glass, smiling. She was enjoying herself, even though – she knew, she knew – she should be the last person to be impressed by the public performance of a drunk; she'd seen more than her share of those.

For example: her father, Victor Woods; his performance one night, unscheduled, at the Ripley hockey rink. The stands are full for the first game of the playoffs. Second period is winding down, fans hooting their disapproval of the ref and the linemen as the Cats fail to close a five-to-one gap in the score.

"That's offside. S'matter with your eyes?"

"Hey ref, hey shit-on-skates!"

Delorie's in the stands with two girlfriends, conscious that her father is also there, only a few yards to her right, coffee spilling from the green-banded, rink kitchen mug in his hand, dripping over his thin fingers. He wears his sloppy brown overcoat; the back of it drapes unevenly over his shoulder blades.

The ref calls yet another penalty on a Cats forward. "That's a bullshit call," Victor Woods shouts. "Bull-*shit*, bull-*shit*, bull-*shit*," he hollers, making a chant of it. But no one joins in on a chant begun by Victor Woods. Delorie, standing there with her friends – who make the generous, or simply embarrassed, effort not to say anything, not to look in the direction of her father, not to comment – knows that the coffee running over his fingers has been spiked from the whiskey flask in his back pocket. There's nothing unusual about that; there are typically a dozen or so hip flasks weighing down pockets in the Ripley rink on a hockey night.

The buzzer signals the end of second period. The teams file back to their dressing rooms, and two boys jump the boards and take down scrapers to clear the ice. Victor Woods takes a shortcut through the penalty box and walks out onto the ice as well. Delorie clenches her stomach muscles to brace herself for whatever will be next.

"Bullshit game," he shouts. A few people laugh, but not in a mean way. "Go, Victor!" someone yells. "Give 'em hell." Victor stands at centre ice, watching the boys with their scrapers. He shrugs out of his brown overcoat and the rink grows quiet as people wait to see what he's up to. Delorie stands still, hands in her jacket pockets, and slows her breathing. The two boys push their scrapers up and down the length of the ice. Delorie's two friends look at each other but not at her. They look at her father out on the ice and then at each other again. Her younger brother Stuart is across the rink among a group of boys, his features unrevealing. He makes eye contact with Delorie. Looks away.

"A rink full of bull," Victor Woods says to the crowd, taking his overcoat by the shoulders and holding it out to one side, empty sleeves dangling. His scarecrow hair, his thin long arms. He slips, and Delorie feels like she is falling with him. He regains his balance. Someone in the stands hoots. Her face burns. Victor Woods steps to the right, placing himself in the path of one of the wide scraper shovels. The boy behind the shovel stops. He grins, not at Woods, but at the people in the stands, looking first to one side of the rink and then to the other. He laughs out loud. The hem of the overcoat in Victor Woods's hands skims the ice. Delorie counts the seconds of her breathing, four on the inhale, four on the exhale. The rink caretaker and the game ref open a door in the boards and begin to walk toward centre ice, the caretaker in his boots and the ref on his skates but going slowly, keeping to the pace of the caretaker, as if he's deciding how to handle this. Victor Woods, his balance uncertain, attempts to flick the coat as if it were a toreador's cape.

"Come on. A bullfight, with all this bull."

Both the boys are stopped behind their scrapers now. They are done laughing and their faces, like those of the onlookers, show uncertainty. Delorie takes half a step backward so she's standing a little behind her friends. They would have to turn to look at her. Her brother Stuart finds her eyes again. They never discuss these scenes. Woods makes another flick with his sagging coat and his feet go out from under him. It is a hard fall and Delorie is glad the ice has punished him. "Son of a bitch," he says quietly. "Son of a goddamn bitch." The caretaker helps him to his feet and off the ice; the ref moves his arms as if to help, but he isn't much use.

Across the rink, Stuart pulls his hand out of his pocket, looks to make sure she's looking back at him. What's that he's holding, too small to see? A tiny flame appears. He's lit a wooden match, one-handed, with his thumbnail, the way he's been practising. Hello you, way over there.

And here a few years later in the Student Prince on a Saturday night, a drunken man lifting one end of a pool table in her honour was enough to make her feel generous. There's the kind of attention a person doesn't like to have, and then there's the kind she does like. She could afford to give Phil a hand with the broken glass. She fetched the whisk broom and the dustpan from behind the bar. Before she swept, she picked up the larger fragments and put them directly into the garbage bin, handling them gingerly. The way to handle glass, that was one thing she knew about, and it wasn't always obvious; you had to learn the hard way. You could be brushing off a terry tablecloth with your bare hand and be caught unaware; you'd feel the multiple stabs and there you'd be with a cluster of tiny slivers sticking out of the pad of your little finger, sparkling. And you'd have to call on Vivien, who kept a pair of tweezers in her apron pocket and a needle behind the counter. She'd lead you over to the bar where the light was good and go to work on your hand, while you focused on the dangly silver Capricorn earring peeking out from her dark hair in order not to feel the dig of the needle.

Delorie finished with the broken glass and put the dustpan away, punched in her order and waited at the bar. Phil had returned and was waiting ahead of her.

"You neglected to say thank you," she said.

He looked at her.

"For cleaning up your mess."

"You didn't give me time," he said. "Don't rush me."

Scavenger, pouring shots behind the bar, looked from Phil to Delorie then back to Phil. He raised his eyebrows.

"What?" Delorie said.

"Idle speculation," Scavenger said. "None of my business."

Phil's elbow rested on the bar close to Delorie's own. Let's try it, she thought, for here I am, suddenly a damsel worthy of attention. She closed the gap, sleeve to sleeve, and, though he didn't look, she felt the press of Phil's elbow against hers before he moved away.

SMOKY REALM

The bus rolled across the bridge, wheezed and farted diesel exhaust along Fourth Avenue. Delorie squinted as she looked out the window at the bright, snowy streets; the Student Prince had no windows and her eyes had grown accustomed to inside and nighttime. She arranged her coat flaps over her knees for warmth – the maxi-coat she'd made over from a shorter coat, buying fun fur in the basement of the Army & Navy store and hand-stitching a band of it along the hem. These were good days and nights. She was content to be a passenger, pleased to be on her way somewhere. It didn't matter where, so long as the road didn't end in Ripley.

She rang the bell for her stop and walked the two remaining blocks to the back door of the hotel, moving quickly, her stride beginning right from the hip in a motion people had told her was graceful, her torso steady. She had long ago learned this way of carrying herself. The old trick of walking with an apple on your head. It's a cliché until you try it. She and her best friend Mona had spent hours practising in Mona's bedroom at age thirteen. McIntoshes were impossible; they used Delicious, because the five bumps at the base gave the apple something to stand on. Later, alone in her own room, Delorie had kept on with the exercise: learning control, minding her own business, ignoring the ruckus down the hall.

Delorie pulled open the heavy back door of the Prince. She'd come to associate the smell of stale cigarette smoke trapped in upholstery fibres with arriving at a good place. She felt the surge of energy she always felt at the beginning of her shift. The end of week two. She'd learned a few things by now. For example, that the names of the sections – left wall, centre, right wall and front – were defined from the point of view of the bartender. As were other things, like how many minutes it should take for a waitress to go to the bathroom. Like who got cut off and who still got service even if he was a pain in the ass.

She'd learned the art of the sharp retort, mastered a karate-like chop with the side of her hand, developed a technique for stepping on a customer's foot, apparently accidentally. The technique came in handy when she asked the guy in the blue leather headband for his order and he answered, I'll have a hot buttered waitress with no dressing. He said it as if he was the first customer who'd ever said that and she ought to laugh along with him like a good sport.

And all the while, she concentrated, because Scavenger didn't allow the staff to write down orders. Unprofessional, he said, an inefficient use of time. Fine. Delorie matched orders to faces: Pilsner nose, rye-and-Coke eyebrows, draft-horse jaw.

The Student Prince was appropriately named. Beyond the tables colonized by regulars at the front were three long rows of tables crowded with engineering students, artsies, nursing students, med students. A group of engineering students favoured the back settee. They stacked their winter coats and hats and gloves in a soft tower in the corner. If one of them drank too much he'd burrow into the tower and fall asleep.

The engineers found out Delorie knew a thing or two about words. She'd overheard a conversation, clarified for them the difference between "illusion" and "allusion". They took to calling on her when similar puzzles arose. They said, "What's a smart girl like you doing in a place like this?"

"I guess I don't know any better."

They requested vocabulary lessons. "Delorie, O Knowledgeable One, teach us a new word tonight."

"What kind of word do you want?"

"Any word, as long as it's one we don't know."

"That shouldn't be hard." She tapped her foot, thought for a second, saw Scavenger at the front, arms resting on the bar, eyes scanning the room. "Panoptic," she said.

"What kind of dick?" said the tall one with the freckles.

Okay, she might have made a better choice. "Nothing to do with a *dick*," she said. "Panoptic. It's when you can see in all directions."

"A dick with the power of sight!"

"Let's start over then, why don't we?" she said, transferring empties from the table to her tray. "Panop*tic*. As in, panoptic vision, like Scavenger over there, keeping track. Be careful, he may be watching you."

The engineers, like good grammar students, made much of using their new word in a sentence.

"Scavenger has a panop-dick and the girls love it!"

"Scavenger's panop-dick moves in all directions."

"Pan-what?" said Anna, stopping to clink trays with Delorie.

"Panoptic," Delorie said. "'It Pays to Increase Your Word Power.' The neighbour lady at home always had a *Reader's Digest* sitting on the toilet tank."

The engineers gathered Delorie a tip from the change on the table. They raised their glasses and christened her "Funk & Wagnalls." She performed a mock bow and dropped the coins into her apron pocket. "We like the new girl," one of them shouted down the long room to Scavenger. They started to sing their College of Engineering rhyme, and when they chanted the line about drinking forty beers Scavenger shouted back, "Behave now." There were, after all, laws about what you could or couldn't do in a drinking establishment: couldn't take photographs; couldn't drink and stand up at the same time; not allowed to sing.

"Yeah," said Delorie. "Show some decorum."

"Decorum," said the freckled engineer. "D-E-C-O-R..."

After they'd turned the customers out at closing time that night, Scavenger cracked a beer for each of the staff. The Molson's rep had been in and told him to buy a round. Delorie sat beside Vivien on the end of the U-shaped settee that faced the pool table. She slipped her shoes off and massaged her feet on the rung of an empty chair. She pressed her soles, where the aches from a vigorous eight-hour shift were concentrated, against the wooden ridges. Yes. She lifted her free beer. It was good to be in a place where a party could be rustled up at a moment's notice.

Phil reached for his bottle and took a long drink. He took down two pool cues, handed one to Anna, and racked up. "Let's see what you know about the properties of balls," he said.

"Let's just," Anna said. The tacks she'd pushed into the heels of her shoes clicked on the tile as she walked to the table. It made a person look, that clickety-click, tacks on tile. Made you notice the fine curve of Anna's ankle as she leaned in to line up her break shot.

Further down the settee, Max stretched out full-length, put his forearm over his eyes, and said, "Turn out the lights when you leave." Max: childish round face with rough blond curls; a part-time student, part-time waiter. The settee was his bedroom. He'd lost his place on Avenue J for nonpayment of rent and now he was living out of the walk-in fridge and showering at the university before class. Scavenger said it was okay as long as he was tidy and always closed the Johnny Walker boxes that served as his chest of drawers and laundry hamper and filing cabinet, in case the man from public health happened by.

Scavenger put a quarter in the jukebox. "Brandy, You're a Fine Girl," his usual first choice. Delorie was betting the next song would be "China Grove." He favoured the upbeat tunes, liked to sing along, drum on the table with his fingers. He played the jukebox with special quarters that were painted black. Before the man from Griffin Amusements came to empty the machine on Thursdays, Scavenger would unlock the caddy at the side, pick out his black quarters, and slip them into an ashtray he kept in a drawer behind the bar. He never paid for a song. "The bar's entitled," he'd explained to Delorie when he showed her how it worked. "I never take out any more than just the black ones I put in."

"Give me one of your painted quarters, Scavenger," Delorie said when "China Grove" had finished.

"Why would I do that?"

"Because," she said, "tonight's my two-week anniversary on the job."

"Reason enough," he said. "Catch."

She tapped her fingernails on the glass of the jukebox and considered the titles. B3, "Queen of the Silver Dollar." Phil had been threatening to make an example of that tune, smash the forty-five and nail the vinyl bits to the wall above the jukebox to illustrate what happens to a song that's played too often. She watched him now as he bent above the pool table. He glanced up at her for an instant through the screen of his forward-falling hair, then concentrated on the table again as he lined up a double bank manoeuvre. Delorie pressed the keys for B3.

"Ah, my theme song," Vivien said. Phil groaned as the others, all but Max, belted out the mawkish words about the jesters vying for the favour of the queen. Vivien laughed her brown-eyed laugh and raised her bottle to Anna and Delorie. Here's to we three queens.

Max rolled over on the bench. "Have you people no pity?"

"None whatsoever," said Delorie.

An hour later Delorie put on her boots and her made-over coat and went to call a cab. Phil followed her out the back to where she waited between the two sets of doors. "Happy anniversary," he said. "Want to go halves on the fare?"

"Sure... Why didn't I think of that?"

They stood and waited in the small, warm space, looking out the glass doors instead of at each other, coat sleeves not quite touching. Phil shifted his stance and touched her winter boot with the toe of his.

"How can you balance on a heel like that?" he said.

She didn't speak. She pressed back against his foot with her own.

They sat close enough to each other in the back seat that by the time the cab was turning left toward Broadway Bridge it felt only natural, necessary in fact, to bring their foreheads together and open their coats to each other.

NAKEDNESS

Over the following weeks Delorie and Phil developed confused living arrangements between his two rooms on Main Street and her bachelor suite on the third floor of an old house near the river. They moved back and forth carrying her denim tote bag, into which they threw their essentials. They had trouble keeping track of toothbrushes, hairbrushes, birth control devices, favourite shirts.

Phil's place on Main Street consisted of a bedroom and a kitchen. In the kitchen, the larger of the two rooms, they spent little time. Most often they were in the other room making use of the single bed.

"Phil the First," she called him one day as they lay together, her finger tracing circles around his nipple. She was making an admission, though he'd probably guessed it by now. Back in Ripley, virginity hadn't been so much a matter of principle as a means to an exit. A pregnant girl was scripted to settle down and stay there. Imagine that: imagine staying there.

When she said "Phil the First" he raised his eyebrows. He didn't put a number alongside her name. He wasn't the type to admit he hadn't been around, but she suspected he'd been looking for a place to get started too.

He took the heavy glass ashtray from the floor by his bed and rested it on his stomach.

"Isn't that cold?" she said.

"Of course." He lit two cigarettes and handed one to her. Smoke rose and hung in front of Jimi Hendrix's face on the wall.

Delorie left the bed and wandered about the room, smoking, practising nakedness. Walking, standing; it wasn't easy being wrapped in nothing but air. She came back to the bed at intervals, let her small breasts hang as she leaned in to knock ashes into the ashtray. How vulnerable a pair of nipples with no cloth to cover them, as if they're open channels to a person's whole insides. Phil watched her, smoked, stopped watching, blew a smoke ring and tried to catch it on his big toe.

Underneath the window was a plywood bookcase Phil had made in grade twelve shop class. It was crowded with socks, sweaters, window envelopes from the phone company, also half a dozen heavy textbooks bought and paid for in September when he'd registered to do a teaching degree, then failed to show for classes after the first week. (It took two months for his mother to figure out he'd quit without starting, he told Delorie. His mother had been through grief over this; after all, she was the one who'd convinced his father that a degree wouldn't hurt. Don't worry, she'd argued, he'll come back to the farm, and anyway, he'll need a way to supplement the farm income. The joke was on her, Phil said to Delorie. He had no intention of farming.)

Delorie picked up a weighty sociology text from the bookcase, opened it, read out headings from the dense table of contents: "English Kinship Structures"; "Social Deviance and Control"; "Communities and Groups." So people actually made a study of these things. University: she might try it herself one day, once she'd put away a few bucks. First things first, though. "What have you got to eat?" They'd been awake since eleven. It was one thirty now, and they had to be at work by three.

"Toasted relish sandwiches," he said. His cupboards were outfitted with plates, glasses and cutlery he'd liberated from the hotel kitchen one or two items at a time, but these weren't as useful as they might have been, since rarely was there food in the fridge. For staples, he kept instant coffee, which they'd both developed a taste for, and graham crackers. Most of his meals he ate half price from the hotel kitchen. Maybe for Christmas she'd give him a gift certificate for Safeway.

"Relish sandwiches. Is that the best you can do?" Delorie returned to the bedside and put out her cigarette. She climbed onto the bed so she was standing over him, then stepped across and sat down in the narrow space between Phil and the wall. Resisting the temptation to wrap herself in a blanket, she moved her free hand over his abdomen. The ashtray wobbled. Her hand travelled to his biceps and she prodded. A bench and a set of weights were hidden in the corner of his bedroom beneath an unstable formation of laundry. He still used the weights once in a while, he claimed, though Delorie had never caught him at it. He used to be a runner too, but she didn't catch him at that either. She had to laugh the day she met his high school friend Eric the Red, and Eric said what an impressive runner Phil was, all those miles he covered on the country roads at home. "No shit," Eric said. "He ran almost every day."

Phil as a runner: hmmmm. He'd quit bumming smokes off Scavenger and Max and started buying his very own pack every second day. But apparently it was true. He used to run, so he told her, with a stone in each hand for weight. Stones from the roadside back on the farm, smooth stones with rust-coloured patterns from the iron inside. The markings, Phil said, sometimes looked like little stick figures. He'd shown her the stone he brought to the city and kept under the bed. She'd held it, a smooth grey egg with brownish red markings that made a picture of a running man. At high school track meets, the runners had always attracted Delorie. She'd watched from the sidelines, admiring the way, when the pistol sounded, they looked as if they'd been released; their bursting speed evidence of a letting go she wasn't capable of herself.

"Why do you keep it under the bed?" she'd said when she saw the running-man stone.

"To chase away the bogeyman." He'd roared at her like a make-believe monster. She'd shielded her face with her hands, then been ashamed of her failure to face him down coolly.

Now Phil grabbed the hand that prodded his arm. "What?" he said. "You're still looking for muscleman?" He kissed her finger, then bit it lightly.

"Maybe. Someone strong enough to lift a pool table. Can you do that?"

"Watch me, I might."

"Okay."

"But only for you, Delorie. Or should I say, *Delorie-baby?*"

He was too deft a mimic, plucking Hammer's voice from the nighttime bar and delivering it here where the light of noon stripped it to a pathetic whine. She didn't like the resulting edge to the words, an edge that mocked her as much as it mocked Hammer. Delorie curled her fingers into Phil's chest hair and tightened.

"Jesus, Delorie! That smarts!" he said, squeezing vice-like at her wrists until she released. "What the fuck!"

He left the bed, sat in the beanbag chair, skin against yellow plastic, and glared at her. "Jesus," he said again, rubbing gingerly at his chest. "You better do something about that."

"About what?"

"*About what* – hah! You're madder than anyone I know." He looked away from her, took from the floor a copy of *National Lampoon*, said in a flat voice, "Pass the ashtray."

Delorie did so, then walked to the window and stood, naked you bet, looking out at the sun-dazzled snow and the traffic crawling through it and the brick apartment buildings across the street, full of people whose names she didn't know. Mad: she hadn't thought of it that way. She was just ready to loosen some of the self-control she'd so determinedly laced together. Hello city, she whispered to the window. I'll show you mine if you'll show me yours.

Delorie preferred that she and Phil spend their time together at her apartment, an open third-floor space converted to a bachelor suite. Along one wall, under the slope of the ceiling, were a short, round-cornered fridge, a two-burner stove and a sink with a small counter. Her dishes came from the cupboards at home in Ripley – four matched plates, cereal bowls, large, friendly coffee mugs in different colours – discards her mother had packed into boxes for her months before the big blowup and the bus ticket to Saskatoon and the silence that persisted between daughter and parents. *Number one bowler,* one of the mugs said, gold letters on blue. *Bob* said another. There were no Bobs in the family.

Delorie managed her groceries better than Phil managed his – rice and spaghetti in the deep lower drawer, cans of sauce and soup on the shelves, cheese in the fridge, occasionally carrots, often milk. The pullout couch was roomier than Phil's bed, though he was right when he said it wasn't as comfortable, too much definition of the springs under the wafer of padding. She'd added extra blankets between the mattress and the sheet, but still they had no trouble tracing the heavy skeleton under the surface.

Her paperbacks were lined up along the baseboard, two deep, from the dresser to the corner. On the windowsill was a trophy made of wood and shiny silver plastic with a brass plate that said *Academic Achievement, Herbert Powell High School, Delores Woods, 1973.* Phil liked to snicker at the trophy so that Delorie would swat him, which she dependably did, and then she would laugh, because high school had so little to do with anything now that she'd escaped into life, now that she answered only to herself.

As a gesture of yuletide goodwill, the hotel gave everyone on staff an eight-pound turkey. Neither Phil nor Delorie left the city for Christmas. They spent the day itself at Delorie's bachelor suite. Her number was unlisted so that her parents couldn't call. Phil had called his mother and father on the afternoon of Christmas Eve, before work, to give them his long-distance greetings. He had to work Boxing Day, what a shame, he couldn't come home. You take care, though.

Delorie cooked their scrawny turkeys one after the other in the small oven and the room smelled like a banquet. "We'll take half the leftovers to your place. To supplement your relish sandwiches."

No stuffing, she'd never learned how, but Delorie made potatoes and gravy and opened a can of cranberry sauce she'd had the foresight to buy. She was pleased with what she produced. This was so much better than a family dinner with its overblown expectations. The room was extra warm thanks to the hard-working oven, and Delorie took off her shirt and sat at the table in her bra and her jeans.

After they cleared away the plates, they smoked a joint and ate chocolate instant pudding for dessert, Delorie's favourite. They poured milk over it and sat on the mat by the window and shared a bowl, taking turns with the spoon.

"When my Mom used to make this," Phil said, "I'd get her to pour it into a cookie sheet to set. Because the best part is the skin on the top."

"We'll do that next time," said Delorie, aware that by saying this she was implying a future, another day to come when they'd find a reason to pour pudding into a pan. Beyond the window the bridge spanned the river, and Christmas lights slung between the streetlight standards dipped and rose from the east bank to the west. Delorie and Phil sat close to each other on the fuzzy red mat drinking sparkling wine from tumblers that turned out to hold a lot more than you'd think just by looking at them.

RUNNING MAN

Years ago Uncle Kenton had sat, one fall evening, at the kitchen table in Ripley and talked about the doe he bagged that afternoon. How the animal raised her head and looked at him the instant before he shot. The look of alarm, unreadiness... Her uncle had abruptly stopped speaking, as if he'd been ambushed by some unseemly emotion. His hands rested on the knees of his stained orange overalls. In the brief pause before the table talk began again, Delorie had tried to imagine the animal's eyes. But she hadn't been there in the clearing, she didn't know; so it was not the animal itself, but Uncle Kenton's uneasy pause that came to her mind when a body showed up in the alley behind the Prince, and Max referred to the dead man as "John-Doe-a-deer."

Scavenger, on his way to a hotel management meeting on a Saturday morning, found the frozen corpse curled on the leeward side of the dumpster near the back entrance. In the late afternoon he led the staff out the back door and pointed to where the last of the man's body heat had melted a bean-shaped depression in the packed snow.

"What did you do?" said Anna.

"Called the cops."

"What did he look like?" Max said.

"Not too attractive. I'll spare you the specifics."

"You don't need to spare me anything."

Just the kind of remark you'd expect from a guy who's living out of the fridge, Delorie thought.

"Then I'll spare myself the specifics," Scavenger said. "It isn't the most fun I've ever had – coming on a corpse on a Saturday morning. No one should see a dead body until after their hangover has passed."

"Right," Delorie said. "Only after the hangover's properly done with should a person encounter a dead body." She credited herself with a talent for denying emotion, but here she was, a journeyman among masters.

"Don't you think so?" Scavenger said.

"Let's go in." Delorie rubbed her arms. Cloth is just a gridwork of threads with holes between them, that's what a day like this made you realize. Thin red shirtsleeves, cold coming through. Poor guy didn't know when he curled up last night that he'd wake up dead.

Inside, Max sorted coins on the hard steel countertop and slid them into the columns in the changer hooked at his waist. "John Doe," he said. "John-Doe-a-deer. Do-re-mi."

"I heard he was young," Vivien said.

"What'll they do with him?" Delorie asked.

"No funeral," Scavenger said. "The radio says no funeral till someone comes forward to claim the body."

"We should claim him," Vivien said. "Take up a collection and get him decently buried."

"You'd have to be a relative," Scavenger said.

"I'll save my money for the living," said Phil.

"First among them yourself?" said Max.

"First among them myself," said Phil, reaching for the pack of smokes in Max's shirt pocket.

"Smoke your own, why don't you?"

It happens every winter – a week or two of unbroken frigid temperatures, the kind of weather that keeps people indoors and creates a market for T-shirts that boast, I survived twelve straight days of thirty below. Icicles hanging off the letters. People call it a cold snap, but it's more of a slow, merciless squeeze. The night of the same day that Scavenger found John Doe, a blizzard chased its tail through the city. Delorie borrowed Vivien's heavy-duty boots to walk down to the Briarpatch at suppertime, wished she'd borrowed her knitted tuque as well. On her way back the snow slanted into her eyes, clung to her lashes. She tried to imagine summer. No. Even the warmer channel in the river, fed by the excess heat that spilled in from the power plant upstream, might freeze on a day like today.

When she walked back into the Prince, there was Phil, waiting tables in a Hawaiian shirt and cut-offs. Winter-white legs and thick orange socks. Oh cripes, prince of fools. Delorie felt herself redden, then wondered: if she wasn't sleeping with him, would she be entertained instead of embarrassed? Old Glad, her parents' next door neighbour in Ripley, used to warn her to watch who she got mixed up with. Mixed up she was, but not in the way Old Glad had meant.

"*Cut-offs?*" she said to Phil.

"My good friend Max granted me access to the Bacardi carton where he keeps his summer clothes."

Anna, emptying ashtrays into a grimy coffee can, gave her diagnosis: "Phil's having an extreme reaction to the dead man in the alley."

"Dead man nothing. When I came back from supper and saw all these sorry people sitting with their Jesus-big parkas on the backs of their chairs I thought we could do with a touch of the tropics."

"Scavenger said okay?" Delorie said.

"We compromised. I wanted bare feet but he said runners and socks."

Sheilah the Bear came in the front door, snow on her jacket, frost in her hair. She used a glove to wipe the fog off her glasses, looked at Phil and laughed out loud. "Far out," she said.

Scavenger poured the draft short that evening, a little below the line on each glass, holding back enough to justify a free round for staff later on. At closing time they had more than the usual trouble herding the stragglers out into the cold. Anna convinced the last of the engineers to file out, telling them no, they couldn't take the fitted terry tablecloths to keep their necks warm. The man Vivien so disliked, the one with the red pile coat, the one who kept calling her "wench," gave her grief at the door and she had to get Scavenger to threaten a call to the cops.

"And don't call me 'wench,' asshole," Vivien said as the door closed. She took two draft and sat down.

Max said, "There are worse things to be called."

"Seriously," Vivien said, "does anyone else get 'wench'? Anna? Delorie?"

"'Barmaid,'" said Anna. "That's not so bad. I get that."

Funk & Wagnall's, thought Delorie, but she said nothing. Vivien had a point. Names had currency here. The regulars carried their credentials in their nicknames: Hammer, Twitch, Shuffleboard Mike, Stan the Hippie Indian. Sheilah the Bear, so named not for her size so much as for the bone-crushing hug she gave her opponents after she won at pool. Delorie's own name had been customized. She was christened Delores and that was her name all through school. Mom said she'd chosen it because it sounded so pretty; anyone who looked it up, though, could tell you the word meant grief. She came up with "Delorie" on the bus ride to Saskatoon. New me, new name. Goodbye to grief.

"Gaffer," Phil said. "Someone called me 'gaffer' once. But I prefer 'asshole.'"

"We'll get you name tags," Scavenger said, looking pleased with himself. "That's what you need. Name tags."

"Like that'll help," said Vivien.

At Phil's the next morning, Delorie sat up in bed and took the mug of instant coffee he handed her. He sat down on the bed, naked. She thought of his white legs against Max's orange socks last night, thought again of the words "mixed up." She knew so little about this person. "So, beach boy," she said. "You don't talk much about your family."

"Where did that come from?"

"I'm curious, that's all. Just pick one thing about someone in your family and tell me. Whatever you want."

He made a stretchy morning face and rubbed his eyes, reclaimed the coffee mug to take a sip, handed it back. "Okay, one thing."

"One definitive thing," she said.

"*Definitive*.... Now you're adding conditions." He reached to the bookshelf for a pair of undershorts.

"No more conditions, I promise."

He stood up and pulled his shorts on, then sat again on the edge of the bed. "My father," he said, "built himself a platform on the roof, two foot by two, cedar so it won't rot. Beside the chimney, so he can lean against the bricks. He climbs up there with his thermos after lunch every day, two-and-a-half stories into the sky, and sips his Lipton tea and surveys the land. He loves his three hundred and sixty degrees of land."

Delorie waited silently. She wanted to raise the cup and drink, but she resisted. If she were quiet, if she didn't move, he might say more.

"And *I* do not," Phil said. "I do not love his land. The definition of 'farm' is 'work'." He reached for his wrinkled black waiter pants and put them on. He brushed his fingers through the hair on his chest. "I used to run the square, six days out of seven. Down the lane to the grid, then four miles of gravel roads and dirt tracks, just kept turning right at the corner. Wind and sun and open fields, crickets scuttling into cracks in the earth. Then a stretch through the poplars close to the creek, and the rock pile at the final corner. I would feel so far, far away from the house." He reached for his shirt and shook it. "One day after the old man went out to the shop, I climbed up to his cedar platform. From the roof, those four miles I was running don't make a very big square."

He took the cup from Delorie's hand. "Time to get up," he said, not looking at her.

"When do I get the next installment?"

"You said I had to tell one thing. Your turn now." He took her bra from the chair and tossed it to her.

"I don't talk about home," she said.

"That's true, you don't."

Delorie waited but he said nothing more. She wanted him to ask again. He didn't, just took the cup around the corner to the kitchen. She put on her bra and reached for her shirt. The feeling she'd had moments before, the feeling that she'd received something of value, slid away.

With a flourish, Scavenger opened a cardboard box and spilled half a dozen plastic rectangles onto the bar. Each rectangle had a pin on the back and a blank depression on the front. He produced a hand-held label maker and the staff took turns printing stiff red plastic tapes with their names embossed in white capital letters. "You look very professional," Scavenger told them once they had the tags pinned to their red shirts. VIVIEN, PHIL, DELORIE, ANNA. Then he saw that Max had made his tag out to say JOHN DOE. "You," he said, "could be replaced."

Max peeled JOHN DOE off his name tag, picked up the label machine, and punched out M-A-X-I-M-A-L, which was what he was trying to get the others to call him.

That evening a man with stubby teeth made a point of leaning in close to read Delorie's tag, sending his warm, liquory breath filtering down through her shirt, making her want to climb into a shower and scrub off. He softened the middle syllable and drew it out: De - *lorrrr* - eee.

After work, Delorie sat sideways on the counter in the women's can and washed her feet in the sink. The relief of bare feet, the warm water on her toes, the smell of soap. Her black pantyhose hung off the edge of the counter beside her, still holding the shape of her legs. They made her think of Christmas stockings waiting to be stuffed with small surprises, oranges filling out the toes. The door opened and she heard a series of rapid clacks from a break shot at the pool table. Vivien came in. "I'm looking for a change of scene, what do you say we head for the Lion?"

A change of scene. Yes. The Lion was classed as a club, not a bar; it didn't have last call until an hour after the Student Prince closed. They caught a cab, leaving Phil and Scavenger and the others playing pool inside the hollow, after-hours space. Delorie laughed, thinking of the way she and Mona used to run away from their kid brothers. The taxi drove along Twenty-second Street past the dark hatchery and the tire store and the Chinese bakery. Past the five-storey garment factory where, to Delorie, the dim lights shining through rippled green glass made the building look as if it were full of water, a massive, empty aquarium. "We should get spray cans one night," she said to Vivien, "and paint big tropical fishes on the factory windows. Multicoloured."

At the Lion, Delorie and Vivien ordered Scotches. A couple of guys asked them to dance. Out on the dance floor, under the lights, the guy Delorie was dancing with read her tag and called her by name and it took a few seconds for her to figure out how he knew. She liked him for the joke. Gary, he said, pointing to an imaginary name tag on his chest. Beside them, Vivien's partner pointed to his chest and said Slick, and they all laughed. They were the best of friends. Later, at Vivien's place, they poured drinks and the four of them shared a joint, the smoke from a cone of sandalwood incense curling through the air and meshing with the smoke from the joint and their cigarettes. Delorie lay beside Gary on the rug as he read aloud in a slow voice the captions of the posters on Vivien's walls: When you know the answer you will cease to understand the question; Keep on Truckin'. He managed the first few lines of the Desiderata before he broke down. They laughed for a ridiculously long time. Finally Gary said, "Jesus, gotta work tomorrow," and Slick groaned into his hands. They fell asleep separately – on the rug, the couch, the bed, the giant cushion Vivien used for an armchair. In the morning Gary hugged Delorie goodbye and Slick hugged Vivien goodbye. The pairing seemed arbitrary, as it had last night on the dance floor. Delorie lay back down on the couch and thought, that was fun, but it wasn't Christmas, with oranges and surprises. No length of Gary's thigh touching hers until the pressure increased, no sparks jumping between their fingers as he passed the joint. He wasn't the right boy for that. The right boy must still be out there somewhere. He was entertaining and undemanding, this Gary, but he was a daytime person with a job in an autobody shop. Now he'd have to show up at work with his hangover leaking out through his pores.

Phil was allowed, sometimes, to work behind the bar, where Scavenger showed him how to change the kegs and draw draft. The two of them were proud of technique. A perfect head of foam was a work of art created with just the right degree of slant to the glass. There's nothing like head, they liked to say, looking around to see who would smile at their joke. Kings of the castle.

On evenings when it wasn't busy, and if he was in the right mood, Scavenger would let Phil and Delorie take the same half-hour for their supper break. Usually, they'd slip down the street to the Briarpatch for two draft and a turkey sandwich. One night, though, Phil stashed two beer in the pockets of his parka. "I've arranged a nature outing," he said. He picked up two burgers-to-go from the hotel kitchen and led her along the sidewalk and across the street to a bench on the riverbank. The snow was just right for sculpting, and after she finished eating Delorie scrambled around in the winter twilight and made a snowman. Not a standing snowman, a lying-down-drunk one. She shaped a mound into a body, scraped snow together to mould arms and legs, added a head. Snow came in over the tops of her boots, melted through her pantyhose, made cold rings around her ankles. Phil smoked his cigarette and watched. When she'd made the head he worked his empty beer bottle into the snow so the tip of the brown stubby stuck out to make a nose. For eyes, he made Xs out of short grey twigs fallen from the surrounding spruce trees. "Blotto," he said. Delorie swept her gloved hand through the snow near the bench, found their bottle caps and pressed them into the front of the snowman to make buttons. She giggled, thinking of her brother Stuart, when he was little, telling his snowman joke:

Q: What did one snowman say to the other snowman?

A: I smell carrots.

She said to Phil, "What did one snowman say to the other?"

"I dunno. What?"

"I smell beer."

"I think I get that," he said. "But it might not be very funny." He punched her arm. "Let's go."

But Delorie stayed back, took off a glove and printed a message. *Phil + Delorie were here.* The snow melted cold against her finger and she slipped it into her mouth to warm it before she put her glove back on. The streetlight shining through the early darkness left blue shadows inside the letters. "Wait up, you," she shouted to Phil, who was half a block away and showed no sign of slowing his pace.

By the time Delorie arrived at the bar, Phil had already tied on his black apron and picked up his tray. He stood in the corner by the cupboard of empties sharing a smoke with Vivien. Delorie put her coat and boots in the fridge and joined them.

"They should bury him," Vivien said.

"Bury who?" Delorie said.

"The news said this morning John Doe's funeral has been delayed two weeks already because no one's claimed the body. No identification, no belongings except for a cheap watch and a garnet ring."

"Makes you think," Scavenger said. "Doesn't it?"

Yes it did, but it wasn't like Scavenger to say so, even from inside the safety of the worn out phrase. Delorie looked at him and nodded.

Phil laughed. "About what, Scavenger? What does it make you think about?"

"Makes you think about death."

"Whose death?"

"Anyone's. Mine. Yours."

Phil shrugged and handed the shared cigarette back to

Vivien and walked away. Delorie watched the shadows move across his back. She wanted to touch that back, run a finger down his spine, something she'd felt more at home doing when she first met him than she did now. Now it would beget the wrong reaction entirely. On what day had the rules changed? When you're just flirting, you get to touch in public. Once you're sleeping together, it's too possessive a gesture.

In the beginning: waking up naked late in the night, shivering, pulling the extra blanket over themselves, warming with the second breath of arousal, kicking away the covers. Afterward, kneeling on the bed to open the window and cool off. When had he begun to turn sideways from her when she spoke?

You can't just quit without saying. Do me the courtesy.

"We should raise the money to buy him a headstone," Vivien said.

Delorie pictured a block of chiseled stone: Philip Turner, RIP. Restlessness in Person. Reversal in Progress.

"Raise money how?" she said to Vivien.

"Like I said, take up a collection." She handed Delorie the communal cigarette and went back to work. Delorie ground it out; she was finding tobacco increasingly off-putting. Queasy stomach, like yesterday and the day before. *Don't tell me.* Memory of Phil waking her in the dark once they'd slept off an after-work drink, his hand on her hip. "Where are you?"

"Right here."

"No. What part of the month?"

"It should be okay." She pressed into his hand as it moved across the hollow beside her hip-bone.

"Yee-haw," he said.

"Where are the safes?"

"Uh...over at your place."

"It'll be okay."

A conversation they'd re-enacted, with variations, on a number of occasions. And afterwards he'd say again, "Why not the pill?" "I'll get around to it," she'd say. And she would, she would, she fully intended to. Any day now. Just pick some doc out of the yellow pages and go ask, right? What was stopping her? Surely not embarrassment, surely not shame.

LISTENING IN THE DARK

Vivien brought to work a washed out peanut butter jar with a slot cut in the lid. After work she used Scavenger's label maker to punch out a tape that said JOHN DOE MEMORIAL FUND. She set the jar on the off-sale counter. Delorie started things off with a five from her apron pocket.

"No one's claimed him yet," Vivien said. "No one knows who he was."

"Garden variety vagrant," said Phil.

"Alfred E. Snowman," said Max.

Phil started the belt on the dishwasher. Over the noise he said, "Frozen stiff."

Delorie unhooked her changer and emptied it and thought how they had no practice in talking together, the group of them, about things no one should joke about.

"Wait, wait, I got it." Max raised both hands in a gesture that promised a punch line. "He's Popsicle Pete."

"Jesus you guys," said Vivien. "A person *died*. An actual person from somebody's family." She looked at Max; she looked at Phil. "He was someone's little *baby* once."

Delorie said nothing. Vivien had a way of ignoring the unwritten service trade code of conduct – the understanding that there were certain things you were allowed to think about but you must not discuss out loud. Sentimentality would not do.

"J. Edgar Hoarfrost," said Phil.

"No," said Max. "Not as good as Popsicle Pete."

"Christ," Vivien said. She threw an empty box into the cooler and slammed the door.

"Relax," Max said. "Take an aspirin. It's called black humour." He lit a smoke. "Don't be afraid of the dark, now."

"You're the ones afraid of the dark."

Max laughed. Vivien cracked a beer. "Isn't anyone curious who he was, why he was sleeping in the alley?"

"So give him a story if it makes you feel better," said Anna. She folded her apron, sat down close to the pool table, took off her clickety-heeled shoes and stood them side by side on the floor. "Say he was a stranger and he came through town looking for his runaway girlfriend. He was checking all the bars in the country."

It was hard to tell with Anna. Was she making fun of Vivien or sympathizing? Delorie watched to see if Anna would exchange conspiratorial looks with Max or Phil, but she didn't. "Maybe if he hadn't died," Anna said, "he would've been in the Prince that Saturday asking questions about her."

"Nothing far-fetched about that story," said Phil.

"Well, why not?" Anna said. She patted the heart-place on her chest, pretending drama. "It doesn't matter so much what story you give him as long as you admit he's got a right to one. He's entitled." Delorie was struck by how Anna had managed to be flippant and serious all at once and by how her combination of comment and gesture settled her own feelings, satisfied her need to see John Doe as a human being, but without swinging too far in the direction of earnestness, not in this company, not after midnight.

A week later, Anna of the clicking heels and sensuous wrists moved away to Edmonton, following a man. Delorie returned from her supper break on Thursday night and saw a new waitress tying an apron around her waist and strapping on Anna's old changer.

"That's Fern," Vivien told Delorie as they watched her settle the changer into place, head bent, hair light brown and shining, hanging in careless ringlets. She was no more than five foot one in her sling back shoes. She had a small mouth and a widow's peak that brought her dangerously close to looking like a cutie on a valentine card. A look that some guys, thought Delorie, probably couldn't help but find attractive.

"Her clothes are wrong," Delorie said. Staff were supposed to wear red tops and black bottoms, the guys in black pants, the women in black skirts, short. The new girl was wearing the opposite, black shirt, red skirt.

"She showed up that way," Vivien said. "She told Scavenger she got it mixed up. She said to him, 'I've spent the money now, two shirts, two skirts, I can't change it.' Anyway, you better give her a hand," Vivien said as she left for her break. "I had to tell her what a screwdriver is."

Time after time that evening the others came to Fern's aid. "You gotta pick up those empties as you go along or you're playing catch-up the whole shift," Phil told her. "Never go back to the bar with an empty tray."

"Right, thanks. Help me if you get the time?"

Delorie showed her the proper way to change an ashtray, how to cover the old one with the new one when she lifted it so the ashes wouldn't fly out and settle in people's drinks. She wondered how a person could have so little common sense.

"Oh, *I* see. Got it."

Max, helping her with empties, said, "Didn't your mother teach you to fold down the flaps of a beer box before you put the bottles in?"

From the moment Delorie saw her, with her uniform the opposite to what was prescribed, she wondered if Fern had deliberately gone against the grain or if she really was as unlike the rest of them as she seemed. Vivien might separate herself from the cavalier attitude the others adopted, but she wasn't naïve. This Fern seemed the born yesterday type. She dug right in though, and it was hard not to be won over. During a lull she'd even clean the empties off a table that wasn't in her section and turn over the tips. She took the tablecloths down to the laundry when Vivien had a sore ankle, washed a Coke stain from the front of Phil's shirt while he was still in it, went to the drugstore for 222s when Max had a hangover so fierce he crouched in the corner by the empties and cradled his head. She had a way of touching. Not the gratuitous flirtation the rest of them engaged in; no, a touch that left a sensation of warmth. She heard about John Doe and said that, honestly, she found the whole story very sad. By the end of Fern's first week, Delorie knew she wasn't faking it. A genuinely sincere person. If not born yesterday, then born only the day before.

It was a Tuesday night and should have been accordingly dull. And it did start out to be dull, until Twitch's sometimes disobedient arm, the arm responsible for his nickname, flipped into the aisle at the wrong moment and struck – though not with any force to speak of – the thigh of a chemistry student passing by on his way back from the can. The student was new to the Prince, not clued in, and he responded by landing a fast punch on Twitch's shoulder and asking him, What's the idea? Efforts made by friends of Twitch and friends of the chemistry student to mollify failed quickly, and more than a dozen people who'd seen each other across the floor of the Prince for, in some cases, years, were brawling.

Delorie stood beside a wide, square pillar halfway down the house to wait it out. She was the only staff person south of the fracas. She wanted to be over near the bar with the others, but the fight was wall to wall; the only way back would be to walk through the middle of it. A few feet in front of her, Hammer had someone in a half nelson. A pair of eyeglasses landed on the floor near her foot. Carefully she reached for them and put them on her tray. She swallowed and leaned against the pillar and – she'd seen Scavenger at the phone – settled into stillness as she waited for the cops.

She'd learned to be still and quiet when there was a battle on in the house. Delores, in her bed, listening to the two of them, their thundering hatred. Topic for tonight's fight: how

Mom's sister Lenore showed up this afternoon, a rare visit, without warning, and no decent place for her to sit. The living room full of Dad's leftover roofing supplies: narrow pathways running between buckets of nails, stacks of shingles, sharp-cornered remnants of flashing. It's a disgrace. A disgrace! This visitor from the city drinking tea at the kitchen table, sitting on the least precarious of the wooden chairs. Her with her boots still on so her stockings wouldn't pick up splinters from the plywood floor.

For a while, lying there, Delores holds her breath. If you can control your breath, you have the power to control *something*.

She has to pee. You don't get up to pee at night in this house if there's a fight on. You don't get up even if there isn't a fight on, for fear that a disturbance as insignificant as the closing of the bathroom door will flare some smouldering resentment. You take great care not to upset them. You hold your pee at night.

Also, she's thirsty. She thinks about the logic of this: parts of her body too full, other parts empty. She reaches over to the dresser where earlier she put the necklace of fat blue pop beads Aunt Lenore brought from Saskatoon. She tugs one loose to suck on, smooth and plastic. The sucking releases saliva and she convinces herself this lessens her thirst.

Stuart appears beside her bed, arriving, as always, silently. "I'm thirsty," he whispers under their shouts.

"Yeah."

"Can I sleep in your bed?"

"No."

"Can I sleep on the floor then?"

"Got a blanket?"

"Course."

"Okay."

He wraps his blanket around himself so it will do for sleeping mat as well as for cover and settles down. She reaches to the dresser and pulls away another bead and holds it out to Stuart. "Put this in your mouth. It'll make you slobber. You won't feel so thirsty."

The fight ricochets from theme to theme, wearies from shouts to sarcasm, finally rests. There's the creak of the cot in Dad's cluttered office – he moved out of the bedroom years ago. She hears Stuart's breathing and the little click of the bead against his teeth as he exhales.

She's almost dropped off when she hears a new sound. Not sure at first what it means, she holds her head off the pillow, neck rigid. Mom or Dad making some small noise down the hall? Then she hears a muffled gasp, realizes the bead is choking Stuart. She scrambles out of bed, gets her hands underneath him and rolls him from his back to his side.

"Don't!" she says, whispered desperation. "Just don't." Timidly, she hits his back. He is so small. She strikes him again, harder, all the time talking to him in an urgent whisper, all the time afraid of making noise, of disturbing the peace. With one arm, she hauls his torso off the floor and delivers a full-force hit with the heel of her other hand. Again. Again. If she can turn him so he's face down? She snakes both arms around his middle. As she pulls up hard and sudden with her forearms, the bead shoots out of his mouth and onto the floor. A small click and a quiet roll. She lays him down and clambers over to where she can see his face, his eyes big and teary in the dark, snot and slobber around his nose and mouth.

"What happened?" he says.

"Shhhhh...shhhh. Sit still." They listen in the dark. Nothing. "You better go back to your room. I'll walk you."

Moments after she gets into bed again, Delores hears the springs of her father's cot. She lies still, wishes for a toilet. She hears his footsteps in the hall; then he's in the open doorway to her room. Her eyelids are almost closed, letterbox view: he stands in his pajama trousers, skinny chest bare, thin arms hanging at his sides. Whiff of whiskey even at this distance. He just stands and looks in – that's all he's ever done when he's come to the door in the night. She doesn't know why he looks in like that, and she isn't afraid, only disgusted. She doesn't want him to know she's awake. Tonight, before he goes along the hall to the bathroom, he says, voice soft and not quite sober, "My little baby girl."

She closes her eyes then so she hasn't even a slit anymore to look through. Not your little baby girl.

The cops loaded six live ones into the paddy wagon after the fight that began with Twitch's arm and the chemistry student. The dozen or so who'd been part of the fight but avoided the wagon took their coats and straggled out. The Prince was three-quarters empty now. Delorie saw to her few customers and then leaned on the low off-sale counter beside John Doe's jar. Sheilah and Stan were playing a half-hearted game of pool. Phil stood beside Mike near the shuffleboard table and watched with him as he studied the opposition. Delorie looked at Phil and tried to remember how many nights, this time, since the two of them had gone home together.

A shuffleboard player miscalculated a bank shot. "Nothing to worry about there," Phil said. Mike frowned and furrowed his continuous eyebrow. "We'll see." He looked away from the game and said to Phil, "The new girl – Fern – she's a looker, yes?"

Delorie did her best to shut out the other noises around her, the better to hear their conversation.

"So she is," said Phil.

"I tested her last night," Mike said.

"Did she pass?"

"Three and a half minutes from the time I gave my order until my Molson Canadian was in front of me."

"Not bad," Phil said.

Delorie's right leg was going pins and needles from the way she was leaning against the counter but still she didn't move.

"It wasn't a busy night," said Mike. "It should have taken two minutes and fifty, tops."

"I guess she had other things to do besides bring your drink."

"Aren't you generous. Maybe you're thinking of testing her yourself – with a different set of criteria."

Listening hard.

Phil didn't answer; he watched the game as if it was hugely entertaining. His unreadable face. She was the girl, Delorie reminded herself, who could walk with an apple on her head. She could manage a run-of-the-mill heartbreak.

After they'd cashed in that night, Fern sat down beside Delorie and said, "Turn sideways. I'll give you a shoulder rub."

"You're kidding, right?"

"No. I happen to give a very good massage."

"I can't think of anything that would feel better right now."

Delorie turned sideways and put her feet up on the settee. Fern gathered Delorie's hair, gave it a single gentle twist and moved it forward and out of the way.

"You're too good to be true, aren't you?" Delorie said looking over her shoulder at Fern. Phil stood, beer in hand, and looked on, taking a long drag off his cigarette.

Fern's fingers and thumbs went to work, beginning at the base of her skull, and Delorie dropped her head forward. "I'm too old for this business."

Fern laughed. "How old is that?"

"Nineteen. Jesus, I could fall right into bed."

"With who?" Max said.

"That's some question," Phil said, "coming from someone who doesn't even have his own bed."

Delorie closed her eyes as Fern worked on the lower region of her neck. It was hard not to feel self-conscious, hard to loosen her shoulder muscles and give herself over. Fern's hands kneaded deeply, down along her spine, across her lower back. Up again. Gradually, Delorie let herself relax, be caressed.

A hand touched her ankle, Phil's hand, warm. He said, "I'll get us a cab." She nodded. "Thanks, Fern," she said, sitting up and working her feet into her shoes.

"Think nothing of it."

On the way out the back door, Phil stopped at the off-sale counter and held up John Doe's jar; several coloured bills were inside, peeking around the squirrel label. Delorie took a five from her pocket and slipped it through the slot. Phil opened his wallet, found a two and stuffed it in on top of Delorie's five. She had the sense he was doing this only because the others, including Fern, still over by the pool table, were likely to see.

In the back of the cab Delorie arranged Phil's arms into a hug she could burrow inside to keep warm. He laughed and took one arm back so he could slide a hand inside her coat to find her breast. "That was something to watch, that back rub," he said.

LAST ACT

Scavenger flicked the lights and called "Time." A few minutes later he turned the lights up to full glare and a scatter of last drinkers sat blinking at the empties and near empties in front of them. Twitch finished his drink, struggled into his parka, opened the door and said, "Oh right, winter." Hammer, on his way out, paused to drop some change through the slot in John Doe's peanut butter jar. Delorie picked up the jar. It was stuffed with dollar bills and fives, the occasional purple ten. She delivered it to Vivien.

"Johnny had a good night," Vivien said. "I'll count. Anyone know what a headstone costs?"

"What would it say?" Delorie asked. "It's so impersonal just to put 'John Doe.'"

"What about 'J. D.'?" Fern said. "Somehow that's more like a real person. Like it could be someone's nickname."

"Cheaper," Phil said. "If they charge by the letter."

"J. D." said Max. "Jelly Doughnut. Just Dead."

"This guy has some kind of staying power," Phil said. He fished a buck from his pocket and handed it to Vivien. She gave him a steady look. "Thank you, Phil."

"I just want to move this along," he replied. "Who wants a game of shuffleboard?" he said loudly. He looked directly at Fern. "Shuffleboard? Pool?"

"Rocks or balls," said Vivien.

"Rocks, balls, and angles," Max said. "Don't forget about angles." He looked from Phil to Fern and back to Phil. "The angle of incidence equals the angle of reflection."

Phil took two pool cues from the rack. He extended one toward Fern. Delorie saw the attention in his look as he waited for Fern to take up the invitation. Her black shirt, her short red skirt, the colours opposite to everyone else's. Privacy wasn't easy to come by among this group but that didn't prevent the natural progression of things. Anyone could see how Fern's hand moved over Phil's as she took the pool cue.

Scavenger set down a Scotch, neat, in front of Delorie. "Feeling better, I hope?"

"Not a whole lot," she said, and took a drink. She kicked off her shoes and looked for a chair with the rungs still intact so she could do her nightly automassage.

It was time to move on. It wasn't just the hand-play between Phil and Fern – that was only the latest detail. Delorie had begun the week by spilling two drinks and Scavenger had taken the retail price out of her tips, as he sometimes did, depending on his mood; then there was the customer with the crooked smile who'd shoved his hand way up inside her skirt. And last night an underage drinker had bitten her on the wrist when she had cut him off. Add to this her fatigue, which she preferred to believe was a consequence of shift work, nothing to do with her and Phil's occasional failures to locate safes or foam.

And tonight – the last day of classes before reading week, and the students had brought their delirium to the Prince. Scavenger dragged all twenty illegal stacking chairs out of the women's can where normally he hid them from the cops. The place was way over capacity. The engineering students had too much to drink. They sat in a dishevelled line on the back settee chanting, "We want our Funk & Wagnalls, We want our Funk & Wagnalls," but in their drunken voices, the consonants liquid and open to interpretation, it didn't sound like "Funk & Wagnalls." Scavenger cut them off.

"You tell'em, Scavenger," Hammer said.

Delorie set her overloaded tray down near the washer and failed to balance it properly. It made a spectacular smash when it went down. Shards from draft glasses, highball glasses, beer bottles bounced off the floor, sprinkled her feet, skittered toward the pool table. The regulars rose as one and delivered a standing ovation. She walked to the bar to cash in.

"That's it for me," she said coolly to Scavenger. She would not cry or collapse with her head in her hands. She would not hide in the bathroom pressing toilet paper to her eyes.

"You can't quit just like that, and on a weekend too."

"Don't go," said Phil, "Don't be a poor sport." He goosed her back. If she hadn't been taken by surprise she wouldn't have slunk her spine in response to his touch. She was ambushed by arousal, felt the current travel all the way to the arches of her feet. Scavenger looked at Phil with an implied nudge and wink. Delorie reddened.

"Two weeks notice, then," she said to Scavenger. What the hell, she could use the pay. Temporize: a word in bold letters from the damp-riffled pages of the *Reader's Digest* Old Glad kept on the toilet tank.

Later, in Phil's bedroom in the dark of early morning, they made impatient love, their clothing a nuisance. Peel and tug and kick free. Her skin once more impatient for his hands, here, and here. Yes, there. Wanting it to go on and wanting to get it over with, both at the same time.

Afterward they sat in yellow lamplight, pillows behind their backs, and leaned against the wall. They'd been too quick about it; they should have taken the time. Delorie was left unsatisfied. Something had been squandered, not just tonight, but over the last few months. Not virginity – a technical barrier she was glad to have out of the way; and she didn't have – she didn't think she had – romantic notions of what type of guy should be her first. It was something more, the thing that had been squandered. She'd been so busy leaving home she'd failed to take note of where she'd arrived.

Phil lit two cigarettes; Delorie declined and he smoked them both, left hand, right hand. Their bodies barely touched. Wanting it to go on, wanting it to be done with. This would be the last time, and she wondered whether there'd been two people in the bed or three, herself and Phil and Fern. Four, if you counted the spectre of possible pregnancy. Delorie's gaze took in Phil's crowded room, Jimi Hendrix presiding over the scene, pain on his face. The bookcase full of old mail and socks and magazines, *National Lampoon*'s split beaver issue at the top of the pile. The labelled dissection of a beaver, the colours kindergarten-bright – they'd had a laugh over it on a different night, weeks ago. The usual mountain of clothing was piled on the weight bench.

"Nice, the way you keep your shorts on the summit like that."

"It's handy," he said.

"Your room is too small, Phil. There is no *room* in your room."

"I don't deny it."

STANDING STILL

Delorie sat with her coffee and looked out the window at March: damp white sheet of a month, hanging there, unmoving.

Maybe it wouldn't be true. Maybe there was another explanation. An irregularity. In grade eleven, Mona had gone six months without a period and then one day she came looking for dimes for the Tampax machine. So: maybe it wouldn't be true.

Was there something wet in the crotch of her underpants? She stood up and unzipped her pants and tugged them down and checked. Nothing. A headache beat its way up the back of her neck and around into her temples. She pulled her pants up and went to the couch, punched her pillow and lay down. My kingdom for a cramp. She groaned, a long, low *aaaargh!* that rasped in her throat like the slow turn of a drill bit.

Her final cheque had included a little extra for accumulated holiday pay. The entire amount would carry her for another month at the outside. Her radio played songs of consolation for women and men whose lovers had walked out the door. A relatively uncomplicated problem, that. The news reported that Howard Hughes was in a hotel room in Vancouver growing his fingernails.

By the time Delorie had put in her last night at the Prince, it was clear that Phil had transferred his attention to Fern. The new new girl. Phil and Delorie had both quietly managed to collect their own things from each other's rooms on their last visits, without comment, the way they did so many things. And last week Delorie had made a trip to the Prince, found a table in his section, ordered a beer. It was only that she was curious, she said. In his answer he used the word "repetitive." Things were getting repetitive.

Ah. "The Queen of the Silver Dollar." Mawkish too? she wondered. Bust it up, then; nail the vinyl bits to the wall.

"Well," she said to him. "Well, well, well," she repeated, and she laughed a quiet, sore-throat laugh. He laughed too.

"Keep that sense of humour," he said. "You'll need it, being among the unemployed."

"Where's Fern?"

"On her break."

Delorie reached into her pocket but he stopped her.

"Beer's on me."

He stood beside her table, not speaking, not leaving either. He looked almost ready to sit down, and she didn't know whether she wanted him to or not. Was there something she could say that might bring him back, some word, attitude, movement of her hair? But she didn't want him back, she only wanted to be the one in control, to have the power to make him change his mind and then to say, Sorry, we're through.

She stared at his wrinkled shirt. "Where's your name tag, beach boy?"

"I put it through the wash. Scavenger's finding me a new one." He spun his tray on the palm of his hand. "So," he'd said, turning away at last, "take it easy."

She'd left the beer on the table, half full, her small refusal of him. He wouldn't be hard to forget. Three days, she'd told herself after that conversation. Three days at the most for moping.

Scavenger called on day four to check in, to see how she was doing he said, just being friendly. "Guys like Phil," he reminded her, "are six for a nickel. I could find you another one easy, if that's what you want."

"That's not what I want."

"You wouldn't be this upset except he happens to be the one that took your cherry."

"I don't care about that."

She'd moped for one more day, because it could be she did care about that, though she'd rather not.

Delorie's schedule inverted itself: she hardly knew anymore what it was like to be out after dark; daylight was relevant once again. She would put on her made-over coat with the brown pile trim and walk down one bridge and up the other, stopping to stand on the west bank beside the slim channel kept open by excess heat from the power plant upstream. Even during the coldest months the river didn't freeze completely. Even in Saskatoon in winter, cold doesn't always beat warm. She liked to pull loose a piece of bark, lay it on the surface of the water and watch as it floated there hardly moving, sheltered by last summer's reeds from the current that would otherwise sweep it away. Words occurred to her: intermission; hibernation; hiatus. She liked these words, the idea that there was time to rest before things moved forward.

Phil faded in the daylight. She didn't miss the person so much as she missed the idea of Boyfriend. And she missed the Prince, the call and response, the merry band of regulars at the front tables who toasted her for keeping their party afloat. It was her party too. A bizarre and vital assortment of people had evaporated from her life overnight. She didn't know any daytime people. Her black-and-white TV kept her company. She was relentlessly sleepy; some days she set her plate aside, stretched out and closed her eyes partway through *Mary Tyler Moore* or *All in the Family*. She woke up for the national anthem that signaled the end of programming but she didn't turn off the set – she slept more soundly if the TV snowed quietly in the background through the night.

She declined the invitation to the service Vivien helped organize for John Doe. She couldn't imagine going back out into the world that way. Vivien reported the attendance to her: seven or eight of the regulars, all of the staff except for Max. The guys wore suits, picture that. Called their moms and had their good clothes sent up on the bus.

Delorie registered for a library card, borrowed books by Irwin Shaw, Mary Stuart, Phyllis Whitney. They were absorbing tales, family sagas, hero stories, romances and mysteries, thick covers she could disappear into for hours at a time. Some days she stayed inside around the clock, reading. Climbing the stairs became an effort. Time after time she switched from book to book without reading to the end, wanting to stay in the city of Rhodes, on the Isle of Avalon, on the streets of New York City.

One evening she was hungry for resolution and she read four gratifying endings; then, not ready to crack a fresh book and invest her emotions in an untried set of characters – their fears, their quirks, their vain desires – she fidgeted. She sat on the couch and slid open her pack of stale Player's and studied the calendar on the back. She counted once more, as she had counted repeatedly during the past week. Now what, oh please, what now?

As soon as she woke in the morning, she ran down one flight to the shared bathroom with its shared grit on the floor. Coarse bits of dirt dug into her knees as she knelt in front of the toilet and puked. The woman in the suite to the left either slept soundly or knew how to ignore these things. The man in the suite to the right heard her and knocked on the door.

"Are you okay in there?"

"Don't worry about it." She swallowed over the acid in her throat.

"You should cut back on the booze."

It was early afternoon, mid-week, almost a month since she'd turned in her tray at the Student Prince. Time to face this thing head-on. Last night she'd pulled the sofa bed out fulllength; this morning she'd slept until eleven, which made sixteen hours straight. A sore place in her spine corresponded to the place where the bed folded to be stored away. She opened the yellow pages to Physicians and Surgeons, did a mental sort according to bus routes, then dialed the numbers until she found one who had an opening the next morning.

Dr. Audette had early-Elvis hair. He might burst into a cover of "Jailhouse Rock" any second. He should turn up the collar on his white lab coat to complement the look. This is what Delorie thought about instead of thinking about the reason she was there.

"This has to go to the lab," he told her. "Come back next Wednesday and I'll fit you in between appointments."

It was another week of counting and reading novels and contemplating the balance in her bank book. The following Wednesday Dr. Audette confirmed the pregnancy. On the table in his office there was a jar of wide wooden tongue depressors with a chrome lid. There was a box with limp rubber gloves spilling out the side. And there was a box of Kleenex, which he handed to Delorie. She took one, but she had no reason to use it, no tears. The baby wasn't real, didn't exist. Phil was in the past, the distant past, and any baby she might have was in the distant future. It was impossible to believe the two were coming together inside her.

What do you do with a baby? Where do you put it?

When Delorie was a girl, her mother had shown her how to make something go away. The thing her mother could make disappear was a salesman's knock. You had to sit quietly and not respond. Before her mother developed her strategy for avoidance, Delorie remembered tense afternoons in the Ripley kitchen: a man in a brown suit setting out twenty uniform volumes of *The American Encyclopedia;* a rouged woman with floppy yellow sleeves opening lipsticks one after another and dabbing at the insides of her wrists to display the shades; a beefy man offering cleaning liquids and stain removers. All this in the never-finished kitchen with the unsteady light fixtures and the exposed gyproc on the east wall, the kitchen Delorie thought should have the words "some assembly required" stamped across the cupboards.

Delorie remembered the blender man who had demonstrated how to make a health drink without even cracking the raw egg ahead of time, just throw it in there whole with the rest of the ingredients. If you would oblige me by supplying an egg, Mrs. Woods, I'll perform a small demonstration. He smiled and took the egg and dropped it into the whirring machine along with a cup of water and his packet of powder. Imagine the calcium, he said, his beseeching smile. They drank the chalky chocolate/egg mixture, Delores and Stuart and their mother, while the blender man directed them to observe, in the bottom of the machine, what was left of the ground eggshell. Mom gave the children a charged look that meant they weren't to let their father know they'd allowed a stranger to use a perfectly good egg.

Delorie remembered the siding man who drew samples and photographs out of a brown leather tote the size of a suitcase, open on the floor at his feet: No disrespect Mrs. Woods. It's just to illustrate the difference between what is and what could be. No offence, Mrs. Woods, but this house just down the street here – the house in the "before" picture – looked worse than yours does. Now, look what we were able to do with it.

There was an afternoon when Mom saw the stain remover man carrying his sample case into Dorothy Schmidt's front entrance. She told Delores and Stuart, "Don't move." Her voice was sharp. "Sit here where no one can see you through the window. Don't say a word and don't make a noise." They sat on the floor in the central hallway, Delores and little Stuart, back to back, looking away from each other so as not to laugh. Five times the salesman knocked on their front door and waited. Eventually he went away and Delores and Stuart rolled on the floor, their laughter let loose. Mom turned the radio back on. Delores looked at the iron expression on her mother's face and knew it was shame that made her hide: the unfinished siding, the halfhearted carpentry, the unpainted walls where stains caught and spread. The fact that she hadn't allied herself with the right man. The difference the siding man didn't know he was referring to when he talked about what was and what could be.

Inside her third-floor bachelor suite, Delorie made a sanctuary of her armchair, her legs up, feet crossed on the seat cushion, knees resting against the arms, eyelids half-lowered like windowshades. She couldn't make the fact go away, but if she sat quietly enough for long enough maybe she could drag time to a standstill. She had told Phil nothing. Once he knew, time would begin to move again. Once he knew, sober discussion would be required of him, of the two of them together. Unaccustomed as they were. She envied Phil, imagined him walking around unaware, working, playing, moving unencumbered through his days and nights.

SUCH A FINE SPELLER

Delorie recruited her energy and ventured to the bus stop wearing her job-hunting clothes: blue blouse, square-heeled black patent shoes, pressed slacks – were they snug at the waist already? She'd been meaning to do this since Monday and here it was Friday. On Third Avenue she disembarked, walked a block to the post office and climbed a demanding flight of stairs to a glass door that said Personnel. Once she'd filled out the three-page application she handed it back to a pleasantly smiling man who wore a too-white shirt and offensively noticeable aftershave. She raised a hand to baffle the odour, scratched an imaginary itch on the side of her nose. He placed her form in a wire basket on a stack of identical forms. On her way out she looked at him over her shoulder, asked when she might hear something. "Sweetheart," he said, "everyone wants to work here. Don't hold your breath."

Down the street at the phone company they performed a short interview right then and there, followed by a quiz. They must be serious about hiring. Delorie began to feel optimistic, enjoyed the coffee the woman brought, worked out the elementary math problem. She neatly printed the names of the Saskatchewan towns the woman asked her to spell. When she left the telephone building to walk back up the bridge she felt a rare energy. Writing exams had always been easy. Instead of making straight for home she treated herself to the special at Matt's Lunch. Oh so hungry. Mushroom soup, sausages, fried potatoes, peas and apple pie. She didn't mind spending the money because soon she'd have a job.

Early Monday afternoon she sat listening to the radio and waiting for the phone to ring. She tapped her fingers to "Madman across the Water." The prospect of employment was enough, for this moment. Elton John faded and gave way to the news: Nixon was caught cheating on his income tax; someone streaked the Johnny Carson show; Patty Hearst was part of the revolution now. Life goes on, Delorie thought. Mine will too. The phone rang and she jumped to pick it up. When she heard the voice of the woman who had interviewed her on Friday she smiled into the receiver. "Yes, speaking."

The woman from personnel was sorry. Anyone who did that well on the quiz would never stay with the phone company. Delorie's only error had been the spelling of "Radisson": she'd given it two d's when it should have had only one. The telephone company was looking for long-term employees.

"You mean I did *too* well?"

"I'm sorry."

"I just need a job," said Delorie, her smile now nothing more than a leftover muscle contraction. She fiddled with an unlit cigarette.

"You understand. We have to worry about turnover."

"What kind of job would you recommend then," Delorie said, "for such a fine speller?" She slammed the receiver into its cradle. The radio said someone had tried to kidnap Princess Anne. Delorie switched it off. If only she'd known, she could have made the appropriate errors. She could have passed herself off as more limited.

On Friday afternoon she took the Number 5 across town and got off in front of the double wooden doors of the garment factory on Twenty-second Street. Five stories of red brick, windows of pebbled green glass embedded with chicken wire. At night, from the back of a taxicab, she and Vivien had thought it looked like an aquarium. In the daylight she could see how the dust from passing traffic had settled on the grey stone windowsills and how the cracks in the windowpanes followed the pattern of their chicken-wire skeletons. A cardboard sign was taped inside the glass doors, facing out: Yellow-tab Casuals. Inside, she coughed in the fabric dust, found the office half a flight up and asked if they were hiring. The woman at the desk had red fingernails and tall hair and sipped a 7UP through a straw. She handed Delorie an application form and smiled and pointed to a chair.

There was no table, and Delorie used her white drawstring purse as a writing surface. The pen poked a hole through the paper and marked her purse. She licked a finger to clean the vinyl, turned the application form over and worked the edges of the hole in the paper back together so it looked less messy. Would that sort of attention to detail work in her favour or against her in this situation? She heard a buzzer and then footsteps, many footsteps, on the creaking stairs outside the office door. For references she filled in Scavenger's real name, Duncan, and the names of two high school teachers. She took the completed form to the woman at the desk, who some time in the last few minutes had stopped working on the letter in her typewriter and switched to reading a paperback. The woman smiled and said she'd deal with it as soon as coffee break was over.

Delorie sat. She massaged her cuticles into place, slipped a shoe off and flexed her toes, wished she'd brought a novel. Eventually a buzzer rang and she heard footsteps again. She turned her head and saw dozens of women climbing the wide, creaky stairs; they came up from the basement, crossed the landing outside the office and continued to the upper floors. The receptionist left her desk and disappeared through a door at the back of the room. She re-emerged, trailed by a coral-shirted man with greased brown hair. It was the right day to come looking for a job, the man told Delorie – he needed to replace the woman whose appendix had burst the day before yesterday.

The secretary gave Delorie a punch card and showed her how to use it. "I hope you aren't one of those ones who's going to leave us to go off to school in the fall. He hates those ones." Delorie shook her head. She was aware that the waistband of her pants was under strain.

A supervisor in a brown smock, Mrs. Torgerson, led her upstairs and through the whirr and clatter of the second floor to a muscular grey serger and gave Delorie a brief lesson in its operation. "It's almost quitting time. Work with these scraps today, so you learn the machine. Bring your own scissors on Monday."

The next day Delorie walked along the riverbank path from one bridge to the next and back again. The season was turning, the air was warm, the sky a full morning stretch of blue. Soon she'd get a paycheque – far more than she was bringing in from pogey – and she wouldn't have to go back and stand with the others in the government building and scan the matrix of typed index cards that said "experience required" even for the worst jobs. She'd have to learn to get up in the morning. She was aware of the rumour that garment factories were set up so it was almost impossible to earn the piecework bonus – you had to switch your task just when you got quick enough that you threatened to qualify for the extra money. It didn't matter.

She took the bus to a pawnshop on Twentieth where she found a used sewing machine. Twenty-five dollars; not cheap for Delorie, but less than you'd expect to pay. It sewed just fine forth and back, the man told her, but don't expect to use the zigzag. She caught a bus home across the river and lugged the machine upstairs, set it down just inside the door and collapsed on the sofa. She breathed deeply and slowly. Could you miscarry from hauling a sewing machine half a block and up a flight of stairs? Would a miscarriage be a good thing or a bad thing? Oh, stop. There were no twitches or stitches or cramps, not even that roving gas bubble feeling she'd had a few times; just an all-over flush from physical effort. She took off her outdoor sweater, bunched it underneath her pillow and curled up on the sofa.

She knew abortion was possible. Legally awkward but possible. Not common. The grapevine at Ripley had supplied that sort of information, she could name names. Girls her mother said had taken the easy way out. She realized she admired them now – those girls who'd been the subjects of giggles and loaded stares during the high school years – for having the guts to make a clear decision one way or another. When they came back to school people left a buffer strip of empty desks around them in the classroom. They'd had to go to Manitoba or Montana or Saskatoon and walk into a room full of half a dozen people and say they were nuts. That's what it took, an exercise in shame. That and more. You had to ask yourself impossible questions and then answer them, go spelunking through places where who-knows-what emotions lay waiting. It didn't *seem* like the easy way out. Delorie was looking for the path of least resistance.

The clothing production line had its own code of behaviour. No one pinched Delorie in the ass anymore; no one left her tips either. There were time sheets to keep track of piecework, and a union and a punchclock, and no one stayed a minute past the end of shift. Those who worked on the second floor were from half a dozen countries. At lunchtime they sat across from each other at plywood tables and ate their sandwiches. The silence amplified the sound of their chews and swallows. Delorie imagined they were all moving about in the kind of quiet you would find underwater. She thought of the fishes she and Vivien had imagined painting on the factory's nighttime windows.

After lunch, Delorie stood outside and watched the Chinese women walking up and down the sidewalk in front of the factory, arms around each other's waists, and she thought it would be nice if Vivien came to work here too.

She knew hardly anyone's name. Mentally, she christened her co-workers. Across the aisle to her right the Bearded Lady made double inseams. At the machine in front of her a slight woman stitched zippers to facings. She had radiant clean cheeks and when she arrived in the mornings her hair would be hanging in still-wet ropes. This woman was The Baptism. Across the aisle at the bar-tack machine was The Obituary. She had pasty white skin and heavy eyeliner. Occasionally, The Obituary looked as if she was trying to smile but she never seemed to make a success of it.

Work was about repetition. Serge, clip, stack, bundle. Repeat. Once Delorie had the motions down, there was little to do but think. About whether they sold maternity clothes in the factory outlet store downstairs. About her constant hunger. About the white card Dr. Audette had handed her with the name and number of a social worker. You have to make an appointment, Dr. Audette had told her, a girl in your situation, it's the law.

And there were thoughts of her mother. Was it time, finally, to call her? Last summer she'd left her there in Ripley, left both her and Stuart there with him. Apologizing as she packed, then shouting to make it easier. If her mother wanted to live with a drunk, tinkle her store-clerk wages into his bottle, that was up to her. People like him don't change. Her mother had insisted he *was* changing, she could tell.

As she worked, Delorie ran the words to songs through her head. It passed the time. Songs that told stories worked the best; one line led to the next and it was easy to remember the words. "American Pie," "Bad Leroy Brown," "Our House."

It's a type of architecture, making a piece of clothing. A garment requires form the way a building requires form. Delorie felt cheated that only one insignificant step in the construction happened on her machine. One small step, over and over. It took more imagination than she commanded, to see her modest pocket-facing operation in relation to the whole pair of pants. Which was how she'd managed to botch things her first full day on the job. She was serging the edges of facings, twenty to a bundle, a task deemed simple enough to be assigned to a beginner. First thing in the morning, Torgerson had demonstrated what she wanted, then left her without checking back until two hours later. For grunt work, it wasn't bad. There was satisfaction in doing it well, guiding the cloth past the blade so the machine finished it cleanly, shaving only the minimum off the edge. Delorie would have bet they hadn't found many beginners who picked up the technique so quickly.

"Stop. Stop!" It was Torgerson in her dun-coloured smock, her face grey under the banks of fluorescent lights. "What are you *do*ing?"

"Serging pocket facings. Aren't I supposed to?"

"You're putting them in exactly the wrong order!"

There was a right way and a wrong way to stack pocket facings. All morning Delorie had been sending off bundles of ten pairs each, twenty small, important scraps of cloth out of sequence in each bundle. The chain of error she'd set in motion could result in a hundred pairs of substandard jeans that would have to be sold as seconds in the shop downstairs. The facings and their respective pant legs would be from different dye lots; they'd show up in mismatched shades of blue.

"Don't move an inch," Torgerson said before she stormed off to see if there was still time to abort the chain reaction. Well if it was so bloody important, if they couldn't manage to get the colour the same from one time to the next, then maybe someone should have told her about dye lots. It made sense, once it was explained.

In Herbert Powell High School, being smart was a matter of memorizing your notes. There were no damn notes for this. She was flunking out in matters practical and commonsensical. She was a small mess surrounded by larger messes: the president of the United States was cheating on his taxes, the phone company wanted people who couldn't spell, and she, Delorie, was stupid as well as pregnant. It was the stupid part, not the pregnant part, she was most ashamed of. There should be violins, there should be special exemptions, there should be signs that said Reduce Hope for the next ninety miles.

Once the supervisor was out of sight, The Baptism turned around, spool in hand. "It's okay," she said.

"It is?"

"It will be. My name's Tracy."

"I'm Delorie."

"Hi Delorie. Don't worry about Torgerson. She's okay when she's not having one of her fits."

"You're an optimist."

"Well, yeah. I am."

"Wonder what that's like."

"You could find out. I hear it's open to anyone."

"I'll keep that in mind."

"See," Tracy said, turning back to her work. "Already you're starting."

Delorie took the next bundle from the bin beside her machine. Torgerson had told her not to move, but she knew what was required now and she couldn't see why she should wait. She fanned through the bundle and saw how the shades of blue changed subtly from one layer to the next. Of course. That's what it means, she thought, when people use the expression "of a piece." Each pair has to be of a piece – one part matches the next which matches the next which matches the next, and then you have *order*. Order is good. She ran the facings through her machine and as she finished each one she flipped it over so the bundle would end up the right way around and in the proper sequence when she passed it along to the next operator. Pay attention. Stop with the mistakes.

BASIC NEEDS

A story ran in the back pages of the city weekly: "Refuge Sought, Found." The story featured a home for young women "shunned by society because of their condition." The home was sponsored by a religious outfit "motivated by the love of God." And by practical concerns. Practical concerns were something Delorie had plenty of; as for the love of God, she could pretend to pray as convincingly as the next person in need of rent money. Would they talk about Eve and the serpent and the price of redemption?

The Department of Social Services, the article explained, sorted out financial arrangements. Delorie had no idea how long she'd have a regular paycheque, how long she'd be allowed to keep her job once she started to show – really show, that is. Clamped in the teeth of her plastic alligator memo clip on the kitchen counter was the social worker's card Dr. Audette had given her: Bonnie Semchuk. The same worker was quoted in the article, referring to the home as a "safe and caring environment." Delorie made the call.

A few days later she booked off sick for the afternoon and walked downtown to keep her appointment. In a white room inside a great grey block of a government building she met Bonnie Semchuk. Below the jawline on the left side of her neck, Bonnie had a toffee-coloured birthmark. It was just over an inch from side to side and its shape was solid at the top edge, irregular below. It reminded Delorie of the ink blot tests in Phil's underused psychology textbook, but she couldn't extract a meaningful image from the birthmark. She sat down opposite the social worker expecting rebuke, possibly a lecture on morality, at least a few words about carelessness. But this social worker was no lecturer. Maybe she was aware of the berating already going on inside Delorie's head.

Bonnie Semchuk held a stylish blue and silver fountain pen; she removed and replaced the cap as she spoke. This repeated tic, the way the motion seemed to measure and mark time, reminded Delorie that Bonnie had had an appointment preceding this one and she'd have one immediately following. Bonnie said many things very quickly and as she spoke the birthmark moved as if it might be a live thing – no specific animal, just a creature with life in it. The irregular lower outline transformed itself into legs. Bonnie asked questions off a typewritten page and wrote Delorie's answers in the open spaces. She told Delorie not to worry; she asked about her state of health and the relationship with the father and whether Delorie had told her parents. She slowed her voice, looked at Delorie, and told her there were options. To keep, to release. She said also, as if it were something she had to say to meet the requirements of the job, "Abortion is legally possible now."

This could all be over, Delorie thought, but even as she thought it she shook her head. She'd always been the one unable to take a plunge. All those Sunday afternoons she'd stood at the end of the dock on Bird Lake and missed out on the swimming because she couldn't leap from heat into cold.

"I'm not recommending it," Bonnie said, "but if you're considering it, you should know there's a twelve-week ceiling." She looked at her papers. "That would give you just over a week." She paused. "And the arrangements," her voice trailed off. She uncapped and recapped her pen; tick, tick.

Delorie shook her head again. Time was pulling that decision out of her hands. She remembered a saying: Not to decide is to decide. Did that mean she should give herself credit for making a decision, or did it mean the opposite?

"There's a new group home," Bonnie said, "a different set-up from the one you read about in the paper."

"Different how?"

"A co-op. I'll see if they can take you."

Delorie nodded. She left the office carrying a booklet about prenatal nutrition. Questions of nutrition were the ones with the easy answers, relatively speaking. Delorie wanted the bigger answers. Can you really give away a person? What will the pain be like? Answers that couldn't be found in an eat-healthy pamphlet, nor in a birthmark no matter how much you wanted to make an oracle of it. Once she was on the street she realized that for the whole time she'd sat in the office she'd been holding her stomach in. She breathed out and relaxed her abdominal muscles, and physical relief moved out from the centre and through her body. She *had* made a decision, really she had.

She attempted a stern approach with herself. She could do this. Begin with clothing. She made her living in the garment industry; there was no reason she couldn't construct her own maternity clothes on her pawnshop Singer – sews forth and back just fine, the man said – provided she found a thorough set of instructions and paid close attention. After work the next day she went to the library and found a book with hand-drawn illustrations of hugely pregnant women wearing garments stitched together from head scarves and recycled jeans. The book promised to teach her a step-by-step method for constructing a four-scarf skirt and an eight-scarf sundress. At the Mennonite Clothes Closet you could buy second-hand scarves for five cents apiece. Delorie bought a dollar's worth, enough to allow for mistakes and for changing her mind about colour combinations. On the inside cover of the book was a photo of a pregnant woman who gazed up at a blue sky in sheer joy. She wore a small bikini, the bottom slung underneath her seven-month belly. Fronds of curly hair bordered the cloth triangle. No thank you. Delorie turned to the instructions for making a skirt.

She called Vivien and broke the news. Best not to talk about it over the phone, she said, and invited her for Sunday lunch. While Vivien made small talk, Delorie cracked eggs into a bowl and whipped them with a fork, anticipating. Eggs, bacon and toast. She was constantly hungry. The first forkful of scrambled egg looked delicious, smelled appetizing as she lifted it. The first taste made her gag. She sipped a little juice, set her fork aside. Food, shelter, clothing – she'd never been so preoccupied with the three basic needs.

The skirt she'd almost completed was draped on the back of the couch, and she picked it up to show Vivien, who admired it out loud, then shook her head.

"I have to ask, Delorie. Not to be too blunt, but why the hell weren't you on the pill?"

Delorie rotated her juice glass slowly on the table and watched Vivien move her food around with her fork. She didn't answer. Her cheeks filled with heat.

Vivien moved her fork loosely in the air, waiting.

Delorie felt an ache in her eyes. She cut a small rag off a slice of bacon, knowing she couldn't eat. She had invited Vivien here for comfort, support. Not for this.

"This will be so complicated," Vivien said.

Delorie moved her plate to the counter so her uneaten food would be out of her immediate sight. She set the plate down calmly enough, but the knife and fork she threw forcefully into the sink. She was rewarded with the clatter of steel on steel. Of course, of *course* it will be complicated. She took a long breath and then another, folding up her anger as if she could slide it inside an envelope. She turned around and told Vivien there was no need to worry, the social worker had seen dozens of women like her. There was a place to stay before and after. There was no shortage, she told Vivien, borrowing words from the social worker, of grateful, loving couples waiting for babies.

"Phil doesn't know, does he?" Vivien said.

"Not yet."

"You have to tell him."

"Eventually." Delorie sat down.

"No, right away. You have to tell him right away."

"Is that any of your business?"

"It's Phil's."

"Fine, you tell him," Delorie said.

"As a matter of fact, I will. If you don't."

"Vivien," Delorie said, "why are you being this way?"

"It's seems to be what's called for."

Delorie rested her hands on her belly. "What's called for, Vivien, is a little *help*. You're supposed to hold my hand and tell me things'll be all right."

"Jesus," Vivien said, her foot leaving the rung of her chair and stamping hard on the floor. "I'm new at this, okay?" She paused and then reached across, took Delorie's hand and held it and said nothing for a long moment. The two of them looked at their joined hands.

"There," Vivien said quietly, and squeezed.

"There," Delorie said, and squeezed back and let go.

Vivien straightened in her chair and grinned. "I know a trick," she said. "Lie down on the floor."

"You want me to lie on the floor."

"Trust me."

"Oh good, a diversion," Delorie said with a sarcasm meant to be friendly. She rearranged things to make room, settled herself awkwardly between the coffee table and the couch and caught the dry smell of the air at floor level. Vivien asked her for a ring but Delorie didn't wear one. Vivien improvised, taking a flashy blue earring from the dresser and tying it to the end of a hair ribbon. She suspended the pendulum above Delorie's stomach.

"Wait now," she said. "If it swings side to side that means it's a girl; if it swings head to foot, it's a boy." They laughed and waited but the pendulum hovered. Finally Vivien moved her wrist to make the earring swing from side to side. "Let's make it a girl."

Delorie still poured herself a Scotch and water after supper occasionally. Any more than one and her stomach acted up. She took a long time with her drink, moved it in small circles to colour the walls of the glass with an amber swirl. Do they let you name a child that you're giving away? The liquor slid over the ice cubes like oil. She half seriously considered Amber as a name if she was, in fact, carrying a girl. No one needed to know she'd thought up the name while she peered into a glass of Scotch.

On a trip to the library, after she'd chosen three novels, she found an encyclopedia and looked up "amber." She wanted to make it a legitimate name. She couldn't name a baby after the colour of whiskey; this was a more serious exercise, after all, than her game of mentally christening the women at the factory. There were colour photographs on the shiny pages of the encyclopedia – wonderful, changeable, honey-coloured ornaments and jewelry and an entire glowing room with amber furniture and walls. Artists in the Stone Age carved pendants of amber, figurines, amulets. Amulets are for protection, for good luck. So Amber was a lucky name.

Phil called. Vivien had told him. He was more than civil, even concerned. Acted like this was his mess as well as hers, up to a point. He'd help pay for an abortion, he said. "My cousin had one. As long as you agree that a baby will endanger your health, you're home free. Mental health counts too. That's all you have to say – it'll endanger your mental health."

"I know," she said. "No thanks."

"Why not?"

Silence.

"Why not, Delorie?"

He seemed to be looking for logic. She didn't answer. She thought how his telephone voice was unfamiliar and how odd it was that she could remember so little about being with him.

That evening she scrubbed out the tub in the shared bathroom, undressed, and stretched on tiptoe to look at herself in the mirror above the sink, frontal view, then profile. She wondered how big she'd be allowed to get before the unit supervisor would ask her to quit. Wondered how it would be to walk about with the baby's roundness in front of her. People like to touch a pregnant belly, she'd heard. Strangers would come right up to a woman in a department store and put their hands on the bulge without asking.

The job left its traces on her skin. Fabric fluff worked its way inside her clothing during the day. Blue lint coated her ribcage, nestled in her belly button. In the bathtub the lint floated away and gave the water an indigo cast. Delorie stretched out in the deep, old-fashioned tub. She'd tacked a sign to the outside of the bathroom door: Try again in half an hour. She leaned back against the sloped enamel and concentrated on not creating a ripple. She wanted to suspend the baby at its present state and size, no bigger than a fist, folded around itself.

Phil came around. He walked in the door and immediately Delorie remembered a cluster of details about him: he had an oddly placed patch of hair on his right shoulder; he couldn't stand crumbs on the countertop; his favourite undershorts were printed with red triangles.

She hadn't bothered to close up the sofa bed that morning, and Phil hesitated beside it. Delorie remembered another detail:

how after waking her and making love in the early hours, he would curl behind her and breathe sleep back into her spine.

The springs creaked when Phil sat down. He pulled at his sideburns in a way that distorted the shape of his face. He looked at the door, at the dresser, at his feet. Delorie, too, was uneasy. She told him she'd been thinking about names, said she liked the name Amber for a girl. Phil nodded, looked at her belly. She hadn't meant to talk about names, to have the baby enter their conversation as a real person that way. She told Phil that, at any rate, the social worker said the people who adopted the baby would have their own name for it.

He asked why, then, would she bother with a name at all?

She had posed herself the same question. It was little enough, she'd concluded, giving someone a name and not much more. She had to be responsible for *something;* a name was the only thing she could manage. It would go on record on a birth certificate at least. But this wasn't the sort of rumination she was prepared to share with Phil. She thought of the words the nurse had used when she went for her first prenatal: "*prima gravida,*" she'd said, smiling, yellow round collar like petals below her face. "First-time pregnant." But to Delorie the word *gravida* sounded as if it should mean serious. First-time serious. Here was Phil beside her on the open bed and she didn't believe he was made to be serious about or serious with. He was here, she believed, to be told not to sweat it. And it wasn't as if he could *do* anything. She was giving the baby up, and frankly she didn't want him complicating things. He certainly hadn't expressed any wish to be a dad. So Delorie gave him the same list of practical reassurances from Bonnie that she'd repeated to Vivien. Loving families, food-shelter-clothing. Poof.

In answer to his question about why bother with a name, Delorie shrugged and said, "What the hell." No big deal. She fiddled with her earring, then rested her hands in her lap; he played, again, with his sideburns.

"Please stop." She reached up to still his hand.

"Stop that and do what instead? Just what am I supposed to do?"

"Nothing I suppose. It's nothing to do with you anymore."

"Fine, then." He stood up. Raised his hands and slapped them back down against his legs as if something must be hit. "Fine!" he shouted. "Nothing to do with me. Right. I don't know why I came here. I show up to see what I should... Never mind. Obviously you don't need me."

"So you're mad!" she yelled. It frightened her to be sitting down while he shouted. She stood. "Welcome to the club."

"You want me out of here Delorie? Here! Watch me go!" He stormed out and down the stairs without closing the door.

You be mad, she thought. You can be mad and forget about it tomorrow. She blinked hard to battle her tears. She kicked the metal frame of the sofa bed. Hurt like hell, ball of her foot, what if she'd broken it? She limped to the still-open door and stood there, her head full of noise, as if the personal details she'd moments ago remembered were clattering down the stairs after him, bouncing like marbles. She slammed the door.

Her slacks didn't meet around the middle any more. She would do the zipper up halfway and continually hitch them up as she walked or keep them up by awkwardly pressing her arms to her sides. The number of bathroom breaks people took was closely monitored at work. Delorie was being careful; she'd heard rumours that no one more than six months pregnant was allowed to stay. One morning as she sat at her machine repeatedly singing "Our House" inside her head in order to train her awareness away from the physical facts of life, she admitted to herself, finally, that she couldn't make it until the ten fifteen buzzer without a pee. She stood, hitched up her pants, clamped her arms to her sides and walked quickly along the row of machines to the bathroom. As she sat in the stall she heard the door open. She expected it would be Torgerson coming to hassle her. It's a bladder infection, she was ready to say, hoping that if it wasn't an explanation that made sense, Torgerson wouldn't know any different. She came out to wash her hands and found not Torgerson but Lyla, the inseam girl she hardly knew: short bleached hair with an untamed cowlick to the left of her part; a lazy style of gum chewing. Delorie didn't like gum chewers.

"You couldn't make it to break time either," said Delorie. "I never can seem to."

"I've noticed," said Lyla. She had her sewing scissors in her hand, and she leaned toward the mirror and fingered her hair. Delorie thought she was about to chop at the lock that strayed out from the root of the cowlick, but Lyla turned away from the mirror. "I've also noticed," she said, "your big shirts and the funny way your pants hang." She said this in a matter-of-fact way, sounding neither friendly nor unfriendly.

Delorie hesitated; finally she said, "What do you mean?"

"It's okay," said Lyla. "There are ways to hide it. I worked right up till the day before I popped and no one was the wiser. Of course he came two months early. I don't think I'd have kept on fooling Torgerson if I'd gone full term."

"You had a baby and kept your job?"

"Yeah." Lyla let out a small laugh. "It can be done."

"So it's true – they'd have made you quit if they'd known you were pregnant?"

"Six months. That's policy."

"They can do that, then. They can fire you for being pregnant."

"Course they can. And they'll dock your pay for morning sickness," Lyla said. "Self-inflicted illness." She chewed her gum with her mouth open and Delorie could see the slick pink wad move across her tongue. "But follow me, I'll show you something," Lyla said. "Torgerson's gone upstairs. If we're lucky she'll be a few minutes."

Delorie followed her out of the bathroom and they slipped into an alcove where industrial spools of elastic hung on metal rods, attached to the wall like giant rolls of toilet paper. Lyla cut a length of elastic and looked around to be sure no one could see. "Here." She lifted Delorie's loose shirt and looped the elastic through the buttonhole on her pants, then back around the button and made a slip knot. The elastic was long enough that it could be knotted short for now and let out gradually over the months to come. "There. Now your pants won't fall down." For an instant Lyla rested a warm hand against Delorie's belly. "Wow," she said, "there's something in there all right." Delorie missed the warm hand as soon as Lyla lifted it.

"As for needing to piss every fifteen seconds," Lyla said. "I can't help you with that. Except did anybody tell you about those twat exercises?"

Delorie nodded. She never remembered about those muscles until it was too late.

"Keep doing those. Can't hurt."

"Thanks, Lyla."

"Sure." Lyla rolled the loose end of the elastic back onto the heavy spool.

"Lyla," Delorie said, "what finally happened?"

"The morning my water broke I had a friend call in to say I went for emergency surgery. Appendicitis. They never asked no questions. Three weeks later I was back at work."

"No, I mean with the baby. What happened to the baby?"

Lyla looked at the scissors she was holding. "Don't know. Somebody got him. They don't tell you who, you know." She lifted the scissors, opened and closed them. "It's better that way."

"Jesus."

"There's Torgerson."

Delorie headed back to her machine, walking more comfortably now. Mrs. Torgerson did her walkabout and paused next to Delorie's machine. Delorie straightened in her chair and lifted her shoulders; the shift in posture pulled her belly in. They had begun work yesterday on a new line of clothing, next winter's holiday dresses. By the time women were wearing them to parties this baby would be long-born and long-vanished, and Phil would be no more than an anecdote. The fabric was soft and finicky; it caught in the feed dogs and frayed easily; it clogged the machines with lint. Self-conscious with the supervisor looking over her shoulder, Delorie slowed down. Thread tangled underneath the plate.

Behind her Torgerson let out an impatient sigh. "That machine needs the hose," she said, and moved on.

Delorie untangled the threads and went to the pillar a few feet away and uncoiled the compressed-air snake. Back at her machine she opened all the small, hinged metal doors that hid the bobbins and the threading mechanisms, pointed the snake and blew out the lint that the fabric had left behind. Wads of fluff flew out to the side and floated to the floor where they rolled and danced and gathered. They would wait there until the sweeper came through with his push broom to take them away.

BOOK OF CHANGES

They sat on the floor in Vivien's apartment. Delorie – cross-legged on a folded blanket, pillows around her – adjusted and readjusted her position. Vivien loosened the drawstring on the small silk pouch in her hands and turned it upside down. Three bronze coins clinked onto the hardwood floor, rolled, circled and lay flat. Each coin had a small square hole in the middle.

This was Vivien's idea. *I Ching: The Book of Changes.* She was worried. Worried, she said, that Delorie was letting circumstances decide things for her, that the fact she'd chosen a name for the baby meant – didn't it? – that she was more attached than she would admit.

"The pregnancy," Delorie had said in response to Vivien's worries, "is an accident, and all it needs is to be gotten through. End of story."

Vivien had replied, "Humour me."

Smoke unwound from a cone of incense in a saucer; the odour cloyed. Delorie ground it out. "Sorry, Viv, can't stand it."

Vivien opened a window and the flame of the fat pink candle on the coffee table flickered in the summer evening air.

"How do we do this?" Delorie said. "Is it supposed to make decisions for me? Heads I give the baby up, tails I...." She had nothing to put at the end of that sentence.

"Don't miss the point. It doesn't decide anything. It helps you see patterns."

"Wow. You read that in your book, didn't you?"

"Quit making fun." Vivien opened the paperback and leafed through it, taking her time. Watching her, Delorie felt her own mood shift. It was just a diversion. She could go along.

"You have to cast the coins six times. I'll keep track of how they fall. You have to think about the question while you do it." Vivien looked up from the book. "Really concentrate."

Delorie gathered the coins and shook them in her hands but didn't cast them. Her mood shifted yet again. Think of a baby. Think of watching it grow up. She could imagine the one, but not the other, couldn't transform the imaginary baby into a person who walked and talked. She opened her hands, tried to put the nail of her pinkie finger through one of the tiny square holes. "Vivien?"

"Yeah?"

"There's no shortage of loving couples, et cetera. I can't *keep* it."

"Like I said: humour me."

What the hell. She did the first four casts quickly, stopping in between only long enough for Vivien to look and record. They were all the same. Four yin lines, Vivien told her. Each one the same, as if her imagination had failed her. To mother or not to mother. She cast twice more.

A yang line, Vivien said, and a moving yin. She flipped through the book and consulted a chart. "Hexagram eight. Auspicious." She brought the book fully into the light from the pink candle. The words she read aloud to Delorie sounded like spells, like nonsense.

You risk becoming incapable of closeness to others....

The third entity is the pair, together....

Recognize that this chair is your brother, the sun and stars are your brothers....

You seek union but hesitate to take the steps....

Delorie moved impatiently. "It's like those horoscopes in the paper – there's always one line that rings true no matter who reads it."

Vivien held up a hand to ask for patience. "That doesn't mean it's useless."

Vivien had finished reading. Delorie shifted her position and fanned her face. She was uncomfortably warm most of the time. "What's it supposed to mean?"

"Shit, Delorie, *I* don't know. You figure it out. You're the smart one."

"And you're the one who knows about *I Ching*."

Vivien read from the book again. "The pattern of the cast depends upon the forces of yin and yang within you. The question and the answer are both part of you." She paused. "Within *you*," she repeated, looking at Delorie.

Delorie wiped her forehead with her hand. "I feel stupid: get out the magic kit, light a candle, read the oracle." She dried her damp hand on her smock. "Not that I don't appreciate your efforts."

Vivien sighed.

"No, really. It's very nice of you."

"What'll you do?"

"Eenie, meenie," Delorie said. "But seriously – I'll do what I've said all along. Have the baby and leave the rest up to the worker."

She'd left the overhead light on in her room and she winced from its glare as she came in the door. She switched it off in favour of the lamp in the corner. Easy for Vivien to talk about attachment and choices. There was no choice. Delorie wanted to melt into the cushions. She sat with her feet up and her eyes out of focus and tried to relax. You seek union but hesitate to take steps. Oracles, horoscopes, lame mumbo-jumbo. She was bothered by a persistent sense of pressure close to her right hip. She went to the phone.

She dialed, heard the line ringing, knew just the sound it would make in the nook built into the ash cupboards in the kitchen in Ripley. *She'll hate me.*

"Hello."

"Mom?"

"Delores! Hallelujah! Where are you?"

"Is he home? Can you talk?"

"He's out."

"Good."

"It isn't like that anymore."

"Sure."

"He hasn't taken a drink in twelve months, Delores. I can talk anytime. You don't have to worry."

"Twelve months. He must be due for a bender."

"It's different this time." Her mother waited but instead of responding Delorie listened to the empty line that stretched from here to Ripley.

"Delores?"

"Still here."

"Delores, it *is* different. No fights, nothing to speak of anyway."

"Even at Christmas?"

"Even at Christmas."

"Some kind of record." She paused. "How's Stuart?"

"Stuart's fine. He misses you. *We* miss you. Delores, I'm so glad you called."

"Don't say that until you hear why.'"

"What is it?" The voice was calm.

Now that she at last was speaking to her mother, she couldn't say it. She stared at the counter, at her alligator note holder and the pamphlet held between its teeth: *Exercises for the Expectant.* Groin stretches, abdominal strengtheners, pee-blockers. She'd been doing them faithfully since Lyla reminded her, her way to retain some influence over the changes to her body. The peripheral changes, that is. The fundamental change had its own momentum, and in the purposefulness of this process she sensed the direct connection from her own mother, through herself, to the child.

Her mother waited in silence. *Pregnant,* Delorie thought. She hadn't the courage to use this true, plain word in conversation with her mother. "I'm in trouble."

The slightest hesitation, and then her mother said, "Oh, Delores. You should be home." Delorie detected no anger in her voice. "You should be home with us."

"I won't live with him."

Evenings: the clock ticking past suppertime while they waited to hear his step on the walk, Stuart sliding up and down the hall in his sock feet, sliding and sliding. Mom finally taking the potato pot to the sink and draining the cooking water. "They've turned to mush." The margarine slipping over the hot potatoes in the serving dish.

And if supper was over and still he hadn't shown up and if it was a good night for TV, Delores would take Stuart across the street to Glad Barrett's house to watch for awhile. Some nights it was *Huckleberry Hound*, which Glad didn't watch but let the kids sit there, didn't mind the company. Other nights it was *Don Messer's Jubilee*, for which she would join them. Marg Osborne with her hair sprayed up and wearing a modest, dark barrel of a dress, singing "Smile the While" at the end of the show, the credits rolling over her chest, her face, over the wave of hair above her forehead, giving Delorie a sense of motion sickness as she tried to guess whether this would be a good or a not-so-good time to leave Glad's small room with the delicate glass bell on the windowsill, the bits of lace on the backs of the chairs, the softly ticking wall clock. Leave this and take Stuart and walk back to face the unforgiving planes and angles of the kitchen across the street.

The calm was gone from her mother's voice now and in its place was a mix of pleading and anger. If Delores wouldn't come home, she demanded, if Delores was so all-fired proficient at looking after herself, then why had she called? After so many months of silence, of not having the decency to even say where she was living, not being good enough to let her parents know she was still alive?

"You have no idea, have you, of the fear I've had to fight off just to get to sleep at night? No idea!"

Delorie listened with the part of her mind that she'd cordoned off from emotion. She waited in silence for a moment, then told her mother she was welcome to come and see her in the city.

"You're ready to give out your address, then?"

Yes, she was. To her mother. There was no reason her father had to know. "You have to promise you won't tell."

"I don't know if I can do that."

She had another meeting with Bonnie in the gray building downtown, in the cube of a room with the blue green chair that let out a slow wheeze under her pregnant weight, leaving her feeling as if she sat on a slab.

"You don't need to sign anything just yet," Bonnie said of the adoption arrangements. Delorie wondered what it was in her speech or manner that had prompted Bonnie to make this statement.

"No rush," Bonnie said. Then she made a quiet suggestion. "You could write the baby a letter."

"Pardon me?"

"A letter. Many girls in your situation find that it helps."

Despite her flippancy about casting the *I Ching*, after that evening at Vivien's Delorie had let herself imagine keeping the baby. At first the scenarios amounted to no more than tourism: picturing a flannel-lined bassinet, teething rings, touchable skin and downy curls. Then her imaginings went further: diapers, rent money, crying in the night.

She'd called home again, during the daytime on a Monday when her mother would have the afternoon off and he wouldn't be there.

"But how would you live, Delorie?"

"I'd get a job; they'll take me back at the factory."

"And the baby?"

"I'd get a sitter."

"And pay her the same amount you bring home from a minimum wage job?"

"That's not how it works, Mom."

"Then tell me how it does work. You pay her less than you make?"

"Well, yes."

"Which would leave both of you with?"

Silence. Then:

"Okay," Delorie said. "So maybe welfare."

"Maybe welfare?"

She sat on the front steps listening to a Bob Dylan tape, "Don't Think Twice." She was staring absent-mindedly along the ragged line of elm trees on the boulevard and thinking wasn't that quite a sensation, that slow shift in her belly, like a bubble looking for a pathway, as the baby realigned itself, when she saw a bicycle round the corner at the far end of the block. Phil. He took to the sidewalk, ducking under low branches. He slowed and braked in front of her and stood, straddling his bike, moving it back and forth as he stood there. Back and forth.

He said it first: "Hi."

"Hi back."

"You like my convertible?"

She watched the motion of the pine tree air freshener that hung from the handlebars, flick, flick, flick against the chrome. "Wouldn't be much use at a drive-in movie," she said.

"I don't suppose."

After a moment she asked, "How's Fern?"

"She's good."

"I'll bet," Delorie said. She meant it to sound funny, not sarcastic, but she knew by the look on his face that she hadn't managed the right effect. He shifted his gaze, studied the sidewalk that led to the front door. She didn't see a need to ask him up.

"So?" he said. One word rising into a question mark; he could mean any one of a number of things – could mean, Tell me everything that's happened since I was last here; or, You're not going to keep it or anything dumb like that; or, simply, Nice day if it doesn't rain.

She tried a smile. No reason the two of them shouldn't get along. He smiled back. Unreadable. Like someone she'd only just met.

"Sorry about last time," she said.

"Me too."

Armistice.

"There must be some reason you're here," she said, looking at his front tire.

"Out for a ride."

She repeated: "There must be some reason you're here."

He set his bike on its side on the sparse grass beside the walk. He sat down, faced Delorie and shrugged.

"I just wanted to make sure everything's okay." He moved his hand. He might have been reaching for her hand and then changed his mind; he might have been reaching for a blade of grass in the first place.

She snuck a glance at his face and tried to imagine kissing that face now. No.

He tugged at the weeds along the edge of the sidewalk, pulled a wide blade of quack grass and lined it up tightly between his thumbs. When he raised it to his lips and blew he coaxed no more than a squawk out of it.

"Everything is *not* okay," Delorie said in even tones. She felt an ache in the muscles around her eyes. "Nothing is okay. Everything is different. But it's a helluva lot more different for me." They weren't angry words, they were just the appropriate ones. She used her sleeve to wipe at her nose.

He moved to her side and put his arm around her. It felt foreign and she shook it away.

"Want me to stay, want me to go? What?"

"You better go," she said.

He didn't move.

"You better just go," she repeated, holding her face steady so the tears rimming her eyes wouldn't spill. Restraint was the appropriate approach. She shouldn't have tried to abandon it. It was a comfort to return to the known way of managing. To hold her head still underneath the apple and know she wouldn't be responsible for it rolling off.

"What can I do?" he said. And when she didn't answer, again: "What can I *do*?"

He got up and moved toward his bike but didn't lift it. She didn't want him to go away angry again. A gesture was called for.

She waved and gave him an awkward smile. She picked up her silent tape player, its motor straining against the played-out cassette, and retreated up the sidewalk, went inside and closed the door. She sat for ten minutes on the bottom stair, waiting for him to be long gone, before she went back outside and flipped the tape. If she were to take Bonnie's advice and compose a letter to this child, what would she say about the father? She should have asked him.

LONG DISTANCE LESSONS

Release. It had the ring of something a child would thank her for one day.

"It's entirely your decision," Bonnie said, "but I will say this: If you're ambivalent at all, it's best for everyone if you release the baby. A teen mom, all alone – it's hard. It's too hard."

This time they were not meeting downtown. Bonnie had come today to Olivia's Place, where Delorie was now a resident. They sat upstairs under the gently sloped ceiling of a former bedroom that had been made into a case room. At seven months, unemployed, tapped-out and tired, Delorie had skipped on a month's back rent and moved to Olivia's. In her bachelor suite she'd been waking from bad dreams; each time, once the adrenaline summoned by the dream had jolted her awake, she would think, What if it were to start this minute and here I am, alone?

Tracy had taken the afternoon off on moving day and helped Delorie load two suitcases and three boxes into the back of her Austin Mini. "Meep meep," Tracy said, mimicking the radio ad for the Mini. "Still the lowest-priced new car in Canada." Delorie obliged with a smile for purposes of friendship. She manoeuvred herself into the passenger seat and thought it was good that her entire life could be packed inside a car, and such a tiny one.

Vivien showed up too. She was working the split and took the bus to Olivia's between shifts. "Who's Olivia?" she said as she carried a suitcase up the stairs.

"Haven't the foggiest."

"What does it mean, the co-op part?" said Tracy.

"I think it means we're supposed to be grown-ups."

Now, sitting with Bonnie, Delorie looked out through the dormer window at the balconies of the apartment building across the alley from Olivia's. She saw geranium pots and small black barbecues, homes. She felt the direct gaze of Bonnie's mauve-shadowed eyes.

"The most important thing," Bonnie continued, "is that you make a decision, soon, one way or the other. Any decision, even a painful one, brings relief."

The word "decision" twice in two sentences.

"I *have* decided," Delorie said. "I'm going to release the baby." Not give her up, she told Bonnie. It was better to think about releasing than to think about giving her up.

"You should see it in terms of both those things," said Bonnie. "Releasing it and giving it up. You have to release the baby emotionally at the same time. For the baby's sake; for your own too. I'll bring papers next time."

"Yes," Delorie said. She imagined long pages crowded with legal sentences. A place to sign so that after delivery she could get on with things, all the wiser.

"I'll see you next week." Bonnie closed her file and smiled at Delorie. "Good girl."

Good girl. Bonnie is kind. Bonnie is understanding. Bonnie is doing her job. But she just said "Good girl" to me as if I'm a puppy. How fitting. Sitting quietly and waiting for things to end, the way I did when I was little, trying to radiate stillness.

They were six at Olivia's Place: Darlene L.; Cindy; Darlene T.; Bridget, who was older than the rest of them; Marjorie, who was rumoured to think herself too good for this place and these people; and Delorie. They were told to think of each other as family. If you counted Lea, they were seven. Lea was working toward her social worker ticket; she caught the bus to class on Wednesday nights. Delorie wasn't sure if Lea was supposed to be a paid friend or a kind of boss. Or whether she was a kind of boss and you were supposed to be fooled into thinking she was a friend. At Delorie's intake interview, Lea had helped her establish what her contributions would be to the household. Each resident took regular rotations for cooking and cleaning. Beyond that, Delorie would add a few items to the communal maternity closet. Lea had seen her four-scarf skirt, how it managed to emphasize her belly rather than soften it, how the hem trailed longer in the back than it did in the front, but evidently it hadn't put her off. She had, however, directed Delorie to visit Penn's Fabrics and buy bona fide dressmaker patterns and quality yard goods. Olivia's Place had room in the budget for proper fabric.

And could she help the girls who were doing their high school correspondence?

Oh, and when you answer the phone in the hall, say "hello," nothing else. Above all, don't say "Olivia's." Some of the residents don't want people to know. They've told their families the phone number but nothing more.

The sewing machine was set up near the living room windows to take advantage of the natural light. Delorie sat at a card table close to the machine and pinned a facing to the front of a smock. The slacks and smock she'd already completed had a fine, finished look. Both the Darlenes, one after another, had worn them to go out to the movies with friends. It was satisfying to follow a pattern, with its diagrams to illustrate the relationships between the pieces. Facing D, yoke E.

There was a knock at the front door and Lea let in Dr. Moore. Delorie folded her sewing and stacked it on the card table. It was time to go up to the case room for BP. You couldn't be too careful, high blood pressure being so common among unwed mothers who've decided to give up their children – a statistical fact, Lea said. Now you couldn't find salt in the kitchen. Delorie sat on the chair outside the case room and waited her turn. She closed her eyes and tried to relax. The BP checkup was a test she didn't want to fail.

Last night her mother had called. Delorie had given her Olivia's unlisted number and they spoke regularly but said little. It was difficult over the phone. There were no visits.

"I can't come to Saskatoon without telling your father where I'm going and why."

"But you *can't* tell him."

"I don't know what I'd say to him, Delores, if not the truth."

"Can't you figure something out?"

Breathe in, breathe out. She wanted her mother. Breathe in, breathe out.

The woman from Tresses came one morning to lead a session in beauty culture. They wound each other's hair up in rollers and took turns with the bonnet hair dryer. Delorie did a practice updo for Darlene L., who was to be married soon in the living room of her fiancé's parents. Her own parents would not be attending. While Delorie worked on her hair, Darlene hand-stitched purple ribbon roses around the hem of her wedding dress. Her future mother-in-law had insisted colour be added to the dress – the circumstances did not allow unbroken white.

"What's your night class?" Darlene said to Lea.

"Unofficially we call it Laws and Loonies. On the books it's Deviance and Social Control."

"I suppose we're covered under that," Cindy said. "Unwed mothers."

Lea nodded. "Yes. You are."

"What've you learned about us?" Bridget said. "What's the solution?" She took off the hair dryer bonnet and patted her rollers.

"To what? To unwed mothers?"

"Yeah."

"The policy solution?"

"Whatever you call it."

"There's a guy in class who's for mandatory sterilization after two illegitimate kids."

"For the girl, he means?"

They were good at diversion, the residents of Olivia's. Every day at noon Cindy and Delorie carried sandwiches and milk to the living room and watched *The Flintstones*. It seemed the shortest half-hour of the day. Each week a librarian came with ten new books, and each week Delorie would sort through and find at least two that could take her away from now and here. In the kitchen in the evenings they played game after game of cards. (In bed at the end of the day Delorie would close her eyes and playing cards would float through her field of vision. Ten of hearts, two of spades.) Together, they talked about anything but babies. Sentimentality would not do. The contradiction they lived with: if you love your baby you must give it up; if you give your baby up, you must achieve indifference.

They were teaching themselves about distance. They'd been told by their workers and by Lea that when you gave up your baby the best thing you could do for it was make a clean and final separation. For yourself as well, so you'd be able to move on. It was a form of abstinence: one drop of sentiment would be too much, one drop might lead to binges. Delorie had moments when she achieved a fine, clear disengagement, a stepping off to the side, a place where her breath came slowly and her bones and muscles felt pleasantly heavy. From there she saw how her life was a little life with little trials, griefs that were only small.

Still, some nights she wrapped her arms around herself, cuddled her own shoulders and cried. It seemed the tears sprang not so much from sadness as from the need to complete a physical function, perform a service, the way washing dishes readies them for the next meal, the way using the pressure hose to blow out her machine back at the factory had cleared out what clogged the gears so it would operate again.

Delorie stood alone in the kitchen, pleated a paper napkin into a fan and made a breeze across her cheeks. She checked the work schedule. She took rubber gloves and a pail from under the sink, grabbed a scrubbing cloth and headed for the upstairs bathroom. Stairs. The work in her thigh muscles and the downward pressure on her perineum.

Surprising how comfortable it was to get down on her hands and knees to scrub – the weight in a different position for a change. Still, she wouldn't want to keep it up for long. The key to comfort was variety; keep shifting things from here to there. She was thirty-five pounds above her regular weight. Sometimes it seemed as if the food lifted itself and entered of its own accord, like paper clips to a magnet.

She washed the floor, working backward from door to bathtub. Her scrubbing cloth had a raggedy edge and the unraveling threads caught on the stopper chain when she rinsed the cloth in the tub. She broke the longer threads off and draped them over the side of the tub. She climbed inside to scour the wall tiles while the linoleum dried.

Cindy came to the doorway. "None of us ever do the tiles."

"Maybe you should." Delorie pulled another loose thread away from her cloth.

"Scrubbing your way to redemption?"

"Could be. How much farther, in your estimation, have I got to go?"

"No but seriously – that's what it was like when my sister went into the home with the nuns in Edmonton."

"Yeah?"

"Damn right. The first thing they did was take away her real name and give her a religious name for the duration. Second thing they did was hand her a mop and a bucket and tell her to get started on scrubbing her way to redemption."

"Is she there yet?"

"Is she where?"

"Redemption."

"Good question."

Delorie climbed out of the tub. As she wiped the sink, she didn't think about redeeming herself, she thought about how if Cindy's sister in Edmonton had a baby and gave it away, and Cindy had a baby and gave it away, those two people could one day end up working side by side in a bank or office or restaurant and not even know they were cousins. It was hard to bear, the thought of these babies – her own baby too, she realized with a wrench – their lives an unpredictable unravelling in any old direction out in the world. Not knowing who they were. People should know who they are.

MESSENGERS

Best to write the letter without too much thought ahead of time, otherwise she'd never begin. Sit right down after supper and do it. Delorie hung her wet jacket in the hall. She'd been out to see Phil – a fact-gathering mission. They'd emerged from the Red Lion to find the city shining wet under the street lights. The long wait for the cab home had made her back sore; her bladder felt ready to burst, and she hurried upstairs to pee. What – she'd asked Phil, sitting in the Lion – should she tell the baby on his behalf? What did he want the child to know, in the future, about her biological father?

After supper she arranged a swap to free herself from kitchen duty. To her favourite sitting place, the firm end of the couch where the pole lamp cast a beam of light, she brought the notepad they used for keeping score when they played cards. The pages were small and they filled up quickly.

Dear Baby,
All I can say is I'm sorry. I'm sorry to let you go. Sorry I

won't see your face as you grow up; they say it will change week to week, day to day even.

Sorry I am not equal to this.

Your father wants you to know he wishes you the best. That you be strong and healthy and have a good time in life. He says to tell you a sense of humour will get you through a lot. He says be a good sport and it will save you some grief.

Lea came to the doorway. "Delorie? Your friend Vivien's here, but there's a guy with her. I told them to wait in the kitchen, in case he's someone you don't want to see."

"What's his name?"

"Duncan, he says."

Scavenger. Dusting off his given name to be presentable, to gain entry to Olivia's. "It's all right," Delorie said. She lifted herself off the couch.

"Vivien," she began as she entered the kitchen, "you're not supposed to tell people even where this place *is*, let alone bring – "

She stopped. Vivien's hair was dripping and her face was wet, tears mixed with raindrops.

"What?"

The Darlenes, gathering the cards and the cribbage board and getting up from the table, said, "We'll go now." Lea stood behind Delorie in the doorway, on call.

Scavenger said, "Delorie. It's Phil. He had an accident. It's bad. It's bad. Delorie?"

Their stricken faces. Delorie said, "He's dead."

"No, he's alive, but," Vivien stopped speaking and looked steadily at Delorie.

"What does 'but' mean?"

Scavenger pressed his hands together. "He's hurt bad. All over." He paused, and when no one else said anything, he added, "I mean everywhere."

"You mean his head," Delorie said. "Him. You mean brain damage. Don't you?"

"His legs." He paused. "Broken back...."

"His head."

Scavenger's orphan lock of hair clung damply to his forehead. "They say it's very bad."

Delorie made her hands big across her belly, as if she could shield the baby's eyes and ears. She saw the room, the furniture, the cupboards, the clock, and the kettle, as if from far away. They were miniatures: she could have picked up a person or a chair or the kitchen table with her thumb and forefinger. Scavenger came around and moved a chair into place behind her. The three of them sat. Water puddled around Vivien's and Scavenger's feet.

An accident, a couple of doors away from the Prince. As he spoke, Scavenger passed his hand over his eyes, rested his forehead on his spread fingers. The bus stop, the street flooded from a clogged grate at the corner, troubles with visibility, with braking, one bus after another pulling into line. Phil coming back to put in the second half of his shift. His habit of aiming for the low spot on the curb, jumping his bike up to get to the No Parking sign where he would chain it. Sheilah, who saw the accident, came into the bar white and shaking and yelled for Scavenger. He was the one who phoned the ambulance, who hoisted the mangled bicycle onto the sidewalk and called the hospital every half hour until Phil was out of surgery.

Delorie could not face these two; they were looking at her now and she didn't know how to look back. She held the cool chrome tubes on either side of the seat of her chair. Tears fell on the roundness of her smock.

Scavenger got up from his chair, and water that had been trapped in a fold in his jacket streamed noisily to the floor. He reached carefully into his pocket, pulled his hand out again slowly and extended it toward her. On his palm, limp and soggy, was the cardboard pine tree Delorie had last seen hanging from the handlebars of Phil's bicycle. The peak of the tree had begun to tear away.

"What the *hell* did you bring that for?" she shouted. "His stupid corny goddamn *joke!* What am I supposed to do with that?"

It was the first thing she'd said since Scavenger had started his story. Fresh hurt showed on his face. Vivien's hand moved toward Delorie's shoulder but hesitated, then touched her arm before withdrawing.

"Stupid," Delorie muttered. "Stupid."

"There it was," Scavenger said, "in the water by the curb. Looked like it would get lost. I thought…I don't know." He set the wet tree on the table and gently nudged the ragged bit at the top into place. He put his hands in his pockets. "I'll just leave it."

Delorie stared at Vivien's wet pumps in order not to look at the table or at Vivien and Scavenger. After a moment she said, "Was Fern there, at the Prince?" It seemed important to know.

"She's out home for the weekend," Scavenger said. "I'll try to reach her."

"They aren't together anymore," Vivien said. "Weren't."

"Oh. He didn't tell me."

Scavenger shifted from one foot to the other. "What can I say?"

"He could get better, " Delorie said.

"No," Scavenger said. "He won't get better Delorie." He made a for-God's-sake-take-over gesture to Vivien, who said, "I'll stay with you tonight, Delorie. I'll sleep on the floor."

Delorie shook her head. "No overnight visitors."

Lea, in the doorway still: "It's okay, Delorie."

But Delorie said, "No. Come back tomorrow, Vivien." She didn't want someone in her room, worrying in case she cried all night, in case she didn't. She watched as Scavenger followed Vivien out the door; she noticed how his hand touched her back as she stepped outside. She remembered Vivien's brief touch on her arm, how Vivien had seemed afraid to let her hand rest there. Delorie wished now that she'd taken that hand and held it for a moment, but she didn't call out to Vivien to come back.

In her room she rolled her extra blanket and tucked it under her pregnant belly for comfort as she did every night. Intermittent darkness; beams from headlights moving across the walls; the sad music from the traffic below on Avenue H – thrum of car motors, swish of tires through the wet. A scorched feeling began in her throat and traveled in the direction of her gut. Let. me. just. sleep.

The fact of the accident was still there in the morning, like an object almost, a thing she could pick up and turn over, like you would a dish or a knife. A stone. It would not disappear.

RECONNECTION

She stayed in bed. Lea came to the door and Delorie asked could she please bring the Phyllis Whitney up from the library shelf. She reread the whole thing, carried it downstairs with her to read through lunch, spoke only when absolutely required. She took the book back upstairs and when she finished she began again. Solving a mystery in the sunshine on the Isle of Rhodes. Not a nice man, that fellow in the book.

Cindy came to tap on her door and tell her Vivien was on the line. Delorie went out to the hall phone. Vivien said, "We'll get you to the hospital. You can see him."

"No." Pause. "Did you see him, Vivien?"

"Yes."

"And?"

"It was...hard."

"I think I won't go."

"Another day then. Can I come to Olivia's?"

"Another day."

Delorie heard a commotion downstairs and Bridget's shaky voice saying, "No turning back now. Lea, can you carry my bag out?" She hung up the phone and went into the empty case room. The car was parked at the back of the lot. She watched Lea help Bridget into the passenger seat and then hurry around and get behind the wheel. They backed out into the alley and Delorie went to her room to begin chapter three again.

The next day at lunchtime Lea reported that Bridget had had a healthy baby boy. Four days later Bridget returned to Olivia's. They were allowed that, a week of transition time back at the house, two weeks if they needed it. Lea organized tea and cupcakes in the living room that evening to welcome Bridget back. Talk was low-key; most of the girls went off to bed without lingering. By nine o'clock Delorie and Cindy were almost finished with the dishes.

"She didn't even get to see it," Cindy said. Delorie didn't respond. She didn't see the point of conversation. She could almost have recited her mystery novel. She was still refusing offers from Lea and from Vivien to take her to visit Phil. She put away the last mug and looped her dishtowel through the fridge handle and went upstairs to bed.

She fell asleep finally with her book in her hand, then woke, startled, not knowing how long she'd been out. Was there a noise? Never mind, she was always hearing a noise. She let the book drop to the floor, pulled her cold hand under the covers and closed her eyes. But then Cindy was jiggling her shoulder. "Wake up Delorie, wake up!"

"What?"

"Bridget!"

"Bridget what?"

"I heard noises from the bathroom – coughing and spluttering like someone was dying of pneumonia."

Delorie sat up, braced her hands on the mattress and started to heave herself off the bed.

"No, no," Cindy said. "Stay there. It's okay now."

"What's okay? What was it?"

"I went for Lea and she used her skeleton key to get into the bathroom. Bridget must've held her head underwater and tried to drown herself in the tub."

"You can't do that. That wouldn't even work." Delorie pushed down with her fists and stood up. She told herself she wasn't going to gawk, she was going to help. From the hallway she saw into the bathroom: Bridget naked on the toilet and Lea in her sleeping shirt, bum resting on the edge of the tub, leaning forward to rub Bridget's back. Bridget's slack, empty belly-skin; snot streaked across one cheek; the mole near her nose black like a beetle against her white skin.

With her foot, Lea nudged the door so it swung shut.

The next day Delorie called the house in Ripley. She said nothing about Phil, nothing about Bridget, said only, could her mother come, please? Find a pretext that would preserve the secret, and come to Saskatoon for a few days. She gave her the address.

"I'll be there on tomorrow's bus."

She would say nothing about Phil. That story was immaterial. That story was over.

What notions would her mother have about this house? She recalled a day three years ago when her mother had first seen the Sally Ann home in City Park that served the same purpose. They were on their way to City Hospital with Aunt Lenore to visit Uncle Bailey near the end of his life. They turned left at Queen and as they neared the hospital Delorie's mother took note of the brick building on the north side of the street. "Look at that – it's a mansion." Aunt Lenore had explained about the Bethany Home, referring to the residents as wayward girls. The three of them had stood in the hospital parking lot and looked at the house: its warm brick walls and its abbreviated stone turret, the multiple windowpanes in their clean, white frames. Delorie remembered her mother's raised eyebrow and the precise parentheses either side of her mouth. *My, those wayward girls live in a lovely place.*

Her mother was here, standing in Olivia's entryway in her green double-knit pantsuit, the good one. It hung more loosely than it used to. Delorie was shy, didn't reach for her, stood back after opening the door, a few feet of floor space between them. Their history was not one of physically demonstrated affection. Delorie, standing there, her hand on the newel post for stability, seeing how unexpectedly slender her mother was, said the first thing that came into her mind, "Mom, you've lost so much weight."

"Yes, I have. Exercise classes at the community centre." A smile came and went, answered briefly by one from Delorie. Silence.

Her mother's reading glasses hung around her neck on the same damn stray length of pink plastic skipping rope she'd rigged for the purpose a couple of years ago, stretching the open tubing around the arms of the glasses like sleeves. Delorie had tried to train her not to wear it in public. But. No reason to expect something like that would have changed. And hadn't she decided she needed the comfort of the familiar, the known?

"Come upstairs, Mom."

In her room, Delorie closed the door and sat on the bed. She was about to gesture toward the chair, but she saw her mother's careful balance, feet hip-width apart, her face both familiar and changed. A calmness Delorie didn't remember. She patted the quilt and said, "Here."

She accepted her mother's embrace. She cried for a long time.

"It's all over now, Delores. All over now."

They were standard words of comfort, and they weren't true. It wasn't over. Her mother didn't know what had happened to Phil – and Delorie wasn't about to tell her – but she did know the baby was still to come. And go – who knows where. Delorie gripped the sleeve of her mother's jacket, held the machine-knit fabric between her fingers, then stopped gripping empty fabric and held, for real, her mother's arm. Maybe this was what her mother meant – that the separation between them was over. New tears traced the paths of the earlier ones; they tingled, burned.

"I suppose this boy's gone," her mother said.

"Yes. He is."

"Why am I not surprised?"

"Stop it, Mom." Delorie pulled away. "He had an accident." Her voice was a blend of anger and defiance, as if she feared she wouldn't be believed. "He was on his bicycle. The night of that big storm." But no, she hadn't meant to talk about this.

Her mother drew her into a hug again. "What kind of accident? What on earth happened?"

What could she say? There was nothing to be done. A man pedaling away on a ten-speed, the streets slick. She closed her eyes. Enough of this emotional binge. "He's gone," she said.

"My baby," her mother said. "My baby."

Her mother took her to supper at the Chinese café two blocks from Olivia's. Delorie talked more than she'd planned to talk. She told her about Cindy and Cindy's sister and their two babies out there in the world passing each other on the street twenty years from now and not knowing each other. "But I guess there's nothing really wrong with that," she said. "I guess."

She told her what Bridget had tried to do that night in the bathtub. She stopped abruptly at the end of the story, surprised that it led her nowhere, as if she'd been walking along the flat top of a cement wall and the wall had run out.

"Delores…"

"My name's Delorie now."

"I keep trying. I'll get it yet. Delorie, I never knew life could be so good as it has been this past year. You won't believe that, I know, but it's true."

"So he waited until I was gone and then, miraculously, he became a different person. I leave and right away things are fine."

"It's just that he was finally ready to quit. His body just said stop. Or his soul, if you can think of it that way. So devastated, seeing you go off like that."

"It's hard not to take it personally," Delorie said in a voice that she willed to come out sounding steady and casual.

"Delores…Delorie, don't say that, don't. He wants to see you. Wants you to see him, to see who he really is."

"The past twelve months – that's really him? Who was the

guy we lived with all the other years? Let's make a deal, Mom. Let's see if we can go twenty-four hours without mentioning him. He's miles away and still he manages to occupy centre stage."

Her mother looked down at her plate, fingers at her temples. "You've told him," Delorie said.

"You're right, Delorie," said her mother, "we don't need to talk about your father. We need to talk about other things." She looked up and leaned on her forearms. "We need to talk about where this baby will grow up."

PROTOCOL

The final conversation with Bonnie in the case room under the eaves wasn't a long one.

"I'm going home to Ripley with my mother and the baby."

"You don't have to do that. Don't forget, Delorie, it's *your* decision."

"I know. It is."

"I see," said Bonnie, looking past Delorie. "I see," she repeated, in a way that made her sound as if she was in fact trying to see but didn't. Delorie allowed the fleeting thought that her meetings with Bonnie had been more about finding someone a baby than they'd been about helping her get through this. It was a lie, what she'd told Bonnie. She wasn't going home with her mother, but the thought of explaining – she wanted to be delivered of that responsibility as well as the other responsibilities. There'd be paperwork required sooner or later, she supposed, and Bonnie or another worker would no doubt come back into the picture. But leave that for another day.

"Delorie, this is your chance, now, in this room, to talk about anything you want to talk about." As she spoke the motion of the birthmark on her neck was slow and fluid. She leaned back in her wooden chair now as though it were a padded recliner and she'd comfortably sit there for another hour. If she noticed that Delorie was staring at her neck, she didn't appear to mind.

There was nothing to say. She and her mother had cooked up a strategy. Delorie stared at the blank wall. No. Her mother had come up with a strategy and she had agreed.

"I need to go back to my room," Delorie said. A person can come unlaced about these things, or she can maintain her self-respect. Bite back on it, as the song says. The matter was, at any rate, settled. *Settled.* The image coming to mind of a cat kneading and pawing as it makes its bed, turning and turning, a final look about before at last it settles, tip of its tail over its nose, restlessness not so much overcome as temporarily quelled.

In the Chinese café the other night she'd looked across the table at her mother and tried to imagine how this would work. She'd remembered her mother making supper in Ripley, waiting to see if Dad would show, slamming cupboard doors, mashing the piss out of the turnips.

"Suppose he drinks again."

"I'll take the baby away somewhere, the baby and Stuart both."

Delorie put down her fork. "You didn't do that before, why should I believe you'd do it now?"

"I know I didn't; I know. And I am," she looked up, "I'm so, so sorry. I had no savings. I know that isn't," her voice trailed off as she rubbed beside one eye with her fingers. "I would now. I would take the children away if he drank again," she said, her voice emphatic.

Delorie looked hard at her mother and believed her.

"But that won't happen," Mom said. "Your father wants to do this too." She paused. "And he wants to apologize to you, Delores."

Delorie rolled her unused chopsticks against the tabletop with her palm. "I've heard of that. The apology. It's one of their steps, isn't it? Which one, what number?"

"Delores..."

They were quiet for a moment.

"Why?" Delorie said. "Why do this?"

"Dear, it would give you a degree of peace." She paused. "And with the father dead..."

With the father dead.

Two days ago Delorie had said to Vivien, "The broken back is the least of it. For that there are wheelchairs. For the other...." Dead. Yes. If *she* wasn't the one to say it, did that mean it wasn't an actual lie?

Now her mother said, "Delores, sweetheart. You would know where the baby is. With family. Loved."

With family: of a piece. Delorie thought how she'd been cradled by her mother at Olivia's, the comfort of it. Yes, maybe. She would know where the baby was. Not that loose, uncontrollable, unpredictable unravelling who knows where.

Her mother would go home to Ripley with the baby and Delorie would stay in Saskatoon and carry on as if. Find her own little set of rooms. Phil would go to the place his parents had found in Moose Jaw where he would be, as Scavenger had pointed out, closer to family. Not that he knew them anymore, his family. Delorie would go back to work, where they were always happy to see the return of someone with experience, as though none of this had ever happened. With any luck, she'd settle in behind a familiar, second-floor machine and work on a single operation until she mastered it. She would do it repeatedly, efficiently, and so fast that the bonus for piecework would be a regular occurrence.

At her mother's insistence, they would follow the unwritten protocol for the situation. It hadn't been called into play in Ripley for a number of years, but there was a rumour of a recent case in Morris. Mom would go to stay at her sister's house in Regina for a couple of months with the baby. Dad would spread the word that she was in the city because she was undergoing a complicated pregnancy and needed to be near the specialists. A woman her age. Yes, there would be raised eyebrows, but the community would participate in the fiction that the long-suffering Mrs. Wood had managed, at forty-four, with a daughter nineteen and a son thirteen, to be either sloppy or complacent about birth control or merely surprised – and here there would be more than one person who winked – by an act that had become such a rare event she'd been caught unprepared. Mrs. Woods would begin once more, in middle age, to pin diapers on the clothesline. The baby would be introduced as "the afterthought." And who knew – at least some of the good-hearted souls would think – maybe she was.

It was the best course of action.

UNFINISHED

The doctor shouted for forceps and the nurses moved quickly in response. Jesus, she'd seen pictures of forceps. No way. She wasn't letting them put those industrial egg tongs up inside her. Emboss her mother's baby's soft skull, damage her. She summoned her strength and pushed, kept on pushing, heard someone say, "Stop now, stop pushing Delorie! The contraction's over." She couldn't tell when a contraction began nor when it was over. It was supposed to be plain as day, or so the prenatal nurse who'd visited Olivia's had her believing.

"Lodged in the canal," the doctor said in a clipped voice. He waved dismissively at a nurse. "Forget the forceps. Tell the surgeon to scrub." Delorie wanted to do this without a surgeon. Push now. Is now the time? Keep pushing. Stop when?

But there was no getting it right, and they put her to sleep. After the Caesarian she woke and retched into a shiny, kidney-shaped pan and realized that the moaning she'd been hearing as she drifted in and out of consciousness had come from her own throat. She felt the raw incision and thought, I know I could do it now if I just had another chance. A person should get a practice run. It's a matter of timing, knowing when to push. Let me – please – let me have another try.

The nurse brought a bundle that cried desperately, but almost without sound. Tiny face, red and straining. Immediately there was so much more to think about than the feeling of not completing the delivery. The baby eyes looking up at her. The fear of holding such fragility in her arms.

For years, the sense that she hadn't finished her task would unsettle her at odd moments, would catch her in an emotional clutch accompanied by a tensing through the muscles a woman depends on to expel a baby. She would remember the unexpected weight of the tiny head on her arm, and how the baby had radiated heat; would remember being aware, after the nurse lifted the baby away, of the cooling circle of dampness where the sweat-warm head had rested on the sleeve of her nightgown.

Del would remember these sensations not as a sequence, first this and then this, but as a cluster that didn't separate themselves from each other; any single one would present itself out of the blue and all the rest would be implied. She would close her eyes for a few seconds until the cluster dissolved, and then she would carry on with what she'd been doing – rinsing cutlery, choosing stalks of celery from their bed of ice at Safeway, reaching for a bundle of sleeves at the factory.

PART 3

SALVAGE

Last night Amber had fallen asleep on her living room floor holding the sock doll she'd found in the box; wakened after midnight and pulled the throw off the couch to keep warm. Sunlight came now through the northeast window. Her reluctant eyelids struggled open and fell shut, open and shut. The tingle of a nerve, beginning in her right hip, moved along her leg like a procession of needle points to the base of her second toe. The same long line of sensation she felt whenever she woke from sleeping on the floor. Since she was a toddler, she'd spent occasional nights on the floor, as if getting into bed would be an admission the day was over. She used to sit on the floor in her quiet room in their peaceful house and play in the dark for hours after Mom and Dad thought she was asleep. Finally she'd drop off, her head resting on her latch hook rug with the yellow sun and silver grey moon.

In the shower, she turned slowly under the warm hand of the water and thought of the small heap of articles she'd dumped from her stuff box onto the floor yesterday. She dried off and let the towel lie where it fell. As she crossed through the kitchen on her way back to the bedroom her bare feet slapped past the red candle with its unmeltable outside – the candle she thought of, now more than ever, as the Del candle.

She reached into the bedroom closet for a work shirt. Her careless movements disturbed the windbreaker Cal had given her last year. The fabric was slick and the jacket slid sideways on the hanger, then slipped to the floor, followed by a slinky top from the next hanger over, then a mock-satin shirt. She grabbed, too late to make the rescue. Ignorant damn shirt! The anger reflex took her by surprise. As she tried to right things, more clothing, more hangers, tangled and fell. Sleep deprivation spiked her frustration. She smacked the door frame with the flat of her hand and felt the burn in her palm. Fuck! She needed short words with sharp edges. Fuck! She snatched up the windbreaker and threw it back down with a force that was mocked by the jacket's flimsiness. She dropped to the floor and her knee bumped the door jamb, hard. That was more like it – definite impact – short, sharp, satisfying pain. She watched as two empty hangers on the rod touched each other in a rhythm of quiet ting-tings, their movement slowing.

She reached for a hanger lying on the floor, flipped it back and forth against her leg as if it were a lid on a hinge, open-shut, open-shut. You can make something out of almost anything – or out of almost nothing. You can start with a clothes hanger. In grade eleven art class back in Ripley, Mr. Bowler had required that they construct mobiles. They were to begin with what he called "found objects": bring one thing from your bedroom, one from your backyard, one from an open field, others at your own inspiration; suspend them from hangers with varying lengths of fishing line. When Amber's older brother Stuart heard about the assignment he told her Bowler had given him the same task years before. He'd made his mobile entirely from product labels, including the tag from his Maple Leafs comforter that said New Material Only, a corner from a faded Weed and Feed box, and a weathered chocolate bar wrapper he'd found caught in the clover in Uncle Kenton's pasture. Bowler loved it, Stuart said; Bowler told him it was real art. "I think I offended him when I laughed at that," Stuart said. He'd thrown his creation in the garbage without bringing it home. On second thought, he said, maybe it *was* art and he should've held onto it. Stuart the roofer; Stuart the artist.

For her own assignment, Amber had used an old rhinestone necklace that changed colour according to the light, a few leaves from the elm tree out back and a collection of small stones from the alley. No one had called her creation meaningful, but Amber still remembered thinking hard about her choices: the changeable beads; the stones that she'd added because of their definite mass compared to the weightless leaves.

Her friend Tamara was the real artist. From feathers and dry grass and her own hair she'd created an ethereal arrangement that shifted in the slightest air current. "Nothing like the mobile Mom made when I was born," she'd said. She was referring to the school of enduring goldfish that hung from the ceiling in her bedroom, woven out of tiny ribbons, iridescence shining from their bellies. It had been there since Tamara was in diapers; maybe it still hovered above the tableau in her room, undisturbed since her death. Or had Mrs. Blanchard finally boxed things up? The rag rug, the inflatable snake, the biology books – dozens of them – and the fading fishes. And the vivid wardrobe

Tamara had accumulated on trips to Value Village in the city, her resounding colour combinations, her reds against greens, blues against oranges, her bright pink scarf threaded through a buttonhole, trailing, the way Amber's chartreuse scarf trailed now from a lopsided hanger. She'd wear that scarf today. Carry the idea of Tamara around with her, visible, touchable. Amber's white work shirt lay on the floor. She stood and shook it and pulled the scarf through the buttonhole.

In the living room she stopped beside the window that looked out over the gently sloping roof of the downstairs addition. Out on the slope, secured to the shingles with duct tape, was the stuffed dummy she'd inherited from the previous tenant.

"What about him?" she'd said pointing out the window after he handed over the key and told her he'd left eggs and ketchup in the fridge and she was welcome to them, he was off to Fort McMurray.

"I forgot. That's from Hallowe'en. Would you mind dumping it in a garbage bag? My truck's running and I gotta go pick up a guy."

The dummy was made from an old shirt and a pair of stuffed pants; yellow rubber gloves for hands. His balloon head had disintegrated to a few tatters, which were still tied with string to the top buttonhole of his striped shirt when Amber moved in. This spring she'd bought a succession of yellow helium-filled balloons to replace it. She'd given him a Magic Marker smile and Elmer Fudd eyes.

"You and I, balloon man," she said now through the window. "We both have to be so careful not to lose our heads completely."

On her way to work she passed the lot where the Burton house had stood, the basement a gaping hole littered with chunks of collapsed concrete. Chain-link surrounded the basement and the long, chewed-up stretch of side-yard that Cal called the Estate. By the end of summer a multiple-unit dwelling would stand here. Amber thought of the doorbell plate with the empty space in the middle. She thought of Del yesterday at the house. How could two people standing inches away from each other be so far apart?

On the bridge she saw a woman and a boy on the sidewalk, looking downriver. The boy gestured insistently, trying to make the woman see what he saw. Amber slowed her steps, dread and a guilty excitement mixing inside her. What was so important? This wasn't the bridge of choice for a jumper. Suicides favoured the train bridge. As Amber approached, she saw that the woman finally recognized the source of the boy's excitement. He relaxed and the two of them brought their heads together, both smiling. Amber once more picked up her pace.

"Look," the boy said, turning toward her as she came near, "beavers building a lodge." She followed his gesture and saw the brown head of a beaver trailing a shallow wake as it swam toward a mound of twigs on the east bank. She smiled and hurried on. She liked the idea of this animal building a new house so close to the place where an old one had come down.

The air was humid and, after yesterday's thin attempt at snow, surprisingly wrap-around warm. At five to ten she was turning onto Second Avenue, nodding hello to the short man with the uneven gait and the fidgety hands who roamed about downtown telling stories to himself. Ahead of her, casting a slim, ten o'clock shadow over the sidewalk, hung the sign for

Poor Man's Treacle with its carved and painted bulb of garlic. The über-garlic.

People hear the word "treacle" and they think of molasses, if they think of anything. Poor Man's had nothing to do with molasses. There was a complicated explanation for the restaurant's name, and Donna-the-boss taught it to all the servers on the day they were hired. They were to repeat the explanation to customers, but only if they were asked:

In medieval times rich people would go to the doctor and pay for an expensive concoction to ward off disease. The doctors called the mixture treacle. Chaucer – the poet, they were to say, in case people didn't know – said garlic was "the poor man's treacle" because the peasants would eat it instead of paying for the doctor's overpriced mixture. Strong antiseptic and germicidal properties.

Donna-the-boss liked bits like that, and she liked to share them. Every Friday morning she had Shari clip the "Twenty-five Years Ago This Week" sidebar from the paper and post it inside the door to amuse lunch customers as they waited for tables. (Last week it was Diefenbaker announcing he'd seek a twelfth term in the 1974 summer election; the week before that, an infestation of caterpillars so severe people out in the country had to shovel them aside to get their doors open.) History lessons, Shari called these clippings.

"Nothing wrong with lessons," Donna told her.

"Plenty wrong with history," said Shari. Shari was, as she put it, part Cree, part French, part Scot, and parts unknown.

Donna waited a beat before she said, "Point conceded."

This morning Billy was on the sidewalk outside Poor Man's, his plaid cap upended in front of his crossed legs. Donna would be grumpy about that. Only a loonie and two quarters sat in the cap; he stashed most of his take so he wouldn't look too flush. Before leaving home, Amber had put a loonie for Billy in her shirt pocket, but he was sitting too close to the window of Poor Man's. Donna would see. She decided to save it for this afternoon when he'd be at his other corner. Donna had explained her position about Billy: "I *do* give to charity, just not on the street. We have *programs* for people like that." Amber didn't bother to argue, but she preferred a more direct connection. As she passed Billy this morning, she gave him a nod and a smile but no money, feeling disloyal both to Donna and to him. She opened the door and smelled stock simmering in the back.

Despite her lack of sleep, Amber had no trouble staying awake at work, but it was a surreal wakefulness. The furniture and fixtures seemed to bob gently up and down: the tables and chairs, the muffin cases on the counter, the plants along the windowsill, dipping and lifting as if they were elements of a makeshift mobile. Light-headed, she thought of balloon man, his head anchored only by a length of string. Keep it on man. Her movements were too quick; she had small accidents, dropping cutlery, spilling leftover soup. Only herself to blame, sleeping on the floor, waking at intervals, shifting position to keep the glare from the street light out of her eyes.

"You're wired on something," said Shari. "Am I right?"

"No."

"Oh. Is it your thing again?"

"Yeah, it's my thing."

This fragile energy. A filigree moulded around a bubble of emptiness. The feeling that the filigree might any moment collapse into a heap of filings. She took a break, went into the bathroom, and sat on the cool, tile floor. Leaned her head where the two walls met. She pulled her scarf free of the buttonhole, wound it around her right hand like a bandage, and held on tight. Jiggled one knee just for the motion. She thought about endings. When married people got a divorce they signed papers to show it was over. When people died there were funerals and graves. When she and Cal split up she'd gone out for drinks that night with Shari and come back to her suite alone with a rediscovered feeling of ownership. He was gone and she could be as messy as she wanted. She'd made a start on reclaiming the place by leaving her clothes where they fell. But the ending she and Del had arrived at yesterday didn't come with a ready-made tradition, didn't suggest an appropriate gesture.

Amber didn't know how long she'd been sitting on the bathroom floor when Donna knocked. "The girls could use some help when you think you've got a minute." Donna had a gift for making sarcasm sound as if its raw material were warmth, not contempt. When Amber came on staff, Donna caught on quickly to the vagaries of her emotions. She was patient, didn't even blink when a couple of months earlier Amber had presented her with a doctor's note that said, "Amber would benefit from a week off work." Donna laughed and ran her fingers through her coarse blond hair and said, "I would too, but no one's writing notes for me." Followed by, "Go on, then, get out of here."

When Amber came back the next week, Donna had said, "Better now?"

"Yes, thanks. For the time being."

"What's it about, Amber?" Donna's eyes wide open with the question, the arch of her pencilled eyebrows acute.

"Nothing. It isn't about anything. It just is."

After work today, sitting on her couch and eating a cheese sandwich, Amber took herself to task: at *least* look after the plants. Phred the philodendron (so named by Cal before he moved out) drooped pathetically atop a speaker; the others were lined up along the squat bookcase, leaves pallid, stems flaccid. She last watered them when? She took a mug and slopped water into the pots. They were offspring of the plants at Poor Man's, cuttings wrapped by Donna in bread bags for the journey, instructions for care written on the backs of unclaimed till receipts. Don't tell Donna the misery they've been through.

Donna who cared so well for plants and for her staff, but who would chase Billy off Second Avenue. ("Leave them alone and they'll multiply like fruit flies, colonies all over downtown. 'Help me pay for a haircut,' my ass.") Donna with her dress codes and her very own initiative and her drive to succeed – which, she would remind people, had brought her to where she was today. She'd made that restaurant out of nothing. Donna with her stringent sanitation policy emphasized by the red-letter notices that said "HANDS?" tacked up in two locations in the kitchen and two behind the coffee bar. Who was normally so sure of herself, but who turned curiously more strict with her staff when Steve from Mock Turtle Books was in Poor Man's, as if she wasn't sure of her personality in his presence.

Amber lay down on the couch with her feet on the armrest and looked past her toes at the print Cal had left behind when they split up. *Concert of Angels*. The fun tack that held it up was old and the top right-hand corner periodically left the wall and curled across to hide the angel that played the triangle.

"What kind of atheist puts angels on the wall?" she'd said to Cal when he brought the print home from the poster sale on campus. He skimmed his palm over his ultrashort hair. He bought it, he told her, because when he saw it, something he'd been trying to explain to himself became suddenly clear – why human beings invented gods and angels. He looked at the benevolent faces of those angels and he understood that we'd pretended a whole race of beings into existence because we wanted someone to be interested in what goes on down here. Someone to care what we do.

"Like little kids," Cal said. "Look at me, Mom and Dad. Look at me!" He waved with both hands and Amber supposed from the gesture that he'd done a lot of this when he was little and now he had to make fun of the boy who'd done it. He hadn't rolled the print up and taken it away with the Olitski and the Miro prints when he left the Burton. Maybe by then he'd made his point to himself. When she moved out of the Burton and over to Temperance Street, Amber took down the angels and reused the drying dabs of adhesive still on the back to put it up in her new living room. It was like having a Christmas card on your wall all year. It was pretty and colourful and she kept it because of that; it did not, however, make her feel there were special beings watching her.

If there were such creatures, she thought, they'd hardly be impressed if they chose this moment to check in. *Take yourself in hand.* She got up and fetched the broom from its hook on the back of her kitchen door. She moved a chair out of the way, opened the window a couple of inches and slid the broomstick out so the brush end hung out over Temperance Street and the long blue handle jutted into the room four feet off the floor. She pushed the window down tight to hold it in place. Over the broomstick she hooked a clothes hanger. Clouds were building in the northwest; she heard the faint crackle of thunder. Through the narrow band of open window came the tang of approaching rain.

Amber sat on the floor amid the scatter of objects from the condensed milk box. Salvage, she thought, remembering the letter someone had written to the editor about the dismantling of the Burton house: salvage is possible. She crossed her legs, and her knee nudged the red zodiac candle, making it roll a few inches.

"Fine," Amber said, and she extended her leg and kicked. "I'll make myself without you." The candle rolled across the small kitchen and stopped underneath the radiator. Amber fished through the jumble on the floor and picked up two mementos: the jagged-edged handle from a broken teacup and a hat badge from the Army Service Corps. Mom and Dad.

NIGHT, LITTLE ONE

Amber set the hat badge down and held the handle from the broken teacup in her palm. It was a souvenir from a freak explosion that had happened when Amber was nine. She'd been in the backyard practising a skipping rope trick when she heard the blast, then screams. She ran inside to see. The explosion had scattered the contents of the refrigerator. Broken bowls and shattered jars. A chair leaning against a chair, another toppled on its back. It looked like a scene from cartoons on TV, and it made her giddy. She giggled a little as if the mess really did belong to Daffy Duck.

Her mother ran into the room, blood trickling down one side of her face, obscuring her eye. Amber swallowed so she wouldn't be sick. Dad grabbed the towel from the hook above the sink, pressed it to Mom's face and said to Mom, "Hold that! Steady." He rushed her out the door, stopping only to be sure Amber was unhurt. "You stay here," he said. "Your mother...!"

Amber stood alone in the kitchen, frightened by the fact that something as ordinary as a fridge could explode. What if her mother had lost an eye? What would it be like to see only half of everything? Amber covered one eye with her hand and walked across the kitchen, the soles of her shoes sliding through pickle juice and crunching over broken glass. She could hardly funnel enough information through that single pupil. Pause, sweep the room with her narrow beam of vision, step, pause again.

Until now, she'd never been left alone in the house. She used a tea towel to wipe off a chair and sat down. None of the neighbours, apparently, had heard the explosion; no one came to the door. After a while she started to shake, feeling a chill as if the fridge had let the cold air out into the room. Should she go find Stuart over at the Murray place where he was shingling the roof? Should she call Del? The person in the city who – Mom had explained on that awful, horrible day when the kids at school had blabbed – was another mother of Amber's. The kind of mother who didn't live with her. Who hardly ever showed up in Ripley, not even now, when Amber knew, and Del knew that she knew. She wouldn't call Del. She wouldn't call Tamara's mom either, or Old Glad. She would just wait here for Mom and Dad to come home. She would be fine.

They were gone only an hour, Dad told her later, and when they got home – Mom with a row of stitches, and a swollen face – there was his little girl sitting with a dish towel in her hands and staring at the open kitchen door, faintly blue at the lips and fingers. Amber remembered not wanting to look at her mother because her face was wrong; she remembered Dad's cable-knit sweater being wrapped around her shoulders; remembered being carried upstairs and, later, Stuart peeking in to say, "'Night, Little One. I missed all the fun, huh?"

Mom hadn't even been in the same room as the fridge when it exploded – she'd been in the living room, but the fridge and the china cabinet backed onto opposite sides of the same wall. The blast sent slivers of wedding china and fragments from the glass cabinet door flying. Amber helped her father clean up the mess. When he saw that she'd fished one of the bits of broken china out of the dustpan and was studying it, he said, "That goes in the garbage."

"Can I keep it?"

"What for?"

"Just to have."

"Sure," he said. "You and your stuff."

She'd slid the broken cup handle into her pocket. Here it was now with the other things from her box, a reminder of good luck, of the bad thing that didn't happen to her mother. Its colours were violet on cream, with a dark area that might be a residue of bloodstain on the sharp raw edge that hadn't quite managed to take out her mother's eye; it had succeeded only in leaving a long scar, most of which retreated inside the crease of her eyelid as she grew older. Amber rubbed the china fragment's two facets with her thumb, its smooth surface and its raw edge. Her mother lived in the smoothness.

The rain came heavily now, sluicing through the eavestrough above Amber's kitchen window. The air was muggy; her curly hair had swelled with the damp, and thin twists of it were pasted to her forehead. She got to her feet and took a coil of white string from the drawer by the stove. Cut a length from it and suspended the teacup handle at one end of the hanger. Hung her father's hat badge at the other end. It was heavier than the bit of china and it weighed down one end of the arrangement.

The badge was all that her father had saved from his uniform. He'd tossed it into the thing drawer in the kitchen just before Old Glad came by to collect the uniform, which she took to the Legion Hall and laid out in the display case the Legion inherited when the school was renovated.

Dad hardly talked about the war, but then he wasn't one for conversation. (Although – Mom used to say – in the old days his voice was like a tap you couldn't shut off, his mouth open more than it was closed, either talking or shouting.) Sobriety had turned him into a man who, when he wasn't at work (his roofing business had grown to a three-employee concern), spent most of his time sitting in the easy chair reading, a cigarette between his fingers and a streetscape of empty coffee cups on the table beside him. He browsed the weeklies – *The Western Producer* and *The Ripley Advance* – and stacked them for recycling in a box by the chair. When he'd finished with the weeklies, he'd pick up the Bible or one of the other books he read over and over, books about his Lord Jesus. He'd memorized the Epistle of James. If any of you lack wisdom, let him ask it of God. He bought the current issue of *Awake* when the Jehovah's Witnesses came calling. Mom didn't like to answer the door to them, but Dad gave them a loonie and took their colourful booklets and, though their mission was to speak, they smiled and went away, as if they knew the deal would fall apart otherwise. It was as if, her mother once said when he wasn't in the room, he spent the first half of his adult life spilling words out and the second half reading them back in. He had to fill himself up one way or another, she said, and taking in a stream of words was less toxic than taking in booze.

The day of Dad's funeral two years ago, so soon after Mom's, Stuart had told Del and Amber what he could remember hearing about their father's war – though he had to admit it wasn't much – from the days before Dad went quiet. The three of them sat in a line on the couch, Stuart in the middle. "Come on," he said to Del, "you remember. The way he'd sit at the kitchen table and ramble. Remember? Usually it was about the goddamn politicians." Stuart smiled as if he were talking about a colourful, long-dead uncle who had no direct effect on his life. "Yeah, the politicians, or sometimes it was about who was out to get him for no good reason. Once in a while it was the war."

Del said no, she didn't remember, she'd mostly found ways not to listen those nights.

Amber tried to imagine that same quiet man with the pale, vein-laced skin talking non-stop, but she couldn't. The man who spoke so little, but who knew how to tell her something of love by shyly patting her arm at the right moment.

Stuart recalled bare themes from their father's ramblings, few specifics: that he was stationed in the tropics, took quinine every day, but ended up with malaria anyway. That they worked even when they were sick with fever. That all through the war his two great fears were that he would kill or be killed. The men didn't talk about those two great fears, but they must have felt them just the same, he couldn't be the only one. So young. They weren't engaged in battle, the Corps, but they were at war. They were the ones who moved food and people and munitions; they were targets for snipers. He shouldn't even be alive, he'd said, but according to Stuart he'd followed this claim with no details.

Even when it was over it wasn't over. It was supposed to be done with, but no one told that to the Japanese in Burma. They just kept on fighting, and Dad and his squadron stayed on for months. "He used to say, everyone but the enemy forgot about them."

This was all Stuart could say. He'd read about it, there was information to be had, but nothing that could tell you what Dad was referring to when he shook his head and said, "I've seen some things."

Such mystery compressed into a hat badge, less than two inches either dimension, a circle within a star, and a crown at the top. "He talked and talked," Stuart said, "but he said the same things over and over."

The day after Dad's funeral, Aunt Lenore drove Del and Amber back to Saskatoon in her nearly new Accord. Del sat in the back, pressed into the upholstery as if she'd surrendered to the seat belts, shoulder and lap, eyes closed for most of the trip, red rimmed. Amber realized, turning her head to look at Del, that even angry people mourn. Though what they mourn must have its own set of properties.

The road from Ripley to Saskatoon was long and level and the smooth-riding car carried silence like ballast. Finally, Aunt Lenore spoke. "Your mother told me once that she never knew life could be so good as it was with your father after he," she paused, "climbed on the wagon." Clumsily put, as though she'd mentally sorted through a set of expressions (sobered up? quit drinking? renounced the bottle?) and still couldn't find one she felt would bear being pronounced out loud, as if to speak of recovery were as embarrassing as to speak of what came before. She's ashamed for him, thought Amber. For a version of him Amber had never even known.

Aunt Lenore had turned her head to the side as she spoke, so it was clear her words were directed toward both Del and Amber. Amber waited to see what Del would say in response. Nothing. Did she at least wish she'd tried to know their father when he was sober? Did she at least wish she'd given him a chance? At the graveside Del had said to Amber, "We had two different fathers, you and I." She wasn't referring to the biological facts – they'd had that conversation, and it had been a terse one, on a different occasion – she was referring to Victor Woods the drunk, and Victor Woods, sober.

The downpour outside was too much for the eavestrough now, and water cascaded past Amber's kitchen window, carrying with it bits of twig and last fall's uncleared leaves. Gusts of wind brought drops of water in through the narrow band of open window on either side of the broomstick, and Amber welcomed the wet. She touched her hands to her hair and felt the extra spring the humidity gave it. At the end of its white string, suspended from the hanger, the badge rotated slowly, showing by turns the back with its narrow brass clip and the front with its crest and motto *Honi soit qui mal y pense*. One side, then the other. One side, then the other.

When they'd arrived back in Saskatoon after the funeral that day, Aunt Lenore had dropped Amber off first; Del had waved from the back and hadn't bothered to move up front for the drive across town. Hadn't called Amber in the weeks immediately following. Two separate griefs for their two different fathers.

Amber moved the badge along the hanger wire toward the centre, to compensate for its weight. She stood and saw water running in the street below, rushing toward the low ground, toward the river. She wanted to feel the force of the rain on her head, wanted to soak her hair so its spirals would be, for the moment, tamed. So as not to disturb the broomstick and the hanger jutting in from the kitchen window, she went to the living room and lifted open the window that served as her door to the gently sloping roof where balloon man sat, his round yellow helium head with its Magic Marker smile and Elmer Fudd eyes pummeled by raindrops. This was the gable end of the house and there were no gutters, no leaves and twigs washing out, just clear rain falling past the short eaves. Amber braced herself against the windowsill, hung on and stuck her head out far enough that she cleared the angle of the eave and felt the rain on her scalp. She looked at the dummy, his face wet and ridiculous. Like my own, she thought.

She returned to the kitchen and placed her palms on either side of the hat badge and pressed them together until her arm muscles ached. Then she did the same with the jagged cup handle. The sharp and smooth and rough of first the one and then the other. She opened her hands, then, and looked at the traces of their imprints overlapping on her palms. She pushed the strings together so she could take both objects between her hands at the same time. *Squeeze.* These two the only parents that matter. Wet hair dripping down her shirt.

ANOTHER STUDENT PRINCE

The man with the charmingly crooked jaw smiled and made indecisive clicking noises inside his mouth, drummed his fingers on Poor Man's counter as if there were not four people behind him waiting to pick up coffees-to-go. Forgive him, Amber thought, he has no flippin' idea.

They'd multiplied with the coming of spring – the people who left the store or the office or the copy centre for their breaks now that the weather had improved, the browsers and grazers who were fond of the perfumed concoctions listed on the blackboard. Amber stood behind the counter next to Shari, who handed a customer his Saskatoon-berry 'cino, looking judgmental as she did so. Shari had little respect for people who, because they didn't like the real bean, ordered it disguised, combined with berry syrup or chocolate whip. When people ordered these brews she responded with spare service; she herself was a double espresso girl. Coffee inside, coffee outside, she liked to say. She had dark skin and blunt-cut black hair with a shining streak of purple, which became her, beginning at the part and running across her forehead and down to where she tucked it behind her ear.

Amber had no use, either, for the adulterations listed on the blackboard, but she filled the orders happily enough. Finally the man with the clicking tongue asked for a mocha latte and Amber told him, Good choice. Achieving a decision had been such a challenge for him that a reward seemed appropriate. When Amber wanted coffee, she poured herself a cup of Just Old Joe. Which she did as soon as she'd sent the man away with his latte. She allowed herself a sip after each customer. Don't tell Donna-the-boss. Donna's rule was, Coffee only when things are slow.

She had her worries, Donna. Yesterday as she'd loaded the dishwasher Amber had listened in on a tense conversation between Macy and Donna. Macy had done prep in four different restaurants over six years; based on her experience, she'd come up with the law of the third owner. She set out her theory for Donna. Macy, all in black with her hard-edged haircut and dramatic eyeliner. "The first owner," she said, "spends more on leasehold improvements than they can ever earn back – the kitchen installation, everything to meet code. Like you did. The second owner spends more than they should to buy the place because the stubborn first owner has to get something for all the money they spent. The third owner scoops the place up for cheap, after the second owner gives up. The third owner's the one who's going to make a profit."

Donna looked at her steadily, not smiling, not quite frowning.

"Just an observation," Macy finished.

"What are you saying? That I'll go belly up?" Donna, who had proudly created Poor Man's from scratch.

"Not *necessarily*."

Amber watched for Donna's reaction. Poor Man's was fine, wasn't it? No reason to think otherwise.

"I refuse to be classified as endangered," Donna said.

Macy fiddled with a stalk of lemongrass. "I'm just saying, because I thought you should know."

"So your point," Donna had said, "is that I might as well give up. Which, as a general approach, pardon me, sucks." She'd smiled her don't-take-it-personally smile.

"I'm just saying what I've seen."

But today they were slammed at lunch, all thirteen tables plus the counter – a rare enough occurrence – and Donna was smiling. Knots of people waited near the door, beside the twenty-five-years-ago clipping – an obscenity hearing in Edmonton to do with *The Joy of Sex*. Two hundred copies seized from Coles bookstores. A psychologist claimed the book promoted defiance of established leaders in society. "Not only that," Shari had read aloud to the rest of them this morning as she taped it up, "the book has no bibliography and shows ambivalence in the use of the semicolon."

Steve from Mock Turtle Books, who probably had a copy or two of the original edition on his shelves and who could have made good use of a clipping like that, walked right in past the people waiting at the entrance and started busing a table for himself. Donna, who seemed to have a feedback system that alerted her when Steve came through the door, appeared from the kitchen and told him, Back of the line.

"Amber-Amber," Shari said, "trade you my table three for your table five. One of the suits thinks I'm his very own Indian princess."

"You don't want to be a princess?" Amber said. Shari rolled her eyes.

Amber had two specials on her arm, plates overlapping, soup threatening to slop onto the miniloaves. Slow down. Enjoy the scent of garlic wafting from the soup. Chelsea scooted past. Chelsea was perpetual motion, delivering plates one at a time, multiplying the number of steps between the order window and the tables by the number of orders. She said it was one way to stay skinny. Donna said it was one way to drive away customers, and what was so great about skinny?

The buzz of multiple conversations, accelerated, compressed into the noon-hour envelope. What did all these people do when they weren't sitting in Poor Man's, when they disappeared back through the looking-glass doorways of their office buildings and storefronts? Amber imagined them busy with a multitude of tasks: faxing pages of pie charts and bar graphs; developing film in rooms that smelled sharply of chemicals; unscrewing the backs of computers to perform electronic surgery. She felt slightly panicked, as if she were responsible to see that each of those activities continued.

By quarter past one, to Amber's relief, only two customers remained, Terry at the front with his bowl of chowder cooling on the counter and his laptop open, and, in her regular spot, Dorothy from The Rolling Pin, who worked through noon hour and came in for salad after help arrived.

Amber ferried empty plates and cups back to the kitchen. Clatter of dishes, clang of a knife as it hit the blue and yellow tiles. Chelsea moved right and left, north and south, straightening tablecloths, eyeing the distance between two tables, correcting it. Muttering asides about the lunch ladies who'd stiffed her on the tip. Amber wished Chelsea would, Christ's sake, stop moving for one second. She turned her back on her and felt immediately more relaxed. A hand at her waist startled her. Shari's cool fingers slipping coins into Amber's pocket.

"Jumpy or what? Your tip from table three."

A cup of Just Joe to smooth out the bumps. Amber chose a clear glass mug because she liked to watch the yin and yang as the milk swirled in and made its way through the coffee. She turned and leaned against the counter beside the Pavoni, looking away from a cluster of dirty cups and toward the sidewalk traffic on Second Avenue. As she stood there, leaning and looking, the glass front door swung open, and in walked a wrong number. Amber liked to watch the wrong numbers who ended up in Poor Man's. This one removed his baseball cap and stood just inside the door, blinking as his eyes accustomed themselves to the change in light. It made her think of her own first impression of Poor Man's, the day she came in on spec to fill out an application. Tablecloths stylishly knotted at the corners; yellow and blue ceramics. The place looked more formal when you first entered than it really was. By now it felt like home, but Amber had almost walked out that first day, thinking she'd have a better chance at one of the doughnut shops.

He was forty or more. Wore jeans of no brand that mattered, a green plaid shirt, running shoes that had lost their form. His hair looked as if a relative cut it at three-month intervals and he was due to go under the scissors again. He seemed the type who would prefer a pancake house but wouldn't admit his mistake. He took a seat by the window, where the sunlight reached inside and where the view was of the street rather than the walls with their glazed finish and their eye-level art. The window where he sat was the one staff had dubbed the display window: anyone who sat there was visible from the street. The early afternoon sun had come around so it caught his hair and drew out a glint of red amid the dark, irregular layers. Amber took note of the red. Maybe him, she thought. Out of all the thousands of possibilities, maybe him.

"I'll get this one."

"Um, coffee," he said, tapping the table, and – maybe because he'd noticed that across the room Dorothy was lifting a parisienne bowl to her mouth with two hands – he added, "in a cup."

He wouldn't likely take too well to the dark roast of Old Joe. She brought him a mug of Columbian and retreated behind the counter. For now she left the loading of the dishes to the others. She knew he wouldn't stay long, the ones who wandered in by accident never did, and if she wanted to look she should look now. She bent to take the rag from underneath the counter and began to polish the steel casing of the Pavoni, all the time aware of him in the way she'd be aware of a sock-wrinkle inside a too-snug shoe. The ghost of a red gleam in his hair. She played with the question she asked herself from time to time when she saw certain men roughly his age: Could he be her natural father?

She stole glances. Looked from his profile to her own distorted face in the shiny steel strip that ran along the side of the espresso machine. Nobody's child. This was her fourth possible father in as many months. (Since Dad died, she'd been seeing them more and more often.) One of them she'd spotted eating a plate of fries at the Midtown Plaza, another walking along Broadway, a third at the library, paging his way through *Building Your Deck* while she sat at the Internet terminal. It wasn't always red hair that drew her attention; sometimes it was the line of the jaw or a way of moving the arms that echoed her own. Grasping for straws.

The official story ruled out this kind of speculation. Her natural father, of course, had died years ago. Mom had shown her his name on her original birth certificate, the birth certificate that didn't count because of the adoption: Philip Turner. Where's the grave? she'd asked Del, after she'd turned eighteen and decided she had the right to any and all information about her father. (That timid assertion of her rights had been limited to one brief visit to Del's house the year Amber moved to the city.)

The grave? It would probably be, Del told her, in a country cemetery somewhere in the southwest near his parents' farm. No, she hadn't gone to the funeral, she'd told a shocked Amber, it was out of town. Hundreds of miles away. The relationship was over by then, and Del had other things to see to. Ah, yes, Amber thought. The baby. Herself. She was what Del had had to see to. She tried to imagine Del's small frame resculpted by pregnancy, Del's quick stride altered by the roundness, the awkwardness, the weight. To imagine her small breasts engorged to the proportions of motherhood; to picture her scanty arm muscles lifting a bundle in a blanket. She could conjure up portions of these images, but inserting Del's face into the picture, the hard blue eyes, the delicate nose – that exercise was like writing a fairy tale, something made more for amusement, possibly for comfort, than to be believed. She, Amber, had been something to be seen to. That's what she still was, sitting there that afternoon almost seven years ago in Del's cottagelike house in Caswell Hill asking questions about Philip Turner.

Amber was of two minds when it came to what Del said about her biological father. She hadn't looked for evidence to disprove the official story. She'd made no effort to complicate her life by tracing grandparents who would no doubt be shocked to learn she existed. In any case, a name to put on a birth certificate, a story about an accident – these were things that could be fabricated. The kind of things a girl *would* make up if some guy knocked her up and wanted nothing to do with the consequences. Amber knew her Mom and Dad wouldn't have lied to her, but Del might have lied to all of them. A pregnant girl in 1974 looking to simplify things. So even though Amber didn't outright dismiss the official story, she kept the door open to the possibility that it was false.

It wasn't that she wanted a father she could get to *know* – she'd had one of those and one was all she needed. Having two mothers had been confusion enough. Still, she wanted him to be out there, wanted someone to point him out from a distance, then show her to a pillar she could hide behind and watch as he walked and talked. Did they have the same pattern of smile or scowl? Was he tall, the way she was, strong in the legs? That day seven years ago when she'd sat in the saggy velour chair in Del's living room and dared to ask, Del had said no, she didn't have a picture of him. It wasn't that kind of relationship.

Del had told her she met the man who fathered her when both of them worked at the Student Prince. (That was how she put it: the man who fathered you.) On the free Internet terminal at the library, Amber had tracked down a plot summary for the light opera that gave the bar its name. She'd spun a rag of plot into a family history. When you need a story for someone, and the ones that are offered don't satisfy, you're left to fabricate your own. In the play, the prince said goodbye to his true sweetheart and went home to marry the princess next door.

Maybe her natural father long ago moved back to whatever rural route he came from and, without even knowing he had a kid, took over the family farm. She wondered about her half-brothers and half-sisters on the farm: what did they do for fun and did their features mimic hers?

Delusions, sure, but delusions were so seductive – the idea that he was out there to be discovered, the way, when you take last winter's jacket out of the closet you might find a twenty in the pocket. Unexpected wealth. Straw into gold.

The man with the red glint in his hair gestured for a refill. When Amber brought it he pointed out the window toward the wooden sign hanging over the sidewalk on its wrought iron arm. The lettering was ornate, hard to read. "What does that say?"

"Poor Man's Treacle."

"Say again?"

"Poor Man's Treacle." Amber smiled.

"Treekle?"

"Treekle."

"What's that thing beside the words?"

"Garlic."

"Looks like a pumpkin."

"Well, it's garlic."

"Whatever you say." He smiled and looked at his coffee in a way that ended the conversation.

She stood by the table and waited for the next question, coffee thermos still raised and gaining weight the longer she held it. He plunked a sugar cube into his cup and stirred. Took a drink and looked out the window.

"Thanks," he said, still not looking at her. She walked away. She would've liked to talk to him about the uses of garlic. She would've liked to talk to him about whatever. He finished his coffee, dropped a toonie beside his cup and left. Amber watched as he walked away, the display window a frame and the man disappearing from it. She hurried out to the sidewalk and watched as the plaid shirt and the hair that was red in the sun moved away down the street. The short, fidgety, mumbling man who roams the sidewalks of Second Avenue bumped her shoulder, and then she was jostled by a skater who was dogging the fidgety man, making fun because he wasn't all there, or because he was too much there.

"Stop that," Amber said to the skater, as if it would make a difference. She looked ahead along the street but the green plaid shirt had disappeared. Probably Phil *was* dead, just as they'd told her. Anything was possible. In Amber's kitchen, held to the refrigerator with a magnet, was a clipping she'd brought home from Poor Man's.

TWENTY-FIVE YEARS AGO THIS WEEK

This morning Saskatoon bid farewell to John Doe in a memorial service attended by a small group of mourners.

"The death of this stranger has somehow moved people," said Reverend Tim Bennett. "He's touched a part of us that says human beings must care for each other, in death as well as in life."

Staff from the Student Prince, a popular downtown beverage room, helped organize the service. A waitress from the establishment said, "We did this because he died alone and no one knows who he was. People feel it isn't right for someone to pass from the world without their life – or at least their death – being marked."

John Doe's body was discovered four months ago in a downtown alley. No identification was found. The coroner's office accounted for the delay before the burial by saying they were waiting in hope that a relative or friend would come forward. Police Staff Sgt. Bill Warner said there are no new developments in the case, though they believe the man was travelling through Saskatoon on his way from the West Coast, and was possibly bound for Ontario. Sandler Memorials has worked with a local group of citizens to provide a headstone engraved with the name John Doe.

John Doe had become a presence for Amber, and she reread the clipping from time to time. He was lying somewhere among the thousands of graves in a city cemetery, his history surviving only in his bones. That reference to the Student Prince. She didn't believe John Doe was her father, not really, no more than she believed Del was the waitress who talked about the importance of a life as it passes, but she couldn't let go of the way he was linked to that time, and to the place that Del had so grudgingly mentioned. She couldn't let go of delusions, no matter how unlikely.

So Amber ran parallel ideas along three father tracks in her mind: he was a man found frozen, curled in an alley twenty-five years ago; he was a man dead in an accident, the details of which she didn't dare imagine; he was a former student prince – a farmer who visited the city from time to time, with or without his wife and his other children.

GODMOTHER

Amber would rather be alone right now, listening to Ani Defranco's funny little number about the fish and the plastic castle instead of minding her posture and trying to guess at the reasons for Vivien's visit. Loved that plastic castle song. Loved sitting on the living room floor and looking out the window at the smiling dummy and listening to it. Amber hadn't recaptured the bright-white-room feeling she'd had just before the Burton house came down, but she'd had a string of three good days in a row. There were things to laugh about. There was Chelsea, today at work as they cleared after lunch, appropriating old jokes and customizing them to the trade:

Q: Why did the waitress cross the road?

A: Donna sent her over there to get the goddamn chicken.

"You're not waitresses, Chelsea," Donna said, "you're servers."

"Right," said Chelsea. "Of course." Followed by:

Q: How many lunch ladies does it take to calculate fifteen percent?

A: Lunch ladies don't know it's supposed to be fifteen percent.

Donna frowned.

"Right, okay," said Chelsea. Followed by:

Q: What do you call a hundred lunch ladies at the bottom of a lake?

"This one I know," said Shari. "A hundred lunch ladies at the bottom of a lake is a good start."

See, things to laugh about. But now here was Vivien in her kitchen. This was the second time Amber had noticed her looking toward the music coming from the living room as if it were a child that should be shushed. As if she had something important to say and required all other sound out of the way before she began. Amber went in and pushed the stop button. Better to listen to Ani when she was alone anyway, when she could read along with the words, pay attention, the way Dad used to concentrate on the hymns in church.

Amber's watch timer beeped. Three minutes, the optimal steeping interval for this particular tea. She pushed her chair back, careful not to bump the horizontal broomstick still clamped in the window frame, and went to the counter where she lifted out the tea ball and set it in the sink. She swished hot water through two cups and glanced at Vivien, who still looked purposeful, both hands palm-down on the table, though a little less urgent about whatever she'd come to say.

The house call was unexpected. Vivien would drop in at Poor Man's at rare intervals and say hello, but she'd only sat at Amber's kitchen table twice before today, and those two visits had happened when Amber lived at the Burton, shortly before Cal moved in. The first had been a few days after Mom's funeral and the second only a couple of months later, after Del and Amber had been out to Ripley to help Stuart bury Dad. That day, Vivien had come with flowers. A courtesy call from an unofficial godmother. How was she doing, Vivien had wanted to know on that visit after Dad's funeral. How was she doing and could Vivien help?

"Thank you but I'm all right," Amber had said. Loss, she reflected, being not subject to patching over from the outside, the emotional ambushes catching her at any time of the day or night, so she couldn't just call someone up and say, Now; come hold me while I cry. In the end, though, Vivien had coaxed her into conversation and then tears. She'd stayed through two pots of tea that time, stayed and heard not only about Amber's father, but also about her mother, the two griefs knotted together.

Today Amber was on guard. Vivien had the ability to disarm; words would spill from Amber in her presence, and afterward she'd ask herself why she'd said so much to someone she hardly knew. Vivien had a trick of arranging herself in her chair so it seemed as if the act of listening involved the whole of her body. She sat that way now, palms no longer flat on the table but resting open in her lap. Amber's table was small and its angle of placement in a corner nook meant that when Amber poured the tea and sat down again they were at right angles rather than across from each other.

"Good tea," Vivien said.

"Kenyan." Amber lifted a lemon wedge above her own cup and squeezed out a few drops, for the scent as much as the taste.

Vivien sipped again, offered no clues to why she was here. The woman who comes to visit me when a parent dies. But none of my several parents have recently died. Just be polite, Amber decided. Status of an aunt, and let's keep it at that. Resist tumbling into discussions of the feelings ignited at the Burton house. The thought that Del, stickwoman, had lived on the top floor; that Phil, the live dead man, had walked up and down the stairs. No need to study the physics of emotion with a near stranger.

A source of confusion, Vivien, her cotton skirt, white flowers on navy, her husband Duncan the milkman, their several teenagers in the three-storey fixer-upper over on Tenth Street that looked from the outside like it was never quite fixed up. Teenagers Amber didn't even know but that she imagined to be barefoot throwbacks who patted bongo drums and used expressions like "far out." Vivien either refused to have a haircut or didn't think of it. She parted it in the middle, two braids. Amber amused herself with a fantasy of taking Vivien to Et Cetera, of buying her a butterfly clip, demonstrating how to twist her hair, gather it high and let it fan out from the top of the clip. What I couldn't do with those silky locks. I could remake you, the hair, the skirt, the sandals with no heel to speak of.

The toe of one of those sandals pointed now past Amber's chair toward the messy arrangement of hanger and broomstick and memorabilia cantilevered from the window.

"What have you here?" Vivien looked at Amber over the rim of her cup, smiling.

"Just stuff. Mementos," she said, in a voice that almost made fun of the word, though she didn't feel it should be made fun of. "Mementos," she repeated in a voice she liked better.

"Of?" Vivien tucked one foot underneath herself, and the folds of her skirt hung loosely from her knee. Nothing stylish about that skirt, but it was pretty to look at.

"Things and people. My Mom and Dad, so far." And, oh, she wanted Vivien's approval – she saw that now – was pleased to be showing her this commendable evidence of the good daughter honouring her parents.

"Will your brother be part of your creation?" Vivien was stocked, as usual, not with commendations but with questions.

"I don't know. I just started."

"Will Delorie be part of it?"

Amber had rarely heard Vivien slip back into using the old version of Del's name. "Like I said, I just started. It's just a thing." Vivien's question had brought Del, the idea of Del, into the room with them, to be addressed before she would go away. Let Vivien do it, since she was the one who summoned her. Amber waited.

"I saw her a couple of days ago," Vivien said. "Del."

"Yeah? Where?"

"Bought her coffee at the Grille."

"That's nice." Ask how she's doing, Amber coached herself. "How's she doing?"

"I'm not sure."

Welcome to my world. "How do you mean?"

"When was the last time you talked to her?"

Amber wasn't about to go into last week's encounter at the Burton. "Not long ago. She came by Poor Man's on a Saturday."

"When exactly?"

"I don't know, couple weeks maybe."

"Weeks."

"Maybe. Maybe not that long." Can't see how it matters.

"What did you talk about?"

"Del and I don't talk *about* much of anything, Vivien. We make parallel statements about the weather and the construction on Twenty-first and the pros and cons of cream versus two percent milk in coffee."

A series of sputtering efforts by Amber, answered minimally by Del. Finally, that most recent Saturday at Poor Man's, before the encounter at the Burton, Amber had said to Del, "Want a muffin? It's on me." Making an offering.

"No. Thanks."

Like throwing a penny down a well, Amber thought. Like leaning in and listening for a splash, waiting long moments but hearing no evidence the coin found water. "I'll get back to work then."

When Amber was a girl, Del was hardly a presence. She would come for Christmas, or not, staying only for the few busy hours that were focused on helping Mom cook, then clean up after the meal. A meal that disappeared speedily from the table, impeded by a minimum of conversation. Dad saying his stubborn grace, naming first his wife and then each of his three children as blessings for which he thanked the Lord, long and patient spaces between the names:

Delores

Stuart

Amber.

Those Christmases when she did appear, Del would choose her seat at the dinner table so her line of sight included her father only obliquely. Once, in the kitchen as they cleaned up after the meal, Amber had seen Del sniff the dregs in Dad's water glass and coffee cup before she emptied them down the sink. A few minutes later she'd seen her do the same with the cup she'd taken from beside his chair in the living room.

Del would bring along or send in the mail for Amber a Christmas sweater or a shirt or a book. All five volumes of the Hitch Hiker series for the Christmases from ages fourteen to eighteen. Instructions for living embedded within the stories, older sister to younger. Clearly the role Del had chosen: distant older sister. They were great reads, laugh-out-loud funny, but even at fourteen Amber couldn't help wondering – was *The Hitch Hiker's Guide to the Galaxy* supposed to substitute for conversation? This cast of characters who made astute observations: things may not be what they seem; you should always carry a towel, for you don't know when it might save your life; embrace boredom, for in the event of an airplane crash only those who were bored enough to peruse the safety card will have a hope of saving themselves. In grade eleven she'd studied *Hamlet*, and the teacher declaimed for the class Polonius's speech to Laertes: neither a borrower nor a lender be; reserve thy judgement; to thine own self... It was as if Del had chosen Douglas Adams to deliver her own version of that speech. Standing in the margin, inside parentheses (*This message sponsored by Del*).

Amber loosened the dishtowel she used as a tea cozy and touched her palm to the side of the teapot. She topped up Vivien's cup. A pleasure to make a good cup of tea; lessons from Old Glad back home. Amber hadn't even tried to convince Donna to reform the way Poor Man's handled tea: gauze bags in tin pots that cooled too quickly and dribbled from the spout. Jasmine, Earl Grey, Rose Hip Sunrise, and a type of green tea called Envy. Amber liked to hear a customer say, I'll have a cup of Envy.

Vivien sipped her freshened tea, and with her shoulders she made a slight, expectant motion. As if the silence in the kitchen had an appetite she was bound to feed, Amber spoke.

"Del is not, I don't think, especially interested in talking to me."

"Don't give up."

"Why not? She did." Amber cringed at her own satisfaction in saying this.

Vivien took a moment to respond. "She named you. She gave birth to you. Those aren't things a person does if she's giving up."

Right. The name. Amber recalled Stuart sitting at the table in Ripley with his rye and ice. His rye nice, as he called it. Mom trying not to be obvious about checking the level in the bottle. What we inherit. Stuart looking at his drink and saying, "The colour of Amber," and winking at her. Amber feeling her pale cheeks warm to crimson, thinking, I suppose that's where Del got the idea. Saying so out loud and ending with, "I wouldn't put it past her." Stuart, surprise on his face, saying, "But it's a beautiful colour. Look." The glass, the light through the liquid, the condensation trickling onto his rough, roofer's hand. Amber realizing he was right about the beauty, not knowing how to feel about that.

"I was an accident."

"Amber," Vivien said, moving her hands impatiently, "*lots* of people are accidents."

Silence.

"What do you want her to do, Amber? Maybe you just have to ask."

What did she want? Sloppy and extravagant use of the word "daughter"? Would that make her feel more like she ought to exist?

Del didn't deny the facts. They'd been pulsing in the background since Amber was eight, there, but hardly spoken of after that first day of revelation. When she was in grade two, Amber heard the other kids saying the kinds of things kids say on the playground, things they hear from older brothers and sisters or from parents who talk while kids play quietly behind the couch. It seemed everyone knew but herself. And after foot-stamping, screaming denials, after being led home by an unusually quiet Tamara, after hearing from her distraught mother-grandmother that what the others said was true, she had refused to eat supper. She wondered what it was she was supposed to have done wrong to bring on such mockery. She didn't even know what it meant, to be her sister's daughter, but she knew it wasn't nice; she'd seen the look on Sue Mitchell's face, the meanie eyes that didn't normally belong in that face, as she swung the double-dutch skipping rope:

Sugar, butter, salt and pepper,
Amber's sister is her mother,
Who's your daddy, who?
A, B, C, D....

That evening Mom searched through Del's old things in the basement and found a booklet filled with black and white drawings in the style of cartoons, but without the funny punchlines. There were the labelled parts of a woman's insides, and a girl's smiling face with the caption, You're a young lady now. Mom turned the pages and pointed and explained. This was how she responded to the crying and screaming – by walking Amber through a pamphlet about menstruation, egg and sperm. But be fair: she also said, again and again, during the following days, "We love you so much. You are our real daughter." And Dad would touch her arm or her head as he walked past the table where she sat with her homework. Amber had agreed that evening, finally, to be cuddled and to eat homemade soup with garden peas. Her throat was sore for days, first from her screams and denials and later from shouting Stop! in the schoolyard. And they did stop, after a week or so.

Her parentage was not spoken of, then, until the time when Amber, fourteen years old and angry at anything within range, had demanded that Mom and Dad tell her about her biological father. They had repeated what Del had told them: he died before you were born. Then the story, solemnly delivered, of the bicycle and the bus and the rainstorm. A likely story. Except for the single brief interview when she was eighteen, Amber hadn't asked Del about Phil; nobody said it in so many words, but she could tell from the silence – Del's, Stuart's, Mom and Dad's – that she wasn't supposed to bring it up. How could she talk about something so intimate as family with someone so distant as Del?

What *did* she want from Del, supposing she had permission just to walk up and ask her? I want her to be alive to me. No, that's what she would have said as recently as a week ago. Now she just wanted a rest. She remembered sitting on the bathroom floor at Poor Man's the other day and thinking there should be a way to mark the ending.

"I used to want to know what was inside," she said to Vivien now. Yes: shake her small frame until something fell out – until any old damn whatever fell out. Maybe because Vivien was sitting so close like that with no table between the two of them, and maybe because the flowered skirt draped so softly from her tucked-up knee, Amber said more: "I used to want her just to put her arms around me."

"That doesn't happen?"

"Of course not."

"Maybe she's waiting for you to ask." Vivien sounded hopeful.

"I doubt it."

Vivien half rose from her chair and for a moment Amber thought she was getting up to give her a hug, but she was only shifting so she no longer sat on her foot. "That's what you used to want, you said. And now?"

Amber shrugged. "It isn't so important anymore."

"What makes it less important?"

"Um. Fatigue?" She straightened in her chair and pulled both cups toward her to signal the end of the conversation. "It's time I stop thinking so much about her, time I move ahead. A quarter century, a symbolic milestone. I should spend the *next* twenty-five years on something else. Get unstuck." The Rumpelstiltskin voice that lived inside her head asked, Who are you trying to convince, Vivien or yourself? Amber told the voice, Just following through on what I promised myself. If I can't split it open I have to make it not matter. She thought of the tense discussion between Macy and Donna the other day about the natural laws of business. A discussion that if you boiled it down was about not throwing good money after bad, about when to cut your losses.

Amber still had the sense Vivien was here as godmother, but godmother in relation to Del, not Amber. She was ready for this visit to be over, for this long-skirted woman to let those flat sandals of hers walk her out the door and down the stairs. Vivien had adopted a variation of the purposeful posture she'd had when she first sat down, as if her business on this visit was to say something in particular, both feet flat on the floor, both hands on her knees. Amber picked up the cups and walked toward the sink.

Vivien stood. Maybe she'd been about to stand up anyway and her shift in posture had only been preparation for that; maybe she couldn't ignore the obvious dismissal communicated by the removal of her cup. She was biting her lower lip at one side as if to stop a sentence that wanted out. Her movements were hesitant, and she paused beside the refrigerator, one hand on her hip, one at the side of her neck. Amber took a step forward from the counter – a goodbye step. Vivien leaned in to read the curled newspaper clipping that was held to the fridge with a magnet.

"Will you look at that." She smoothed an edge against the fridge. "This is about our stranger."

"You knew that guy?" Amber said.

"God, no. But I remember. See where it says about the waitress. Guess who?"

"It was Del, wasn't it? I knew it. I knew it as soon as I saw that." Not true. She'd known as soon as she'd seen it that it wasn't Del.

"Not quite right," Vivien said. "That was me. I was the one who organized the service."

Amber felt as if Vivien had snatched away a piece of private property. John Doe belonged to her – to her and Del and the space between the two of them. "*You* organized it?" she said.

"It seemed the thing to do. Put him to rest, finally. The two terrible...events that year within months of each other. John Doe. Then Phil's...his accident. It was an awful, terrible time."

Vivien's reference to Phil's accident felt like another snatching away of something that belonged to Amber. Her possible fathers, alive and dead, disappearing. Vivien had no rights to this territory. But if she made reference to an accident, then there really had to have been one. Vivien might be a snoop and a meddler, but she was no liar. Amber blinked and swallowed. She was mad at herself for wanting to cry. She'd never believed, anyway, in her homemade fairy tale that he was alive. Of course there had been an accident.

"Is that your role in life, then?" Amber said. The Rumpelstiltskin voice was talking out loud now. "Are you the designated do-gooder?"

"I don't know." Vivien paused. "There are worse roles. I suppose."

*May*be.

"Amber, I'm worried about Delorie. About Del. I think you should talk to her." Vivien shifted her weight from one sandal to the other, her flowered skirt swaying as she did so. "Do you think you could call her?"

I am not the mother here. And Del doesn't *want* to be looked after.

"You can't fix other people's lives, Vivien."

"I know." Vivien stood looking at the cluster of objects on the kitchen floor: the sock doll, the notebook, the doorbell plate with the hole in it. She leaned toward the broomstick, her hand coming forward as though she was about to touch the hat badge. Amber was about to say, Don't touch, don't you dare, but Vivien's hand stayed a few inches away. "I like this," she said. "Nice." She looked over at Amber. "I'll go now."

As soon as Vivien left, Amber changed her clothes for a run and then stretched and headed out in the direction of the river, toward the Meewasin trail. She was pissed enough right now for a raging long one, and she did run, good and fast for seven or eight blocks, but by the time she reached the stairs at the Broadway Bridge that led down to the trail she was short of breath. She slowed to a walk, descended and looked up at the graffitied underside of the bridge. There were gangs of kids, she'd heard, whose initiation rites involved crossing the river by making their way through the concrete landscape of struts and arches underneath the roadway. They'd have to be resourceful as well as foolhardy. She couldn't see how such a crossing would be physically possible.

She read the graffiti on the concrete footings: gang tags, political declarations, a careless scrawl telling her Stephanie wuz here – a message so carelessly scrawled, in fact, that Amber doubted Stephanie even remembered leaving it. Further along was a featureless stick figure sprayed in thin blue lines of paint. Three short, vertical spikes of hair. Amber bent and picked up a shard of broken glass. Beside the head of the stick figure she scratched a speech bubble and inside the bubble she scratched, after a moment's thought, a blank line. There. Spit to say, just like Del.

If she can't love me, she could at least make the effort to hate me. She dropped the piece of glass and picked up instead a taffy-coloured stone with a smooth hollow for thumb-rubbing. As she straightened, two kids on bikes came around the bend downriver on the asphalt path and raced toward the place where Amber stood under the bridge. Little kids, only eight or nine, a boy and a girl, slithering sideways off the pavement to jump over rocks and skid through the loose stones. They pulled wheelies; they spun out and then righted themselves. Daredevils, risk-takers; they knew who they were. As they whisked past Amber, bits of gravel pelted her bare shin. "Ouch! Watch it!"

"Wussy-pussy!" the girl yelled over her shoulder, and the two of them laughed and pedalled madly.

Amber massaged her smooth stone. Climbed the steps in rhythm: hate me, hate me, hate me, hate me.

EVERYDAY RELICS

She tried again the next day. When she left home she started out walking but soon her legs were impatient and she began to alternate, running for five minutes, walking for two, running five, walking two. The twos made the fives possible. Not the way she'd do it if she were in shape, but still she was impressed with herself. Getting unstuck. Cal might be wrong about other things, but he'd been right about the running. Get off your ass, get on with it, get going while you're feeling good, because you don't know, Amber, when the baffles will go up inside your brain, slow you up as if you're wading through mud.

The day seemed lush, generous, as if it had such a luxury of personality it could lend some to Amber. Push anger and exasperation and yearning away out of her mind and soul. If there were such a thing as God, she thought, I'd offer a prayer of gratitude. She was grateful for the pelicans, the geese, the wind in the grass, for whoever ensured the riverbank and its paths were there for her, wild with bush instead of terraced with apartment buildings. Grateful; maybe even forgiving; just possibly hopeful. Del just another weird person in a world that had to make room for all kinds. One of the risers on the stairway to the bridge was spray-painted with a purple message: "Fuckin-A!" That about summed it up.

Halfway across the railway bridge Amber stopped running and looked down through a space between the heavy wooden planks. Far below, the green water flowed north, but Amber had the sensation she was the one moving, floating southward through the sky while the river stood still. It was exhilarating.

People talk about moderation, the golden mean. Ha. Amber wasn't aligned with any golden mean. She might balance for a while, arms out to her sides, but eventually she'd fall off on one side or the other. She'd heard somewhere that it's important to know what your basic tendency is, whether you're a person who's meant to carry a heavy weight through life or you're one who's meant to keep three golden balls aloft. But suppose you're both. Today the golden balls are in the air and the hands that juggle them are working in rhythm. Who could explain why one day was like this and another day not?

The longest hallway in the city, that's what Cal said once about the railway bridge. It did look like a hallway: the waist-high fences on either side of the walkway that ran alongside the tracks; the five wide wooden planks underfoot, stretching ahead like a lesson in perspective. Cal had walked the length of the bridge once, from the southeast bank to the northwest, without stepping anywhere but the middle row of planks, one foot directly in front of the other. Partway across he'd encountered a warped plank and stooped to print in block letters with his felt marker WATCH YOUR STEP. His balance wavered from time to time and he had to pause to quell the wobble. Cal was working on discipline. For instance, it bothered him that he couldn't look up a word in the dictionary without being waylaid by other words. It was a symptom, he said. He'd been trying to get a start on his thesis, but he kept changing topics or finding something else he had to read before he could write. "But isn't curiosity a *good* thing?" Amber had said. "Isn't it one of the places surprises come from?" He'd answered, "Surprises. Yes. I rest my case."

Amber, this afternoon, stood on the bridge and looked upriver to where the water tumbled noisily over the weir. The famously dangerous weir; the water falls only a short distance, a metre or so, but don't get too close or over you go into the whirl and there'll be no saving you. Amber watched a goose floating so near to the rush of water it looked as if it would be swept into the roil any second. She waited for that to happen, but just as the bird had drifted to the crest, it paddled back upstream, where once again it began drifting toward the edge, then moments later paddled against the current away from the tumbling water. Why didn't it just lift off, fly up and away?

"Dumb-ass bird!" The noise of the weir swallowed Amber's words. What did she know about the habits of geese? Maybe paddling so close to the falls gave the goose an impressive rack of muscles. She left the bridge and headed south again, running, walking, running, energy a gift from out of the blue, surging into and through her, taking her over, propelling her. Running, running. She was the moving northern lights; she was a bouncing ball anointing the words to a song, the singer singing along. She was the top half of topsy-turvy, two heads better than one, a theme and all its unruly variations, extravagant. Inside her head, a circus of possibilities leaping and flashing, and she was the acrobat catching the bar of a swinging trapeze, tracked by a moving spotlight.

At home, still pumped, she stood bathing in a breeze that came in through the living room window. A rivulet of sweat ran freely down her spine. The delicious tickle of it. She braced her hands on the windowsill and stretched her calf muscles. So satisfying, so profound. She opened the window, crawled out onto the roof over the main floor addition and sat down beside the dummy to cool off. If his Elmer Fudd eyes could see, his view would include the huge hand-lettered sign the teenage girl next door had taped in her bedroom window, facing out: HOUSE OF BOREDOM. Amber patted the dummy on the knee. "If she'd just take down that sign," she said to the face on the yellow balloon, "she'd have a pretty good view of you. D'you think that might make her feel better?"

She clambered back inside and flicked on the TV. When he lived with her, Cal had christened the television Ed, because the only channel worth watching, Amber said, was the educational channel that came bundled with the stripped-down cable package. Today though, Ed let her down, offering the opening credits of a documentary on the history of television. TV about TV.

She sat down cross-legged on the kitchen floor beside the condensed milk box and the litter of mementos. The first few things that came into her hand would do. She closed her eyes and reached. A spiral notebook with a shiny holograph cover; a stack of high school track and field ribbons; the silver swan earring of Tamara's that Amber had rescued from the overturned truck the night of the accident.

The notebook contained two point form lists, one in the back that she'd been adding to for months now, and another in the front. For now, she ignored the list at the back – Cures for Melancholia, it was headed – and opened the book to the front. Three pages, begun years ago. Back in grade eleven when she started the list, the first title she'd given it was Reasons to Stay Alive, but that gave the exercise far too serious a tone. What if Mom found it and worried? She'd immediately torn that page out and started over with the title Reasons to Get up in the Morning. Maybe that would worry Mom a little less.

In the seven years since she'd left high school, left Ripley, Amber had made additions to the list. Sometimes on a bad day she'd take out the book just to read through the pages. But today, so far, was a good day, and the list was a bonus not a necessity. She tore a blank sheet from the middle and transcribed her favourites onto a boiled-down list. She made the letters large: Kenyan tea; The river steaming on a cold winter day; Second-hand stores; Wool socks in the wintertime; The train bridge Joni Mitchell sings a song about; The shaggy black dog that lives two houses in from the corner; The Mendel Art Gallery.

Yeah, the Mendel where you can still get in for free and where you can walk through the conservatory and see a banana tree in the middle of the prairies in the middle of January. She folded her best-of list into a paper airplane. Life's redeeming features, so trivial; so much the opposite once you add them together.

She took the bundle of track ribbons from their clip, left the red ones aside and chose the white. She squeezed a second hanger inside the first at right angles, used twist-ties to hold it in place and suspended the paper airplane and the ribbon.

She'd won the first-place red ribbons at interhouse runoffs in high school, but the white was her trophy: the only one she'd ever earned at a unit meet. She'd made it to the unit meet four times, and three of those times she'd placed fourth in her single event, the four hundred. She wasn't quite fast enough to compete in the hundred. The four hundred, that's what she was suited to, not a dash, not a distance run, but a sprint. Those lightning girls who did the one and the two hundred couldn't keep up their speed long enough to win the four.

For the first three years at the unit meet she was a dependable fourth to the same three rivals who traded positions among the top spots. The fourth year that she qualified for the unit meet, the girl from Thompson Creek with the long black braids and bony knees and determined, squinty eyes wasn't there. A place in the top three was up for grabs.

The smell of dirt and grass and sunscreen. Her fingers on the clay. The crack of the gun and immediately the power in her legs, the feeling that her feet were rolling the sphere of the earth like a log on water. She tasted the sweat on her upper lip, felt her stride reach further, knew she was far ahead of whoever was in fourth. After the finish line, after she slowed, giddiness in her limbs. She walked it out, walked it out, breathed deeply, spat. She'd have made it into the ribbons, she told herself, even if the girl from Thompson Creek had been there.

She used to build imaginary trophy rooms, playing in the alley after supper with Tamara, using long sticks to draw houses in the dirt. They drew the walls of each room straight out from the floor so they looked like cardboard boxes that had been slit along the corners and laid out flat. Inside, they drew furniture. Sofas and bookshelves and giant television sets.

Stuart would sit on the back step with his workboots beside him and his beer in his hand, watching. "I'm just drinking in the evening," he'd say, and sometimes he'd say it with the one inflection and sometimes the other. *I'm just drinking in the evening.* Sometimes he'd set his bottle down and strip off his socks, pick up a long stick and draw his own house. A tall thin man with a skinny long stick making pictures in the dust. He had a talent for drawing, and Amber appreciated the perspective, the views he drew out the windows of his house, the disappearing roads and diminishing telephone poles.

Stuart still lived in the house in Ripley. He had by now become a fried-egg bachelor, sleeping between the old green-flowered sheets in what used to be Mom and Dad's bed; sitting on their fortieth anniversary couch to watch TV; keeping up the roofing business. He was thinking, he said last time she spoke to him on the phone, of expanding into soffits and fasciae. She should call more often, she thought after she hung up.

Each house they drew in the alley had a trophy room. Tamara had trophy fish and other creatures of the sea mounted on plaques, and racks of antlers, and guns in a cupboard by the fireplace. *Those're loaded,* she'd say. In Stuart's houses the trophies were for baseball, shelves of them, medals too. Amber's imaginary trophies were for track and field – not just the four hundred, but high jump, long jump and pole vault too. Pole vaulting she hadn't even tried, she was no scream in hell at long jump and she'd never mastered the Fosbury flop.

"The Stanley Cup of high jumping," Stuart said once, looking at the trophy shelf she'd scratched in the dirt. "You're a hero, Amber, a real sports hero, a regular phenom."

Amber jiggled the broomstick and watched as the lengths of white string swayed. Even to think about racing and jumps made her tired. The out-of-the-blue energy that had surged through her earlier had ebbed with as little reason as it had appeared in the first place. Her mind had begun to feel slow and thick. Colour, she said to herself; the arrangement needed colour. Ignoring for the moment the spilled-out contents of her stuff box, she went to her bedroom and surveyed the clutter on the dresser: nail polish; a scatter of makeup; a hairbrush; the half-empty pop bottle still with its earring. Slob; sloth; deadly sinner.

She looked at the brush and the mist of fine russet hair curling from its bristles. Some of her earliest memories were of people remarking on the colour of her hair. People still complimented her on it, as if it were something she'd made with her own hands. She extracted a few strands from the brush, but it wasn't enough and so she reached up under her hair to the nape of her neck and pulled hard. Her fingers came away with only a few wisps. She was aware of an anaesthetic hum inside her head. She found her scissors and cut a four-inch length, thick as her thumb, leaving a blunt stump that she tucked back under the fall of her hair. She secured one end of the lock with an elastic, braided a small plait and fastened it with another elastic. Mom used to brush and braid her hair, seemed almost to worship it. The only redhead in the family, she'd say. And then Mom would go silent and Amber would know she was thinking about the dead man and the possible colours of his hair. She returned to the kitchen, slid the string that held the paper airplane so it hung midway on the hanger and suspended the braid close to one end. There it was, this hair she hadn't done a thing to earn, bobbing opposite the frayed white flag of a track ribbon. To counterbalance the braid and its heavy elastics, Amber weighted the track ribbon with the tiny brass pin coach Mitchell presented her with when she graduated. It gave the cloth an extra torque, made it corkscrew, winding and unwinding. Motion with no apparent purpose. She looked at Tamara's silver earring where it lay on the floor. Not tonight, she thought.

Spring was the worst, statistically; she knew that. Spring and, to some extent, fall. The worst times of year for people with the kind of trouble she had. Its ancestral roots buried in the response to changes in heat, humidity, light? Spring was almost over now. She stared at the two hangers and the ridiculous broomstick above her kitchen floor. This creation, which half an hour ago had been so potent, had now lost its power of enchantment. If this is you, Amber, she thought, so far you don't amount to much. She pictured how the scissors had looked in the mirror cutting through her lock of hair. Pictured how if those same scissors cut through balloon man's string, he'd lose his head completely. With a slow hand she pushed lightly at the arrangement of hangers. Everyday relics. If any one of these items had belonged to, say, Madonna, you could sell it for hundreds over the Internet. But this collection had meaning for only one person. Use it, she told herself. The art gallery, the banana tree, the shaggy, ecstatic dog down the block. Use it. Take yourself in hand. Don't let yourself be lured – don't – into that motionless place that dissolves you alive.

PERFORMANCE ART

Years ago, Amber had watched as Tamara bent to pick up the hoe in her parents' backyard. Her shirt was bright orange like the lilies beside the house. Her signature earring, a silver swan, dangled from her left earlobe. She kept her voice quiet, so as not to scare away the salamander hiding among the rocks; she had plans for that salamander.

"Performance artist," she said, "and scientist. That's what I'll be when I get out of here." She swung the hoe up and back and held it above her head.

"Both at once?" Amber said.

"Of course both." Tamara held the hoe ready to strike. The keys glued to her leather belt glinted in the sun, silver and red and blue; the occasional empty space where the glue she'd used to hold metal to leather had failed. "This is the performance part," she said. "My regeneration piece." Her ready stance, her legs apart, her two stub-toes nestled in her sandals beside their normal, full-length neighbours.

Two years ago, age fifteen, Tamara had gone out in her bare feet to mow the lawn and lost the ends of those two toes. Afterwards, she'd had to relearn balance both walking and standing. Since then she'd been fascinated by regeneration. She'd bought the books, done the reading. She'd decided to make it her future career. Its possibilities for healing wounded human beings.

Tam and Amber had discovered the salamander a week ago in the rocks near her mother's fishpond. "These guys can do it," Tam had said. "If you cut off a part, they'll grow a new one."

"So I've heard. The tail, right?"

"Legs too. They can grow a whole new leg. I want to do an experiment."

"What kind of experiment?"

"I have to think about it."

They'd kept tabs on the salamander, periodically checking the damp dark granite cubbyhole where it snoozed through the afternoons, its acid green belly flesh a startling contrast to the tiger stripes that ribbed its back. This afternoon Tamara had phoned Amber and said, Come over, let's do it today. Now Amber stood near the rocks, feeling squeamish, holding the stick Tamara had given her.

"Ready," said Tamara. Pencil-straight brown hair hanging on either side of her face.

"Shouldn't we – I don't know – hit it on the head first? Knock it unconscious."

Tamara lowered the hoe. "How are you gonna reach into that little space," she said, pointing at the low-roofed cave formed by the rocks, "and hit it hard enough to knock it out?"

"I guess you're right."

"Go ahead. Poke it already." Tamara raised the hoe again.

Amber knelt and reached toward the salamander with the stick. She moved her arm half-heartedly. "How about," she said, holding still for a moment, "how about we scare it into a shoebox and *then* hit it on the head."

"Come *on*, Amber."

"Okay, okay." She prodded, making shy indentations in its flesh. It stayed put. It looked like a lazy creature, there in the dark in the daytime, its stupid round snout.

Tamara shifted her feet impatiently. Amber prodded more forcefully and the salamander scurried from its shelter and darted across the lawn. Tamara struck. The hoe came down in the grass with a thud and still the salamander ran. The hoe hadn't caught even a portion of a leg, let alone the decisive amputation Tamara was aiming for. She chased it, hacking wildly. Finally the hoe found its mark – sort of. Tamara had sliced the hindmost third of the animal at an angle – hindquarters, tail and a single leg – from the rest of its body. The two separate segments churned in the grass, acid green flesh whipping the deep green blades. Tamara chopped with the hoe again and again. Now there were more parts, and they seemed all to be moving, as if they could still flee the blade. Amber turned away.

Finally the thudding stopped and Tamara, her breath coming quick and heavy, said, "I had to put it out of its misery." She let the hoe drop. It made a small, hollow noise as it hit the ground.

They went inside then, away from the wet smell of the pond and the water plants, away from the smashed animal and the slimed hoe, into Tamara's room. They sat on the floor, the placid pretty fish hanging from the mobile above them.

"Not my best performance," Tamara said. "I guess I should wait till I get a lab." She rubbed her face with her hands.

"I guess."

Tamara took her sandals off and stretched her legs out full length. "But see." She pointed at the tough scar tissue on the stubs of her lost toes. "*We* lose a body part and we get scars. Hardening. Layers and layers. A salamander loses a leg and it gets another whole leg. That part of its body doesn't even know how to make a scar. It's like you get the choice, the one or the other, a scar or a new part. So that's the job – to figure out how to build the *thing* and not the scar."

"Creepy," Amber said. The separate parts of the salamander out there in the grass and Tamara acting as if she'd forgotten about them already, while Amber was still feeling squeamish.

They were so different from each other, she and Tam. Amber had sat cross-legged alone on her bed one afternoon and asked herself what the source of the strong attraction was. It was, she decided, like a gravitational pull. From the beginning she and Tam had glided along neighbouring orbits: the same block, same streets, same classrooms, same playground. Tamara had always been there, the way sisters must be for some. They had played, swum and schooled together, pulled the legs off spiders together, learned how to drink, smoke and smoke up. They had drawn their imaginary houses in the dirt, had made up the world together. The sun, the moon, Earth, Mars, Amber, Tamara.

Once in a while she still thought about the failed experiment, about how things would be if people worked the way salamanders did, if you could get replacements instead of scars.

It was the end of grade twelve, parties every weekend. A softball game at Thompson Creek and a wiener roast afterward. Tamara with the fire making lights in her eyes, starting the fight with Jordy, the fight she'd told Amber earlier they had to have. It was graduation time, decision time. "I don't want to look around and discover I'm still standing next to him when the smoke clears. Another version of my dad, destined to work his way up to service station manager. Aren't we supposed to be the generation that leaves this place behind?"

Later, the drive home in the truck they'd borrowed from Wendy's dad, the three girls in the cab together laughing about where they'd be when the smoke cleared. The gravel road, the fierce wind flattening the grass in the ditches either side; the high-bodied vehicle swerving, then launching itself off the road, the fence coming at them in slow motion. The sensation of hanging in mid-air before they crashed and rolled. After the crash, Amber came to alone in the upside-down cab, the shattered casing of the interior light a cluster of plastic splinters under her heel. The smell of torn metal in the chill night.

Tamara? Wendy? Amber ducked her head toward the window and peered up the steep bank of the ditch. Pain lanced from left to right across her back. Hold still and remember how to breathe. The headlights of a car appeared in the distance, indistinct and starry. She raised a hand to feel for the glasses that weren't there, then groped among the shards of glass and plastic that littered the cab and came up with only one bent spectacle arm, and with it the swan earring Tam had taken off and set on the dash when she got in the truck. Amber closed her fist around the two objects. Up on the road, the car passed without slowing.

Favouring her back, she climbed the ditch and sat on the gravel ridge at the edge of the road, scanning the darkness. The truck was a blurred shape, wheels in the air like an animal sleeping or dead. She picked a fragment of windshield glass off her jacket, then raised a hand to check her face, her skin. All that glass, she must have cuts. She tried to shout for the others, but she couldn't manage more than a weak voice. Tam. Wend.

The lights of another car appeared. She half stood and raised her hand. The car slowed and stopped. The man who got out was familiar to her from somewhere – from wedding dances or hockey games or maybe just the aisles of the Kmart in Thompson Creek. A staccato series of questions: What happened? Are you hurt? Can you walk? Amber's answer was to point numbly toward the truck. How many? She held up fingers: two more.

She waited in his car, her back wedged into the corner where the door and the seat came together, a position that at least blunted the pain. Another car slowed and stopped in front of the one Amber sat in. Soon she could see three figures, Wendy between two others, limping up the side of the ditch and being helped into the other car. Headlights now from yet another vehicle. A strobe effect as people walked through the beams. Serious voices said words she couldn't make out.

During the drive to the hospital Amber asked over and over, "What about Tam?" and the man from hockey or Kmart or wherever at first said nothing, then said he didn't know, then finally, "They don't think there's any hope." The only thing left of Amber's glasses, the one arm, black and shiny, bending in her hand around the swan.

Two months later she went off to Saskatoon. Once in a while she'd think, I should give Tam a call. And again feel the loss. She would tell herself there was nothing so especially tragic about being Amber. Even for Tamara, whose family had the normal, the correct architecture, the kind of mother who would spend hours crafting a mobile of tiny fishes woven from ribbons – even then the bogeyman can still come.

RHYMES WITH ANGER

"Did you see the Wednesday morning guy?" Amber said to Shari and Chelsea. He sat near the display window with his buddies. Five espressos and one muffin for the group. Multiple piercings and swacks of hair gel; swags of chain linking wallets to belt loops. And scars. The Wednesday morning guy's upper arm was marked with a formation of scars, evenly spaced, their geometry precise.

"I wonder what happened," Amber said.

Shari glanced at him and then at Amber, "They're for decoration, don't you think?"

"Decoration?" Amber knew plenty about cutting, in the abstract. There were people in the UpBeat chat room who said they slashed to remind themselves they were alive. She couldn't imagine doing it – actually cutting with intention – but she could almost understand it. People looking for a way to cut through the fog around their feelings. Opening a door in the skin to let something out, or let something in. But decoration? Designer keloids?

"A statement of personal style," Macy said. Macy with her darkly outlined eyes and her *Pulp Fiction* haircut.

"But how would he do it?" Amber said. "He'd have had to take a knife and...."

"Sometimes you get someone else to use the knife," Macy said.

Amber stared at her. Would that be better or worse than doing it yourself? A sensation like a scald, a scald concentrated into a line, once for each cut. To show how you can hurt yourself and face it.

"But they're huge," she said.

"Highly visible, right?" said Shari. "Now you're getting it."

"Why not just a tattoo?"

Shari opened the door of Terra Firma, held it wide with the toe of her chunky red shoe, and gestured for Amber to go ahead. They entered the tiny store tucked in among the gone-broke businesses down the street and around the corner from Poor Man's. A mesh of scents from vials of oil, racks of incense, cotton clothing that smelled like coriander. Time for a field trip, Shari had suggested after they'd finished clearing lunch. They were here to find henna tattoos.

"It'll cheer you up. Decorating the body. A cure for the blues as old as the blues."

So it's that obvious my spirits need lifting, Amber thought. She'd convinced herself she was doing fine. She'd held on for a week now after attaching her best-of list to the mobile. Gone through the motions every day without toppling, without missing work.

Poor Man's had been busy for lunch and dead calm since, Chelsea already gone for the day, Donna looking from her watch to the door in hope of customers, Macy ready to leave but standing at the counter talking to Donna. She was still on about her third-owner theory. The new juice and smoothie place down the block would be open soon – tough competition on the way. Donna was talking renewal, reinvention. How about live music at noon, how about pub lunches, a takeout window, an Internet café? Still no customers, and when Shari and Amber asked if they could step out to buy tattoos, Donna told them, Go then, fifteen minutes.

Places like Terra Firma had their regular customers the same way Poor Man's Treacle did, and Amber was one of them. She would come in to gaze into the glass case that held amber trinkets. You could wear amber around your neck, your wrist, your ankle, your belly; use it as a stud in your nose. Amber: the name she'd had to make an effort to accept. Once, back when she was still serving fries at the food court in the mall, a customer had asked her name and, being in a who-wants-to-know mood, she'd answered, Rumpelstiltskin. The inner genie who'd always been there but who'd never had a name, was christened. Having a name like that inside, a name so ugly it was funny, made it easier to wear a name as adorable as the one she'd been given at birth.

On previous visits to the store, she'd stood by the bookshelf at the back ignoring the hippie fixings that surrounded her and read, a section at a time, a colourful small book about amber. Roman peasants used it to cure diseases of the neck and head. Frederick the First of Prussia commissioned his artisans to construct an entire room from it. Nuggets of amber wash up on the beaches of Denmark, the book said. Was it free for the taking, then? Did it belong to anyone? Tears of Freya, the Danes called it. Amber didn't know who Freya was. She imagined a sorrowful woman with tangled blond tresses who lived out of sight beneath the sea and who forever mourned some great, unnamed loss. Amber liked the romance of the image.

Posted beside the shelf of henna tattoos at Terra Firma was a sign explaining that the temporary stain would be discarded cell by cell over a number of weeks. Fun, cool, and painless. The woman at the counter, her single silver braid resting on her shoulder, smiled and told them she'd be happy to answer any questions. Happy, thought Amber. Yes. She'd asked this same woman a question once before, and the woman had worked hard to remain happy as she answered it. The question had concerned two small carved figures that sat among the crystals on the shelf beside the till.

"Who are those little carved men?"

"That's the laughing Buddha and that's the weeping Buddha."

"What are they laughing and weeping about?"

The woman had told her that of course the laughing Buddha laughed for the sheer joy of life and, well, the weeping Buddha, she supposed he wept for (bracelets jangled as she pushed self-consciously at her belled sleeves), for all the sorrows of the...of the world. You know? Her smile denying those same sorrows. Her business was optimism.

As for Amber, she'd stood there thinking this: the world has sorrows that merit the tears of a Buddha, but all I can see in these tiny carved figures is myself, laughing, crying. Here I am, too selfish to weep for anything larger than myself, let alone for the sorrows of all the world.

Shari read aloud from the henna display: "'The time-honoured tradition of Indian body art.'"

"Are you doing one too?"

"Might as well," said Shari. "I *am* a quarter Indian."

"Indian, but not the right kind."

Shari slapped Amber's forearm. "The wrong kind, that's me all right." She spread a fan of red plastic stencils on the shelf. "Pick one."

When they went off shift they caught the Number 16 together. This is good, Amber thought, good to have a friend to laugh with after work on the bus. They got off near the fish and chips window wedged in by the pharmacy and carried their dinner to Amber's place. Shari set the steam-softened fish box on the kitchen table. "Why, Amber, do you have a broomstick and hangers clamped in your window?"

"Long story. Come in the other room."

They sat on the floor next to her supermarket-issue coffee table. Amber and Cal had cruised the aisles of the grocery store with the table still inside its flat box, balanced across the cart above celery and apples and KD. One of the screw-on legs had been unsteady since the beginning. It wobbled now as Amber pressed the folds out of the instructions that came with the henna.

"It says to rub your skin with oil. I'll go get some."

But Shari was already rubbing her upper arm with a limp french fry. Amber picked one up as well and dabbed at the outside of her lower leg where she would paint the mandala she'd chosen.

"I'm not sure this is what they had in mind," she said.

Shari pressed her stencil against her upper arm, tapping and testing until it held. "Paint me."

Once Amber had finished working on her, Shari picked a wedge of fish out of the box and sat on the couch, her back against the arm, her legs stretched out along the cushions. She pointed the piece of fish at the concert of angels. "What's with the religious picture?"

"It was Cal's."

"You're not religious or anything, are you?"

"No," Amber said. She began to paint the mandala through the stencil on her leg.

"You don't believe in God, do you? The Creator and that?"

"No," Amber said. "Here's what I do believe." She looked through the doorway into the kitchen, looked still further, past the broomstick and through the window at the green of the new leaves. "I believe there's goodness inside people. Most people."

She felt shy, but when Shari nodded and said, "That works," Amber dared to elaborate: "And I believe we're supposed to look for that goodness." She went back to work on her leg.

"In ourselves, you mean?"

"In ourselves and everyone else." Except, Amber thought, once in a while there's someone stubborn who won't let you see far enough inside to find much of anything. In which case, don't bother looking.

Shari had left hours ago, her red stencil still stuck to her arm. On her way out she gave the hangers on the broomstick a gentle nudge with her foot and said, "Amber-Amber, you're a little bit weird. I like it when people are weird."

Now Amber sat with her back against the couch and Ed TV for company. A show about the moon, a silvery voice-over: if there were no moon there would be no tides; the moon's speed of rotation is such that we see always the same face. Amber stared at the deep green mud caked on her leg. The paste was to stay undisturbed for at least four hours, preferably six, eight if you could stand it. Was it drying too quickly? Her pale complexion wouldn't respond to the stain the way darker skin would. Shari's tattoo would be more vivid.

Ed showed her romantic shots of the moon, waxing, waning, floating its reflection on bodies of water. The moon looks cold as ice but its daytime temperature is a hundred and thirty degrees Celsius; the moon is moving slowly away from the earth.

The skin underneath the dye began to itch. Where did people find the patience? The air seemed to thicken around her and she shifted about in search of a fresh place to take a breath. Nothing like an itch to make you fume. Amber's hand hovered above the dye, *this close* to scraping at it. A tentative probe with her fingernail to relieve the itch – how much damage could that do? A paring knife came to mind. But no, she'd lasted over three hours already; she could wait it out. Jesus, though – dozens of little pinpricks. She slammed the palm of her hand hard against the coffee table. A stinging in the skin from palm to fingertips, a sharp pain where the wrist bone met the table's hard surface.

"Bitch!" she said. "Am I supposed to feel *guilty* for doing this to you, Del? For *being*?"

She kicked the coffee table onto its side and the remains of dinner scattered. The loose leg buckled when the table went over. She wrenched it free and slammed it again and again on the edge of the upended table, her arm doing just as it wished, with a freedom that frightened her. A barrelful of rage. The downstairs tenant replied with her own noises. She and Amber had their signals. Amber took one last swing with the table leg, then left it lying, sat down and breathed heavily.

Eventually she did fetch a knife, but she used it only to gingerly lift away the last bits of dried paste and stencil wax. The mandala looked hopelessly indistinct. She turned the tap on full and hot and ran the blade of the knife under the water to rinse away the sticky paste. Steam rose from the blade. Clean, she thought, sterile like a surgeon's knife. She imagined pulling the blade sharply across the back of her hand to make a blood-brilliant line. With her thumbnail she tried to dislodge a last crumb of wax from the knife. The water was scalding hot, god-damn! The knife clattered into the sink and she shoved the faucet control to the right, tested with a finger until it ran cold and held her scalded thumb under the icy stream. Freezing cold now, but hold it there. Ten Mississippis, that should do it. No blisters beginning, nothing more than a barely perceptible smoothing of the skin and a slight numbness at the surface.

Once more she checked the instructions for the henna tattoo. There was a final step. She drizzled cooking oil on a wad of paper towel and rubbed it over the tattoo with shaking fingers. Out came the pattern, golden against her pale skin, blurred only in a few places at the outer circle. She had her mandala.

SIMPLE COMMANDS

As if she could see herself from above. Could picture her own form curled on the sofa, limp like a feather cushion, surrounded by empty cracker boxes, glasses with thin lacquers of milk in the bottom, wedges of the lemon she'd cut up and placed around the room, hoping the sharp smell would pierce the heaviness in the air. The toppled coffee table. The grease-shined fish box. Fourth day in the trough now, pull of gravity undiminished.

Earlier, she'd looked at the mobile as she stood in front of the open fridge drinking a bargain cola and spooning cheese-spread out of the jar. The arrangement hung ridiculously from the broom handle, its five pendants drifting in slight, random motions. Mother, father, me, me, me. Her idea of building herself out of pieces of junk. She'd made her way to the couch and had lain there since. The day was a glacier inching through eternity.

Two scheduled days off; then yesterday she'd called in sick, and today was Sunday. She'd better be at work tomorrow.

Donna was great, but she didn't get it. Of course she didn't. Amber had to remind herself not to take it personally. Donna thought a person should be able to wedge her way underneath a stubborn, heavy day and tip it over, send it crashing.

Why don't you see someone? Donna had said one day. Well, Amber had, but she didn't bother going into that with Donna. She'd spoken with a doctor who handed her an enormous book with lists of prescription drugs. Tapped her fingernail to indicate a five-inch paragraph of side effects, the least frightening of which was dry mouth. Of course, the doctor said, there was no reason to expect Amber would suffer *any* of the side effects, but they had to be listed in the book. She said she'd consider a prescription if Amber would at the same time see a counsellor. So Amber went to Dr. Still's office in the bank building downtown with the empty reception desk and the sign that said, Someone will be with you shortly. And shortly he *was* with her and she followed him in and sat in the easy chair. Over the next half-hour they went through a checklist of questions about her feelings and he ended by asking Amber did she sigh a lot. Yes no maybe; what's a lot? He'd recorded her answers to his questions and sketched a little graph, which he held up for her to see, as if its meaning were clear. She was depressed, he said; she should make another appointment. She made one for the following Wednesday at nine a.m., but ultimately cancelled, because the following Wednesday at nine a.m. she was just fine. Never did get a packet of pills. Might have thrown them out if she had.

She lay in the warm burrow she'd made of the sofa. The comfort of misery; the way it would embrace her if she let it.

Begin by getting one thing done. She knew the strategy, she'd even keyed it in at the chat room at the UpBeat site, writing with certainty, as if she were someone for whom it worked without fail. Pinned to the kitchen wall above the sink was a list of simple commands: Make the bed; Tidy one corner of one room; Walk around the block; Repeat; Straighten the closet. The list went on, a confident product of one of her better days. Black pen, for its strength. The idea was to take hold of the set of instructions as if it were a rope and pull yourself along it from one item to the next. Get a grip. But she'd been known to begin, then go back to bed, pull the covers over reality.

"What's wrong? What is it, exactly, that's wrong?!" Mom had shouted, finally, one April day when Amber was in grade twelve. "The thing that's most wrong," Amber had said in answer, "is that I can't say what's wrong." The question didn't even make sense, the way it implied a solution.

Amber sat up and rummaged through the magazines and accumulated food wrappers on the floor. She last ate fruit when? There – she found the remote. Ed was part-way through a program about ancient Mayan civilizations. An aerial shot of step-style pyramids, then a shot of the same steps from below. Insurmountable. The ancient Mayans believed each day had its own god, the TV voice said; each day wanted its own sacrifice. Close-up of a poorly lit figure carved from black stone, its features indistinct. Each day had a spirit, Ed repeated. The spirit demanded a sacrifice of some sort, small or large.

Okay. So *I* am the sacrifice today's spirit demands. This day requires me to sit still for hours on end. Patience. All I have to do is wait for a more generous day.

DANCING

There was no need, today, for the self-help list above the sink; there'd been no need for days. Why would she require such a list, ever? Two days ago she discovered herself dancing beside the radio to the Cuban music the morning man favoured, and she thought, I'm dancing, feature that. Change of state. A mysterious deliverance, and with it the certainty that she'd never again find herself so deep in those hollow caves. She'd righted the coffee table and propped up its legless corner with two cans of beans and a jam jar. Now you're really a grocery table, she'd said. It listed a little; it wobbled when she set down her morning Coke.

Yesterday, out for her walk/run, Amber had crossed the railway bridge, and on the riverbank behind the art gallery she'd come upon an artisans' fair. Handmade soap, stained glass flowers, crystal stalks of wheat. A stallholder sat behind a table stringing necklaces. Arranged in front of him were small containers filled with beads sorted into colour families. These weren't new beads, the type for sale at craft shops; they were from dismantled garage-sale jewelry. Beside the containers was a tangled heap of vintage necklaces and earrings. From this hoard the craftsman fabricated unorthodox designs, older beads with newer, shiny with scuffed, plastic with gems. It was the composition of the finished pieces, the way the colours and shapes ran through them in patterns, the way the strands separated, crossed and came together, that gave the necklaces their stylish presence and saved them from looking like recycled junk. The art of salvage. Their beauty depended on arrangement. Amber had pictured, looking at them, a redesigned mobile that would begin at the ceiling and spiral almost to the floor. She would need proper supplies, fine wires, clippers, thin, strong threads.

She hadn't yet equipped herself with the new gear, but she'd added, yesterday after her walk/run, two more relics, the silver swan earring and the broken fish hook. Two bits of hardware turning, deceptively weightless, at the ends of their lines. For Tamara and for Cal.

FUN AND GAMES, UNTIL

The broken end of the fish hook was still sharp, despite the fact that the fierce-looking point had been snipped off and thrown away by the resident at the emergency ward. The way Amber's mind put the story together – the story of herself and Cal – the fish hook was at the centre. It used to hang from the spindle on one side of the dresser mirror, disarmingly colourful – tied with blue, yellow and pink feathers.

The incident that involved the fish hook happened during Amber's french fry era, when she worked at the fry joint in Midtown Plaza. She'd found the job after finally giving up on the idea of school, admitting she would never, after all, complete her five overdue term papers; the thought of those papers had for weeks lashed her to the mattress in the mornings and kept her sitting in front of the TV late at night promising herself she'd start work right after the nature doc was over, after the space show, after the experimental animated short. From the beginning, university had been a start and stop affair for Amber. She'd enrolled and faltered, enrolled and faltered, eating first into her school allowance from Mom and Dad, later into her one-third share of her parents' small legacy. Cal once introduced her to a classmate with, Have you met Amber? She's having trouble completing her Bachelor of Procrastination.

Plain old survival, she ultimately decided, had to come first; she withdrew from classes and forfeited her tuition. Stood behind the counter and ladled curds and gravy on top of fries. Her clothes saturated with the smell of hot grease by the end of the working day. Cal's clothes stale from the lack of air in his windowless basement office. He had a good gig, for a student, troubleshooting in a computer lab at the university and using the machines to build web pages freelance.

Cal wore a precision goatee and kept his hair ultrashort. His favourite jacket was one she'd found for him at a second-hand store, grey blue with bus-driver tailoring and a darker patch where a company crest used to be. He would say proudly to their friends, Amber dresses me. He wore a digital wristwatch that, every quarter past the hour, displayed in tiny letters the message, Time to fuck. Amber wasn't to take it literally, he said. Not *every* time, ha ha.

They met in the computer lab before she'd given up completely on the term papers. A few weeks after they met he gave her a valentine card, though it was November: Hooked on you. Taped inside was the fish hook. After a week Amber threw out the card, but she saved the hook and hung it, in all its gaudy, feathered glory, so it dangled from the spindle to the right of her dresser mirror.

Cal stayed the night on several occasions and then one day asked for and was granted permission to become a bona fide resident of the Burton house. He parked his fourth-hand Nova on the weedy gravel patch out back, carried his clothing up the stairs, closed the door of the communal medicine chest on his three-blade shaving system and set his Mr. Magoo bobble-head doll on the kitchen windowsill. He rearranged the order of things on the countertop to make room for his espresso pot, and in doing so he tipped over the sugar bowl. With the side of his hand he leveled the hill of crystals into a plain. In the white field he drew a heart and inside the heart traced her initials, AW. "Aw," she said, looking at the heart. "Aw," he repeated and nudged her mouth open with a sugar-coated finger.

He was funny. He had names for things. For the colours of Amber's nail polish: royal blood, scratch-the-vampire, buff baloney. For the part of town where they lived, officially called Nutana, but referred to by Cal as Nirvana. Midtown Plaza was The Plasma. He was working on a revisionist map of the city, he said.

"If you're happy and you know it, clap your hands," he said one morning after they made love. She didn't clap. Lay on her back, gazing at the ceiling.

"Don't take it personally," she said.

"I'll try not." He rolled onto his side and looked at her. "What would it take then, my lady of sorrows. Are you embarking on another of your voyages to hollowland?" When she didn't answer, he relaxed onto his back and said, "What do you want from life?" He seemed to mean it. Both of them lying there, nothing but skin between them. Again, she didn't answer.

"Maybe your problem is that you lack Faith. Upper case eff."

"You mean like church?" He was making fun of her, must be; prescribing something he didn't believe in. His poster on the wall in the next room mocking her.

"Don't make fun of me," she said.

"What if I mean it?"

"What if you *mean* it?"

"Yeah," he said. "It works for some."

Her father at the kitchen table, reading in his whisper-voice from The General Epistle of James. Her mother with her round face, her careful smile, attentively listening. Humble yourselves in the sight of the Lord, and He shall lift you up. There was a false wishing well in the backyard in Ripley, holding soil instead of water. Her mother used to plant a cascade of red petunias in it. When Amber looked at it she would see over-bred flowers and faux brick, but she sensed that her parents, when they sat on the painted bench on the patio and looked at the well, saw something else entirely.

Faith. "You're kidding, right?" Amber said to Cal. "I don't think you can just make it up if it isn't already inside you."

"But wouldn't it be handy for you if you could?" It didn't sound mean the way he said it.

After he fell asleep Amber slipped out of bed and went to the kitchen, where she stood with the door to the freezer compartment open and the frosty air rushing down her skin, chilling her breasts and eddying about her ankles. What? What is needed? She pulled out a box of pizza minis and peered inside. Didn't look appetizing. She let it fall, and the cold hard box slid across the floor. She wrestled the plastic lid from a container of frozen cream puffs, bit into one and confirmed that they were tasteless in that state. She let go of the container and the stiff, tiny pastries rained down her legs and hit her feet. She raised both hands and scooped out everything that was left in the freezer compartment. The box of chicken nuggets glanced off her thigh and landed, thud. Frozen peas came to rest on her foot, flesh-biting cold, and she left them there. A scatter of ice cubes hit the floor. What? What is needed?

He was magnetic. At Sharon's Pub, when he chose a table, people would pick up their drinks and leave their own tables to join him. Not that anything exciting happened at his table, but it might, and you didn't want to be in the wrong place just in case. When Cal pushed back his chair later in the evening, when he stood up and stretched and said he was heading out, members of his congregation would gather their things and make as if they'd been about to leave too.

He'd tell stories and borrow the characters from Hollywood. Since we're all just actors anyway. "In walked this woman," he'd say, "This long thin woman-in-white, this Andie MacDowell from Sex, Lies et cetera." Or, "Here comes Kathy Bates from the Stephen King flick, the first one." Or, "So I'm talking to Julia Roberts's mouth." Amber liked the game. She would ask him, mornings while they ate their Mini-Wheats, to play it using people they knew.

"Billy from the computer lab."

"Randall from *Clerks*. He keeps leaving the lab when he's on shift and neglecting to go back."

"Good one. What about Sue?" Sue, the waitress at Sharon's who complained about the pains in her feet but wore high narrow heels to work every day anyway.

"Teri Garr. *Full Moon in Blue Water.*"

He was on the money: the pout, the fluffy hair, the please-note playing through her voice. Amber laughed.

"Give me another one," he said.

Should she put Del's name out there for him? He'd met her only once, what could he know from an awkward encounter on a downtown street? But she was tempted by the idea of wrapping Del up in a package as manageable as one of Cal's caricatures.

"Del."

He was ready with an answer, as if he'd been waiting for the question. "Data," he said, "*Star Trek*. A copy without an original."

"Ouch."

He shrugged.

"So...you're saying she's a robot?"

"Not quite that simple. More like someone who's got a program of who she's supposed to be and she's just following the program."

"That's mean," Amber said. Those were the days when she hadn't yet given up on Del.

"You asked."

"You've met her what – once?"

"Don't forget, Amber. Almost everything I know about Del has come through you."

"I don't like your movie game anymore."

"It's all fun and games until someone loses an eye. Or an 'I,'" he said, drawing the letter in the air.

"You're not so smart," she said. "Just clever."

They were supposed to meet friends for margarita night at Sharon's. Amber stood in front of the mirror getting ready and at the same time trying to tell Cal about Tamara. How she,

Amber, would see someone on the street with a similar build, straight brown hair, and just for a flash she'd think, Hey, there's Tamara. She moved her hands in the air to give shape to her feelings. Then she dropped her hands, and – too quickly for her to realize what was happening – the fish hook stabbed her hand. There was no blood, just disbelief. The sharp end protruding on one side of the web of flesh between thumb and forefinger, the tail on the other side, feathers fluffing.

"Grotesque," Cal said and turned away. "Let me know when you've pulled it out."

"You think I'm going to pull it back through? It'll rip my hand apart! Find something to cut it with – go get my big scissors." Her voice high and teetering.

Cal grimaced as he tried to snip the hook in two. The wire twisted inside her flesh. She whimpered and he set the scissors on the dresser and walked away. "You better do it."

She made only the one brief effort, to confirm that it couldn't be done. At the emergency ward, the resident took a pair of clippers and snipped away the prong-end of the hook just like that.

"There," the resident said as she tied off the single stitch she'd put in. "A month from now you won't even see a scar."

"What, no scar?" Cal said. "All that agony and nothing to show for it."

Near the end of their time together, he celebrated his twenty-sixth birthday. "What should I get you?" she asked, and he replied, "Anything from the bookstore." She realized once she was at the bookstore that she couldn't risk choosing a book for him – she had no idea what he'd consider stylish enough at that moment; which theorists were in and which were out. Scrap the bookstore, she thought, he'll have to settle for a shirt. She'd be confident about a shirt. Passing the counter on her way out of the bookstore, Amber saw a display of fridge magnets. *The square root of hope is courage. The square root of joy is faith.* She turned the metal drum that held the magnets. *The square root of irony is fear.* That was one for Cal. She bought the magnet, then caught a bus out to Value Village and found him a shirt as well. When he opened the box and read the message on the magnet he smiled with one side of his mouth and said, "Irony is such a misunderstood concept."

She should have known. The meaning of irony was one of those things that turned into a *thing* for him. He couldn't just laugh.

"I expect you're right," she said. "You're more qualified to know about that than I am."

"I like the shirt."

It was shortly after she started working at Poor Man's that Amber asked Cal to vacate her suite. Her new friend Shari asked, "Now why would you do such a thing? Here's a guy who's good-looking and funny and almost finished a fancy degree. Not only that, you get to use his free university Internet account."

"True."

"Why would you dump a guy like that?"

How to explain. Finally she said, "His beard is too perfect."

"Stop. Rewind. His beard?"

"The shape of it. Too perfect. And the way he strokes it with his thumb."

"I think his beard is cool," Shari said. "It's exactly, Amber, exactly the right shape for that kind of a beard."

"That's what I mean," Amber said. "He told me he grew it as a joke, then couldn't let it go."

It still happened that running into him on the street could bring on a sadness that seduced her, that reminded her of how, after he kissed her goodnight and turned away to curl around himself she would take the hem of his t-shirt between her fingers to follow him into sleep, slip through the door after him. It occurred to her how easily it could happen again, how you could find yourself in a relationship overnight – step on someone's toe at the bus stop, answer a customer's question in a friendly way, reach for a CD at the library at the same time someone else did. One thing would lead to the next and there you'd be, in so quick you'd hardly know what had happened. It was extricating yourself that was the tricky part.

BURNING MAN

Business was deadly slow this morning – Saturdays were getting that way. Someone would be sent home early. A lone customer came in, took a seat and opened the *Globe and Mail*. He looked slightly familiar to Amber, but she couldn't place him. He was long-haired and soft about the face; young, she thought, barely over twenty. When Amber approached his table he asked for the full treacle explanation.

"Just to be certain," he said, straight-faced, "there's no garlic in the muffins?"

"Sorry," she said, straight-faced as well. He tucked his shiny hair behind his ears and ordered a muffin and a cup of the daily dark. She served him and he thanked her without looking up.

When she turned away from him she saw Del. Amber was startled, unready. Del's form as she stood in the doorway was dark against the light from the street. This made three encounters in less than a month – a record.

"Coming in?" Amber said.

"No thanks. I was doing errands and stopped to say hello." Del's voice was a halftone above its natural home.

"How are things?" Amber asked. She prickled with self-consciousness; the quiet, hollow restaurant behind her, Shari and Chelsea standing at the counter and the solitary customer sitting with his newspaper, not even a rustle.

"Fine," Del said. "Fine. I'm shopping for necessaries." She turned her leg to show how the lower seam of her sweat pants had begun to separate. "These've had it." Her talk was ordinary, but her voice sounded odd. Shallow ripples of uneasiness.

At Del's right shoulder a twenty-five-years-ago clipping was tacked to the wall: Pierre Trudeau had been through town electioneering, kissing babies outside Eaton's.

"Life treating you all right?" Del said, looking past Amber and into Poor Man's. "Looks like a slow day."

"Saturdays aren't good."

The other night as she'd crashed about in her living room, a storm of questions had whirled through her mind with such urgency that she'd beaten them into the phony wood grain of the coffee table:

Did you love the Phil-man? and

Were you sad when he died? and

Do you love me at all? and

What the hell's wrong with you?

Now the questions had lost their vitality, as if they'd been printed and framed and mounted behind glass. As if, Amber thought, she'd taken lessons from Del herself in how to minimize. In case of emergency break glass. But she wouldn't, not here in the quiet with the people in the background. The silence, still, between and around them. Amber thought about what she'd said to Shari the other day, about how you should look for the good in people. She did believe that, though the day she'd said so to Shari was the first time she'd whittled the thought into so many words. She believed it, yes, but it would be easier to accomplish with a stranger than with Del.

Del said, "I guess I, uh, I'll be off to the Midtown now."

"The Plasma," said Amber.

"Pardon me?"

"Just a silly name for it. Midtown Plasma."

"That's funny," said Del, not smiling. Trudeau with the babies twenty-five years ago on the wall beside her. "See you later."

With relief Amber said goodbye and leaned past Del to push open the door for her. She went back to the counter thinking, diversion please. Chase away the aftertaste.

On the counter they kept a stack of glossy brochures from the travel agent three doors down. Sunshine escapes: Ixtapa, Moorea, Huatalco, La Caravelle. Customers would leaf through the glossy pages and slip copies of the brochure into their briefcases or pockets. Maybe some of them bought the two-week packages, maybe they just tore out pictures of palm trees and babes and pinned them on the walls above their fax machines. Diversion. Amber poured herself a cup of Just Joe and took a brochure from the stack.

Macy came from the kitchen, wiped her hands on her apron, said, "Yes, break time," and sat on one of the high stools at the counter. She too took a brochure and flipped through it noisily. "Beaches," she said. "Beaches, beaches, thongs, beaches." Then she said to hell with the beach, they should close this place down for a week at the end of the summer and all go to Burning Man – Macy, all in black, who looked as if she wouldn't last forty-five seconds in full sunlight, whether on a curve of beach at Ixtapa or at the Burning Man Festival in the convection oven of the Nevada desert.

"I'm with you," Chelsea said.

Donna, in the kitchen doorway, said, "Where's Burning Man?"

"It isn't a where," said Shari, "it's a what. A gigantic party in the desert. They build a giant man and then they set fire to it."

"The Nevada desert," Chelsea said. "Hot-hot-hot." She swung her hips to the rhythm of the words.

The lone customer was engrossed in his newspaper. Or he pretended to be engrossed while he listened to what Macy and Amber and Chelsea and Shari had to say. A trace of a smile played across his mouth.

"All right," Amber said, pretending it wasn't important whether the man-boy was listening or not (blond hair against his blue T-shirt). "Everybody has to say what they'd do if they went. Their performance."

Donna said, "Performance?"

"No mere spectators allowed," Shari said. "Am I right? You can't go unless you do some kind of art."

The words "burning man" repeated inside Amber's head, followed by the words "frozen man." Burning man, frozen man, bicycle man, burning man. *Stop that.*

Donna, holding her clean hands in front of her apron so they wouldn't touch anything that might dirty them, said, "That counts me out."

"You could do a cooking thing," Shari said.

"Yeah, do a cooking thing," Amber said, trying to detach her mind from the burning-man-frozen-man singsong.

"And that would be art?"

"Of course," Shari said. "You're good enough." This might be the most generous thing Amber had ever heard Shari say to Donna.

"The chef as performer," Donna said, frowning. "There are too many of those already."

The lone customer turned a page and refolded his newspaper. Amber put down her cup and opened the fridge to check the milk supply, though she knew there was plenty. She wanted to see if she could make him look just by moving. She found a cloth and wiped the steamer. The man-boy looked toward the counter. He nodded at Amber and lifted his cup.

When she came with the thermos, he said, "I went to Burning Man once."

"You did?"

"Well, no. Truthfully, I didn't, I just thought about it," he said. "But I got your attention, didn't I?" He gestured toward the empty chair across from his.

Got her attention. Well yes he had, but only part of it. Her attention still divided. She was thinking how Vivien was right, how Del did look as if she hadn't been getting much sleep.

She considered the empty chair, his smile, the uncomplicated look on his face. "You had my attention already," she said.

"I did?"

"It's my job. You want coffee, I pour. You leave a tip on the table when you're done. That's the way it works." She sat down.

"Ethan," he said.

"Amber."

He was not, she found out, as young as he looked. He was back from Vancouver for the summer, taking a break between degrees at Simon Fraser. His BA in political studies had taken six years, give or take a term, because, you know, there was so much else that needed doing at the same time.

"So much else like what?"

He shrugged and pushed his empty muffin plate aside, then looked at Amber and changed the subject. "Let's say you did go to Nevada. What would *your* performance be?"

"Do you always go to restaurants to listen to the waitresses talk?"

"Not often. You don't talk about the sorts of things I thought waitresses would talk about."

"How many waitresses do you know?"

"Just one so far. And her not very well."

"My friend Shari," Amber gestured toward the counter where Shari and Chelsea were busy *not* looking at Amber and her customer, "she says the operative syllable in 'waitress' is 'wait.' What we're doing is waiting – waiting to decide what to do next. Could be anything. Could be moviemaking, could be deep-sea diving. Could be political studies at Simon Fraser University. So why would it be surprising what we talk about?"

"Good point," he said, smiling. "You're waiting. Suppose you're waiting for Labour Day so you can go to Burning Man. What would you do there?"

"You first."

"Sure." Ethan leaned back in his chair, long arms and long torso taking their own fair share of space. "I'd paint myself the colour of the sand and stand there with the desert as backdrop and my eyes and mouth closed. Very still, and then, once in a while, I'd smile. If anyone happened to be looking they'd see the desert, looking at them and smiling."

She pictured him naked except for the desert-coloured paint. "That's good. I like that."

He smiled, and she imagined that smile against the desert sand. A stunt like that would only work in the imagination, but in that arena it worked beautifully.

"I have a variation," she said, "on the old question about the tree falling in the forest: If no one's looking...?"

"If no one's looking, there's still a smile, but I get to have it for myself."

"So long as it isn't wasted."

"Your turn."

"I have to go back to work."

"No fair."

"I need time to think of something."

"Okay," he said, standing and pushing in his chair. "Tell me Monday."

Amber wanted two things at once. She wanted to say nothing, so he'd come back Monday to hear her Burning Man project; and she wanted to tell him something immediately, something clever and original, so he'd carry away with him an idea that came from her. She did a mental sift through the Burning Man performances she'd heard about: five days and nights in the desert wearing only body paint and a silver G-string; leaving a trail of flower petals wherever you walked; teaching people the tango; juggling with chain saws, motors running; riding a unicycle and singing to whoever would listen. And after it's over, leaving nothing behind, so that when the burning man has finished burning and the cleanup crew has done its job, not a trace of the week-long party remains.

She gave her long-haired friend a smile and lifted the thermos. It was almost empty, lighter than she had expected, and it wobbled in her hand. She went to find his bill, and as he counted out money for the muffin and coffee and a tip that was decent but not exceptional, she considered telling him that her performance in Nevada would be to count out loud the number of smiles he flashed. But no, she needed something that originated with herself, not with him; her own way to take up space.

"Bye," he said and with a raised hand twisted his hair into a loose long rope. She saw when he turned to go how it lay down the middle of his back.

"You were at the demolition," she said. "The Burton house."

"So were you," he said, looking back.

Shari, at her shoulder, said, "I didn't know you were drawn to the hippie type."

"I didn't either."

That day at the Burton she'd featured him in a Caesar cut. Now she wondered how it would feel to use her own hands to twist his hair into a long coil the way he'd done as he was leaving.

SAFE AS HOUSES

The river was low, its colour lightened by sandbars that showed beneath the surface. Amber strode along the trail Monday morning, underneath the University Bridge and north, in and out of the shade of tall bushes – caragana, wild rose, and wolf willow. She felt lucky to live so close to the river, to have this corridor of water and woods in the centre of the city, lucky to have mornings in early summer and time to walk before she had to shower and get to work. It was just after eight, but warm already. Birdsong surrounded her. She moved through a strobe of shadow and sun. A small ravine cut down to the river at the edge of the university campus. Amber stepped onto the pedestrian bridge above it and entered a green tunnel that belonged in a fantasy. Willow and caragana, rooted below in the ravine, grew tall enough here to make a canopy that reached over the bridge. On either side of the walkway, tied to the branches, were a dozen or so lavender crepe paper bows. Also tied to the branches were slim yellow ribbons holding slips of stiff white paper, some with handwritten messages, some with line drawings – a heart with wings, a flower, a cupid. The papers fluttered in the wind so the blank sides alternated with the drawings and messages. I love you. Marry me.

People still get married. She wondered if the proposal had already taken place. Probably – some of the yellow ribbons were loosening from the branches and one lavender bow lay on the ground. Peaches, read a card at eye level. So this woman's name, or her nickname, was Peaches. Served her right, then, to be surrounded by hearts and cupids and lavender bows. I'll bet Peaches said yes, Amber thought. She saw another card that said Strawberries, and another that said Apple of My Eye. Amber realized the woman's name wasn't Peaches after all; the fruit-words were meant to approximate poetry. How funny. Kiwi, she thought. Grape. Banana. If this were a film, it would depend for its atmosphere on the soundtrack: romance or comedy or – the rough caragana branches with their notes fluttering in the breeze began to look pitiful, then eerie – the set-up scene in a horror flick, just before things go wrong. Rags of paper and ribbon scuttling along the path.

Amber picked up the fallen bow and stuffed it into her pocket. The path left the bush and emerged on the high bank of the river where the full force of the wind swept up and across a stretch of open prairie adjacent to the university. Her hair whipped her face and she reached into her pocket for an elastic to fasten a ponytail.

Further downriver she left the high path and descended the sharp slope of a ravine. Here, the roar from the weir a few metres downstream was enormous. Remarkable, that water could make so much noise falling such a short distance. That it could create a swirling boil that no animal would survive. Once, she'd seen the body of a deer caught in the whirl. Its head and its four rigid legs lifted out of the water, made an arc and disappeared, then came around again. Over and over.

Where the ravine met the river, a rare beach had formed, a narrow strip of silver grey sand fringed with reeds at both ends. Amber sat on a rock and fingered the crepe paper bow she'd picked up. She undid the knots, smoothed and stretched it, used a finger to poke two holes and held the wide streamer to her face like Zorro's mask. Looking through the openings she said to the river and the reeds, Guess who? She hoped sincerely that Peaches, or what's-her-name, had her own self properly sorted out before she answered yes.

Amber picked up a stick and doodled. A rich living smell rose where she disturbed the damp sand. According to tradition, she should draw a house, like the ones she and Tam and sometimes Stuart used to draw in the street. Safe as houses, she thought, wondering where the expression came from, what it was supposed to mean.

She scrambled back up to the trail, passed the weir and climbed the wooden stairs to the railway bridge. Halfway across she stopped to gaze down at the water. Two joggers running from the west bank to the east came alongside her, and Amber moved close to the railing to let them pass. She heard their footsteps slow down. It occurred to her that they might be suspicious, might wonder if she were about to jump. Don't worry, I'm no suicide.

When Amber visited the UpBeat site she ignored the suicide prevention link – she'd clicked it only once and read through the list of things to do and not do, say and not say, if she or someone she knew was on the brink. She doubted she would even remember the advice if one day she were faced with the need.

"Watch your step," Amber said to the runners as they neared the warped plank where Cal had printed his Magic Marker warning. She felt their steady rhythm, how it traveled toward her along the boards under her feet. She turned and jogged home to get ready for work.

After the mid-morning coffee crowd dwindled, Ethan came in with a friend, a curly-haired guy Amber had often seen at Poor Man's. She was disappointed Ethan wasn't alone. She waited until Chelsea had served them before approaching, then said hello to both of them and looked at Ethan.

"I have my Burning Man project."

"Tell."

"Custom-designed houses I'd draw in the sand."

"Dream homes?" Ethan said.

Curly-hair looked from Amber to Ethan and back again without comment.

"Yeah. Dream homes." She felt silly in front of their audience of one.

"Good one," Ethan said. He gave her a generic smile and she left him alone with his friend. Maybe she'd been fooled by Saturday's conversation. Maybe it was only a conversation. She should have trumped up a more dramatic project. Tamara, now, *she* would've come up with a piece of performance art worth noticing.

The fan that sat on Amber's kitchen table said Pleasantaire. She turned her face in the breeze it made. Mid-June and hot already. The blades spun inside the narrowly spaced bars of their white cage. This cage that housed the spinning blades, Amber thought, might be there not to prevent accident, but to prevent impulse – self-destructive acts by those who lose for a moment the buffers that usually hold them back. A good idea, this cage around the blades.

She watched the threads of her mobile as the breeze from the fan strayed among them and she saw how, when the white track ribbon lifted, the small braid of hair dipped, how the handle from her mother's teacup spun and the Service Corps badge flashed its metallic signal about the room. Stir of memory.

She'd rebuilt the mobile, rebalanced its parts using strong, coated wire she'd bought from a florist and transparent nylon thread from the hobby shop. It hung now from a brass hook in the ceiling. She'd added new items, but still it was a long way from the graceful spiral she'd envisioned. A metre of nylon line dropped straight from the hook, a length of emptiness, before the mobile proper began.

The new additions were three: a 1933 King George penny Old Glad had given her when she was a girl and which she'd promptly made a nail-hole through so she could wear it around her neck; a photo of Stuart, glued onto two thicknesses of cardboard; and, in the centre because of its weight, the ornate brass faceplate from the doorbell of the Burton house.

The doorbell plate: The bell used to ring in the main-floor suite where Mark the vet student lived, but everyone else in the house could hear it. It played "Cradle Song," but only the first six notes. Mark and Amber both liked it but the rest of them complained about the way the fragment hung in the air, unresolved. The woman from the bachelor at the top disconnected the doorbell more than once. The guy across from Amber on the second floor would print messages on masking tape and stick them over the button: DYSFUNCTIONAL. Do not Use. Over time, the messages degenerated: How many times do I have to tell you? Don't do it, ASSHOLE. When he got around to it, Mark would rip away the masking tape or rewire the bell. If he was the one unlocking the front for three floors of renters, he said, he wanted to answer to Brahms. Now it didn't offer even the beginning of a song.

The photo of Stuart: Amber had been troubled to realize that in her whole box of treasures the only thing she could come up with to represent Stuart was a photo. It hadn't enough weight to hang properly on its own so she'd glued it first to one piece of cardboard backing, then another, but still it seemed flimsy. The man who'd sat at her bedside for long hours after her childhood accident; who'd moved between herself and Del after both parents' funerals as if he could stitch them together; whom she featured (when she featured him at all) standing on a rooftop looking out over Ripley. The range of vision up there, from the shingles beneath his feet, to the near distance, to the vanishing point. A man like that should be better represented.

Old Glad's penny: Old Glad had died eight years ago, after sixty years a widow and more years an orphan. Mom had told her Old Glad's story: that her father was murdered in long-ago rural Ontario when Glad was just a girl, over a disagreement to do with a bet at a summer fair. And before their second wedding anniversary her husband was killed in a threshing accident. When Amber thinks about Old Glad she thinks of the things people manage to get over. Transcend. Like the reporter whose biography she'd seen on Ed TV. A man who'd been through hell in wartime Europe, who'd never seen his parents after the age of nine. Amber had seen his face for years on the screen – kindly, compassionate, a strong jaw and soft eyes – before she heard his story. A face that was stubbornly human no matter the distress or horror or tragedy he reported. A face that lit with an understated smile as soon as the news took a happy turn. There are people who manage to rise even when the unspeakable has happened to them. And there are people with puny little troubles who never make it off the ground. Does it come down to different sets of equipment?

THE MAGNIFYING GLASS EFFECT

Chelsea was taking a poll, asking people to answer a single question: How old is the average person by the time she gets her shit together? She asked Shari first.

"Twenty-six, which happens to be exactly my age."

"Macy?"

"I was three. It was a day in September, three o'clock in the afternoon...."

"Never mind," said Chelsea.

Steve from Mock Turtle Books sat at a table near the counter waiting for his California club. He'd taken to coming in for a late lunch. Donna was less busy by then and sometimes took a break to sit down with soup and coffee.

"Steve?" said Chelsea.

"Depends on the person."

"Yourself, for instance."

Donna was leaning on the counter and looking at Steve, waiting for his answer.

"I'd say thirty-five."

"I'm not sure I can wait that long," Amber said. She thought, You mean it happens? People actually *do* get their shit together?

"Donna?" Chelsea said.

"It happens over and over, doesn't it? You get your life together only to have it come apart again and need rearranging. You have to keep working at it."

"Wow," said Chelsea.

Steve said, "I stand corrected. Thirty-five is only the first time."

"I was three," Macy repeated.

Amber heard Shari's voice close to her ear. "Amber-chick, shampoo-boy is here." She turned. Ethan beckoned from the doorway.

"Can you meet me after you're finished work?" he said.

"What's up?"

"Something I want to show you."

Maybe their audience of one yesterday had affected him too; maybe it was only self-consciousness that had made him unresponsive.

"What would that be?" Amber said.

"You'll see."

"Um, okay. Quarter past four."

"Out front?"

"Sure."

Amber waited on the bench on Second Avenue in front of Poor Man's. The afternoon was warm, and before coming out she'd gone into the bathroom and changed into the shorts she'd worn to walk to work in the morning. Sitting there waiting for Ethan, she thought how she was now included in the view she looked out at when she was on shift. Like someone framed on a video screen. Ethan joined her and rested his arm on the back of the bench, not quite touching her shoulders. Amber wondered, as he asked about her day and she asked back, whether Shari, still inside, was watching, imagining subtitles.

"I have a tape of Burning Man," Ethan said. "Belongs to a friend and I got him to dig it out after I was here the other day. Come watch it with me?"

"Where?"

"My place."

"Where do you live?"

"City Park, I'm house-sitting, ten or twelve blocks."

She decided to make each small choice as it presented itself. "Why not?" she said.

As they walked they made conversational starts and stops: New Japanese restaurant ready to open on the next block. Look at the hospital, the way they've changed it, doesn't it look different? Wonder what kind of tree that is.

They looked sideways at each other occasionally and grinned.

The house was two stories of brick surrounded by tall elms. "Welcome," Ethan said as he opened the door, his hand touching lightly the small of her back.

The entryway was dim after the sunshine. It held the scent of last night's curry. There was a small room off to the left, the kind of room Aunt Lenore called a courting room — two armchairs and a fireplace, blue curtains, drawn. Amber slipped her sandals off in the entryway. Two basketballs sat on the hardwood at her feet. Ethan took his sneakers off and moved the basketballs aside with a bare foot. They rolled back into her path and she stepped around them and followed him into the sunlit living room.

He sat on the area rug and took the tape from a stack below the TV. Burning man, thought Amber. Since Vivien's visit she'd had recurring thoughts about Phil, about John Doe, about possible fathers and how they disappear. Freezing/burning man. She sat on the rug beside Ethan and watched the small movements of his muscles. Ribs under his T-shirt. He slotted the tape into the machine.

Wide bands of light came through the room's tall windows and made a pattern on the floor, dark, light, dark, light. The TV reflected the pattern, obscuring the images, and it took a moment for Amber's eyes to accustom themselves and filter out the interference. The screen showed a burning figure, arms raised, towering above a crowd of thousands. Lit faces, people dancing, naked and otherwise, orange flames against a black sky. The camera angles were strange and clever. The director was fond of the magnifying-glass effect: noses on talking heads bulged like fungus; bodies were foreshortened and so was the philosophy festival-goers declaimed. The burning man is here to show us what we can *be*, man.

The video cut back in time to the four days of festival before the man was set alight. Heat radiated off the desert sand. Water Woman, a figure ten metres tall and constructed of wood, filled the screen. Someone pulled a lever and Water Woman sent a shower of water from her crotch. People bathed under the spray.

A slender woman wearing a diaphanous gown accosted passersby and choreographed them into a dance. Another woman stood on a hard-sided suitcase and distributed handbills for a pagan opera. A bald man with glitter on his dome had chained himself to a block of wood he was carving, but the carving itself, he said, wasn't the real project.

"Go on, man. Say more."

"It's the idea of being *owned* by this creation – see the chain. The more I try to own it the more it owns *me*. You see how wrong that is? On Monday I must cut the chain and throw the carving into the fire."

If anyone says "far out," Rumpelstiltskin piped up inside Amber's head, I'm leaving.

"Far out," said a voice off-camera.

She stayed. Bandanas and peace signs and love beads. And then it was night again and the burning man was aflame. Ethan's attention was fixed on the rapt faces that watched the gigantic bonfire. He looked enchanted, his mouth open a little. She thought she would like to touch his cheek.

People said things to the camera. They wanted to know, they said, when the burning man would finally fall. They didn't want to miss the moment, as if it would tell them something crucial. The video cut to a shot of the flaming figure, orange against a blue black sky. His arms fell to his sides, fire swooshing from them as they traced their downward arcs, giving the effect, for an instant, of wings. But the burning man didn't fly away anywhere, just settled into a fire that was less grand than before. Those who had kept their distance dared to move closer, watching the flames, transfixed.

In response to a question that didn't register on the soundtrack, a man with a fuchsia face and yellow lips said to the camera, "The ending? No, I wouldn't call it a climax, more of a ritual, a cleansing, a new beginning." The camera closed in on his fuchsia cheek; the word "start," hand-lettered in white, jumped against his skin.

When the tape was done, Ethan touched Amber's arm casually, smiling as if to say, Wasn't that something? He pushed STOP, then REWIND and set the remote on the floor. With a stubby-nailed index finger he touched the indistinct bronze pattern on Amber's leg.

"Burn yourself?"

She smiled. "It's what's left of a henna tattoo." A ghost against her skin. "It didn't last long."

"Yeah. You gotta have darker skin." His finger traced the faded circumference with a gentle but unmistakable pressure, as if he meant not to tease so much as ask a direct question. The warmth of his finger found its mark and she had to stop herself from returning the pressure, from giving a premature answer to what seemed a premature query. She wasn't ready. Not ready to engage in the obligatory mutual interview about frightening diseases. Nor for the awkwardness of latex with someone she hardly knew. Not ready for a new partner. The answer to his query, at least for now, would be no. She moved her leg away from his touch.

"What do you do, now that you're not a student?" she said. "Do you have a summer job?"

"I'm doing research for one of the profs here. Habermas and the Frankfurt School. You probably don't want the whole story."

Deep in the dust underneath Amber's bed were preliminary notes for an essay on the Frankfurt School. The unfinished status of that essay had given her a grade of Incomplete/Fail in a third-year political studies class. "Another time," she said.

Ethan's hand rested close to her. He was looking at the distance between his hand and her leg.

"I should go," she said. "I have things to do." Like what, said Rumpelstiltskin. Coil around yourself on the couch and count the rotations of the earth?

Amber got up and shook the stiffness out of her knees. Ethan did the same. They stood looking at each other for a charged moment.

She moved around him on her way to the entryway. He pivoted and followed her. As she put on her sandals he bent to pick up one of the basketballs he'd earlier kicked aside. He dribbled it on the hardwood a couple of times, then held it in front of himself, one hand on top and one underneath. Amber put her hands on it as well, one on either side.

"North south," he said.

"East west."

"You have beautiful hair," he said.

"So have you." Four hands, still, not touching.

"The colour of it."

"Yours too," she said. The presence of him. She imagined the salt of his skin in the late afternoon heat.

"We won't be seeing each other will we?" he said.

"I don't think so." Not soon, at any rate.

"I'm not what you're looking for, something tells me," he said.

"It isn't that. It's just that I'm *not* looking."

"Everyone's looking."

They stood facing each other, palms of their hands on the pebbled surface of the basketball, separated by inches. Amber thought, There are days you believe in magic and days when you don't. Finally Ethan tugged the ball gently away, tucked it between his elbow and his rib cage and held it there while he opened the door for her. Both at once said quietly, "Bye."

She walked through the shaded streets of City Park and south along the river. The days had lengthened and the sun wasn't yet low in the sky; the calm water shimmered blue and silver.

When Amber was growing up in Ripley, Old Glad across the street had been locally famous for the folk wisdom spin she put on the world. She'd say, for instance, sitting on her lawn chair and looking up at a patchy sky, that when you can see enough blue to make a man's shirt, only then can you be sure the weather will clear. Or she'd tell a fable. A woman went into the woods, she'd say, sitting in her kitchen while Amber helped her sort her pre-war penny collection. A woman went into the woods and found herself in need of a walking stick. She rejected the first likely walking stick, finding it crooked; the second one looked as if it might break if she put too much weight on it; the third didn't have a smooth enough handle to suit her, and so on. She carried on this way, all the while journeying through the woods. By and by she came to the end of the trail and she had rejected all manner of walking sticks that would have made her journey less trying. She should not have been quite so fussy, this woman.

Amber had taken note of the message in the story, and she'd taken note of the anomaly as well. Though she hadn't said so to Old Glad, she'd noticed that while it was true the woman in the story hadn't availed herself of the benefits of a walking stick, she *had* managed to make it through the woods without one. As had Old Glad herself, for most of her life.

The physical charge that had begun when Ethan traced the circle on her leg moved through her still. Beginnings had their attractions, emotional and physical. But no. Ethan might be right when he said that everyone's looking; that didn't mean she was looking all the time. Sometimes life needs to be broken into its pieces. She quickened her stride. If wishes were horses, flirtations would come with rain checks. As in that class of movie where the gentleman says to the lady, with exquisite, ridiculous patience, I'll wait for you. And he does.

When she reached the place where the park narrowed behind the Bessborough Hotel she left the asphalt, crossed the rough trail further down the bank and sat close to the water. The electricity from Ethan's touch had weakened. She pulled her legs up in front of herself and rested her chin on her knees. Across the river, on the gravel slope beneath the Broadway Bridge she saw the saxophone man, not sitting on his stool but standing and writhing, the play of sunlight on his sax making it look as if the instrument was writhing too – and not even a rag of music making it across the water – so that they looked, the man and the instrument, tormented and silent all at the same time.

She'd been carting Vivien's visit around for over two weeks now in an emotional suitcase. Those statements about John Doe and Phil, the two terrible events. She'd mentioned Phil's accident in such a straightforward way, as if Amber had always known. And she had, of course she had. No one had hidden the facts: there was no surprise father out there. Admit it. No wild card she might one day play. The idea of a still-living father was a fairy tale. Say goodbye, she told herself, to the imaginary man and those brothers and sisters on the farm, say goodbye to the student prince and to the game of looking at red-haired men and wondering.

Snatched away. Her grief was not so much that Phil had died before she was born, but more that he seemed to have had so little importance. Transient, like the burning man, the garbage and ashes carted away so the desert would return to its previous state. Was there time to be afraid, a moment when he knew what was about to happen? She imagined a thud that made her stomach leap. She cried, tears on her bare knees and amongst the blades of grass and in the dirt at her feet, tears running over her cheeks and in through the corners of her mouth, where she tasted them and swallowed.

She let herself fall sideways and she rolled to one side and then to the other. Her head grazed a stone but she rolled back over it again and again, faster now. The dirt against her shins like sandpaper, but she kept on, back to side to stomach. Side to back to side to stomach, at a frantic speed, as if there were flames and this was the way to put them out.

POOR MAN'S TREACLE

Amber, lying on her bed wrong-end-to, with her feet on the pillow where her head should be. Skull stuffed with mildewed rags. Had she ever loathed herself more than this?

In her spiral-bound notebook, beginning on the last page and writing in, Amber maintained a list under the heading Cures for Melancholia. Notes she'd made after doing web searches. She'd chosen this wording for the title partly because, when she keyed in a search, the most interesting information didn't surface when she used the term "depression," but when she typed in "melancholia." A state, not a disease. That, and it *was* the more romantic word.

You can find anything on the web. You can find out that sloth wasn't one of the original sixth-century deadly sins: sadness was. Someone who must have thought there was a difference made the switch some time later on. Either way, they'd get her. Thank God I'm not a Catholic, she thought.

– ancient Greek shock therapy for catatonic stupor: two physicians, one at the top of a cliff overlooking the ocean. First guy throws the patient off the cliff to where the second guy waits with a boat to fish him out of the water.

– Motion. Mechanical spinning chairs. (Chinese proverb: the hinge of a door is never crowded with insects.)

– purging. taking black bile out of the system.

– St. Augustine – the sin of sloth, God the only way out.

– B vitamins and zinc.

– St. Paul – hard physical labour. Jesuits too. Greeks too. <u>occupation</u> David tried playing his harp to make himself well.

– Dad and AA – only a power greater than yourself...

– boiled head of a virgin ram; remove the brains and add spices: cinnamon, ginger, nutmeg, cloves, etc. etc. Also marigold, ash, willow, dandelion, tamarisk, roses, violets, sweet apples, syrup of poppy, wine, tobacco, sassafras. Seems the cure is all around us.

– drill holes in the skull to let the demons escape.

– Pilgrimage (needs a shrine and a saint).

– India – tie the person up and lay her by a stream for as long as it takes. The healing sound of running water.

The notebook lay now beside her on the bed. Amber thought, lying there, about how the remedies went back thousands of years; how the genes for this were ancient genes. Did they serve a purpose? A way to store up energy for the next round? She brought her knees to her chest.

A curled seashell, she thought, waiting for some sound to thread out of my inner chamber. I should write a letter of resignation. Leave aside my lists, my point form sets of instructions, and allow myself the luxury of complete sentences, of commas and full stops and room for digression. Dear Balloon Man, I now resign myself. To who I am. There are loads of us, getting along just fine. Dozens chatting at the UpBeat site, some in therapy, some not ready or willing, some who've already been there done that. Cyber-nursing each other. Poor man's treacle.

The world goes on while I lie in my furrow. When finally I walk back down the stairs and open the door onto Temperance Street, it is always still there, the world. Has not packed up and left. A loyal thing. And I come out into it, feeling like I've been in a dark place that other people can't find the door to. I know where the door is. I'm not saying I come back with necessary treasures. Once I'm back though, there are echoes I'm convinced other people just don't hear. I might miss them if they weren't there.

Sincerely.

p.s. Except that. Except that I never get that time back.

She had a way to get herself out of bed. It worked sometimes. She moved to the edge of the mattress, closed her eyes so she wouldn't be able to protect herself and let her body roll right off. Ouch in three places, two minor, one major. Ankle-bone against the bedside table. She climbed the flimsy chemical ladder produced by the pain in her ankle, limped to the kitchen, filled the kettle and set it on the burner. Head thick, stomach at the just-before-panic stage. There was this thing Cal said once – brought it home from a graduate class – that if you believe in God, you only have to explain one thing: suffering. But if you don't believe, you have to explain everything. Well, he said, I don't believe in God but neither do I feel compelled to explain everything. Things just *are*. You deal with them, find your way through.

What he didn't dispute, as he argued with himself that afternoon, was that either way you still have suffering. God at least would have lent it some shape.

The kettle boiled. Slowly she lifted it. She battled the temptation to slip, to pour the boiling water over her arm in order to turn the pain into something more explicable. Something that would require no apologies, that wouldn't provoke the question, What do you mean, suffering? – Nobody's whipping you, beating you, sticking knives in your neck. For shame.

Amber poured the hot water, wrapped a dishtowel around the pot and set her watch timer for three minutes. After a moment she reached in the drawer for the paring knife. Closed her eyes. Pulled the blade across the back of her left hand. It bumped from tendon to tendon, slicing only the top layer of skin. No no no no no, she said, but the word only lent shape to the high-pitched sound coming from her mouth. She opened her eyes. A slim trickle of blood, shiny, darker than she'd expected, crawled across her hand and along her baby finger and dripped off the end of her silver-painted nail into the sink. She set down the knife and turned on the tap. Mingled blood and water swirled down the drain. She took the tea towel, warm from the pot, and wrapped her hand around and around. Her watch timer beeped and beeped. The stream of water from the tap drummed against the steel of the sink. She leaned forward and put her ear to the counter to hear how it magnified the sound. Her watch timer continued its beeping for a full programmed minute and when it was done there was only the sound of the running water and the burning sensation across the back of her hand.

PART 4

A NEARLY PERFECT JOB

Del walks to work along the still-cool morning street. The weather has been moving water through its cycle in a daily rhythm, heat building through the day, thunderheads forming in the evening and letting loose in the night. Del likes the still surfaces of the puddles, the way they look smooth as a mirror and solid enough to walk across. She remembers the story from Sunday school where Peter the disciple forgets that walking on water is impossible and he strikes out confidently across the sea, doing fine until it dawns on him, and he sinks.

Del takes hold of the brass handle, swings open the factory door and punches in. Five minutes to eight. With the heel of her hand, she rubs one sleepy eye. She has a slightly hungover feeling, not from drinking but from staying up late with Audrey Hepburn, first *Sabrina* and then *Roman Holiday*. That doll-like woman with the swimming eyes, exotic in black and white against a European backdrop; the princess and her princes.

Del starts up the stairs. There's Tracy in her pressed yellow shirt, standing in the outer office talking to the receptionist. She and Del exchange a small wave. Tracy has worked her way up steadily, ambitiously, and now she manages the Saskatoon operation for the absent boss. She even knows the man socially, to the extent that she's dined with him and his wife at one of the family's houses, the one at Cathedral Bluffs of course, not the one on the beach in the Caribbean. Tracy makes regular trips to head office in Winnipeg; on airplanes; luggage and hotel rooms and smartly printed business cards. A person can go far in this business if she's a go-getter.

Tracy and Del have remained friends, though they don't go for Saturday lunches anymore. Del's heard the nickname some of the others have for Tracy – DD for dressmaker's dummy – but they rarely use it when they know Del's within earshot; despite the nickname, the people on Del's floor have no serious quarrels with Tracy or her distantly chummy style of managing.

Del's about to open the door to the second floor when she hears Tracy below her on the landing. "Del, can you come down to the office for a minute?"

She can guess what this will be about. Tracy will want to bring her on side. Last week a rumour moved up and down the rows of machines on the second floor, passed from one station to the next like a bundle of pantlegs. An experiment in changing work methods, so the rumour went, would have them all working standing up, their machines mounted on high tables. Someone, the rumour goes, heard Tracy refer to time-motion studies, heard her say in relation to the change, "We have to stay competitive." This could be the development that will insert Del seriously into the uncomfortable space between her co-workers – especially Larry – and Tracy. People aren't about to stand up all day for eight bucks an hour.

They pass through the outer office and enter Tracy's small cube at the back. After the briefest of preliminaries – there's always an awareness of the clock in this place – Tracy jumps to the point.

"Del, there's a position coming open later in the summer. Floor supervisor on second."

"Yongmei's leaving?"

"Around Labour Day."

Slowly Del nods. So it isn't about the standing-up rumour. This would have been prediction number two: formal recruitment, bringing her on side for more than just the one issue. Which means Tracy's next words will be…

"You'd be good at it. I hope you'll apply."

"Oh, Tracy, I don't – "

"Don't say just yet. Go away and think about it."

They've had similar conversations before. Each time that Del's considered applying for promotion she's circled back to this: she wants to do something she knows she's good at – the ordinary work of this place. A film of itchy sweat rises on her forehead at the idea of making decisions that would affect the people around her. She has all she needs, she insists to herself. Eight bucks an hour plus bonus and her little house half paid for. She's been socking money into the pension plan since she was twenty-three, which, given compound interest, makes her more secure than most.

"A supervisory position would give you resumé-able experience." Tracy drops her voice. "You might need that soon. We all might."

"I just want to sit at my own machine and mind my own business."

Tracy cuts the air with an impatient hand and says, her voice still low, "It's not that simple. You didn't hear this from me, but those contracts could go offshore at a moment's notice. Things are changing out there." Her gesture implies the whole of the world. "We can't ignore it anymore."

Yes, Del knows. The trade agreements, the expected flood of cheap clothing from wherever in the world production costs are lower. The industry is at risk, Tracy has said. We're unprotected, Larry has said. She knows.

"My machine's waiting," she says, and, because Tracy means well, Del pauses in the doorway. "Thanks."

"Sure."

Resumé-able. As she leaves the office Del thinks of how, if Tracy's right, it's now a more important word than *dependable*. For twenty-five years Del's been walking up these stairs. Somewhere offstage there's a ravenous giant swallowing weeks, months, entire years, whole. Here's what she knows from two and a half decades as a seamstress: how to ease the knits through the machine without snagging; how to coax Kimmie's machine to run smoothly when a gear slips out of sync; how to nudge a reluctant belt; what to do when two needles are broken on a three-needle rig while the last one's still threaded. She's the one her co-workers call on when they need assistance, peer to peer. She doesn't mind, she can make bonus even with the interruptions. She knows the idiosyncrasies of every machine on this floor, Brother or Pfaff. She does a nearly perfect job.

Whatever she wants to wear to work, she can wear – sweatpants and T-shirts if she pleases, which she does. Winter and summer she wears flip-flops inside the building because they're easy on the soles of her feet and keep her toes from getting too hot. (Her hot feet: when she mentioned them to her doctor he made an offhand comment about perimenopause. Geeze, she's forty-four, only.) Tracy on the other hand has to wear business clothes. Chooses also to wear earrings and knotted scarves and pendants on skinny gold chains.

Having worked under the regimes of three successive owners, Del can tell you what's changed in this business in a quarter of a century: not much. At least until now.

The outside of the building has been restored with the aid of a heritage grant. It's a building with good bones: dark brick with Tyndall-stone trim, woodwork painted the colour of red wine, arched windows surrounding the top floor. So much better looking on the outside than it is on the inside, where all its complications are hidden – the clutter of wires and hoses strung several metres below the high ceilings, the off-kilter, suspended trays of fluorescent lights.

Del works hard, as she always has; needs to be reminded that she's to take at least two of her four weeks vacation every year. Tracy has gone so far as to show her the sentence in the personnel manual: *Vacations are provided for purposes of relaxation and recreation;* in other words, Tracy told her, for mental and physical health. Think of it as a responsibility.

Every year Del takes two weeks of pay in lieu and two weeks of actual holiday, for relaxation and recreation, as ordered. Putters around inside her house, repaints the white walls, one room each vacation, goes days without having a conversation beyond her remarks to the television. This summer she'd rather not concede even the mandatory two weeks of vacation.

The ten years Phil was in the home in Moose Jaw she hadn't once used a vacation day to make the bus trip to see him. Scavenger's kept in touch with the parents all these years and sent Christmas cards right up to this past year, first to Moose

Jaw, then to Victoria after they sold the farm, even though the cards wouldn't mean anything to the unfathoming eyes of the man in the wheelchair. Scavenger had driven down only the once to see Phil and had earned a sharp elbow from Vivien when he told Del he didn't recommend the experience. When Scavenger informed her of the family's move to Victoria, the story Del had let her own family believe for all this time seemed even less like a lie; the idea of visiting him seemed more pointless than ever – all that distance for what?

She doesn't need holidays, she needs the clear and solid walls of a workday. At her machine, Del picks up the bundle of pantlegs to her left. Despite Tracy's dark comments about the state of the industry, they're scoring big jobs, for now: uniforms for auto workers; aprons for restaurant suppliers; the khaki pant in its dozen variations, all passing through Del's lap-seam operation on their way out to the marketplace where they'll compete with each other. She keeps her head down and keeps on sewing, folding raw margins of fabric around each other into a tight, finished seam. Tuck, fold, fasten. She doesn't need a different job, she needs this one. Management will be management and the union will be the union. She'll leave those jobs to those who are drawn to them and continue to do what she does best.

After work today Larry asks her to stop for coffee, but she's expecting Vivien. She's been avoiding her; she's seen her only once in the month since Phil died. Yesterday Del finally said, Okay, come on by.

"We'll go tomorrow," she tells Larry. At home she settles into her living room nest and takes a crossword puzzle from the tidy stack she's cut from the newspaper. Her safe little house. She flicks on the TV to catch the end of the 6:30 news at 4:30.

In Detroit someone has located all six of the blue-ribbon quilts that were stolen from the Michigan State Fair. The auto plants are once more laying off workers. Fire killed a thirty-six-year-old woman in her house on Pingree, and a tornado swept through a golf course and turned all the carts on their sides. A golf bag with the clubs still in it flew through the window of the clubhouse. People talk about their good fortune not to be in the way.

The station cuts to commercial. Oh good, one of her favourite co-optation ads. It begins by complimenting Del on the noble ideas and major events that were part of her youth, then invites her to buy an off-road vehicle. According to the advertiser's leap of logic, the next item in a sequence that begins with Bob Dylan and moves through Volkswagen vans and Mark Spitz's gold medals, is an SUV. If you wore flowers in your hair then, this is what you want now. Del has never felt the need to own a vehicle. On the screen is a muscular four-by-four; she has no wish to be that high off the road.

Her feet are burning hot. She takes advantage of the commercial break and runs two washcloths under the cold tap in the bathroom, wrings them out and tucks them into the elastic at the ankles of her sweats so they cover the tops of her bare feet. You can do this sort of thing when you live alone. For so many years her blood seemed so thin, not excitable enough to even keep her extremities warm. Now it rouses itself for no reason, rises to her face without warning, flusters her by bearing along with it unnameable emotions for which she has no filing system. This began even before the call a few weeks ago from Scavenger, but surely now it's intensified. Scavenger, who'd been contacted by Phil's parents, had told her Phil died as the result of a stroke. Apparently it wasn't uncommon in these situations, he'd said. At first she had the recurring image of an empty wheelchair. Last night, though, when she closed her eyes she saw a wheelchair with a person in it, and the face of that person was a blend of Amber's features and those of the long-ago Phil. The mouth fell into a straight, slanted line as she watched.

Del pads back to the living room, washcloths flapping, and stands in front of the map of Detroit that's pinned to the wall. She finds the fairgrounds on 8 Mile Road, where the quilts were stolen and then returned. She wonders where the auto plants are but can find no clues. She locates Pingree Street. No telling which block the poor woman's house was on before it burned.

Vivien knocks, her upbeat *dum-da-da-da*. Del doesn't answer right away. She would have liked a few more minutes to herself to watch the end of the news.

"Knock, knock, I know you're in there, Delorie."

Of course you know. You've always known. Del opens the door and says brightly, "Hi there." Vivien does not allow this pretense of cheer. She wraps her arms around Del, who hugs back, her cheek against Vivien's smooth hair. She allows that this is better than pretense, for the moment, just as she allowed a heartfelt hug from Vivien a couple of weeks ago at the Grille before she resolutely steered their conversation sideways into talk of Vivien and Duncan's troubles with their oldest, and the fact that as parents they were now on a first-name basis with two police constables. She pulls out of the hug now and leads Vivien to the kitchen. "Coffee, tea or beer?"

"Are you having beer?"

"No, just trying to get rid of them."

"Coffee's good."

"How was your day?" Del says, spooning instant coffee into mugs.

"It was my turn to bring lunches for the school down the street here."

"And how was that?"

"Same as usual except for the kid who spit at me."

Del realizes she still has the washcloths, one white, one orange, tucked into the ankles of her pants. She takes them off and leaves them folded on the counter. "Hot feet," she says with a self-conscious grin. "Why would he spit at you?"

"Don't know. I'm walking in the front door with my box of apples and one of the grade eighters opens the door for me and another one goes pushing past and spits. Lands a gob on my purse. Something against do-gooders, I suppose."

"Did you say anything?"

Vivien shrugs. "Kid's got a right to free expression."

"You're something, Vivien."

"Well you can't take it personally. I mean."

Del unplugs the kettle and fills the cups.

"How about you?" Vivien says. "How was your day?" She looks steadily at Del, who turns away from the intensity and adds a splash of milk to her mug.

In the living room Del sees that Vivien's eyes have found the map on the wall, and she wishes she'd taken it down for the day. Vivien moves closer to the map.

"City of Detroit. Why do you have a map of Detroit?"

Del looks toward the TV, where the news is wrapping up. She tries to divide her attention between Vivien and the prison story on the screen. The inmates have started a self-help university:

each one teach one. She doesn't like to miss an item – it makes the follow-up stories confusing. Let it go, she tells herself and turns off the set.

She hopes Vivien's question will disappear without being answered. She feels silly about the map; it's important, but she can't think of a way to explain why. She refers to it while she watches the news in the same way she used to check obsessively the fly-leaf maps in books; the way, for example, she tracked Bilbo Baggins through *The Hobbit* as he passed from the frying pan into the fire. She likes it when a book has a map; it shows the reader the realm; it completes the tale. Every time Del successfully locates an event from the news on the map of Detroit, some agitation inside calms down a little.

They sit down with their coffee.

"The map?" Vivien says again.

"It satisfies my curiosity. I watch their news on cable."

"What's so important about Detroit that you keep tabs on their news?"

"Nothing. It's interesting." She shifts in her chair. She should have taken it down.

"Do you still watch that soap, Vivien?"

"*General Hospital*. Whenever I can."

"Think of this as my soap."

How can it matter what she chooses to watch? Vivien's playing with her keys, flipping them one after another around the ring as if they make a puzzle she's trying to solve.

"What about here?" Vivien says. "What about things that are going on *here*?"

She's going to insist on a heart-to-heart, thinks Del. If only friends could understand each other perfectly. If they could manage not to judge. But judgements between friends are inescapable. The closer you get, the more easily they come; the more it grates when your ways of looking at the world don't mesh. How to make space inside a friendship for that?

Vivien pockets her keys and looks briefly at the floor, then makes eye contact as if she's recalled the accepted guidelines for this sort of encounter. She takes a deep breath, which Del finds irritating for its dramatic show of patience and during which she braces herself.

"It's as if you're siphoning yourself away across the border," Vivien says.

Del stares past Vivien's shoulder to the map. The City of Detroit: water to the south and east, all the smaller cities that together make the larger city. Her pen has left small marks here and there as she's searched out precise locations. The city has the shape of a fallen leaf, major routes in red, moving out like leaf-veins from the downtown; it's a thing of the imagination.

"It's just stories," Del says. "Like reading a book. Last week they reported on a jilted cop who found love letters another guy wrote to his finacée. So the cop broke into her apartment and set the letters on fire in her bedroom."

"Real enough to him. Real enough to the woman with the burning bedroom."

Del says nothing.

"What about," Vivien says, "what about here? Saskatoon. You, Amber?"

Silence. Del's warm again, excruciatingly so. "I suppose," she says, "you're going to take it upon yourself to tell her about Phil's death."

Silence.

"No. I'm not going to tell her," Vivien says. "I'm not going to because if anyone should, it's you."

"But there's no *point*. He's gone now, absolutely."

Vivien's quiet for a long moment. She picks up her coffee mug and passes it from one hand to the other. "I'll give you that. There is no point. But you shouldn't have lied in the first place." Vivien stands up and sets her cup hard on the coffee table. "Amber should have known. She might have gone to see him." She sits down again.

"And what good would that have done her? What possible use could that have been? What, Vivien?"

"Okay. For all I know you're right about that. But is it right to take your*self* out of her life too?"

"I'm not. Out of her life."

"Yes you are. That's the thing you're really wrong about."

The words are like a punch. Breathe now. Count to ten.

Vivien's gaze cuts to the floor.

"You better go. Please!" It's a demand, not an entreaty.

Vivien looks as if she's about to reach for Del's shoulders with both hands, but Del stares her down.

Vivien moves toward the door. "Sometimes a thing has to be said."

Del doesn't look up until she hears the latch click into place.

She tries to calm herself with routine tasks. Puts in a load of laundry, dusts her bedroom, vacuums the rug. I am *not wrong*. I have followed, for twenty-five years, the counsel of the social worker, who was good and kind. Sure of herself, realistic. Who said when you release a child your most important gift is distance.

Her gut clenches. She fills a pail with soap and water, looks out the window above the sink as the water runs and sees that today's thunderclouds have already formed. She performs a hands-and-knees scrub of the kitchen floor. She is so righteous, my Vivien. Judge not, you bitch. What does she know about Amber anyway? She's been to see her, she said so yesterday on the phone. What do they talk about? Do they talk about me? There's a word for that: betrayal. She empties the dirty water down the sink and it leaves a swirl of dirt and a small white button. She is *not* wrong. She picks out the button and rinses away the swirl. Instead of giving Amber a disintegrating air freshener and an unfinished letter, she gave her a mother and father. She cannot be wrong. That would mean that every day for almost twenty-five years she's thought the wrong thoughts, held back the wrong emotions, commended herself for the wrong behaviour. You can't fix a twenty-five year mistake.

And Vivien. She can talk. Does she think she hasn't made mistakes? That her young Kyle doesn't need a little discipline once in a while? That a seventeen-year-old with two shoplifting episodes on his record might need a tighter rein? A serious grounding, a loss of car privileges? A job?

Del paces through the house. I don't give *Vivien* advice. I could, but I don't.

The lightning isn't even close, the thunder just a distant rumbling far to the west, but the power inside the house dies. The fridge falls silent. The TV makes a self-deprecating *fzzzzt* and a tiny flame springs from the outlet where it's plugged in. It flares and quickly dies, leaving a black smudge on the wall. Damn TV's probably fried. Shit.

Coffee, she thinks. More coffee. She fills the kettle and reaches to plug it in but then she remembers the power's off. She stands beside the cupboard, the jar of instant in front of her; impotent kettle. She turns around and slides down until she's sitting on the scrubbed floor, her back to the lower cupboard doors, their smooth handles pressing into her muscles. She moves her shoulders back and forth to massage herself. There is no way back to the beginning. These people who go searching for their lost children after decades have passed, just what do they have in mind? You can't fabricate something where there's been nothing.

She dreams that night of a house. Later, when she wakes, she'll realize she's never seen this dream-house in her waking life, never known this hallway, these tones of woodwork and paint; but in the dream, standing in the entryway, she recognizes the dark wood trim and the buff-coloured walls that appear to darken in the high corners where they meet the ceiling; she knows the swell in the plaster where rainwater has seeped in below the window frame.

She sees the entrance to a small room, high up, an inaccessible space that teases her, a cubbyhole she can see into but doesn't know how to enter. Peering in, she can tell by the cup on the side table, the rumple in the sofa cushion, the attitude of the armchair, that this is a part of the house where life is meant to go on. The opening is impossibly small for a human form. There is no Alice-in-Wonderland bottle labeled DRINK ME with a potion to make her small enough to enter. Besides, it's too high, above the coathooks fastened to the wall of the vestibule where she stands. She makes herself as tall as possible and puts her hands through the frame of the opening, but she can find no footholds. She tries to heave herself up, scrambles, leaves marks from the soles of her shoes on the flat-finish paint. She lets go, rests her arm muscles, sits on the floor.

GETTING IN THE WAY

Amber dreams of Ethan – of moving his fine shining hair to one side so she can paint the skin of his long back the colour of sand. The voices of two women close by thread their way into her dream. The women's voices speak of the moon, and in Amber's dream the night sky appears above Ethan's head. Gradually Amber lets go of his hair and comes fully awake, listening to the conversation that's drifting in through her second-storey window.

Woman one: "There *is* no face on the moon. I've never been able to find a face there."

Woman two: "Sure there is. Watching us. See – over there an eye, and there a bigger eye."

One: "I'll tell you what's watching us. Satellites. Dozens of them up there. You can't see them in the city – too much light – but last Saturday I saw them. Up at the lake, lying on the dock, I saw half a dozen satellites crawling through the Milky Way, snapping pictures of all the streets and houses and back alleys on earth. We're being watched, but not by the moon."

Amber sits up and puts her nose against the sliding screen that props the window open. At first she sees nothing, then an obscure movement on the lawn, then a brief orange glow as someone draws on a cigarette.

"Did you know," she says through the screen in a friendly voice, "that the moon is moving away from the earth?"

"Christ! Who said that?" says woman one.

Dark and quiet, three bodies breathing into the silence for an instant; then Amber says, "Up here."

One: "Did we wake you up?"

Two: "Where *are* you?"

Amber: "Up here, second floor."

"Jesus! You know how to spook a person."

"I didn't mean to."

One: "What's that supposed to mean, anyway – 'the moon is moving away from the earth'?"

"I don't know. Heard it on TV."

Two: "Whatever you want it to mean. Physics, I guess. We should go now, don't you think?"

Amber hears a rustle of clothing and watches the glowing cigarette ends describe the movements of the two women as they come to their feet. She smells tobacco smoke, an aroma that pleases her at this distance.

Amber: "Good night then."

"Yeah, good night."

"Night."

In the morning she pulls on running shorts and a T-shirt, opens her window and crawls out to sit beside balloon man.

Takes him by his rubber-glove hand. He has two sides to his face now, the smiley side and the one she drew on a couple of days ago. The new face has a droopy mouth and sad eyes and represents if not a full acceptance then at least an acknowledgement. She turns the balloon now so she's looking at the happy side.

Two empty beer bottles lie on the grass close to the sidewalk. Amber's disappointed: she thought the two women would've been the type to clean up after themselves. She's not in the habit of talking to just anyone who stops to rest on the lawn in the middle of the night.

Jiggling balloon man's floppy hand in a wave, she looks next door to the House of Boredom. Over the past few days the sign in the window has peeled slowly backward. The letters on the first part of the sign are out of sight now, leaving only a fragment of a message: F BOREDOM.

"Eff boredom," says Amber. "Yeah." Stop asking what the spirit of the day demands of you; turn around and demand something from the spirit of the day. Get those bottles off the lawn. She crawls back through the window and puts on running shoes.

She runs along the riverbank, underneath the University Bridge, further. The geese have departed, continuing their flight north, ceding the river, riverbank and sandbar to the pelicans, whose awkwardly graceful bodies undulate on the sandbar, wings flapping occasionally, startlingly white. Amber abandons her usual running path, the asphalt that follows the upper bank, in favour of the rough lower trail overgrown with willow whips and scratchy caragana that in places bend so low across the path she has to duck to make her way. She passes over cutbanks where she can hear the river lapping below, eroding the shelf from underneath. The lower path is risky business. Roots and rocks to trip on, pebbled slopes that don't afford a good grip.

It's a low-traffic time of day and Amber has the trail almost to herself. The banks are fenced off for a few hundred metres above and below the works of the weir, and behind the chain-link stands a pelican. Amber slows her pace, then stops and stands on her side of the fence looking through the diagonal grid at the bird: the single eye that this angle allows her to see, the slack lower beak, the cowlick of down at the back of the bird's head. The layered feathers along its wings, the arresting curve of its back, the clownish orange feet. She stares into the bird's orange yellow eye and can decipher nothing in it, can't even tell if the bird returns her gaze or looks straight ahead. How does a bird see, with its eyes placed the way they are? She stands as still as she can for a long while. The pelican stands unmoving as well. How would it respond if she spoke, leaned in, reached a finger through the wire grid? A bird has a line you don't cross; she knows that if she pays it any more attention than she's paying now it will swoop away. She leaves the bird and begins to run again. Looks back over her shoulder and sees the bird lift off and glide, wingspread wider than the height of a man and underscored in black feathers.

The image stays with her, the flight of the bird leaving its trace on her visual memory. Encounters do leave their traces on you – encounters, events, objects, people. This bird; Old Glad with her parables; women talking through a window at night; Tamara with her emphatic embrace; the man who walks up and down Second Avenue mumbling his own long story. Traces that last like needle tattoos or disappear over weeks like henna. Traces to be read now, or five minutes from now or far in the future. Ethan: there's a person she might never see again, but their encounter could still be with her thirty years from now. The line of warmth his finger drew on her leg. She wonders if she left a mark on him.

Up the wooden stairs to the railway bridge. How long did she spend staring at the pelican? If she crosses the bridge for an extra long run she might be late for work, but she wants the longer run today, she's ready for it. She reaches the top step and checks her watch. Just enough time. As she turns onto the bridge's wooden walkway she looks up and sees a woman standing beside the railing halfway across. She's in the process of folding a tan-coloured jacket and laying it tidily on the boards at her feet. Amber hesitates for an instant, then resumes her pace. The long straight planks, the railroad tracks on one side, the railing and the sheer drop to the river on the other. Oh damn, what's this woman getting ready to do? Amber tries to picture the suicide prevention sidebar on the UpBeat website, yellow letters against black.

She's still some distance from the woman, who, having set her jacket down, stands looking over the rail, ignoring Amber. What did that stupid UpBeat sidebar say? She read it once and never looked again. Fragment: *Most have mixed feelings right up to the final moment – they might be persuaded to change their minds.* Amber slows her pace slightly. If she could pull out a crib sheet of handy phrases. Though she's slowed up, she's still running, and she has that remembered feeling from her racing days of the earth rotating under her stride. She sees on the planks of the bridge, too late to avoid it, a sharp fragment of brown glass from a beer bottle. She treads on it squarely and has the absurd, fleeting thought that she'll get a flat in her running shoe.

Don't pretend a person isn't suicidal if obviously they are; you're not about to plant an idea that isn't already there.

The long straight planks. The railroad tracks on one side. The railing and the sheer drop to the river on the other. She'd rather take on a physical challenge, not the type of challenge presented by this still woman standing at the railing, already shed of her jacket. If she hadn't stopped to gaze into a bird's eye, she might have been long past by the time this woman's intent became obvious.

She slows to a walk, glances at her watch and pretends to push a button as if she's making an innocent check of her running time; keeping to a pretense – as the woman at the railing is keeping to a pretense. Avoiding.

She has to say something.

At the far end of the bridge she sees a man who's carried his bicycle up the stairs and who begins now to pedal in her direction. Amber's almost alongside the woman now. She stops and smiles and stands boldly close to her. Between them are only a couple of feet of wooden plank and the folded jacket. Amber looks down at the far green water, its surface baffled by a breeze that blows at cross-purposes to the current.

She turns and looks directly at the woman. "Suppose I told you that you could do this anytime." She pauses for breath. The woman continues to look out at the water without turning in Amber's direction. "It doesn't have to happen today. You could wait forty-eight hours, and if you still felt the same way...." She's at a loss. "It doesn't have to happen right this minute."

"What doesn't?" the woman says, still looking upriver. Dark brown hair woven with strands of grey close to her face.

"The jump. You. Jumping."

"What are you talking about?" Still she doesn't look at Amber.

The bicycle is so slow in approaching. The rider's bright blue helmet and his dark leggings. How to flag him, get some help without making a sudden, startling move?

Use the word. You have to use the word. You won't be giving her an idea she doesn't already have. "Suicide," Amber says in a quiet, unsteady voice.

The woman looks directly at Amber. "Since you're so sure what this is about, I might as well carry on."

Without looking away from the woman beside her, Amber raises her right hand in a cautious, static wave toward the approaching cyclist. "Wait five minutes," she says to the woman. "Just five."

Yellow letters on black on the computer screen. *They will get tired and their body chemistry will change.* She has to trick the woman into staying past that point. Desperately she tries to think of her own notes to herself. It comes and goes; wait for a day with a more generous spirit.

"It isn't your fault you feel this way." Amber's voice carries the indignation she used to feel when her mother demanded to know what was wrong and Amber had no answer. She runs her right palm over the back of her left hand, the thin, raised line of scab.

"Like you know how I feel!"

Amber eyes the massive beam that juts over the river on the other side of the railing, solid enough to stand on, to dive from.

"I only know what it looks like from here," Amber says. "It looks like on the one hand there's the bad stuff, and on the other hand are the things that help you handle the bad stuff. Right now you've got more on the one hand than the other. But maybe that could change."

Too much talk. Shut up and listen. The wheels of the bicycle make a hollow sound on the wooden boards. The woman swings around to see. She grabs the rail as if she's about to climb over and gives Amber a hard look. "What do *you* know?"

"Nothing."

The rider dismounts, slides his pack off with a quick motion and zips open the front pocket. Cellphone, thank you. His bike has fallen crookedly against the rail and the front wheel spins frantically. The cyclist backs off a few steps and speaks into his phone.

Don't argue. It's all in the manner, not the words. Person to person. "What's your name?" Amber says.

"Who wants to know?"

Aggression – is that a good sign or a bad sign? Person to person, she thinks again. "My name's Amber."

The cyclist, his telephone folded, approaches. He isn't as young as she assumed when she saw from a distance the hi-tech helmet and the spandex. "I'm Michael," he says. He extends his hand to the woman, who ignores him. She sits down suddenly, as if her legs have forgotten how to stand. *They will get tired and their body chemistry will change.*

Amber wants to lift the folded jacket and put it around the woman's shoulders, but she stops herself.

"Someone's coming to help," Michael says.

"You don't know the first thing about me," the woman says, looking at her feet.

Amber searches for something comforting to say, something that won't juice her full of adrenaline again. "Someone's coming to help," she says, as Michael said, and she sits down to wait, a few feet of wooden plank and the tan-coloured jacket between herself and the woman.

After they've all gone away, Amber rises to her feet as if some force is lifting her. She puts both hands on the rail. One leg over then the other. Both feet lined up on the beam, close to the edge. She's exhilarated – the air all around, the breeze cooling her legs. She cranes her neck to look past the end of the beam to the water below. Her stomach lurches. Quickly she straightens and looks upriver. The landscape aligns itself: the city on either side; the steady horizon; the University Bridge, the Broadway Bridge, the Victoria. The long view stabilizes her balance. She can look side to side now without fear of falling. Look at me! Look at me! The goose she saw that day, swimming so close to the weir – he thought *he* had muscle. Well look at me, goose, I'll take you on. I'll take anyone on!

Keep steady now. One hand to the rail behind her; okay, two hands. Let go with one hand now so you can turn around. Every muscle she puts to use is strong. One leg back over the rail, then the other. She plants her feet on the walkway. Through the space between the floorboards she sees, far below, the rough surface of the water, green and opaque. The force of her heartbeat rocks her shoulders and chest.

She's late for work by only an hour and, because she explained to Donna over the phone, the others know. She arrives to cheers and backslaps. Amber's grateful for the immediacy of busywork during the lunch hour. After lunch is cleared Shari makes her sit and Chelsea sets a glass mug of Just Joe in front of her, milk and coffee finding their way through each other, yin-yang.

"Way to go," says Macy.

"You're a hero," says Chelsea.

"I suppose." A post-adrenaline hollowness inside her skull; contradictory cravings for coffee and for sleep; the image of the woman, who, by the time the crisis team arrived had condensed into a tight curl, arms wrapped around her legs. Does that woman consider her a hero or a nuisance? The idea of telling someone else what they need.

"No," she says. "It had nothing to do with heroism and everything to do with chance."

Donna says, "As soon as you want, you go on home."

"I'd rather stay."

She does think she wants to stay, but as the pulse at the back of her head gathers force, she wants to be home in bed. She fishes through her tips and finds exact change for the bus.

She wakes up while it's still light. Eight o'clock. The headache dissolved as she slept. If she hadn't been there, in the way, what would have happened to that woman? But of course, she didn't want to be saved; otherwise she wouldn't have been out there at a low-traffic time of day pretending her hardest not to notice Amber. Amber was an imposition.

Starving. Peanut butter and jam – two sandwiches slapped together – and a can of bargain cola. She eats standing beside the counter. Fast food.

She *was* there, and she's glad she was. It's all right to put yourself out there. You *have* to put yourself out there. Be prepared to leave your own traces; be prepared to have an effect.

Her mobile dangles neglected in the corner and she considers it as she downs her pop. Look at me, she thinks, these fragments of my life. The parts of the mobile always moving a little, even when there's no obvious source of air current, the heavy brass plate from the mute doorbell making a quarter turn from time to time. What have I built? A dropout, a waitress, a woman in waiting. A damsel in distress or the hero of the tale?

She begins to rehearse demands. She practises out loud in her inexperienced ask-Del voice:

Were you even sorry when he died?

Why would you leave me in a place that you yourself could only run away from?

And Del will say, Was it the wrong place to send you?

No, Amber will have to say, It wasn't the wrong place. I just want to know why. A well of resentment.

Compact little Del, brittle in a fragile way, as if she's taken the black oils of fear and grief and pressed them over years and years into coal. News flash, Del: There's nothing unique about being sad. Lots of people are sad. Read the websites, watch PB-goddamn-S: *It doesn't matter how you got that way, what matters is what you do with it.* The personal remedy. Or do some people love their lumps of coal? Does Amber? Guilty of picturing herself as a seashell, curled and lovely, listening for that sound, the one she hopes will thread its way out of her inner chamber. She thinks of the word "melancholia" and the way it evokes for her the rich music of a lone cello inside a dim church on a rainy afternoon, and what a romantic conjuring that is. If what you must do is love yourself, how many parts of yourself shall you love?

Amber looks at the smiling, turning photograph of Stuart that hangs from the mobile, taken before his hair lost the last of its blond. The angled tooth at the right of his smile that makes it hard for people to take him seriously when they first meet him. A photograph holds so little of a person – so nearly weightless, so inappropriate a medium. Her brother deserves more than a thin picture glued to a double backing. She's suddenly, powerfully homesick for him.

He answers on the second ring and sounds pleased to hear from her, though a little confused, especially when she jumps in with questions she later will realize must sound bizarre. Their conversation proceeds in the manner of an interview. I want to know more about your life, she tells him, I'm losing track. What do you like to do? How do you spend your time when you're not working?

He coaches baseball in the summertime and football in the fall, but she knew that. He's in the Lions. He's expanding the business. Yes, more than enough work. The usual troubles with his crew, but you have to expect that.

He has a dog now, Pup, a great bundle of muscle, fur and exuberance, and dumb as a bag of hammers. So dense that last night after dinner he dragged the lawn sprinkler, still spraying three hundred and sixty degrees, through the open back door and into the kitchen. Gave the room the first washing down it's had since Mom died. Never a dull moment with a dog like that.

"Maybe you should keep the door closed."

"I like to let the evening light come in."

She remembers him sitting on the back step after supper. "Do you still like to drink in the evening?" she asks.

There's a long pause before Stuart says, with only a hint of defensiveness, "I'm no alcoholic, Amber."

"Of course you're not," Amber says. "Of course not."

Most likely, he tells her, she knows the important things. Clearly her volley of questions has made him uncomfortable.

"Amber?"

"Yeah?"

"You're all right?"

"Perfectly."

"So am I," he says.

As she hangs up she looks again at his photo and the other pendants hovering in the corner. Life could be just this: what each person can pretend to make out of inherited and accumulated parts. Just that and wonderfully that. The school library in Ripley had a collection of jackdaw files the students used to use to research their essays. Elizabeth the Queen; the Magna Carta; Hadrian's Wall; King Tut. Folders jammed with bits and pieces, artifacts to hook a person's curiosity and reel it in, catalogued assortments named after the jackdaw bird that picks up whatever strikes its fancy and carries it back to its nest. By studying these, you were to achieve some larger idea, some appreciation for the historical event or person or phenomenon. Well, here is her jackdaw hoard, or part of it, suspended from the ceiling according to the laws of physics. But if you could trick yourself just for a moment, let your mind escape from the constraint of gravity and other learned laws, would it be possible to think of this arrangement of threads and objects as holding *up* the ceiling? Pushing out into space, claiming the right to occupy territory.

A tall order, and this collection of objects is incomplete. She'll ask Del for something to stand in for Phil. She'll go and claim that right, knock on the door and simply demand something. Anything. Even a fact or two will do.

VISITATIONS

She has to have it out with the place, Del's concluded – have it out with the empty space where the Burton used to be. She has to have it out with *some*thing. Friday afternoon she waits for the rush on the stairs to clear before she takes the handrail and guides herself deliberately down. Making sense of stairs is still tricky with her new glasses. She's postponed her coffee date with Larry. She heads east toward the river for a block but then doubles back home to exchange her flip-flops for walking shoes. She sits on the couch to tie her shoes and looks across the room at the blank screen; the TV hasn't worked since it said *fzzzzt* and died yesterday. Damn. She wants it back, wants Detroit back.

Pull yourself together, she thinks. Why this prowling around in the past? Never has she been the sentimental sort, keeps no journals no souvenirs no hoard of mementos like the one Vivien said she saw evidence of at Amber's place. She just doesn't hold onto a lot of stuff. She looks around her tidy living room to illustrate this to herself. Through the doorway into the kitchen:

clean counters. She hasn't even a trinket, a hair from his head; she's never felt the need. It wasn't that sort of relationship. Not even a snapshot to turn upside down in a drawer.

Over the years, on the rare occasions when she happened to think about Phil's eventual death she expected that – if she were even to hear of it – she'd experience little more than a tepid, short-lived wash of relief, for his sake and the sake of his family. Not this unmanageable rattling of things, as if her world were inside a shoebox and a giant had put the shoebox in a sack and slung it over his shoulder and commenced walking.

Is this guilt? Grief? Change of life? There should be labels.

Just go. She locks up and sets off. It's the hottest part of the day. She passes through downtown, where the heat ricochets from glass and cement, multiplying itself. She wipes her forehead with her palm, wipes her palm on her sweatpants.

Vivien. She's angry still with Vivien. Del passes the Colony Hotel, where the Student Prince used to be. She glares at it and sees her glaring face reflected in the glass front and this makes her even angrier.

The baby. The baby so small, so perfect. In the beginning, rage, guilt, relief. Grief. But it was selfish to grieve. She'd made her bed, made her bargain, forsworn her emotional rights. Get on with it. A week after her mother left with the baby she slipped nursing pads inside her bra to absorb the leaks and went back to the factory.

Early on, there'd been the temptation to find someone to marry, someone who would kindly make her decisions for her. Gary, the man she had met the night she and Vivien went dancing at the Red Lion, worked at the autobody shop across the alley from the factory. He recognized her as she sat eating her lunch one day at the crooked picnic table by the factory parking lot. He strolled over to renew their acquaintance, and more. Gary was an eager man. When she'd almost decided to accept his proposal, she'd stood in the second-floor bathroom, straightened her shoulders and looked in the mirror. The smell in the bathroom was a mix of bad plumbing and synthetic strawberry air freshener. The pale light above the mirror took its tone from the paint on the walls and diffused a hint of green over Del's face. You don't even like him that much, she told herself, and not since that first night at Vivien's has he told a joke you could laugh at.

Three men besides Phil had made it as far as her bed. With each, she had worried about what they would make of the Caesarian scar. Gary didn't mention it, nor did the next man. Whatever they assumed, each kept it to himself. The third waited a few weeks before he asked about it. When she told him the scar was from appendicitis he said, Oh, and she thought, Stupid. He'd been getting on her nerves anyway; relationships had been getting on her nerves.

Vivien had teased her once about being too fussy.

"More like self-sufficient," Del had replied, and when Vivien looked like she was trying to formulate a question about, didn't she miss sex, Del had said, "Party of one."

She's on Broadway Bridge now, controlling her stride, two footfalls between seams in the cement. The image comes to her again of the person in the wheelchair with the sideways-slipping, melded face of Phil and Amber. It's Amber who remains. Herself and Amber and Stuart. Only three. Surely so small a family is manageable. Her shoelace has come undone and the ends snap against the sidewalk. She stops at the top of the bridge and double knots both laces. She walks the final two blocks under the shade of elms, welcoming the relief they offer from the heat. Roots have heaved the cement in places and she walks carefully, eyes to the ground.

At the construction site stands a huge wooden sign with a showy architect's rendering of the multi-unit building that's about to go up. Del doesn't like what she sees – a group of four apartments stacked two on two, a brick behemoth with a black roof too steep to please the eye; a fence of ornamental iron with pikes on top to keep the riff-raff out.

Del looks through the existing knock-together fence made from panels of chain-link. The basement's already been poured. It's huge. The empty moat of the unfilled excavation pit surrounds it. The site is deserted. A heavy padlock hangs on the chain-link gate, but no particular care has been taken to secure the fence panels. They're meant to be held together with metal strapping in three places, top, middle and bottom, but a few have only the middle strapping and they tilt at slight angles, leaving small triangles of space. Del pulls at the bottom of a listing panel and widens the opening. She has to get down on hands and knees, but she crawls inside easily enough, angling first her shoulders and then her small hips to fit through. She walks to the edge of the pit around the new basement. Nothing to see but a hole, with an empty hole constructed inside it. What good is it, coming here? It isn't even the same place. That place is gone.

She turns to leave and she hears a whistle – a sharp, fingers-to-the-tongue, call-the-dog whistle. A shaggy black dog is squeezing through the gap in the fence. The dog is big and it has to crouch and drag its belly. She hears the whistle again and then a male voice shouts, "Arsenio!" Once inside the fence, the dog bounds straight for her, exuberant as an overgrown puppy. Instinctively, Del takes a step backward. She hears "Down, Arsenio!" Her foot lands partway down the slope of the pit. The clay slides underneath her, and her foot turns. She twists and falls. She shoots her arms out in front of herself and they take the weight of the impact. A clean, loud crack; a pain in her wrist as if the blade of an axe has landed there. She moans, barely stops herself from screaming out loud. She's crouched in the pit at the bottom of the ten-foot basement wall. She cradles her right forearm in her left and turns awkwardly in the space between the steep dirt slope and the new cement. She looks up and sees the shaggy black dog looking down at her. It barks. She sobs with the pain. Her breath comes in gasps.

She hears the voice again. "Damn! Shut up, Arsenio!" She was too preoccupied with avoiding the dog to see its owner before she fell. She hears the person grunt and swear and the fence panels rattle.

The pain overwhelms her – an electrical current surging the length of her arm and whizzing through her head. Her stomach answers the pain by slathering nausea on top. She closes her eyes and tries to breathe slowly, but the pain increases and she lets herself gasp and pant again. When she opens her eyes a teenage boy with a dusty face is grasping the dog by the collar and looking down at her. The sun is at a bad angle and she squints against it.

"Sorry," he says. "You okay?"

Del gives up on trying to hide the pain and lets it out in a sobbing, *Ow-ow-ow.* She doubts she could climb this unstable, seventy-degree slope even with two good arms. Holding herself steady, she squeezes her eyes to clear them of tears. She looks squarely at the boy and says, "I need help."

"Maybe I can get you out of there." He lets go of the dog's collar and gets ready to slide down the slope to where Del sits. The dog disappears from view.

"Shit," the boy says and scrambles after the dog. "Arsenio!"

She doesn't want this boy's help anyway. She wants someone who looks more capable.

The boy is back now, holding the dog by the collar once more and looking stupidly into the pit. Things begin to go dark inside Del's head, a seductive, sparkling dark. She almost surrenders, but in the split second available she makes the decision and puts her head down to stop the faint. Gradually the blackness clears. She raises her head.

"I need help," she repeats to the teenager. "I need 911."

"Oh," he says and she can see relief on his face that someone's told him what to do. "I'll go phone."

If he likes orders, that's what she'll give him: "You get that dog out of here and you find a phone and call 911. You tell them where, exactly. Tell them I'm down in a hole and something's broken." She lowers her head again to wait, her neck sore from looking up. Her legs are stiff from crouching, and she realigns herself along the wall so she can stretch one leg out in front and lay the injured forearm against her thigh. She moves the fingers of her good hand over the cement wall and thinks of the architect's rendering up at street level. The steep black roof: unforgivable kitsch. And did the drawing show columns at the front, underneath a cupola? "My, haven't you come a long way," she says under her breath. Will there be lions, too, paws raised, on either side of the front gate once they finish?

I hope he's got the damn dog on a leash by now. *Arsenio*. Who names a dog after a talk show host? Sarcasm: her dependable, time-tested pain management technique. Don't fail me now. Arsenio. They got the *arse* part right, she thinks. The pain throbs. This is a situation sarcasm isn't equal to.

She grows cold. Is this what it is to be in shock? The pain still there and coursing through her but meeting its match in something dull and brawny that knows how to push back.

She never did pay the last month's rent when she left for Olivia's. For a time she felt uneasy about that, afraid some skip tracer would chase her down and make her pay up. Compounded since 1974 – that would amount to what by now?

After the baby, the unnatural weightlessness. She can remember the cotton blouse she wore the day her mother took Amber. Can remember running her hands over the sleeves after her mother left to feel the softness of the weave, its comfort. Her breasts were heavy. The pressure against her nipples drove her to stand at the sink, undo her buttons, lean over and pump with her hands. The awkwardness of expressing; the sound and scent of a thin stream of mother's milk hitting metal. At night she would trace with her fingertips the smooth stretch marks on her thighs, the Caesarian scar; would feel the lack of tautness in the skin of her belly, the sense of a collapsed, empty thing meant for holding and carrying. Her hip joints loose, arranged according to a fundamentally new alignment. Evidence.

When Amber was a girl, when she was hurt and in the hospital and not waking up, Del went out to Ripley and took a shift sitting by her bed. Even alone with her that afternoon, Del couldn't bring herself to put her arms around the girl. Rather she watched her and listened to be sure her breath was still there. She wasn't sister and she wasn't mother. She could only stand up for so long to the ambiguity. The ambiguity is still there, but the family has shrunk around it. Del, Stuart, Amber. Just we three. It should be manageable. It should.

Del shifts position and cradles her arm. Two separate beings, she thinks: the baby who was carried away in the yellow terry sleeper and the girl my parents brought up. Is that what I've been doing all this time? Is that how I've managed? By dealing with Amber as a stranger who happened to appear in my parents' home. By keeping the baby as the baby, a being I parted company with years ago, an empty space in my life that I closed up and layered over.

She hears, finally, a siren.

Now they'll come, one by one, to sit across from her in her living room. Del feels besieged, backed into a corner. Her arm, inside its cast, is propped beside her on the side of the couch. Her fingers are fat sausages mottled yellow and blue. She called Larry simply to ask about borrowing the little tv that sits on his kitchen counter, and now he's told Vivien. Larry and his little tv are yet to arrive, but Vivien's appeared, with flowers. She's been told the details in a conversation that ignored their last visit together and concentrated on matters of practicality and pain. Three breaks, the one Del heard the snap of and two that she didn't.

"I was sitting in Emergency yesterday," Del says, "and I had to wait for the painkillers to kick in, so I sat there thinking of all the different kinds of falls."

"Hmm?"

"Free-fall, fall from grace, fall of the year. Nuclear fallout.

"Falling off a log."

"Rainfall, nightfall, waterfall."

"Fallen woman?"

"Ha-ha. Fall guy, fall to earth, windfall."

"Can I write my name on the cast?" Vivien says.

"Only if I don't have to move. Hurts like nothing else."

"Do you want me to call Amber for you?"

Silence.

"About the *arm*."

"No, I'll do it." Del doesn't look at Vivien as she says this. She knew Vivien might dare to mention Amber again, and she hopes this will be the first and last of it. She's waiting for Vivien to ask, now, what she was doing at the site; waiting for Vivien to tell her she'd do better to deal with people rather than things. Holes in the ground, television news, a map of an American city.

"I'll call her later today," Del says. "Can you hand me that bottle?"

Vivien opens the bottle of painkillers and shakes a capsule into Del's hand. "Let's go back to your game," she says. "It'll take your mind off. There's fall down, there's fall out, fall over."

"Fall off the wagon."

"Fall in love," says Vivien.

"Oh, that."

They hear a knock and they both, guessing that it's Larry and knowing he could never achieve that kind of timing on his own, laugh out loud. It's what they need – a spontaneous, shared laugh, and it's good. Del suspects, though, that Vivien would stop laughing if she knew what Del is thinking right now – how she can't imagine falling in love with Larry. She can imagine falling into something else, eventually, into bed, into a pattern, but not into love. Life would never have that sort of happy surprise for her.

Larry opens the door without its being answered. "I won't ask what's so funny," he says. He carries his little TV in an awkward football hold. In spite of Del telling her that it's all right, that she should stick around, Vivien leaves a few minutes after Larry's arrival. He sets his TV on top of the old one, but he doesn't plug it in or change the cable connection. That's fine, Del can do it later herself – it'll only be a little awkward with her bad arm in the way – but she really would rather have the TV operational now, would welcome its noise.

"Beer in the fridge?" says Larry.

So he's planning to stay at least that long. "Help yourself." She's to get no break between one person and the next.

"Want one?"

"I've got water."

"Opener?"

"In the drawer." *Make yourself at home, Lare.*

"Which?"

"By the fridge."

He comes back to the living room, beer in hand, reaches to squeeze Del's good hand hello and sits opposite her in the armchair. He seems to notice, for the first time since he came in, the map on the wall. "Detroit," he says.

Oh joy, now I'll have to explain again.

"What's the map for?"

"I was curious, that's all. I watch their news."

That's enough explanation, apparently, for Larry. "Detroit," he says. "Now that's a place where labour's got clout."

Del suspects that big auto unions have, in fact, little to do with

Larry's understanding of how unions ought to work, but there's no harm in allowing him his pronouncements. It's got nothing to do with her.

Larry sits down in the saggy velour chair and takes a swig of his beer. With his thumb he riffles the pages of a booklet of crossword puzzles she's left on the arm. It surprises her again (she's noticed it before) how beautifully shaped his fingers are, and how well-tended. The things you least expect. Not even a residue of brown under the nails from the twill aprons that came up from the cutting room this week.

"How long was the wait at Emergency?"

"Not long; it was a slow day, so I didn't have time to think too much about what was coming. Which is a good thing, because when that guy took my forearm in his two hands and wrenched it! I thought I was going to vomit all over his grey slacks, ruin that ridge of drycleaner crease."

"Hurt much, did it?"

"You wouldn't believe."

"I can imagine."

"No you can't."

"Okay, I can't. But I remember when the brother-in-law broke his wrist. He isn't one to admit to pain, normal scheme of things, but he wasn't afraid to say how it hurt like blazes when they set those bones. And then, after all that, two weeks later the doctor didn't like the way things were lined up and he said it had to be rebroke and reset. Now that, the brother-in-law said – that was damn near unbearable."

"Rebroken," Del says flatly.

Larry nods, still looking full of his story, full of having something to say on the subject.

"You're telling me this why?"

"Oh crap, I shouldn't have said that. It won't happen to you. You'll be okay the way you are. The worst part's done with, I'm sure of it."

It seems like a lot of words, seems suspiciously like a case of quantity over quality. He rushes on like someone who's tripped and puts a hand out to steady himself on the closest wobbly end table. "Amber know yet?"

"I'll phone her tonight. There's no rush. There's nothing she can do."

"She can visit."

"Yes."

"That's a nice thing, visits, flowers – shit, I should've brought flowers."

"No need. You brought the TV." She hopes, by speaking at a measured pace, to slow Larry down as well.

"Flowers next time then. Next time." He moves his index finger back and forth on the arm of his chair.

"It isn't necessary."

"I still don't get it," Larry says. "Geeze I talk to my sister all the time. And she's in Winnipeg."

"We've had this conversation, Larry."

"I know, the party line about separating yourself from your own kid. It was the *nineteen-seventies,* Del."

"Sometimes the prevailing wisdom really is wisdom."

"If your social worker told you, in the nineteen-seventies, to jump off the roof of the hospital would you have done that too?"

"Har-dee-har, Larry."

"You know what I think?"

She braces for the next part of what he thinks.

"I think you like that advice the social worker gave you because that's the way you want things to be. Easy. You just hang onto whatever story you like the best."

Del's good fist pushes into the scratchy fabric of the cushion beside her.

"You need to get over yourself, Del."

There's no place to go. Into her bedroom and slam the door? Stay here and pretend he isn't saying these things? She lowers her eyelids partway. He doesn't know the half of it. Imagine if he did.

Maybe he's right; maybe she's horrible and a bitch and doesn't care about anyone but Del. She feels the mean sting of her own whip. Maybe he's right, but who asked him?

"Why are you here, Larry? Why are you sitting in my living room?"

"Why am I here?"

"Yeah. If you have such issues with me, Larry, what are you doing here?"

He stands up, beer in hand, his breathing a show of exasperation. But the next moment his shoulders fall into a sloping line. "I'm here to lend you a TV, I suppose." He sits down again. His beer, still in his hand, comes to rest on the crossword puzzle book, and three large, fizzy drops splash onto its cover. They both stare as the shiny paper resists the drops for a moment and then succumbs. Anger darts around in Del's chest until she reins it in enough to speak.

"You can't talk to me like that."

"Nobody can talk to you like that."

"You're right. That's not how people should treat each other."

"But if people don't say things, nobody ever *gets* anywhere."

Of course they do, Del says to herself. People *think* about things. You can get somewhere just from thinking about things.

Once, at the Grille, over deep-fried squid, when everything Larry said seemed to be about dissatisfaction, about trying to *get* somewhere as he put it, she'd asked him in exasperation, "What would make you happy?"

"Lots of things. A 1970 candy-apple-red Impala with a white hardtop."

"That's pretty specific. Why don't you save up and buy one?"

"Do you know how hard it is to find a 1970 hardtop Impala that's in any kind of shape? Besides, that's only one thing. Like I said, there's lots of things I want."

People want so much. Did he ever consider just living? There might be other ways, other ways to be, than the one he picked. What about you, Larry? Del thinks. You're hanging onto your own favourite story.

He gets up from the armchair now and taps his chin with the fingers of one hand. "You know Del," he says, "if you're not going to *make* good things happen for yourself, you could at least try *letting* some good things happen to you." He squeezes her hand and says, "Next time I'll bring flowers."

PHRED CROSSES THE RIVER

Good timing, Del, Amber thinks. I'm all set, finally, to come at you, and you take a dive.

But she doesn't truly believe people fall into holes on purpose. They just discover it's happening, the way she discovers some days that her state is changing without asking her permission.

She felt ambushed last night by Del's brief phone call, the news about the triple-broken wrist. Felt unprepared and ungenerous. Now that Del's the injured party, literally the injured party, Amber and whatever demands she planned to make have been pre-empted. She'll go to visit this afternoon, of course. She'll take a plant as a get-well gesture because that's what people do, they offer gifts. She looks at the plants lined up along the bookcase and the speaker. Any one of them will do. Donna-the-boss would be impressed with the way Amber's revived the poor plants. Take your note from the plants, she tells herself: optimism.

Across the river, Del manages to extract a white plastic garbage bag from the package under the sink. She coaxes the bag open, pulls it over the cast and, wrangling a strip of masking tape with her good hand and her teeth, secures it around her upper arm. "You don't want to get that plaster wet," the doctor said. "Wrap it before you shower." Del prefers a bath to a shower, yet she tapes the arm inside plastic even to rest it to one side as she sits in the tub. Before she presses the last inch of tape into place she tries to squeeze the excess air out of the bag. It's an awkward job. "Lie flat, you," she says. Once, when she was little and her mother was getting peas ready for the freezer, she sat Delores down and gave her a straw and instructed her to suck the air out of each bag of blanched peas before she twisted the fastener to close it. She did a good job; her mother praised her. Del remembers the satisfaction she felt in knowing that as the bags of peas lay in their borrowed space at one end of Glad's freezer they were that much safer from freezer burn, vacuum packed. That's how she wants this garbage bag to behave now. This ignorant garbage bag, damn it. Stay down.

She lay one night in bed listening to the two of them fight. She'd been home from school that day with the flu, and she'd found a plastic pail and set it beside her bed before she crawled in. She felt the vibrations through the house as they struggled, and then she felt the slight shudder as one of their bodies slammed into the door jamb between the kitchen and living room. Delores's stomach heaved and sent what little it still held to her throat in an acid wave. She leaned over the edge of her bed and vomited as quietly as she could into the pail. She took the pillowcase off her pillow and draped it over the pail to keep the smell in. Feeling her way along the windowsill to orient herself in the dark, she went to the closet and set the covered pail in the back corner. She found her way back to bed and lay there relieved to have thrown up, to have gotten rid of something for the time being; a cleansed emptiness. She pulled the blanket tight and rolled to snail herself inside it. She remembers picturing as she lay there those tight bags of peas nestled in the freezer inside Glad's safe little house.

Sitting at the kitchen table, the dregs of this morning's Coke in front of her, Amber fidgets with a ballpoint pen. Woods Roofing it says. It's an old one, the kind with a spring inside it and a click-button at the top. She unscrews it and spills the workings out on the table. How to keep herself *nice* today at Del's? How to wait and breathe through the silences? She presses the spring between her thumb and forefinger. Releases it so it jumps to the table. She makes the spring jump again and again. Sees how it finds its original shape each time, how it returns to that taught coil. Optimism, sure, but what reason is there to think Del will warm to an overture any more than she has in the past?

It's time to start out if she wants to arrive at the appointed hour – two p.m., Del's choice; two p.m., Sunday, June 20. Father's Day, in fact. Amber takes Phred the philodendron from his place on the speaker, coils the vines, lowers the pot into doubled-up plastic grocery bags and goes down to the street. As she's crossing the bridge she feels the weight. She switches the bag from one hand to the other. It takes thirty-five minutes to walk all the way to Del's little house. Thirty-five minutes to think about how to be nice, to strategize how to muzzle

Rumpelstiltskin: offer to make tea; busy herself with finding a spot for Phred; smile and look out the window; massage her cuticles.

Del's eaten a one-handed lunch and even managed to wash her plate and glass, which now rest on the draining tray. She unlocks the door so she won't have to get up, settles herself on the couch, takes a painkiller and arranges her arm on its cushions.

Vivien she can speak to sternly when she gets nosy. Larry she can blow up at; they can even shout Let's just forget it! at each other, and then they can forget they've shouted Forget it! and go back to being who they are with each other. It isn't so easy with Amber; a different set of rules applies. They're right, Vivien and Larry; this isn't the way it should be between her and Amber. But she doesn't know how. She doesn't know *how*.

In fact, she doesn't know how other people do so many of the things they appear to do with such ease. How Vivien raises that assortment of kids, how Tracy makes decisions about production streamlining, how Larry assumes the authority to speak on behalf of other people.

Here's Del's square little house sitting at the end of its bit of front walk, the lawn short and tidy. Amber knocks and tries the door. "Don't get up," she says as she lets herself in. Del, sitting there on her couch, looks more than ever like a gathering of matchsticks. Amber sets her plastic bag on the mat inside the door, slides out of her shoes and moves toward Del. Injury amounts to a perverse kind of armour. Del looks more than ever untouchable. Amber hesitates, then gathers her resolve and takes the bruised fingers that protrude from the cast between her own thumb and forefinger and strokes gently. How rare to touch this person the hand belongs to. The fingers are cold from not moving. Amber notices how the swelling gives them a synthetic feel, as if they're covered in a clever imitation of skin.

Tea, Amber coaches herself. "Can I make us some tea?"

"All right. Yes, please."

It's a tidy kitchen for someone with a useless right arm. Amber finds teabags in the logical cupboard, above the electric kettle. She waits shyly in the kitchen while the water heats and then she makes trips to the living room with teapot and mugs and milk and a plastic lemon she finds in the fridge. Amber splashes a little milk into Del's cup and then pours the tea before it's had time to properly steep. Holds the cup so Del can grasp the handle without leaning forward.

Amber thinks: topics of conversation.

Del steadies her cup on her knee. She sees leaves sticking out of the top of the plastic bag beside the door. Amber hasn't mentioned the bag.

If Vivien were here she'd say, Now: your turn, Del. But what is it she's supposed to do on her turn?

Amber's curls are wild from her walk across town. Del remembers the wisps of red hair against the baby's neck. This is the red-haired baby, grown. Admit it. They are not two separate beings.

"Have you talked to Stuart?" Amber says as she squeezes a few drops from the plastic lemon into her cup.

"Yesterday."

"You've heard about Pup, then?"

"I've heard about Pup." Del smiles.

Amber smiles too. "The funny story about the sprinkler."

"It sounds like business is good out in Ripley."

"Yeah, sounds that way."

Silence. Del shifts her weight to keep her leg from falling asleep. Too much sitting, too much keeping her hand propped above her heart to minimize swelling.

"How about you?" Del says. "How are things at Poor Man's?"

"We're closed on Saturdays now. But weekday lunches are still fine."

"That's good."

"I suppose you won't go back to work for a while." Amber gestures toward the arm.

Del doesn't like to think about this part, about how in hell she'll fill the time. The doctor said six weeks, and that's the best-case scenario. She expects Tracy will come by the house with a plan for setting her up as a supervisor-in-training. With this thought she feels besieged again.

"They'll get along without me," she says.

Silence again. Amber wonders, What else? Talking from scratch. It would be good to have slips of paper in a bowl on the table, each with a topic, like the impromptu speeches Mr. Hobbs used to assign in high school. She looks at the wall above Del and sees a street map of Detroit. Screwy old Del, she's different, no question. Amber holds the front corners of the armchair cushion. Up to here with small talk. She strokes the velour nap against the grain and feels how it resists her fingertips.

"What were you doing over there?" she says. "At the building site?"

"I saw the picture of the new apartments," Del says. "A massive thing with a black roof."

The way Del can ignore the question. Amber sees her turn her good wrist and surreptitiously check her watch. She could take her by the shoulders and shake that set of matchsticks until they rattle.

"Thank you, Amber, for making tea."

That would be my cue to go, Amber thinks. Christ's sake. Del on the couch looking like a person who's swallowed herself.

"Any time," Amber says. Resentment drips inside her. There's something about this feeling she actually likes. A marinade of vindication, of sweet, ripe I-told-me-so. Cut your losses, she thinks. Make your exit.

Or. Sometimes you just have to say something and see what'll happen. Inside Amber's mind, Rumpelstiltskin's looking for something to say. In there pulling back on a rubber slingshot and wondering what to load it with. Before Del's fall Amber had resolved to ask for something of Phil's for the mobile. Why let broken bones stop her?

"It's Father's Day," she says.

Father's Day, yes. When the radio mentioned it first thing this morning, Del remembered the squirmy feeling she used to get when she looked through the cards in the Ripley drugstore hoping to find one that said simply, Happy Father's Day – that wouldn't have been *too* dishonest. But no, what she could find on the racks were cards with mallard ducks on the front, and inside, worshipful verses: Very Special Dad; Best There Is; As Wonderful As You. One year, after thinking hard to come up with a redeeming feature, she'd decided Hallmark should print a card with the message: Drunk or not, you go to work every day. I'll say that for you.

Yes, okay, there might be things she's handled poorly, but this one thing she's sure of: she's been right to be strict in her silence about Dad. To take care not to pass on to Amber even a trickle of that bitterness. When Del went out to Ripley all those years ago to sit with Amber in the hospital, her father was leaving the room just as she was arriving. They exchanged their official nods, and Del remembers taking note as they passed each other that he no longer emitted the boozy odour that had defined him when she was a girl. He smelled like a stranger. Good.

"I want to have something of Phil's," Amber says.

"Phil's?" She was expecting Amber to say something about Dad.

"Whatever you've got," Amber says. "Anything, doesn't matter."

"I've got nothing that belonged to him." Del allows herself a slow, complete blink, a split second of darkness behind her eyelids to calm herself. When she opens her eyes Amber is still looking at her. "I'm sorry."

"Nothing?" The vacant look on Del's face infuriates Amber. "Not a single thing? You haven't kept *one thing*?" Has anybody anywhere anytime ever mattered to Del?

"I did have something," Del says. "Once."

"What?"

"Just a small thing. Phil used to have an air freshener hanging from the handlebars of his bicycle. A little joke." Del's talking to her own lap, and Amber has to lean forward to hear. "A cardboard pine tree. Eventually it ended up with me." Del's picking at the leg of her sweats. "I must have lost track of it."

"You lost *track* of it?"

Del looks at the coffee table between them, spread with breakable things. "It was falling apart," she says. Shh-shh, she wants to say. She thinks of Scavenger's hands gently setting the soft cardboard on the table.

"I'm sorry, Amber. I just don't hold onto stuff." And she does regret it now. Look at the way Amber pumps her knee, how she pushes at the skin at the base of a nail, leaving a naked strip between the shiny silver lacquer and the cuticle. Del makes an effort to reconcile the grown woman in her living room and the baby in yellow terry cloth whose small warm head had left a damp circle against the sleeve of her nightgown. Even if they are one and the same, how does a person go back?

What else does she have to offer? In the beginning there was the dear-baby letter, the very first thing she was supposed to have passed along for Amber to have some day. She never did finish the letter. It wasn't supposed to be just from her, it was supposed to be a message from Phil as well. She even asked him what he wanted to say, didn't she? She can't remember what she did with the half-written letter.

Things about that afternoon that she *does* remember: the dim and smoky Red Lion in the afternoon; the wet parking lot reflecting the street lights in the premature darkness brought on by the storm; the curve of his backbone against his shirt as he pedaled away.

Again that infuriating blank expression. Del's power of dismissal: I just don't hold onto stuff. Her few terse words lying there like a fork upside down on the plate. Then the vacant look. Done.

"Honest to God, Del," Amber says. Then louder, "Honest to God!"

"Calm down, Amber."

"Calm down! Of all the stupidest things to say!"

"Can we please just quiet down?" Del says. "Just for a minute?"

"Can we please just make some goddamn *noise*?!" Amber shouts. "Just for a *minute*?" She gets up from her chair, bends toward the coffee table and sweeps everything to the floor. There's a breathtaking crash and then silence. Shattered crockery is scattered across the hardwood in puddles of tea and milk. Amber rubs the inside of her arm where it's hot from touching the teapot. She watches the plastic lemon wobble and roll, wobble and roll to the foot of the armchair. She laughs out loud, though nothing is funny.

"Amber! Oh no, Amber!" Del says. "Please, it'll ruin the wood."

"The wood! Worry about the wood, Del!" Amber says as Del gets up off the couch and moves toward the kitchen. Amber's questions are here now, the framed-behind-glass questions. They're out again. "Did you ever love him, ever?" she shouts. "Were you even sad that he died?"

But neither of these is the real question. The real question is the one she still hasn't asked: Do you love me at all?

Del turns and makes her way back to the couch. She sits, slowly, carefully. She feels very small in the presence of this tall shouting figure. "Vivien's been talking to you, hasn't she?" Del says. "Did Vivien tell you about Phil?"

"Tell me what? Here's what I know about Phil. He worked at the Student Prince and he rode a bicycle and he died. If there's something else I should know about Phil, why don't *you* tell me?"

Del's body quivers. She thinks how it would calm her to be on her hands and knees with a rag, wiping up. She looks at Amber. "I will tell you, Amber. Sit down."

Del isn't sure that what she's about to do is the right thing. All she knows is that she is expected to say something of substance to this young woman, and the territory of Phil is the territory they've landed in. But Amber is so angry. All this anger set loose in the room. And the next thing will only cause more. Del's instinct is to pull her knees to her chest, but she holds steady.

"Phil died just over a month ago, Amber. I should have told you."

Amber stares at her. Del braces her back against the couch.

"A month ago? I thought there was an accident? The famous fucking bicycle accident." Amber picks up the plastic lemon and hurls it at the wall.

Del winces as the lemon hits the wall; it drops and settles against the baseboard. "It's true. There was an accident. That part was true."

"What do you mean *that* part was true?"

"It didn't kill him, but he wasn't Phil anymore. The person who was Phil – he was gone." Del pictures the man in the wheelchair, the straight line of his mouth. She moves her head a little to the side and succeeds in making the image disappear.

There's a tight band around Amber's temples and she sees little explosions of light and colour. She rests her head on her fist. How can Del manage to deliver information like this without one single, solitary tear? Amber had thought Del's personal best to date was holding back the fact that she'd lived in the Burton house. That was just a baby silence compared to this one.

"He was alive," Amber says. "Where was he? Was he here in Saskatoon?"

Del shakes her head. "In Victoria, where his parents are. These last years."

"What else don't I know?"

"That's everything."

Not true. I don't know anything about what goes on inside that head.

Amber feels as if a door has been slammed shut as Del gets up off the couch and disappears into the kitchen. Del reappears moments later carrying in her good hand a plastic bowl and a rag. She looks directly at Amber and Amber looks directly back.

"It wasn't him anymore," Del says. "He wasn't Phil, believe me. He was gone, Amber."

"You could have told me that. I could have handled that. Or did you just not think about me?"

"I'm sorry. I wish," she says and hesitates. "I wish now that I'd kept it for you."

"Kept what?"

"The pine tree. That used to belong to Phil. I wish I'd kept it."

"Jesus, Del, the problem isn't that you lost a piece of cardboard!" Amber says, crying now. "The problem is you didn't tell me the truth." She watches Del kneel and rest her cast on the seat of the couch. Watches her reach for a piece of broken crockery. "You didn't give me any goddamn choice to decide what I wanted or didn't want to do with that truth!"

Del stops moving.

"The problem is you don't ever *say* anything to me. You never say anything!" Amber shouts at her motionless back. "I need you," she says. "I need you to love me."

Del begins dabbing at the tea and milk and drops of lemon juice. Her head is lowered and Amber can't see her face. "I do love you," Del says. "Oh, I do."

"But what do you mean when you say that? I know what it means coming from other people, but I don't know what it means coming from you."

Del rights the milk carton, wipes around it with her rag. "I can't tell you what the words mean," she says. She squeezes the rag above the bowl. "But I know it's true."

I know it's true, Amber repeats silently, trying to replicate Del's voice in her mind, imprint it in case she might not hear such a thing again.

She watches as Del picks up pieces of broken mug one by one and sets them down in a group near the leg of the table; as she gathers the tiniest shards of crockery by pressing the pad of her finger on them until they adhere; as she uses her thumbnail to flick them off her finger into the unbroken base of one of the mugs. Her movements are slow and painstaking and look as if they come at a considerable price. Amber watches Del's small hand pressing a finger on the shards and for the first time sees a person who needs looking after. If only Del would allow it. But no, she's like the pelican on the riverbank – a thing with wings ready to swoop away the moment someone steps closer. An unknowable being.

Amber goes to help, nesting the fragments of cups and teapot so she can lift them in two cumbersome handfuls and carry them to the garbage. When she returns she takes the bowl and rag from Del and rinses them in the kitchen sink.

Del sits down and settles her cast on the arm of the couch. She hurts, but it isn't yet time for another painkiller. She's to take no more than five a day, doctor's orders. Doctor's orders are so straightforward; practical instructions. Situations should come with instructions. But Larry is right, she supposes. Instructions can be wrong.

Amber returns from the kitchen and goes to the door. She's about to slip into her shoes when she sees the plastic bag on the mat where she left it.

"I forgot. I brought this for you." She takes Phred out of the bag.

"That's good of you."

Del's eyelids are half-closed. She looks as if she could fall asleep in the middle of a word. The injured party.

Amber carries the plant to the windowsill and sets it in the sun.

"I'll leave you to rest," she says. "I'll go now."

"I'm sorry," Del says.

"Yes."

WITHOUT FALLING

The door closes behind Amber. Del moves her cast arm down from its propped position to relieve the ache in her shoulder joint. It's so hard. So *hard*. Amber will have more to say. More than she said today. It doesn't matter anymore what was right and what was wrong, because it's out. Can we have a little rest from talking now that things have been said? A few days off to retrench?

The plant on the windowsill catches the afternoon light on its leaves. Del's never been one for plants, but she expects she can manage a little water now and then. She gets off the couch for a closer look. The two longest vines are coiled together; to try to extricate the one from the other would do more harm than good, and she leaves them mounded on top.

Of course she loves her. The way she looked standing in the living room. The flush in her cheeks, the shine in her eyes. Do ordinary mothers feel this astonishment? The length of her form, the youth in the fine shape of her jaw. A picture Del has never until today allowed to arrest her attention so. It hasn't been part of the bargain. The bargain Larry thinks can simply be renegotiated. Compounded since 1974. Amber's face in the light and her hair brilliant where the sun glanced off an untamed wave. In her whole storehouse of words, where are the words for this?

Amber will be back before the week is out. What consolation prize does she have to give her, what to stand in for a ragged piece of pressed cardboard? What can she do about the request for something from Phil?

Larry will be back too. Larry and Vivien and, one of these days, Tracy. All these people with their ideas of who she should be. But *this* is who she is. What ever happened, Del wonders, to a little respect for the introvert, the recluse, the hermit? Leave me alone. Please. As she thinks the word "please" over again, her tense leg trembles and her breath roughens.

She reaches for the pencil and the crossword book on the end table, but she stares without comprehension at the clues. She can't print left-handed anyway. She exchanges the puzzle book for the remote. Yesterday after Larry left she switched the cable over from the broken TV to the borrowed one. It wasn't so difficult. She watches the teaser for the full news report an hour from now. Some stories we're following, says the woman behind the desk. A Southfield man was taken to hospital after a truck plowed into his house and knocked him across the room. He'd been standing in his kitchen talking on the phone.

There's little to tell Amber about Phil. Del remembers him turning away from her one evening at the Prince and the play of shadow on his shirt as he walked away. He was in a state of leaving almost from the beginning. She remembers him sitting naked on the edge of the bed as she tried to fit various emotions to the form of their relationship. What is there in any of that to give to Amber? The fact that he ran with stones in his hands; the winter night he worked in a Hawaiian shirt and orange socks; the story of his father sitting on the roof and surveying a farm Phil couldn't imagine going back to. Such insignificant bits and pieces. Should she write each memory on a separate card and give them out one at a time, birthday by birthday, to this girl; this girl who needs keepsakes. Maybe such fragments will be sufficient for someone like that, a gatherer of small objects.

It isn't fair, Del thinks. That man in Detroit was just standing there in his very own home, talking on the phone, not bothering a soul; and now he's in critical condition. She sees a hospital and tubes and bandages. She wipes at her eyes with her sleeve.

Wincing, she moves her shoulder in a careful, small rotation to work out the stiffness. She massages her cool hand, its mottled skin. She looks at the Kleenex box on the end table and sees that it's empty. Where's a Kleenex? Doesn't she have a Kleenex anywhere? If she gets a good sleep tonight, she'll go on a major excursion tomorrow. She'll walk to the 7-11 to pick up a jug of milk. Of course she loves her. Never mind, toilet paper will do just as well. If she goes out tomorrow she'll have to manage the locking and unlocking of the door with her single good hand, pay for the milk and pocket her change, carry the jug home again. In the bathroom she tears off a length of tissue, folds it to make a double thickness and wipes her eyes. Tomorrow she'll have to simply get to the store and back without falling.

UNDER AND UP

Walking home, Amber misses the weight of Phred in his plastic bag. She has nothing for her hands, and they rise once in a while and then fall back to her sides. Last night she'd noticed, still underneath the radiator, Del's old zodiac candle in its stiff red blanket. For a moment she'd thought of breaking off a flake of that red wax and winding fishing line around it and hanging it on the mobile, but she decided against it. The mobile, suspended in the corner of her kitchen, clumsily made and still incomplete. Each object standing in for a person or event. The silent doorbell plate the stand-in for Del. The stiff wax would be redundant. There's nothing for Phil, never will be, unless she's to let him reside in the doorbell plate as well.

Would she have gone to see him? There's no way to answer a question like that. She pictures the last of her possible fathers – the man with the plaid shirt and running shoes who wanted his coffee in a cup not a bowl – immobile, lying on a cot. She hopes he isn't unhappy. She sees his baseball cap on the bedside table.

She hopes it didn't hurt, being him. Because if it did hurt to be him and if there were as many years of hurting as there were years she'd been alive on earth – there was no room in her for such a thought.

Phil Turner, dead, once more and still. How to live with this information? But I *can* live with it, she thinks. I've dealt with Phil's absence all my life. Even the imagined Phils, the delusions, were put to rest the day I rolled in the sand and grass on the riverbank.

How to live with Del, that's the real question. Do I simply resign myself to the way she is?

Resignation; her second dance with that idea in a matter of days. It sounds like a weak notion, sounds like it might dissolve if it got wet. She shoves her empty hands into the pockets of her jeans. Pulls them out again. Dad, heading out to his meetings week after week, coming home so sure of himself – that wasn't resignation. Acceptance was the way he referred to it once. Such a more solid idea, like a workbench you could set things on top of. The Christmas when Amber was ten or eleven, Del made a rare trip home, caught a ride out and back the same day with a university student. She exchanged few words with their father that day. Not as if she hated him or carried a forever grudge, but stony, as if she felt no emotion toward him that was powerful enough to bother with. And he, despite her near silence, kept his presence at the table quiet and steady as always. Reciting the grace, naming his three children out loud as blessings, a generous pause after each name:

Delores.

Stuart.

Amber.

That must be what acceptance sounded like, the way he slowed his voice as he pronounced those names.

Slow

down.

Abruptly she stops walking. She hunches tight around herself the way she used to do when she trained too eagerly and got a stitch in her side. After a moment she straightens and continues to walk, though she feels as if her guts have contracted into a ball that pulls like gravity at her chest and shoulders.

Halfway across the bridge she stops to watch four rowers as they slide downstream in their long boat; together they look like a sleek insect skimming the water, long slim oars catching in unison. Amber moves the fingers of her right hand across the back of her left and feels the still-rough line the knife made. It will become a thin snail-trail of a scar and later might disappear, might not. The boat slips underneath the bridge and out of sight and a finely sculpted wake trails behind. The wake looks soft and receptive. She imagines arcing off the bridge in a finely controlled dive, entering the water cleanly, tips of fingers, forearms, head, torso. Slide in. Swim below the surface with no need of breath through miles of green caverns. Maybe that's how the woman she met on the railway bridge that day had pictured it. But that isn't how it goes. Slam! –that's how it would sound and feel if a person really were to dive. Crazy pain, broken body, possible death. There are no green caverns hidden in this body of water.

I know it's true, she says in her mind. She wonders if she'll ever be able to believe this affirmation from Del. Things must be going on behind those blue enamel eyes, complicated mechanisms that keep Del moving through life, getting up and going to work, buying groceries and eating and washing the dishes afterward. Her own made-to-measure patterns of resilience, strange and mazelike.

The river breeze drops away and a catch of song floats up from the unseen saxophone on the bank below the arch. Another few notes, another few. Torn-away bits that she listens to as if, even with the spaces between, they make an entire serenade. There she goes, thinking again that she can spin something out of near to nothing. If you can call that faith, after a fashion, then she does have her portion of faith after all. It must be what's holding her feet on the bridge.

There's resignation...and there's acceptance...and there's love. How do you get from one to the other? What does it take to fill in the blanks?

Upstream, a man paddles a bright red kayak, the short kind, the kind the freestylers use for their tricks. The blades on either end of his paddle carve the water left and right by turns. He looks like a monopod bobbing in a shiny red shoe, and under other circumstances Amber would have laughed at the sight. He pauses for a moment, then leans forward and to the left, head down, and pulls with his paddle. He rolls under and re-emerges, dripping, his hair swept into his eyes, his paddle scattering bright drops of water.

Is it possible to melt a space around a cold hard core, a space where two people can negotiate love without necessarily hoping for understanding? Is this one of those days when belief in such a thing is possible?

I know it's true. She still can't quite get the sound of Del's voice saying it. It will take work to make it into something that will be there tomorrow morning when she goes looking for it. Work she's desperate to do.

For a long moment the man in the kayak has rested there, rising and falling with the slight motions of the water, his paddle propped across his small red boat. Now he leans to the left again, and forward, and once more rolls under and up. Around him the green water shimmers with strands of yellow tinsel cast by the sun. In spite of how she feels, Amber smiles at the sight. She remembers again her mother's shot taffeta dress and how she used to take it to the window and play with it, looking for the glimmer.

ACKNOWLEDGEMENTS

Heartfelt thanks to my editor Sandra Birdsell for her skill, enthusiasm, support and hard work. The seed of this novel was a short story, Traces, commissioned by *Between the Covers* at CBC radio for the Festival of Fiction in 1998. Thank you to Sandra Birdsell and to producer Ann Jansen for that opportunity. For their helpful readings of earlier drafts of all or parts of the manuscript, thanks to Brenda Baker, Bev Brenna, Alice Kuipers and George Sipos. Special thanks to Dave Margoshes for his generous, thorough and immensely helpful review of an early version of the manuscript. Thank you Beth, Margaret, Nancy, Norma and Fred for all you do. Thanks to Gord Vaxvick and Kirby Wirchenko for their contributions. Thanks, as always, to Murray Fulton and Michael Fulton for their support, humour, patience and creative input.

I extend my thanks to the Banff Writing Studio, particularly faculty members Joan Clark and Michael (Young Man) Winter, as well as to the Sage Hill Writing Experience, particularly faculty member Robert Kroetsch.

I'm grateful to the Saskatchewan Arts Board and the Canada Council for financial assistance.

Thank you to the literary journal *The Malahat Review.* Part 2 of *The Art of Salvage,* under the title *Long Distance Lessons,* was named a finalist in The *Malahat*'s 2004 novella competition. Thank you to the Writer's Federation of New Brunswick, which administers the Richards Prize for Fiction. Part 2 of *The Art of Salvage* received honourable mention for the Richards Prize in 2006.

I consulted a number of works while writing this novel. Among the most important to the final book were the following: *Night Falls Fast,* by Kay Redfield Jamison (Knopf, 1999); *Touched with Fire,* by Kay Redfield Jamison (Maxwell Macmillan, 1993); *Gone to an Aunt's: Remembering Canada's Homes for Unwed Mothers,* by Anne Petrie (McClelland & Stewart, 1998); *Birthmothers,* by Merry Block Jones (Chicago Review Press, 1993); *The Noonday Demon: An Atlas of Depression,* by Andrew Solomon (Scribner, 2001); *Adoption Reunions,* by Michelle McColm (Second Story, 1993); and *The Anatomy of Melancholy,* by Robert Burton (New York Review Books Classics, 2001).

Interpretations of the I Ching are widely available. The "quotations" that appear in part 2 are very loose riffs on material compiled from a number of different editions. The square root metaphor, used in two places in the novel as a way to speculate about what is central to an emotion or attitude, springs from a comment in John Gardner's *On Moral Fiction* (Basic Books, 1978). John Doe's death and memorial service were inspired by incidents reported by Mike O'Brien in the Regina Leader-Post. The date of the report is lost in the mists of time. Finally, those who worry about accuracy of details borrowed from the so-called real world should be forewarned: Some Detroit and Saskatoon news events referred to were fabricated while others were adapted from headlines from roughly, but not exactly, the period during which the events of the novel take place. National Lampoon's split beaver issue may well have been published long before or long after the timeframe within which it appears in *The Art of Salvage*.

ABOUT THE AUTHOR

Leona Theis is the author of one other book, *Sightlines,* the recipient of two Saskatchewan Book Awards in 2000. She was also one of three writers featured in the 1998 edition of *Coming Attractions,* and has been cited in a number of award programs, including The Writers Union of Canada short prose and Prairie Fire competitions.

Leona grew up in Bredenbury, Saskatchewan, and has lived in Saskatoon since 1973, with sabbaticals in Vancouver, Europe and Australia. She has worked as a freelance editor, librarian and adult education program developer.

also by Leona Theis

SIGHTLINES

WINNER OF TWO SASKATCHEWAN BOOK AWARDS

ISBN: 1-55050-160-7 • $16.95CAD/$14.95USD

"...a kaleidoscopic drama...gathers and offers gratifying connections." – GLOBE & MAIL

The time is right for... **COTEAU BOOKS** WWW.COTEAUBOOKS.COM